AFTERLIFE with Archie®

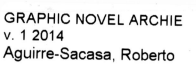

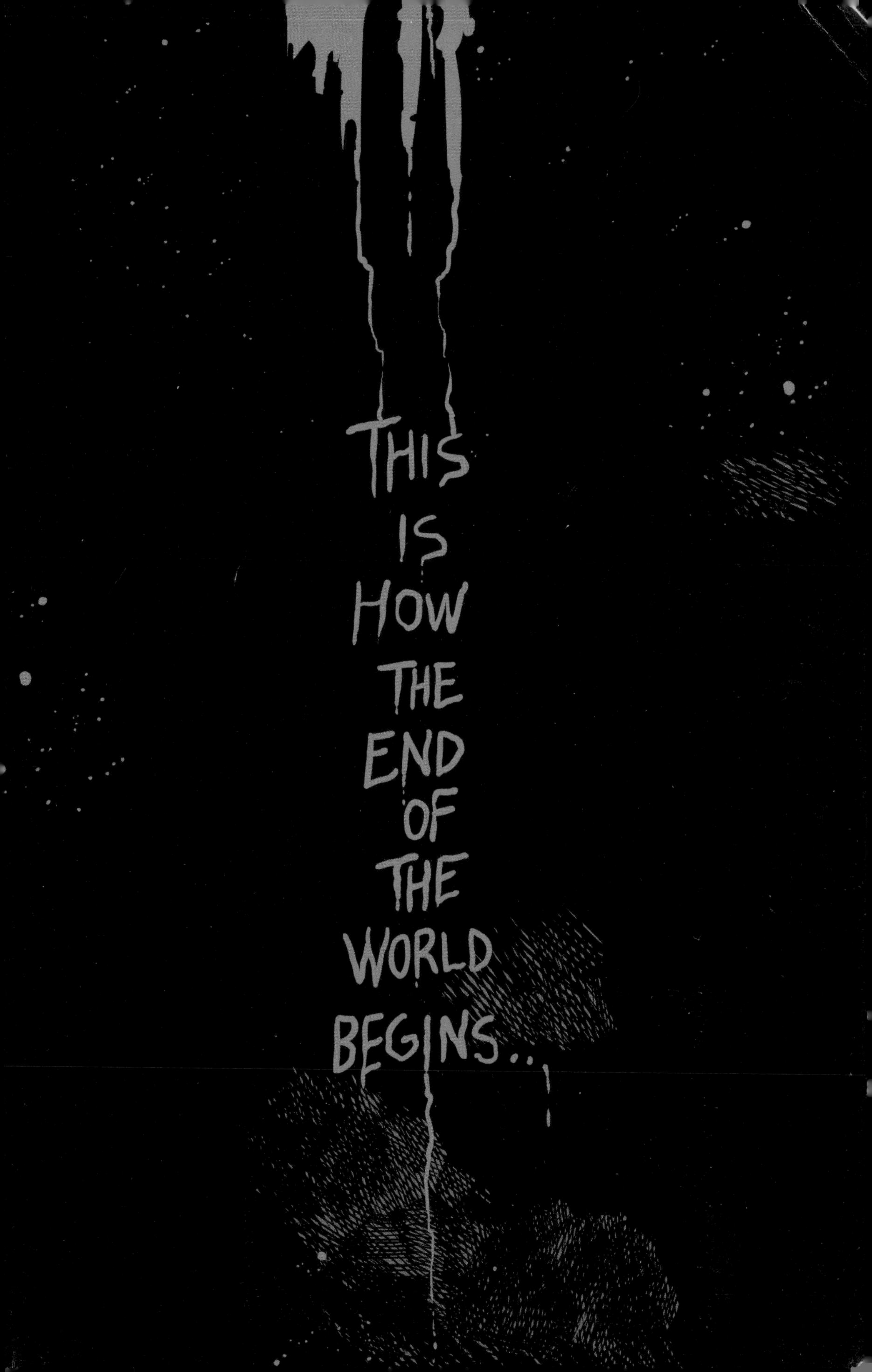
THIS IS HOW THE END OF THE WORLD BEGINS...

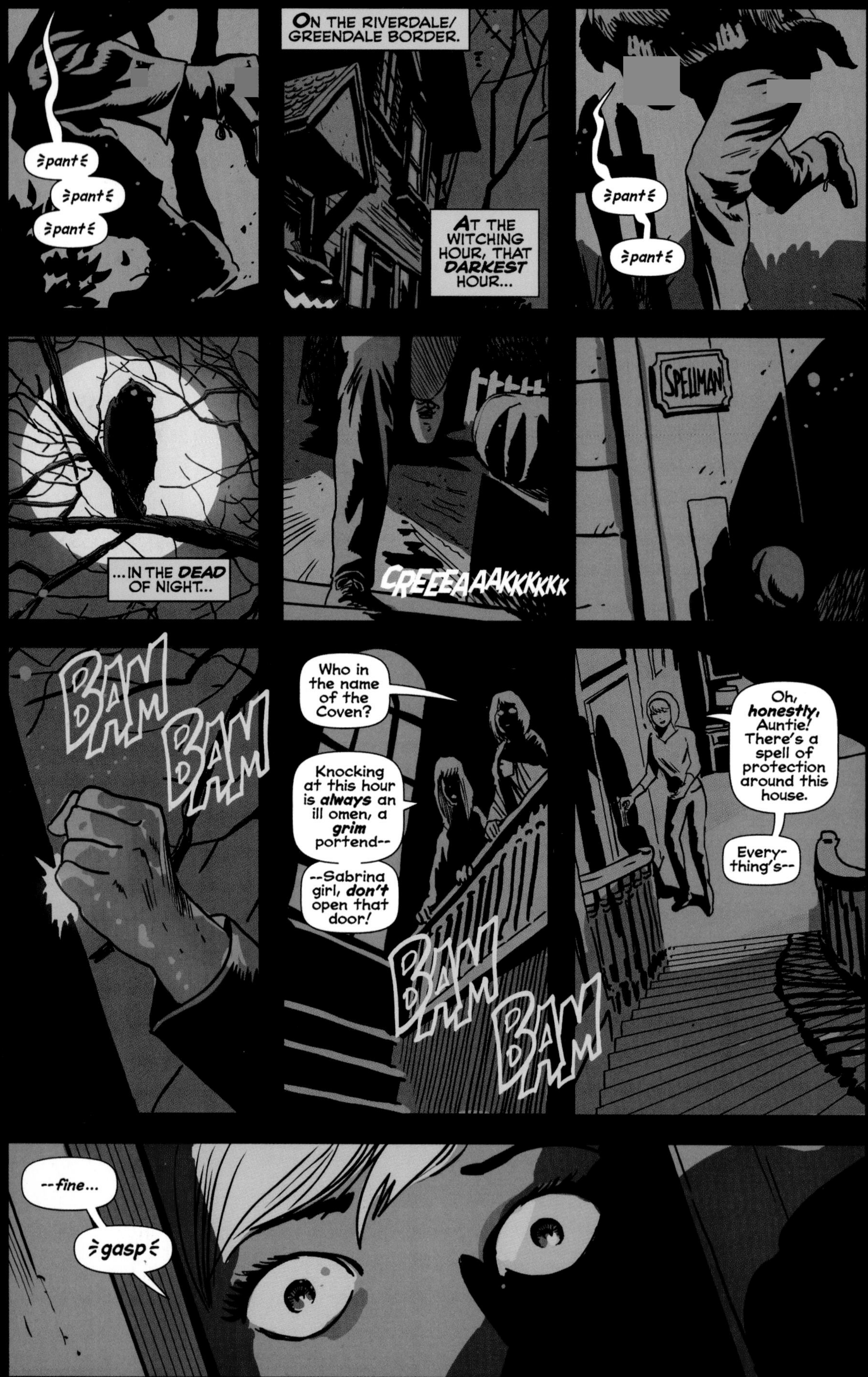

≥pant≤
≥pant≤
≥pant≤
ON THE RIVERDALE/ GREENDALE BORDER.
AT THE WITCHING HOUR, THAT DARKEST HOUR...
≥pant≤
≥pant≤
...IN THE DEAD OF NIGHT...
CREEEAAAKKKKKK
SPELLMAN
BAM BAM
Who in the name of the Coven?
Knocking at this hour is always an ill omen, a grim portend--
--Sabrina girl, don't open that door!
BAM BAM
Oh, honestly, Auntie! There's a spell of protection around this house.
Every-thing's--
--fine...
≥gasp≤

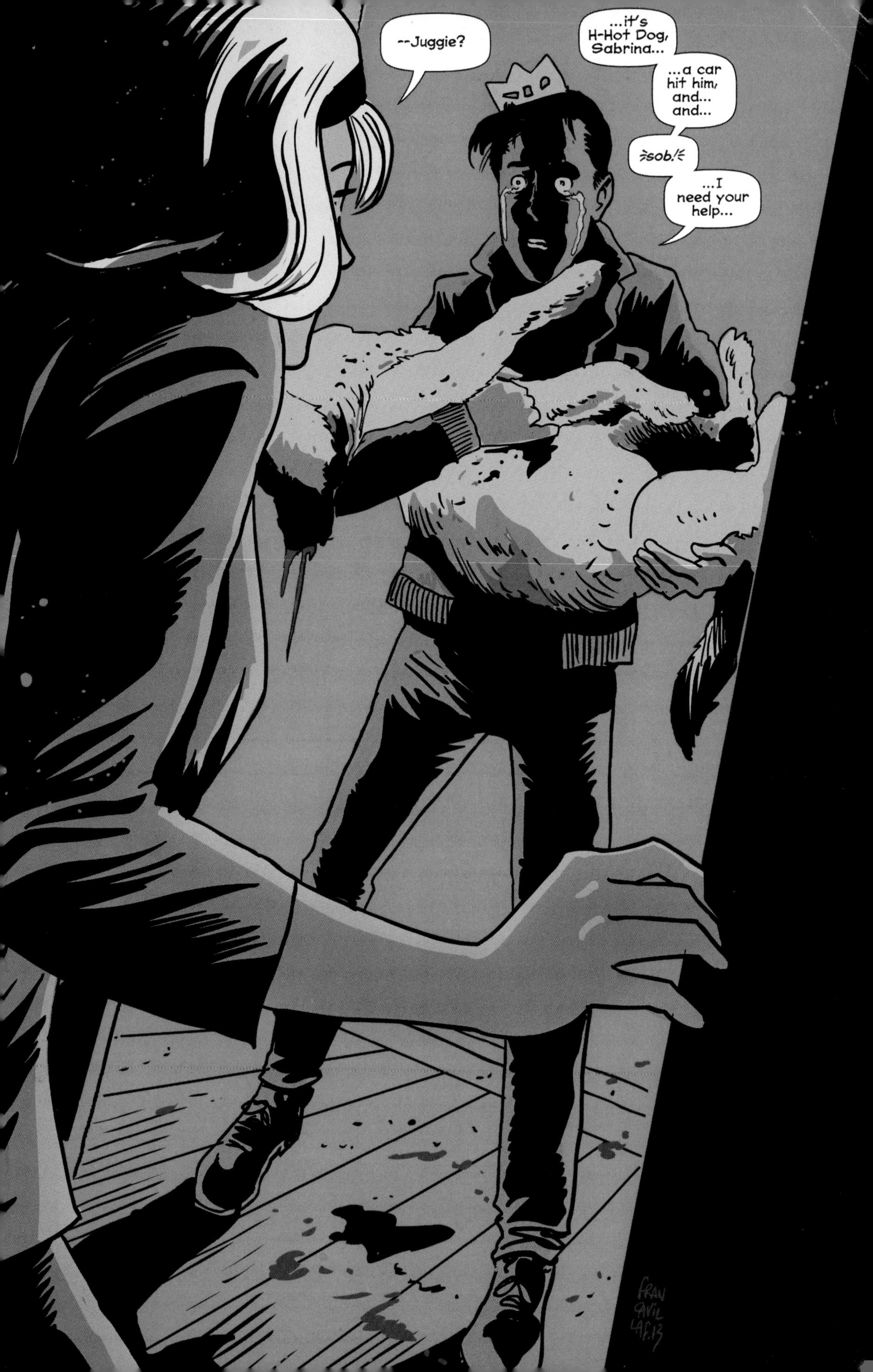
--Juggie?
...it's H-Hot Dog, Sabrina...
...a car hit him, and... and...
≈sob!≈
...I need your help...

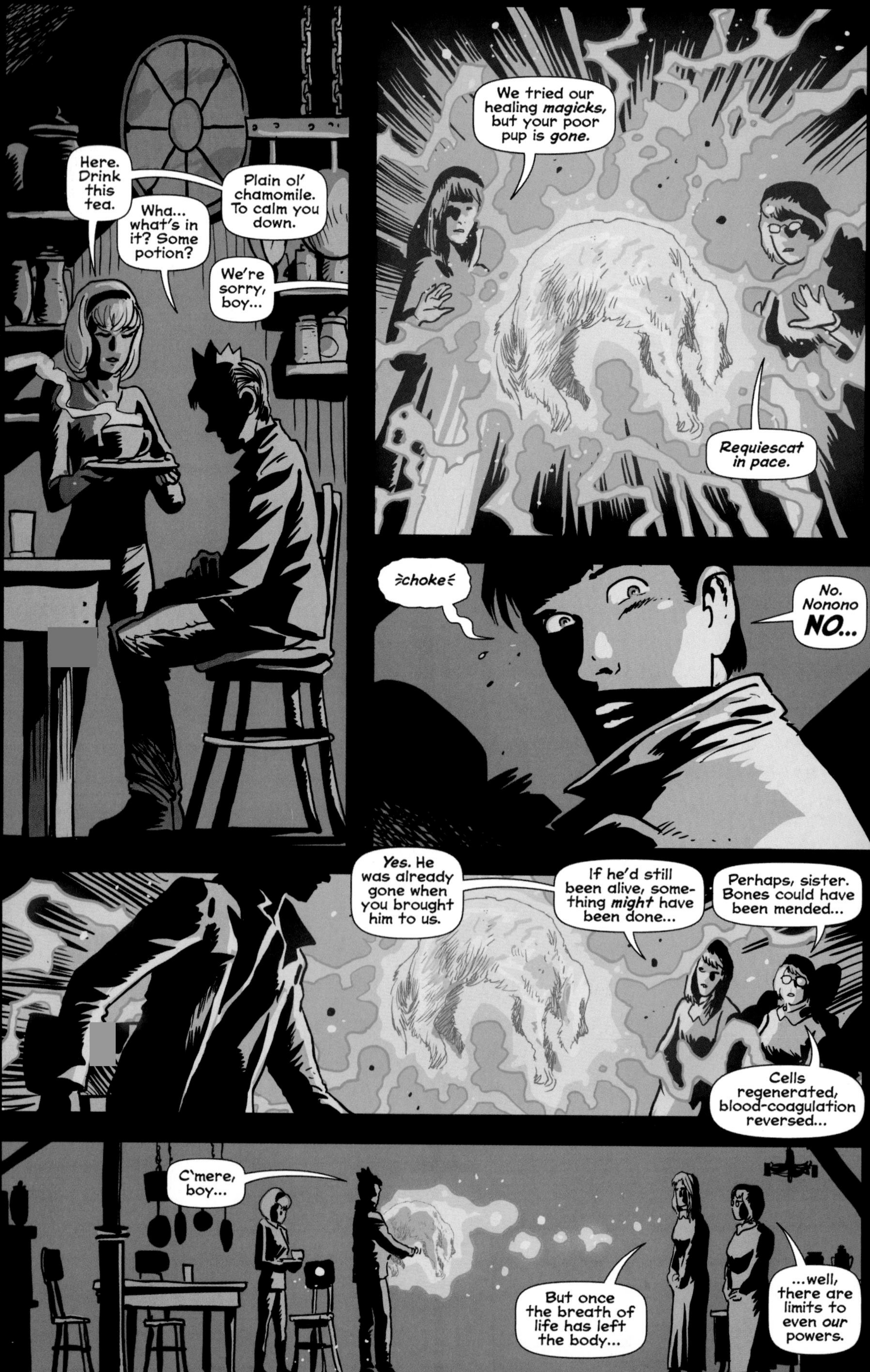

Here. Drink this tea.
Wha... what's in it? Some potion?
Plain ol' chamomile. To calm you down.
We're sorry, boy...
We tried our healing *magicks,* but your poor pup is *gone.*
Requiescat in pace.
≈choke≈
No. Nonono **NO...**
Yes. He was already gone when you brought him to us.
If he'd still been alive, something *might* have been done...
Perhaps, sister. Bones could have been mended...
Cells regenerated, blood-coagulation reversed...
C'mere, boy...
But once the breath of life has left the body...
...well, there are limits to even *our* powers.

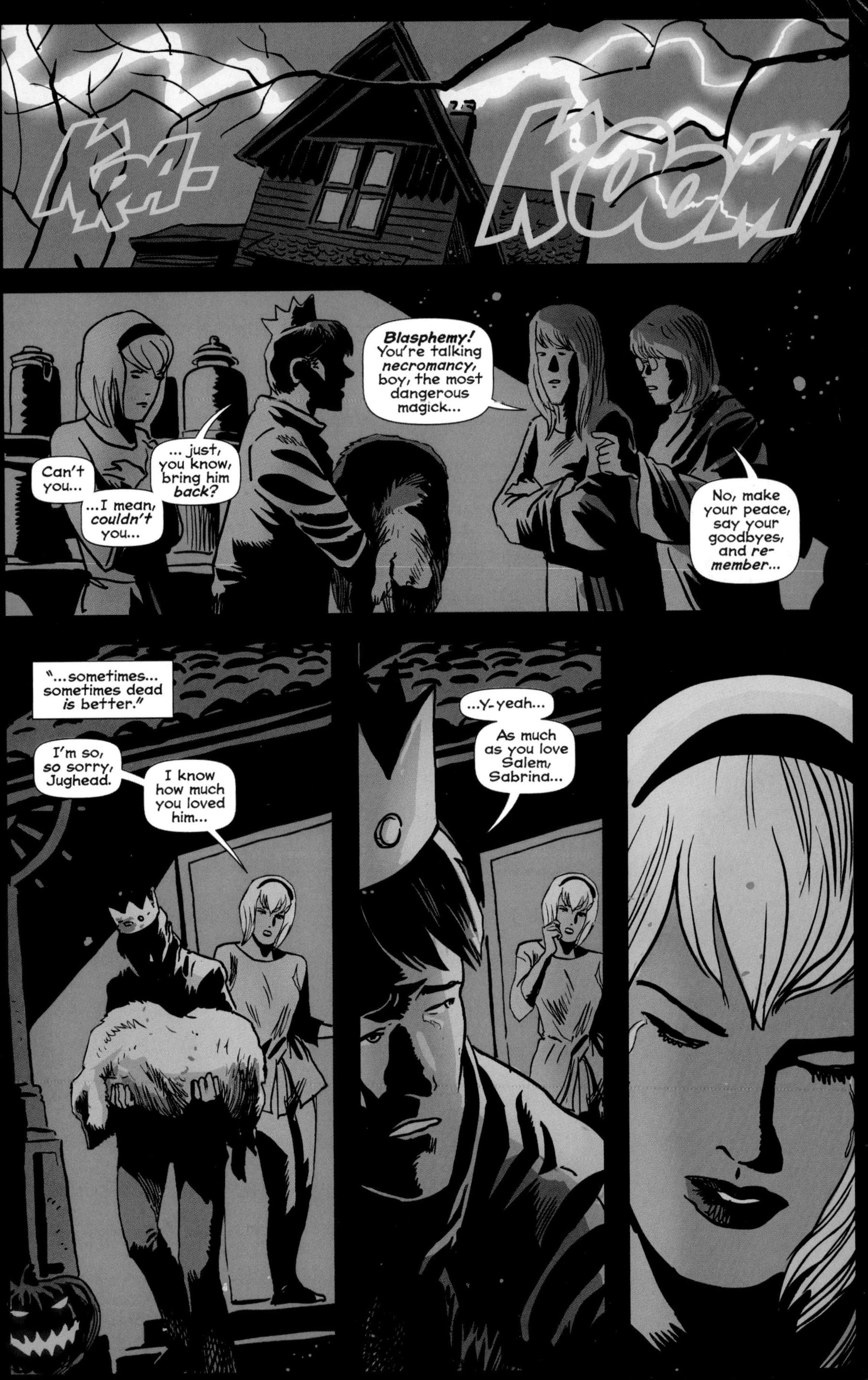
KRA-
KOOM
Blasphemy! You're talking necromancy, boy, the most dangerous magick...
Can't you...
...I mean, couldn't you...
... just, you know, bring him back?
No, make your peace, say your goodbyes, and remember...
"...sometimes... sometimes dead is better."
I'm so, so sorry, Jughead.
I know how much you loved him...
...Y-yeah...
As much as you love Salem, Sabrina...

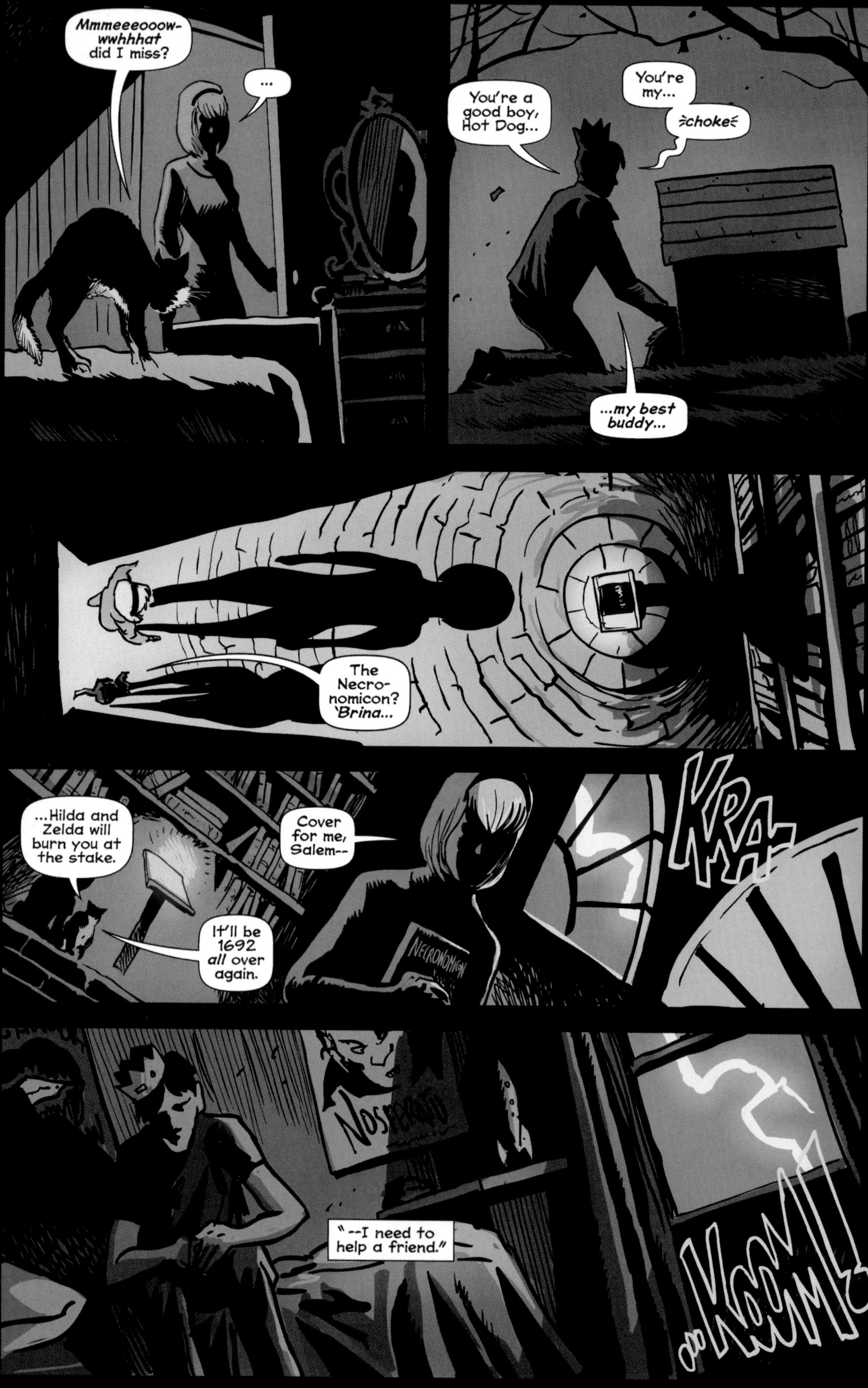
Mmmeeeooow-wwhhhat did I miss?
...
You're a good boy, Hot Dog...
You're my...
choke
...my best buddy...
The Necro-nomicon? 'Brina...
Cover for me, Salem--
...Hilda and Zelda will burn you at the stake.
It'll be 1692 all over again.
NECRONOMICON
KRA
NOSFERATU
"--I need to help a friend."
KOOM

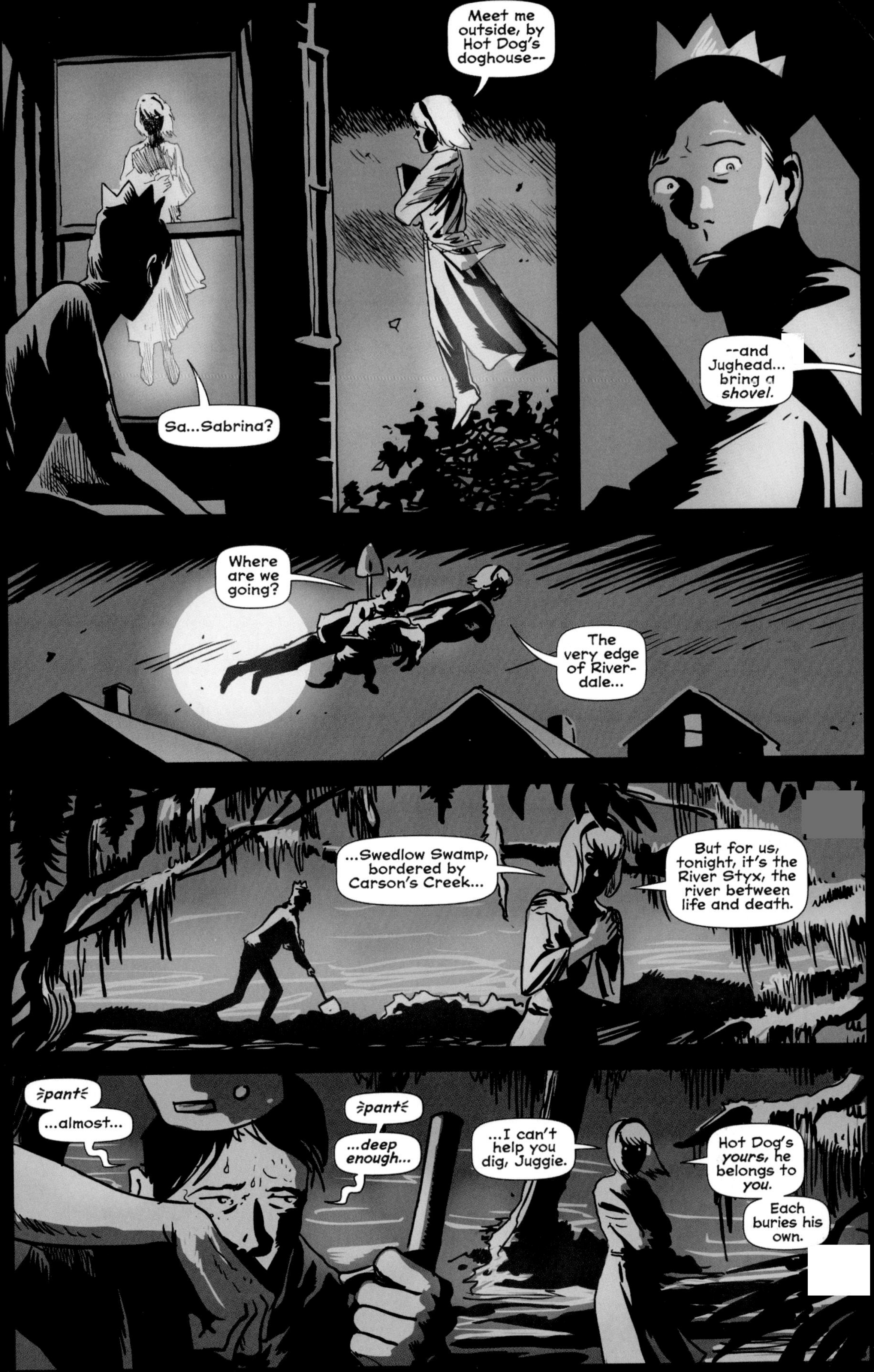
Sa...Sabrina?
Meet me outside, by Hot Dog's doghouse--
--and Jughead... bring a *shovel.*
Where are we going?
The very edge of River-dale...
...Swedlow Swamp, bordered by Carson's Creek...
But for us, tonight, it's the River Styx, the river between life and death.
pant
...almost...
pant
...*deep enough*...
...I can't help you dig, Juggie.
Hot Dog's *yours,* he belongs to *you.*
Each buries his own.

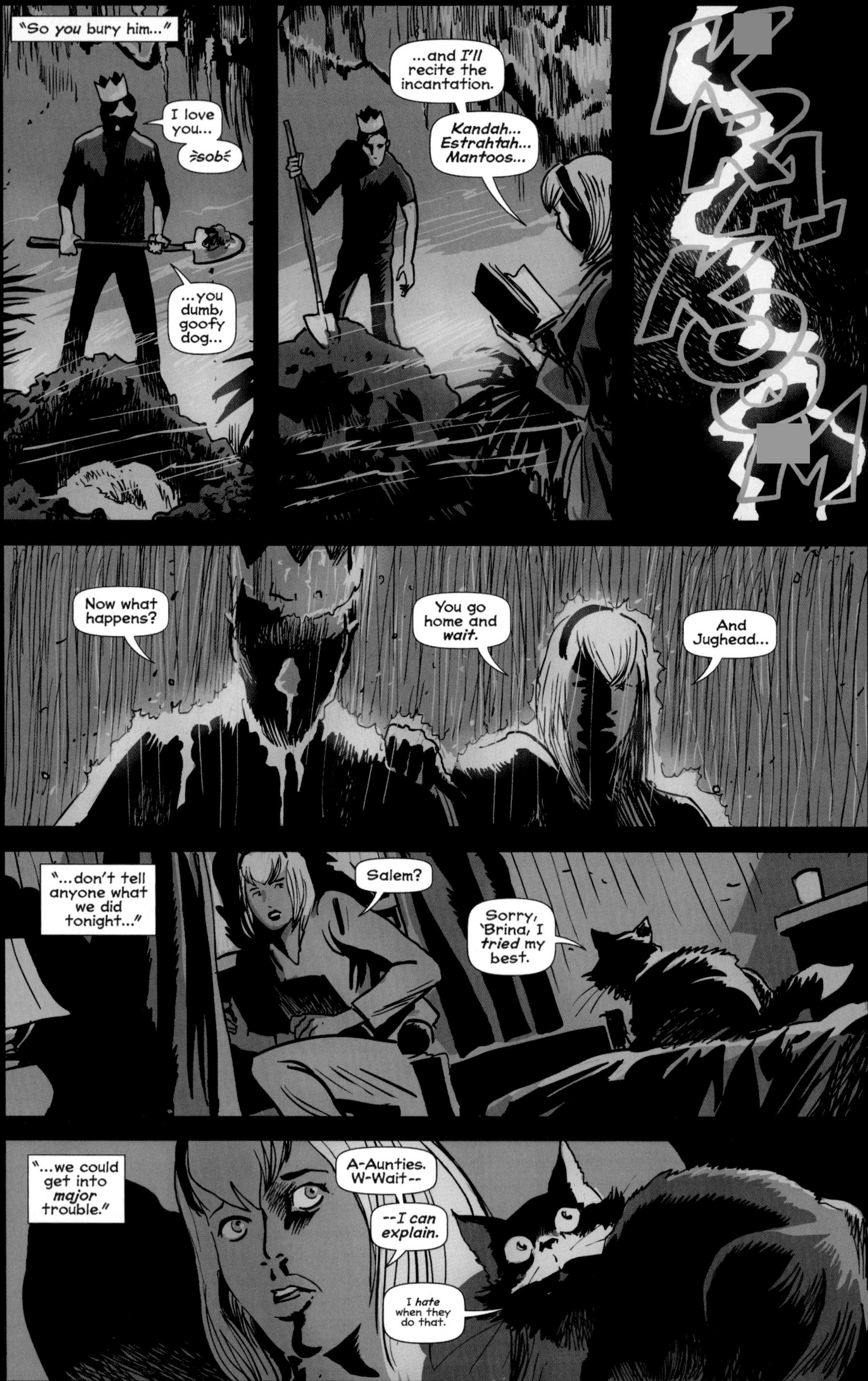
"So you bury him..."
I love you...
sob
...you dumb, goofy dog...
...and I'll recite the incantation.
Kandah... Estrahtah... Mantoos...
Now what happens?
You go home and wait.
And Jughead...
"...don't tell anyone what we did tonight..."
Salem?
Sorry, 'Brina, I tried my best.
"...we could get into major trouble."
A-Aunties. W-Wait--
--I can explain.
I hate when they do that.

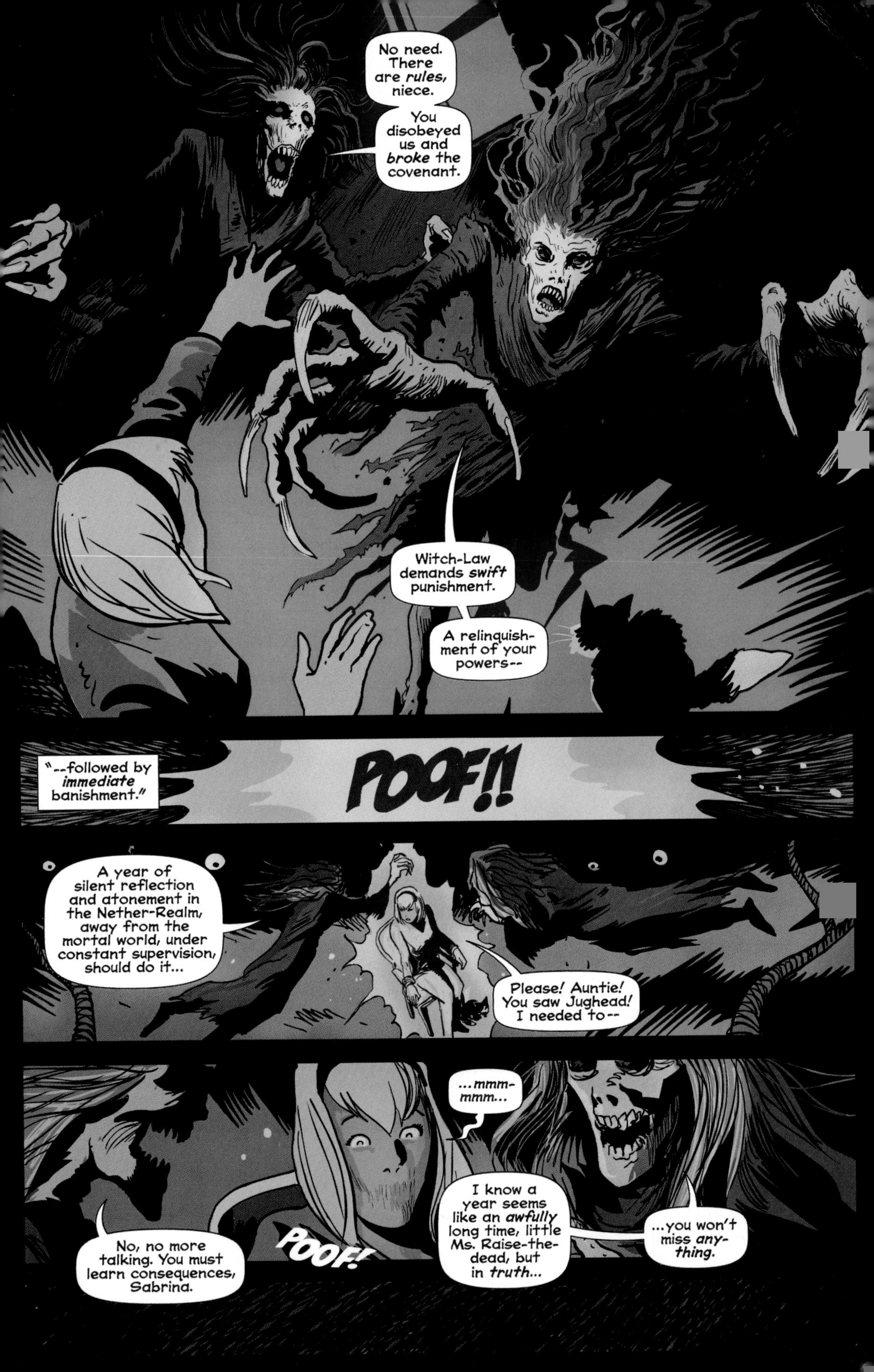
No need. There are *rules,* niece.
You disobeyed us and *broke* the covenant.
Witch-Law demands *swift* punishment.
A relinquishment of your powers--
"--followed by *immediate* banishment."
POOF!!
A year of silent reflection and atonement in the Nether-Realm, away from the mortal world, under constant supervision, should do it...
Please! Auntie! You saw Jughead! I needed to--
...mmm-mmm...
No, no more talking. You must learn consequences, Sabrina.
POOF!
I know a year seems like an *awfully* long time, little Ms. Raise-the-dead, but in *truth*...
...you won't miss *anything.*

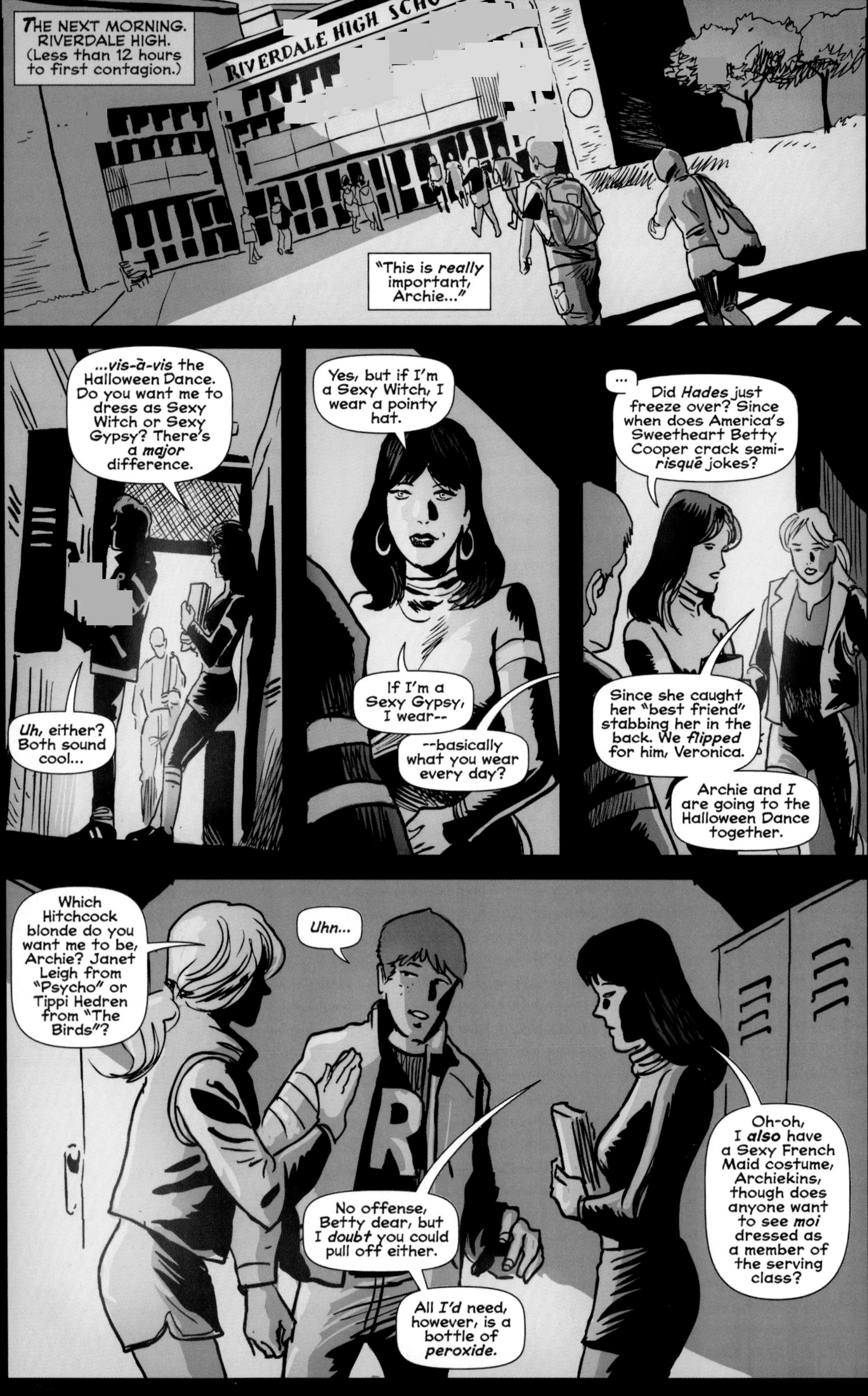

THE NEXT MORNING. RIVERDALE HIGH. (Less than 12 hours to first contagion.)
RIVERDALE HIGH
"This is *really* important, Archie..."
...*vis-à-vis* the Halloween Dance. Do you want me to dress as Sexy Witch or Sexy Gypsy? There's a *major* difference.
Uh, either? Both sound cool...
Yes, but if I'm a Sexy Witch, I wear a pointy hat.
If I'm a Sexy Gypsy, I wear--
--basically what you wear every day?
...
Did *Hades* just freeze over? Since when does America's Sweetheart Betty Cooper crack semi-*risqué* jokes?
Since she caught her "best friend" stabbing her in the back. We *flipped* for him, Veronica.
Archie and *I* are going to the Halloween Dance together.
Which Hitchcock blonde do you want me to be, Archie? Janet Leigh from "Psycho" or Tippi Hedren from "The Birds"?
Uhn...
No offense, Betty dear, but I *doubt* you could pull off either.
All *I'd* need, however, is a bottle of *peroxide.*
Oh-oh, I *also* have a Sexy French Maid costume, Archiekins, though does anyone want to see *moi* dressed as a member of the serving class?

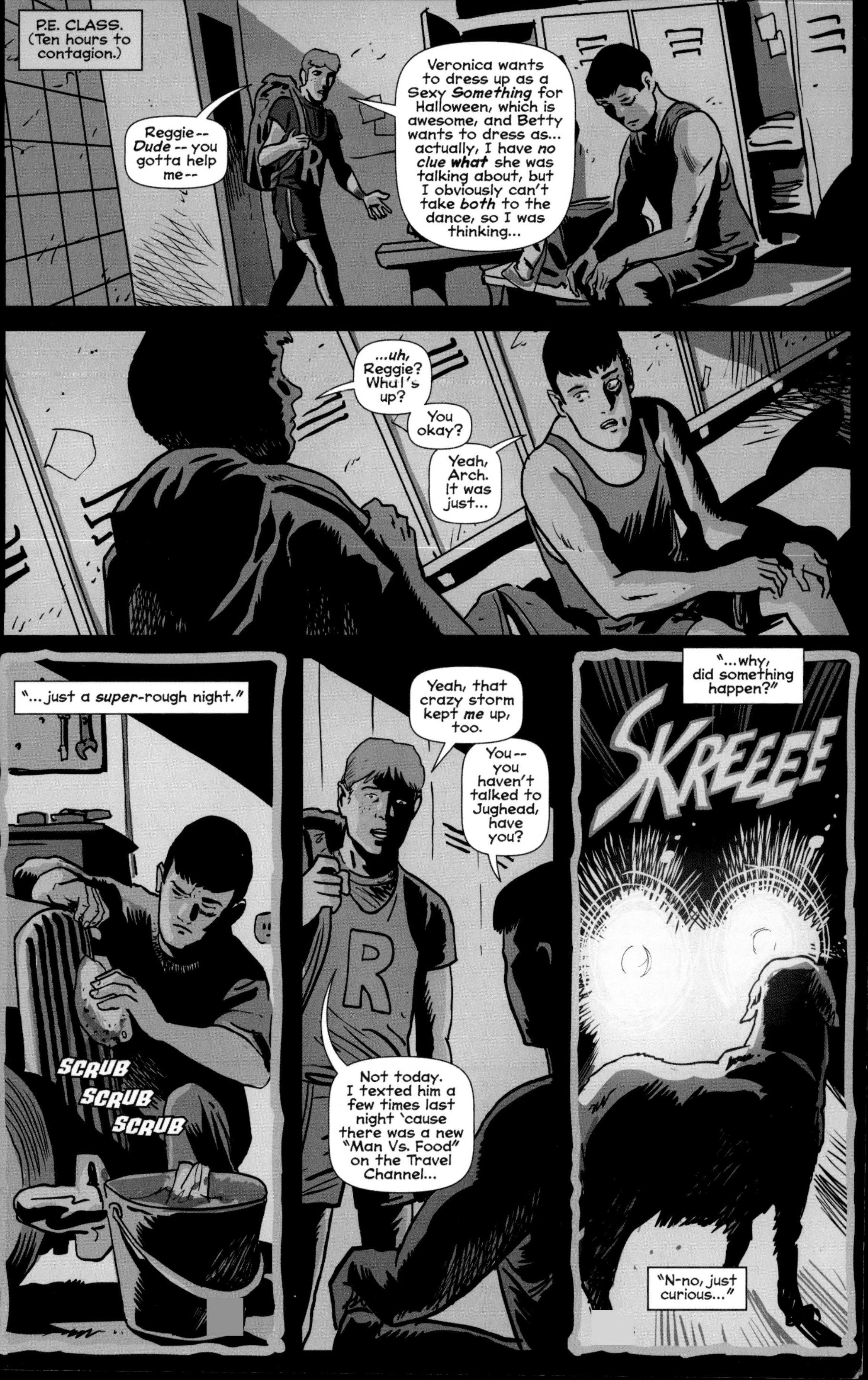
P.E. CLASS. (Ten hours to contagion.)
Reggie-- Dude -- you gotta help me--
Veronica wants to dress up as a Sexy Something for Halloween, which is awesome, and Betty wants to dress as... actually, I have no clue what she was talking about, but I obviously can't take both to the dance, so I was thinking...
...uh, Reggie? What's up?
You okay?
Yeah, Arch. It was just...
"...just a super-rough night."
SCRUB
SCRUB
SCRUB
Yeah, that crazy storm kept me up, too.
You-- you haven't talked to Jughead, have you?
Not today. I texted him a few times last night 'cause there was a new "Man Vs. Food" on the Travel Channel...
"...why, did something happen?"
SKREEEE
"N-no, just curious..."

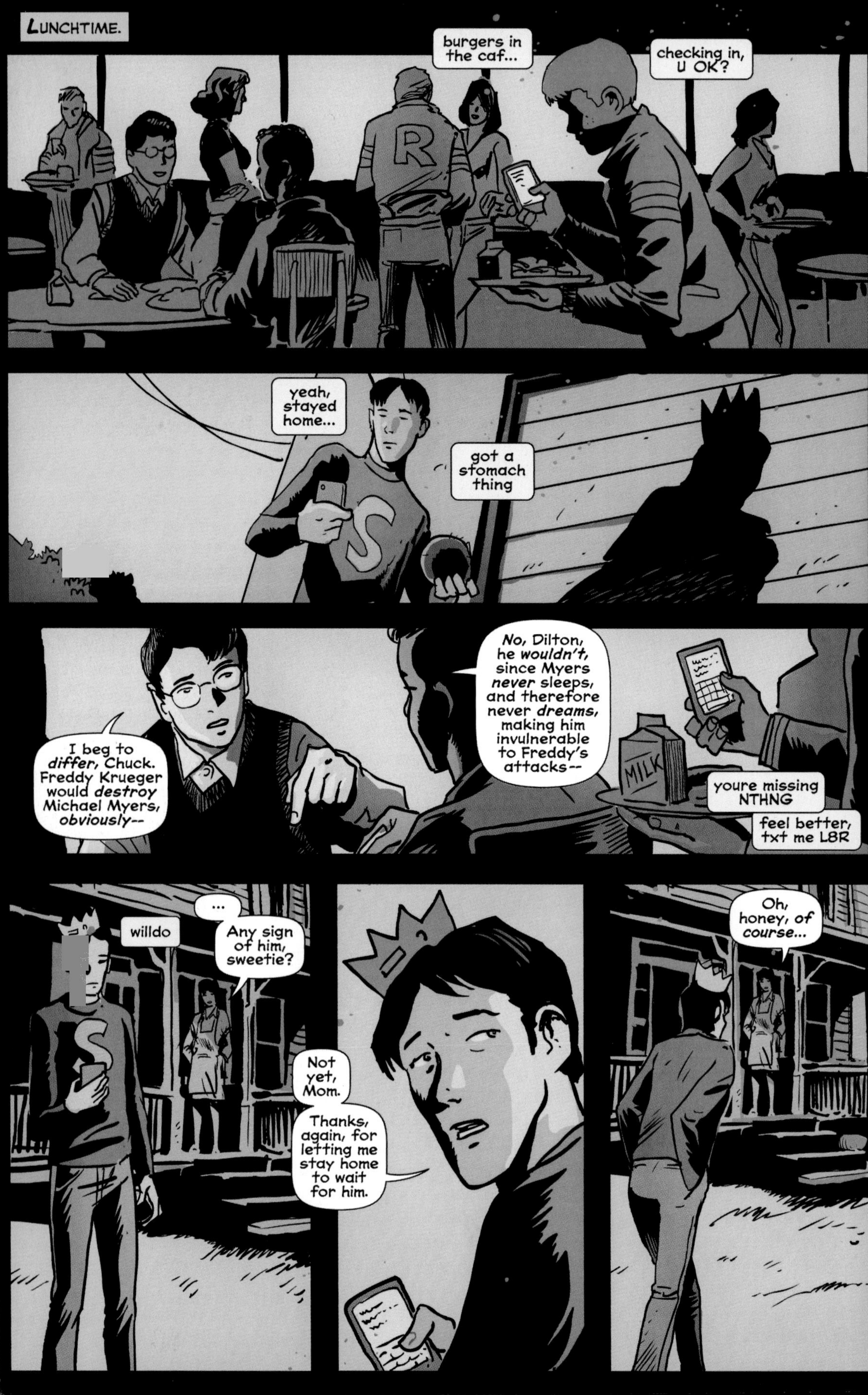
LUNCHTIME.
burgers in the caf...
checking in, U OK?
yeah, stayed home...
got a stomach thing
I beg to *differ*, Chuck. Freddy Krueger would *destroy* Michael Myers, *obviously*--
No, Dilton, he *wouldn't*, since Myers *never* sleeps, and therefore never *dreams*, making him invulnerable to Freddy's attacks--
MILK
youre missing NTHNG
feel better, txt me L8R
willdo
...
Any sign of him, sweetie?
Not yet, Mom.
Thanks, again, for letting me stay home to wait for him.
Oh, honey, of course...

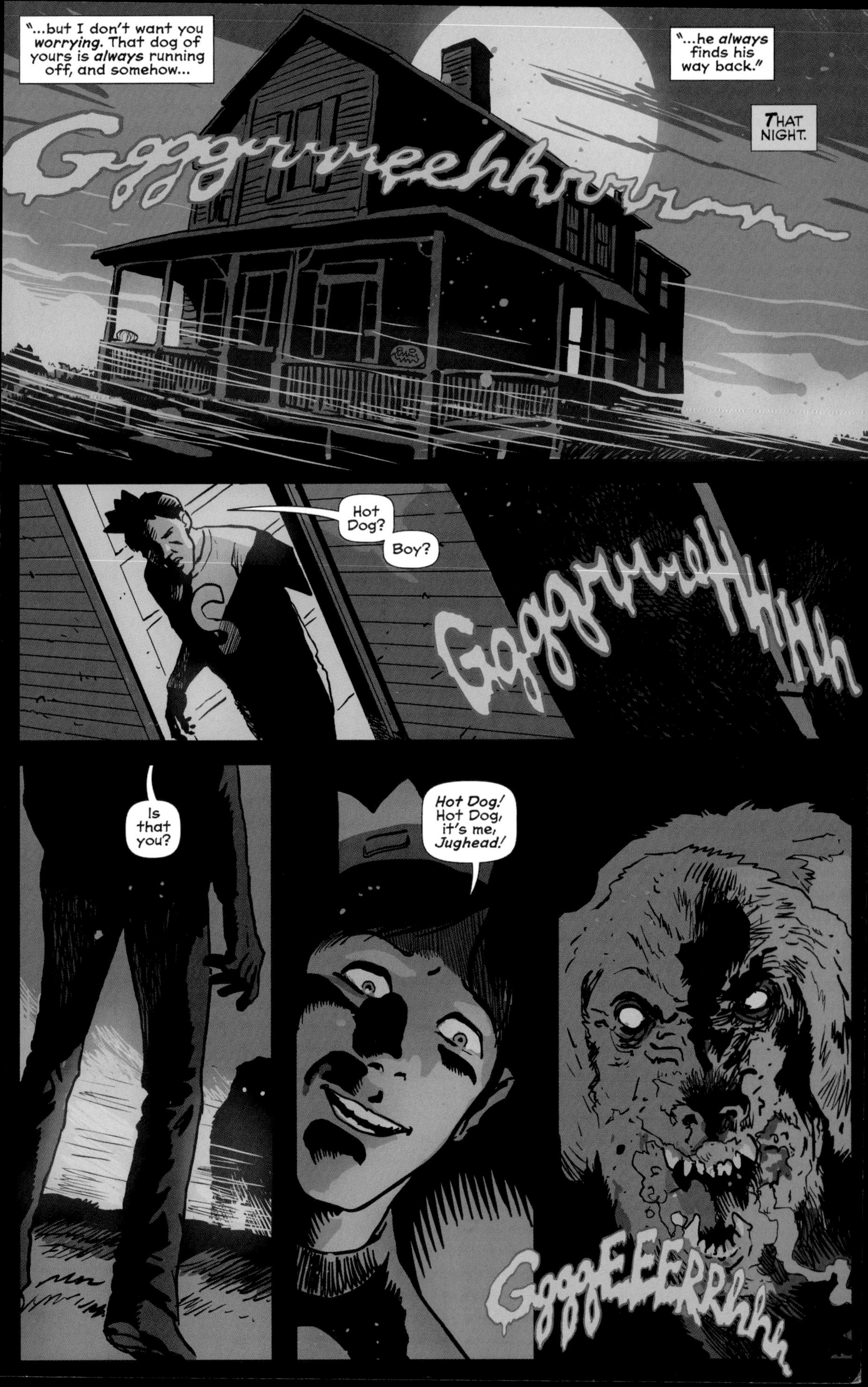
"...but I don't want you *worrying*. That dog of yours is *always* running off, and somehow...
"...he *always* finds his way back."
*T*HAT NIGHT.
Gggggrrrreehhrrrr
Hot Dog?
Boy?
Gggggrrrrrr
Is that you?
Hot Dog! Hot Dog, it's me, *Jughead!*
GgggEEERRhhh

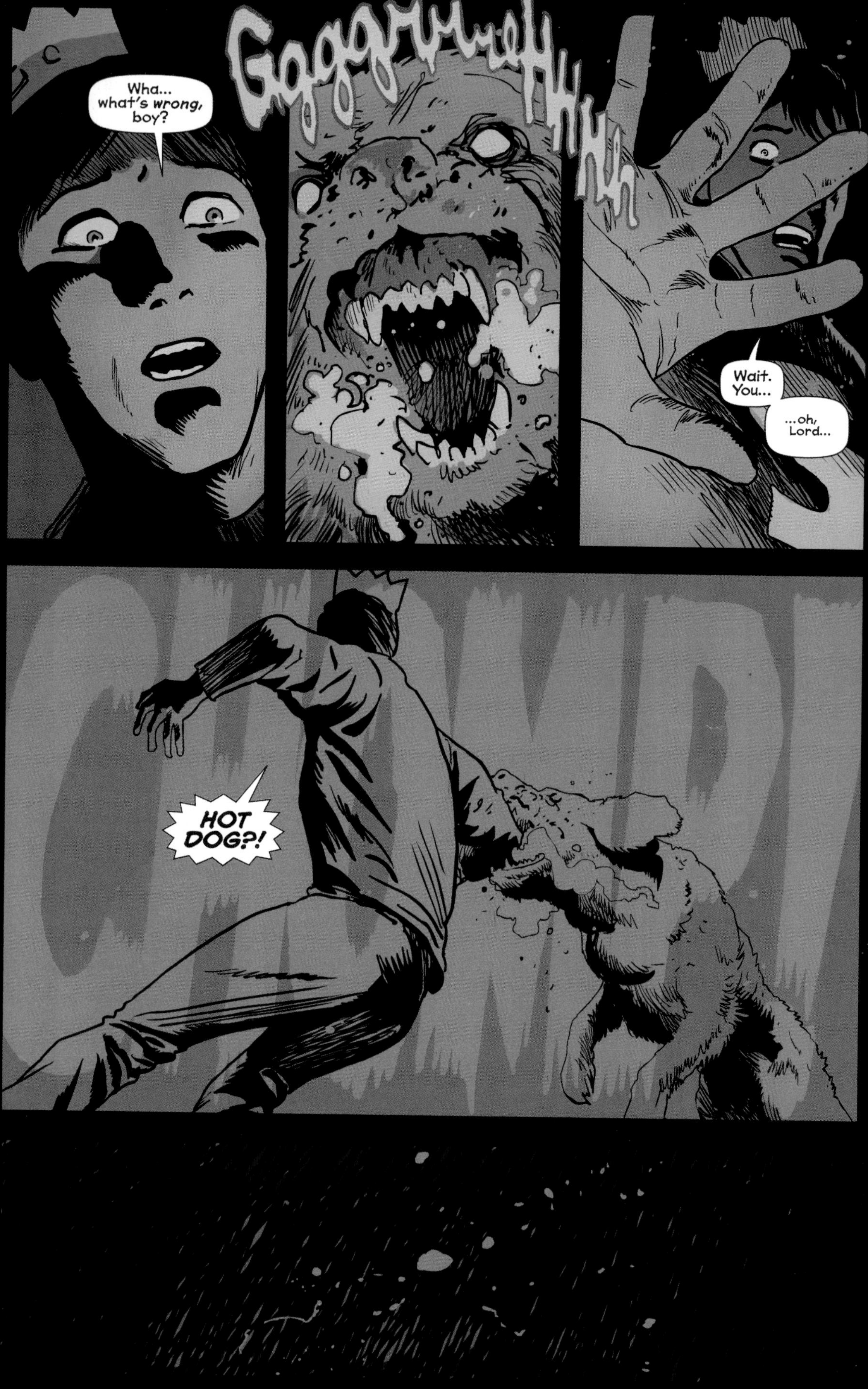
Wha... what's wrong, boy?
Gggrrrrr
Wait. You...
...oh, Lord...
HOT DOG?!

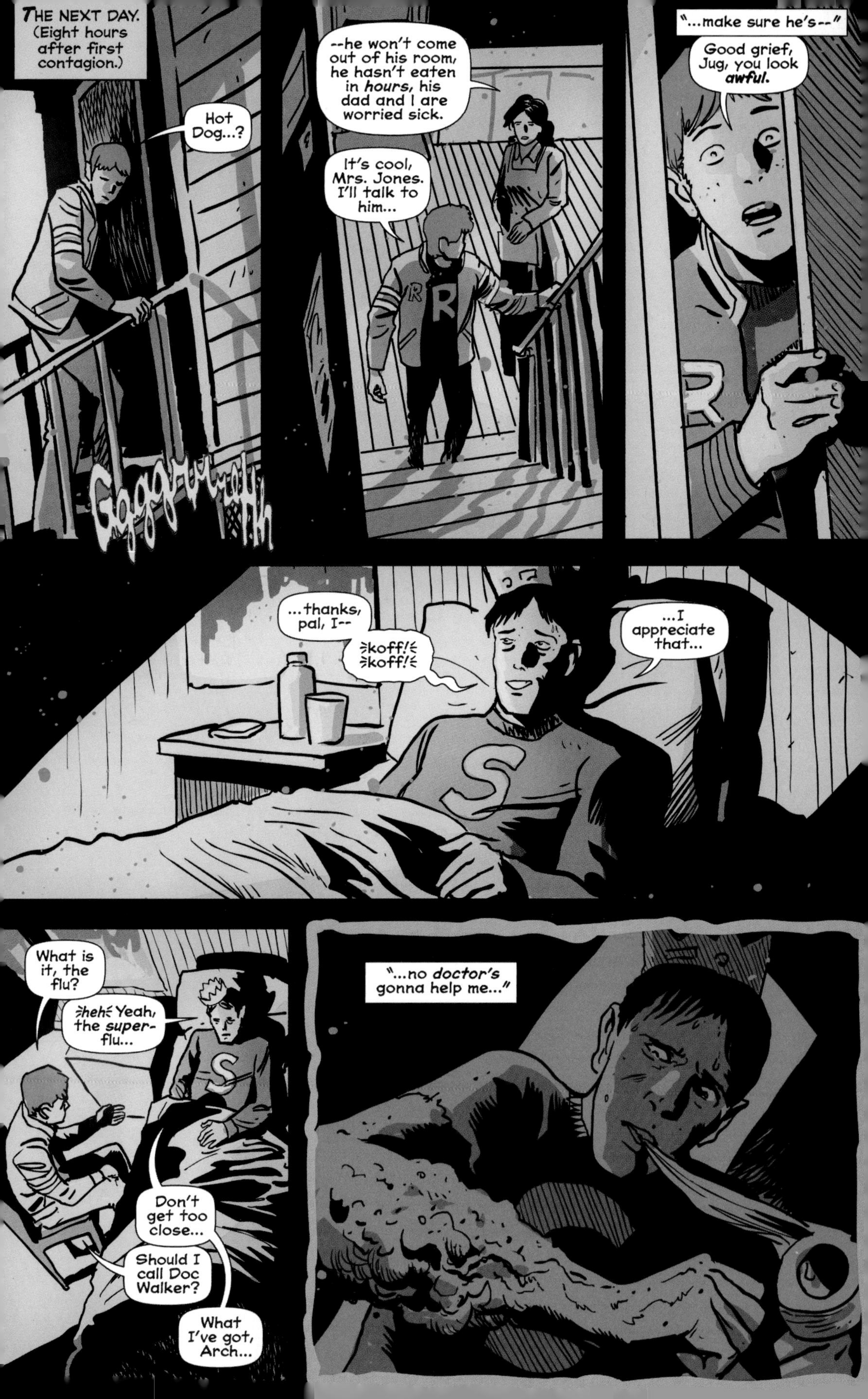
THE NEXT DAY. (Eight hours after first contagion.)
Hot Dog...?
Gggrrr
--he won't come out of his room, he hasn't eaten in *hours,* his dad and I are worried sick.
It's cool, Mrs. Jones. I'll talk to him...
"...make sure he's--"
Good grief, Jug, you look *awful.*
...thanks, pal, I--
koff! koff!
...I appreciate that...
What is it, the flu?
heh Yeah, the *super*-flu...
Don't get too close...
Should I call Doc Walker?
What I've got, Arch...
"...no *doctor's* gonna help me..."

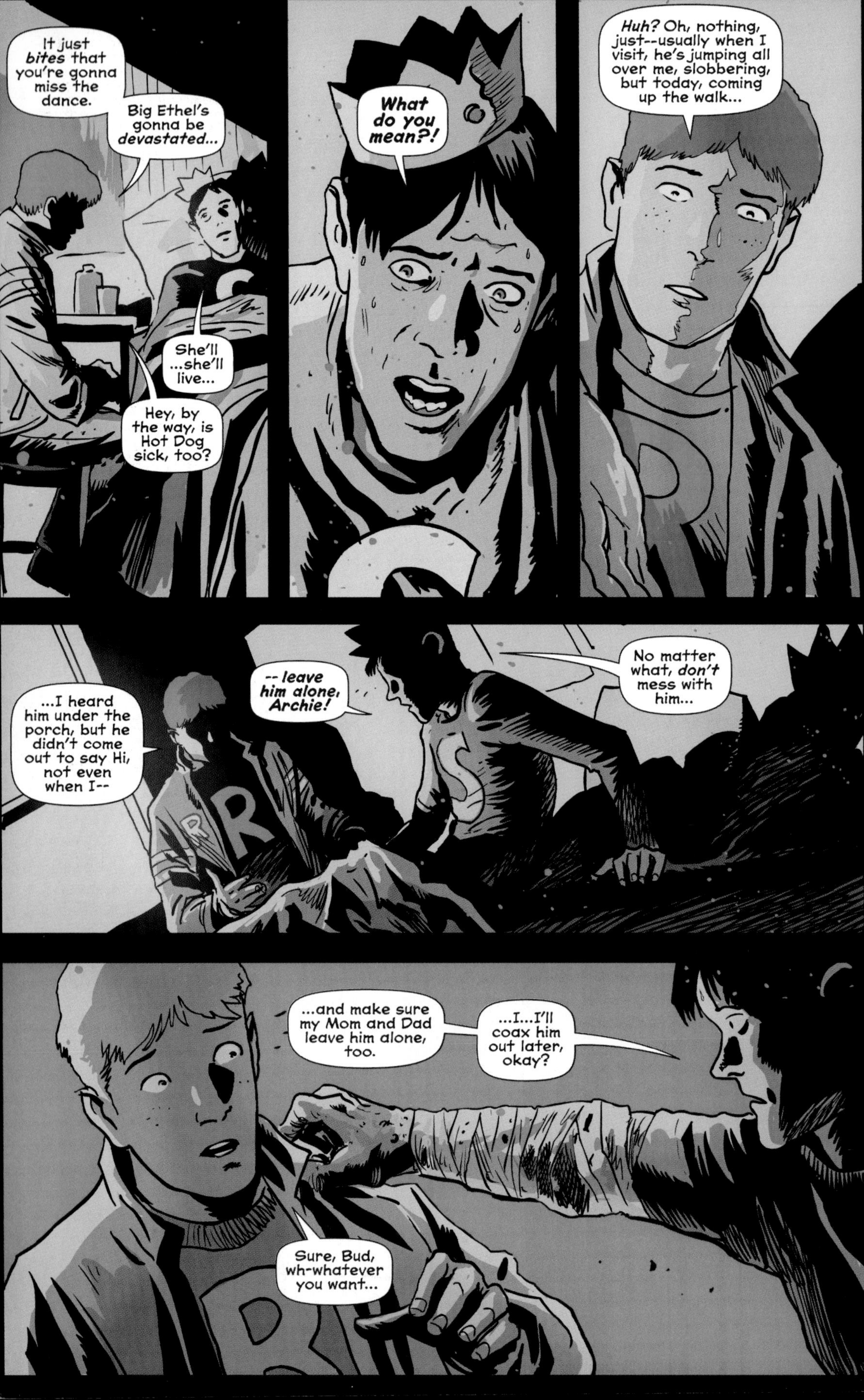

It just bites that you're gonna miss the dance.
Big Ethel's gonna be devastated...
She'll ...she'll live...
Hey, by the way, is Hot Dog sick, too?
What do you mean?!
Huh? Oh, nothing, just--usually when I visit, he's jumping all over me, slobbering, but today, coming up the walk...
...I heard him under the porch, but he didn't come out to say Hi, not even when I--
--leave him alone, Archie!
No matter what, don't mess with him...
...I...I'll coax him out later, okay?
...and make sure my Mom and Dad leave him alone, too.
Sure, Bud, wh-whatever you want...

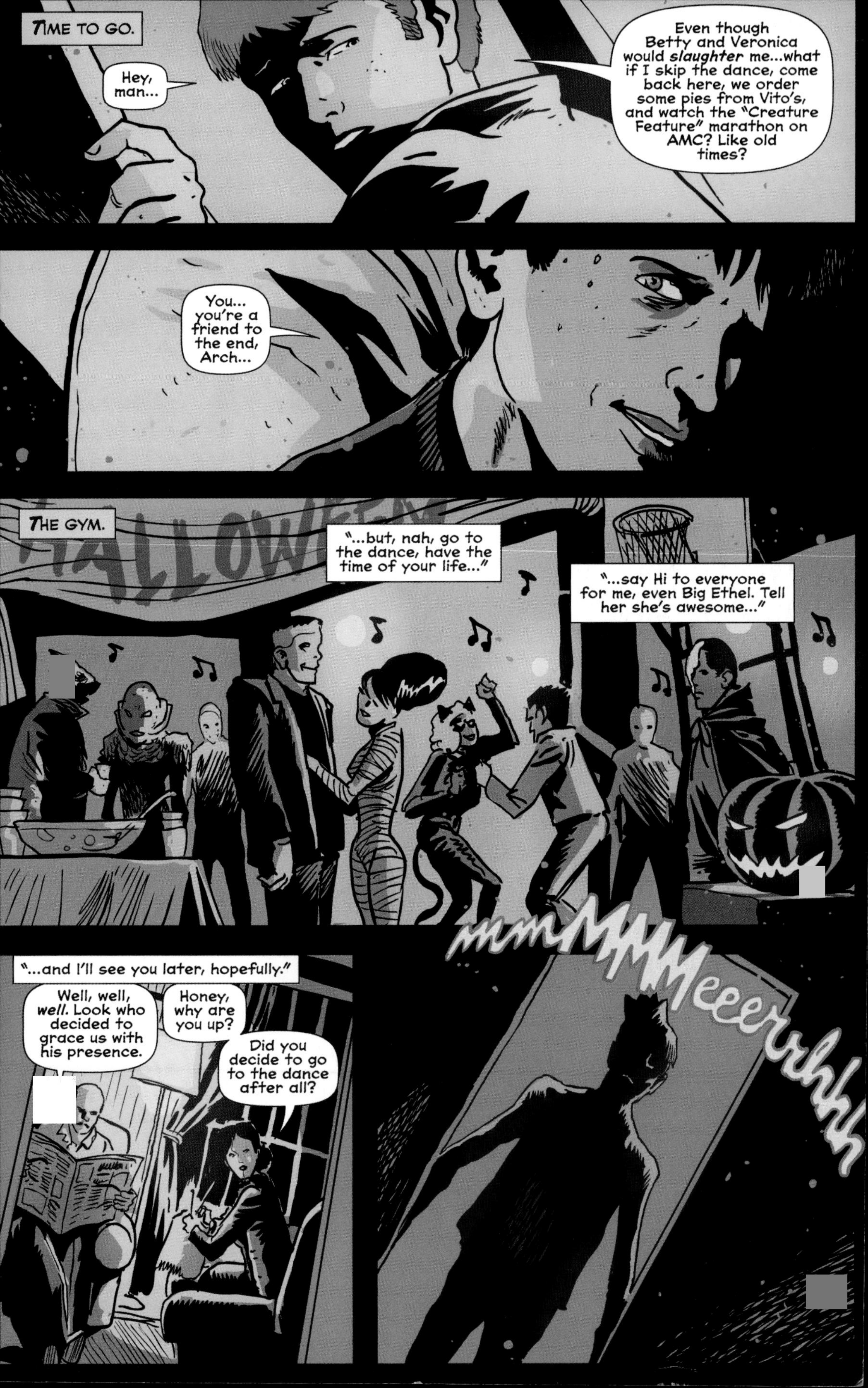
TIME TO GO.
Hey, man...
Even though Betty and Veronica would *slaughter* me...what if I skip the dance, come back here, we order some pies from Vito's, and watch the "Creature Feature" marathon on AMC? Like old times?
You... you're a friend to the end, Arch...
THE GYM.
HALLOWEEN
"...but, nah, go to the dance, have the time of your life..."
"...say Hi to everyone for me, even Big Ethel. Tell her she's awesome..."
"...and I'll see you later, hopefully."
Well, well, *well*. Look who decided to grace us with his presence.
Honey, why are you up?
Did you decide to go to the dance after all?
mmmMMMeeeerrhhhh

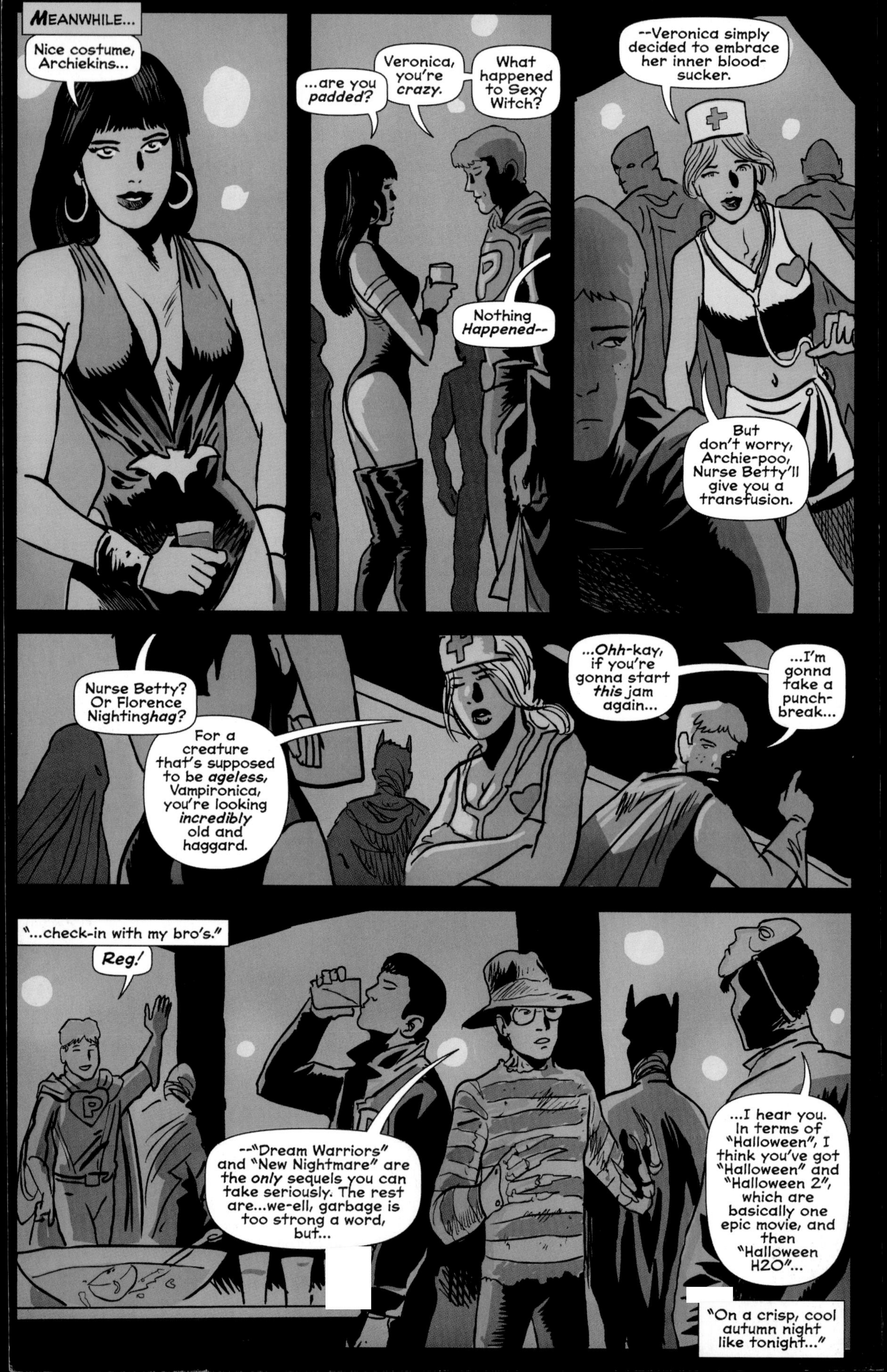
MEANWHILE...
Nice costume, Archiekins...
...are you *padded?*
Veronica, you're *crazy.*
What happened to Sexy Witch?
Nothing *Happened--*
--Veronica simply decided to embrace her inner blood-sucker.
But don't worry, Archie-poo, Nurse Betty'll give you a transfusion.
Nurse Betty? Or Florence Nighting*hag?*
For a creature that's supposed to be *ageless,* Vampironica, you're looking *incredibly* old and haggard.
...*Ohh*-kay, if you're gonna start *this* jam again...
...I'm gonna take a punch-break...
"...check-in with my bro's."
Reg!
--"Dream Warriors" and "New Nightmare" are the *only* sequels you can take seriously. The rest are...we-ell, garbage is too strong a word, but...
...I hear you. In terms of "Halloween", I think you've got "Halloween" and "Halloween 2", which are basically one epic movie, and then "Halloween H2O"...
"On a crisp, cool autumn night like tonight..."

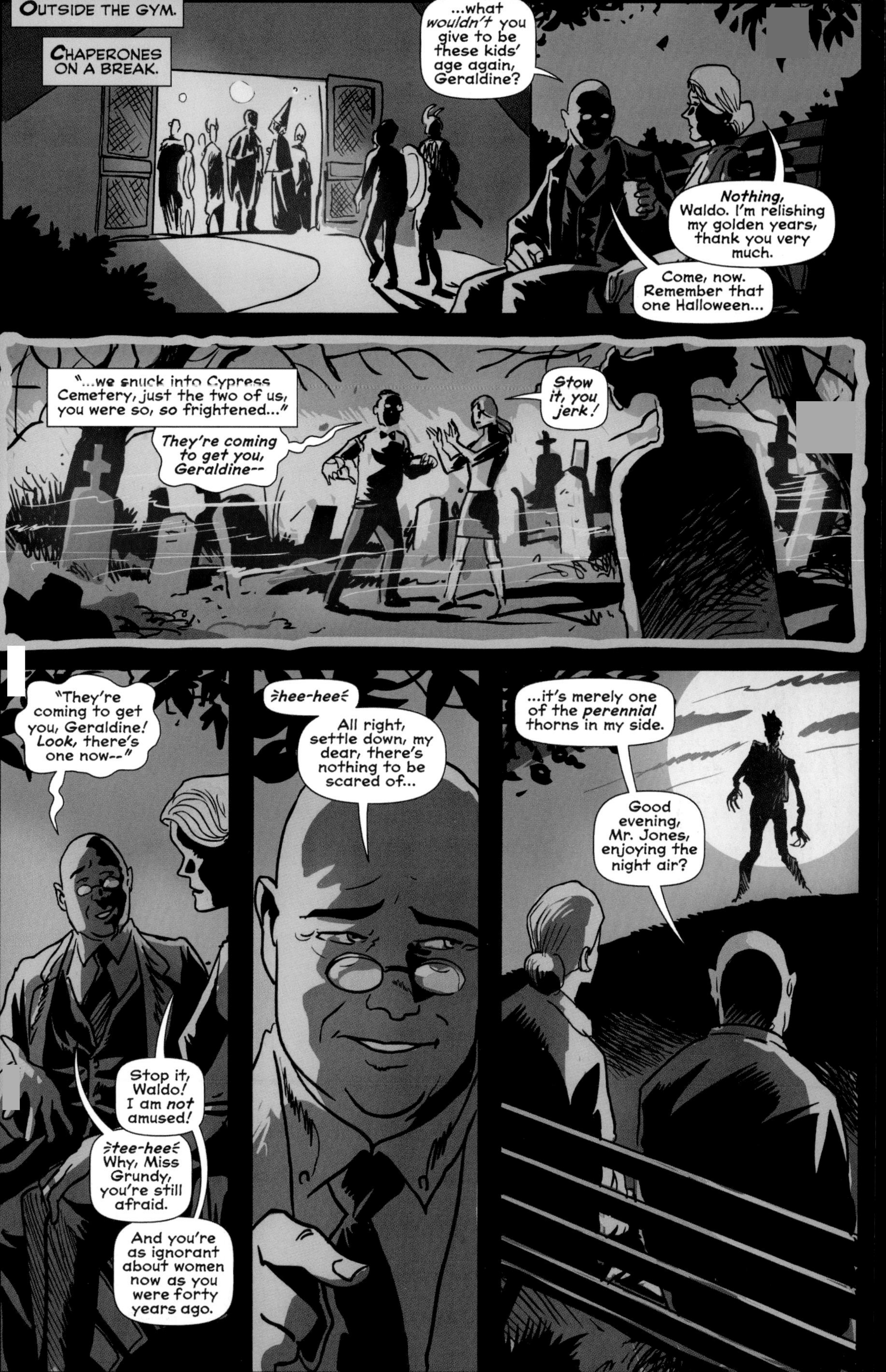
OUTSIDE THE GYM.
CHAPERONES ON A BREAK.
...what *wouldn't* you give to be these kids' age again, Geraldine?
Nothing, Waldo. I'm relishing my golden years, thank you very much.
Come, now. Remember that one Halloween...
"...we snuck into Cypress Cemetery, just the two of us, you were so, so frightened..."
They're coming to get you, Geraldine--
Stow it, you jerk!
"They're coming to get you, Geraldine! *Look,* there's one now--"
Stop it, Waldo! I am *not* amused!
tee-hee Why, Miss Grundy, you're still afraid.
And you're as ignorant about women now as you were forty years ago.
hee-hee
All right, settle down, my dear, there's nothing to be scared of...
...it's merely one of the *perennial* thorns in my side.
Good evening, Mr. Jones, enjoying the night air?

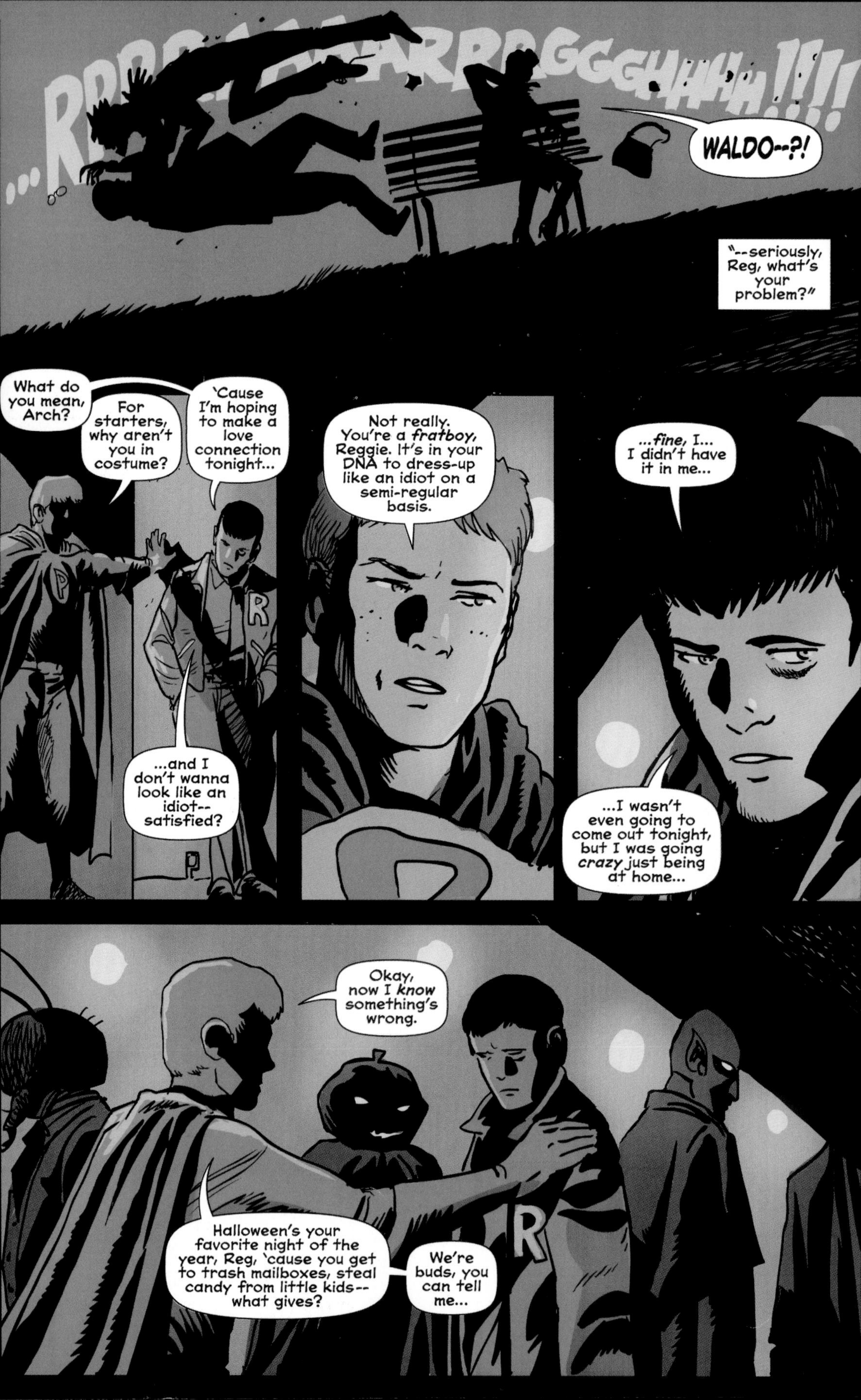
...RRRRAAAAARRRRGGGHHHH!!!!
WALDO--?!
"--seriously, Reg, what's your problem?"
What do you mean, Arch?
For starters, why aren't you in costume?
'Cause I'm hoping to make a love connection tonight...
...and I don't wanna look like an idiot--satisfied?
Not really. You're a *fratboy,* Reggie. It's in your DNA to dress-up like an idiot on a semi-regular basis.
...*fine,* I... I didn't have it in me...
...I wasn't even going to come out tonight, but I was going *crazy* just being at home...
Okay, now I *know* something's wrong.
Halloween's your favorite night of the year, Reg, 'cause you get to trash mailboxes, steal candy from little kids--what gives?
We're buds, you can tell me...

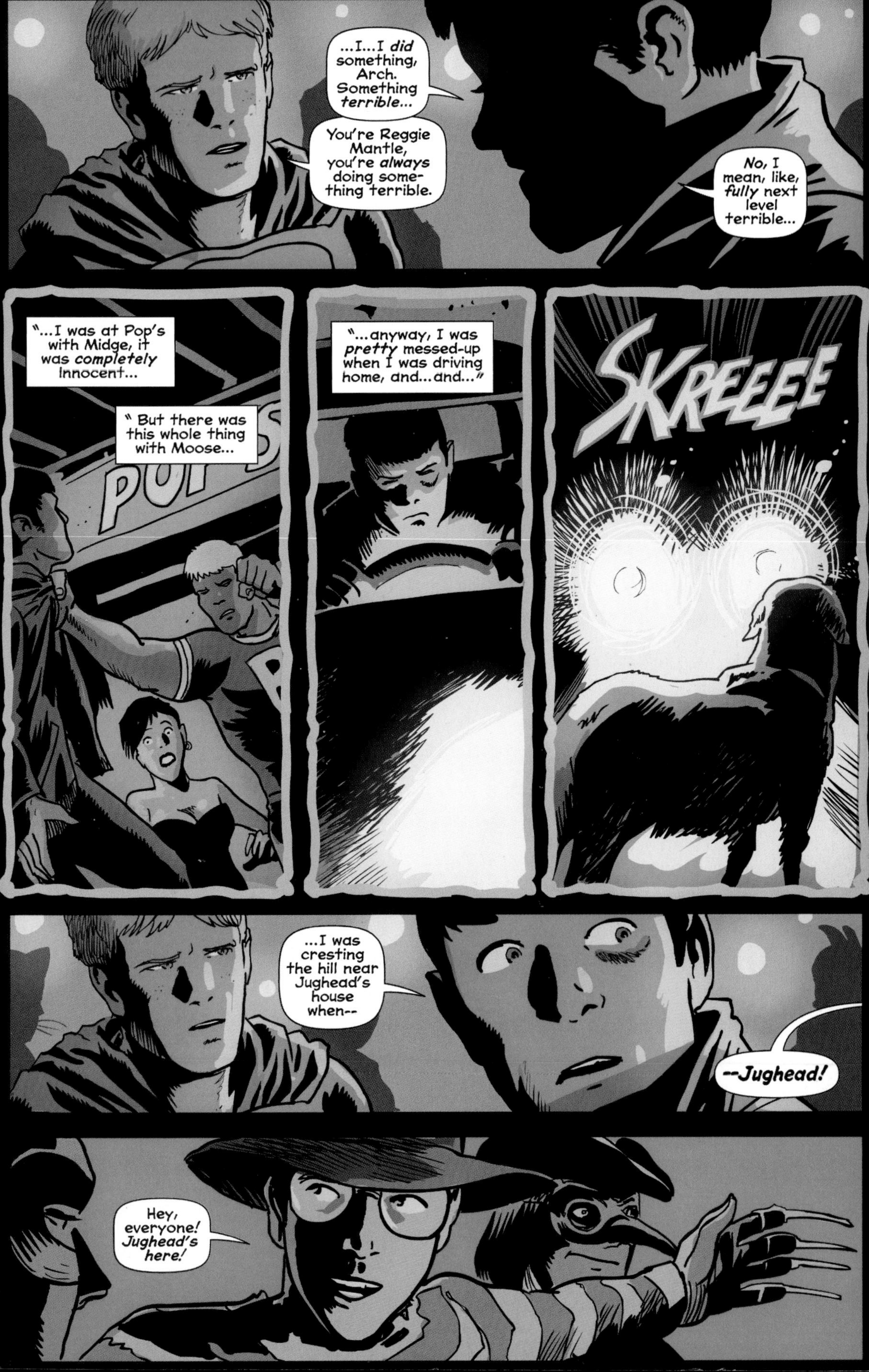

...I...I *did* something, Arch. Something *terrible*...
You're Reggie Mantle, you're *always* doing some-thing terrible.
No, I mean, like, *fully* next level terrible...
"...I was at Pop's with Midge, it was *completely* innocent...
" But there was this whole thing with Moose...
POP'S
"...anyway, I was *pretty* messed-up when I was driving home, and...and..."
SKREEEE
...I was cresting the hill near Jughead's house when--
--Jughead!
Hey, everyone! Jughead's here!

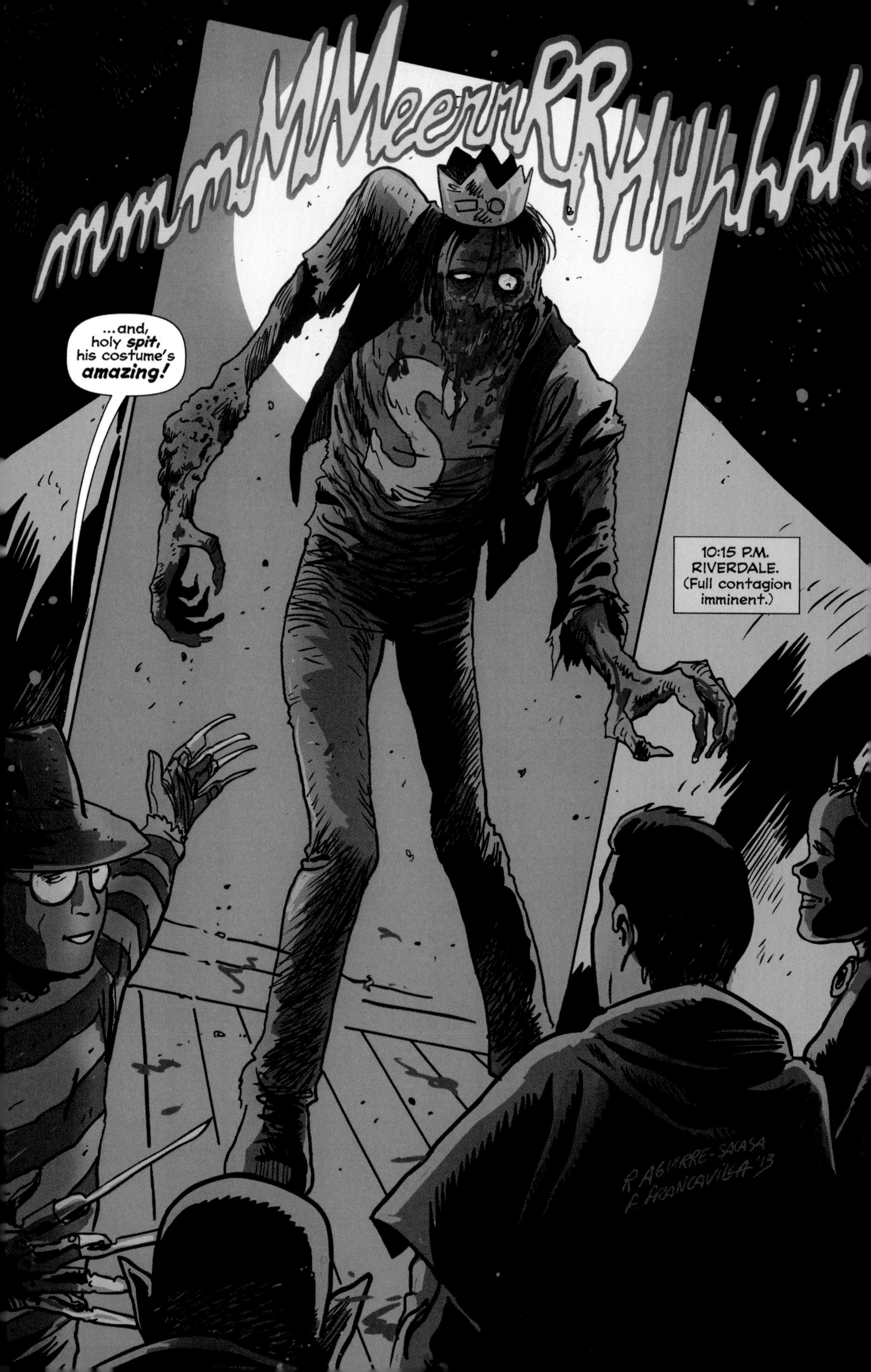
mmmMMeerrRRHHhhhh
...and, holy spit, his costume's amazing!
10:15 P.M. RIVERDALE. (Full contagion imminent.)
R. AGUIRRE-SACASA F. FRANCAVILLA '13

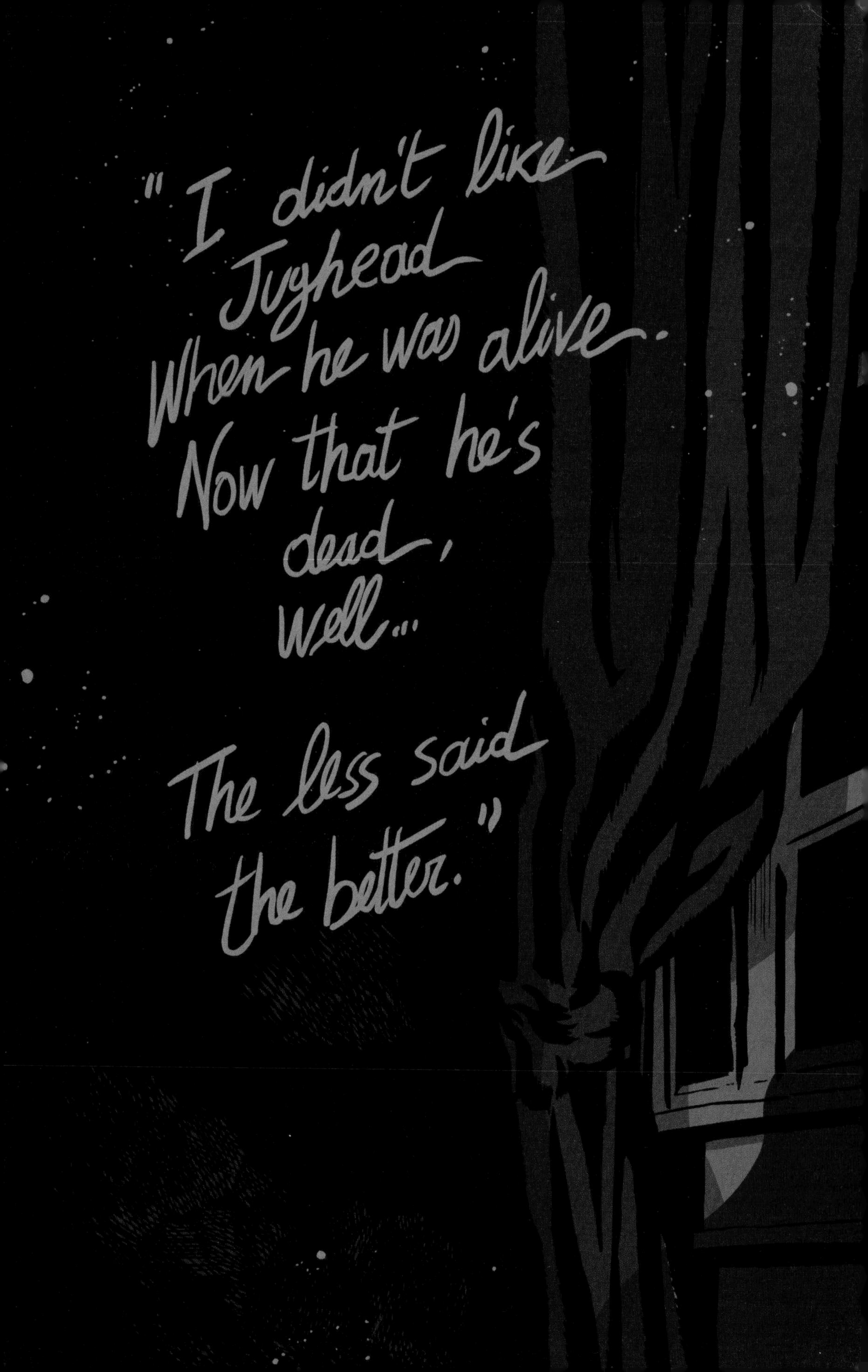
"I didn't like Jughead When he was alive. Now that he's dead, well...
The less said the better."

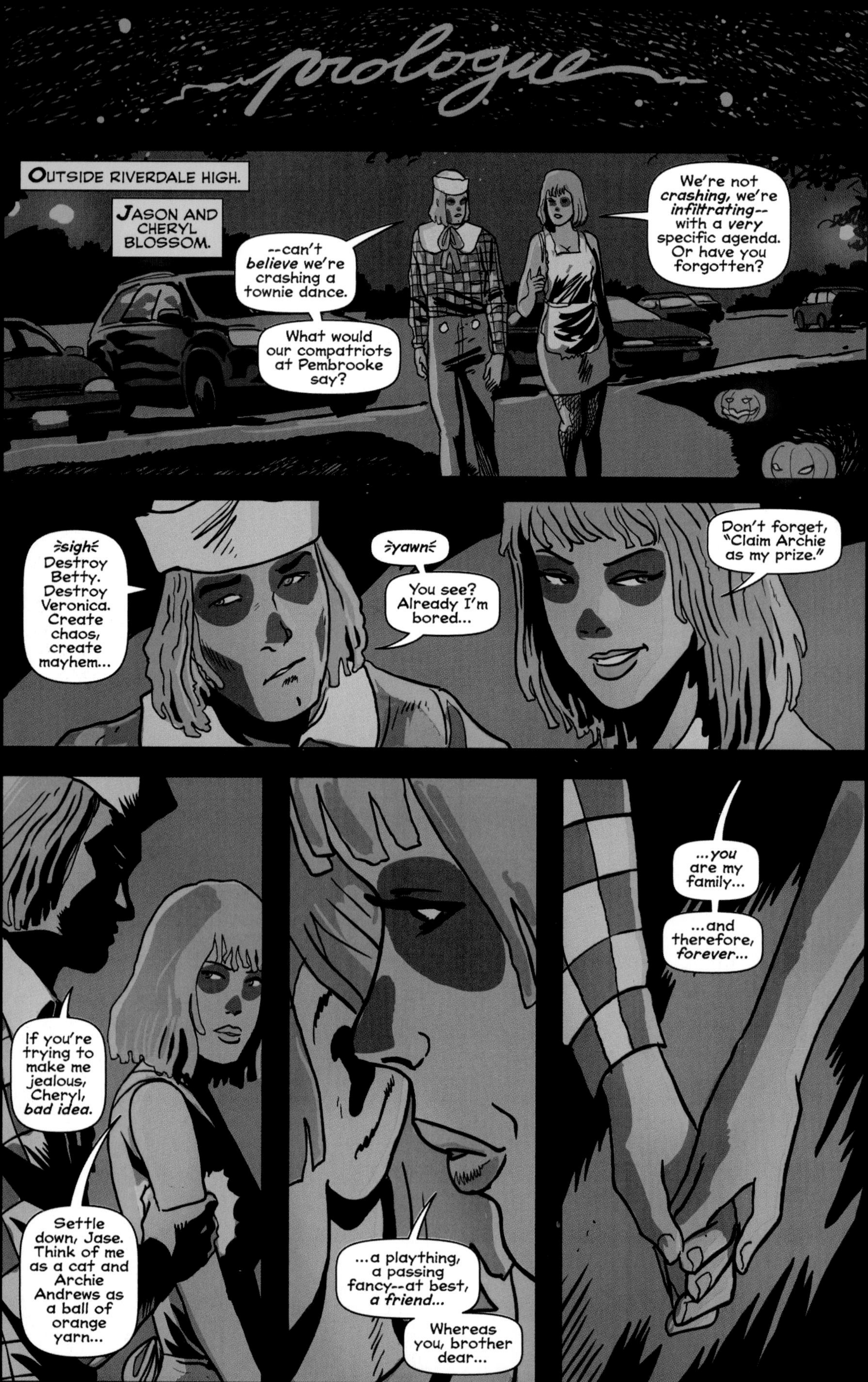
prologue
OUTSIDE RIVERDALE HIGH.
JASON AND CHERYL BLOSSOM.
--can't believe we're crashing a townie dance.
What would our compatriots at Pembrooke say?
We're not crashing, we're infiltrating--with a very specific agenda. Or have you forgotten?
sigh Destroy Betty. Destroy Veronica. Create chaos, create mayhem...
yawn
You see? Already I'm bored...
Don't forget, "Claim Archie as my prize."
If you're trying to make me jealous, Cheryl, bad idea.
Settle down, Jase. Think of me as a cat and Archie Andrews as a ball of orange yarn...
...a plaything, a passing fancy--at best, a friend...
Whereas you, brother dear...
...you are my family...
...and therefore, forever...

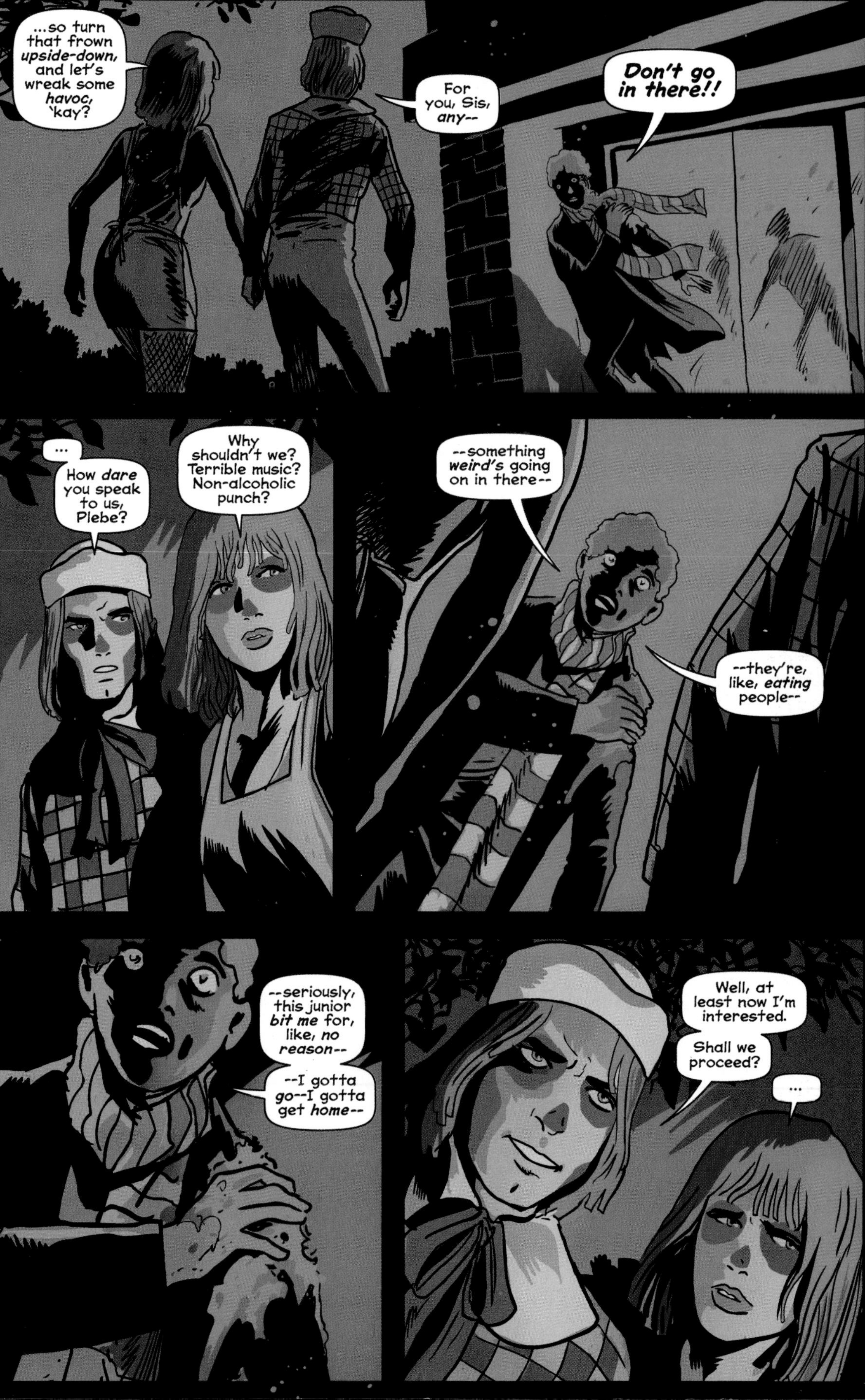
...so turn that frown *upside-down,* and let's wreak some *havoc,* 'kay?
For you, Sis, *any--*
Don't go in there!!
...
How *dare* you speak to us, Plebe?
Why shouldn't we? Terrible music? Non-alcoholic punch?
--something *weird's* going on in there--
--they're, like, *eating* people--
--seriously, this junior *bit me* for, like, *no reason--*
--I gotta *go*--I gotta get *home--*
Well, at least now I'm interested.
Shall we proceed?
...

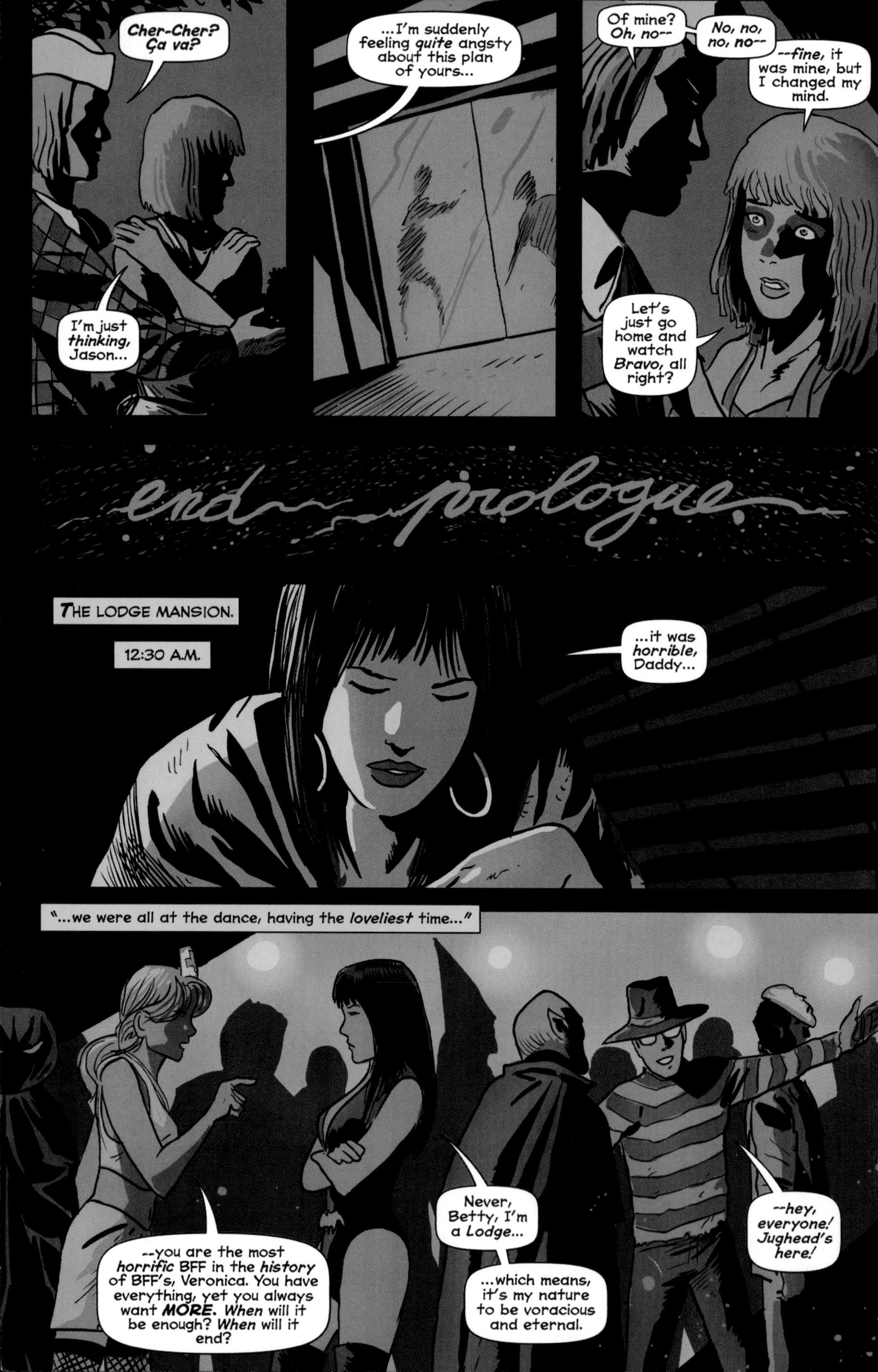
Cher-Cher? Ça va?
I'm just thinking, Jason...
...I'm suddenly feeling quite angsty about this plan of yours...
Of mine? Oh, no--
No, no, no, no--
--fine, it was mine, but I changed my mind.
Let's just go home and watch Bravo, all right?
end prologue
THE LODGE MANSION.
12:30 A.M.
...it was horrible, Daddy...
"...we were all at the dance, having the loveliest time..."
--you are the most horrific BFF in the history of BFF's, Veronica. You have everything, yet you always want MORE. When will it be enough? When will it end?
Never, Betty, I'm a Lodge...
...which means, it's my nature to be voracious and eternal.
--hey, everyone! Jughead's here!

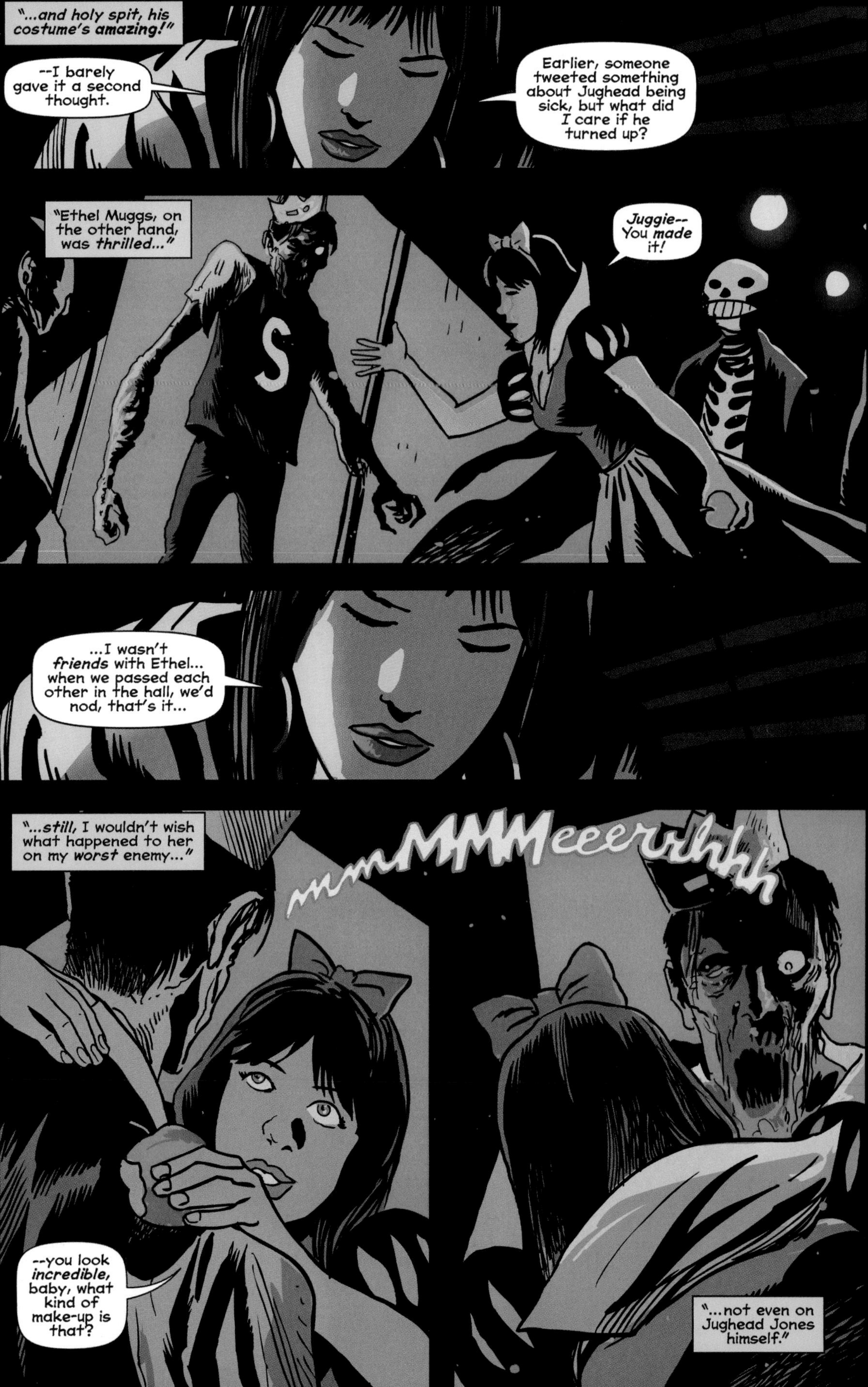
"...and holy spit, his costume's amazing!"
--I barely gave it a second thought.
Earlier, someone tweeted something about Jughead being sick, but what did I care if he turned up?
"Ethel Muggs, on the other hand, was thrilled..."
Juggie-- You made it!
...I wasn't friends with Ethel... when we passed each other in the hall, we'd nod, that's it...
"...still, I wouldn't wish what happened to her on my worst enemy..."
mmmMMMeeeerrhhh
--you look incredible, baby, what kind of make-up is that?
"...not even on Jughead Jones himself."

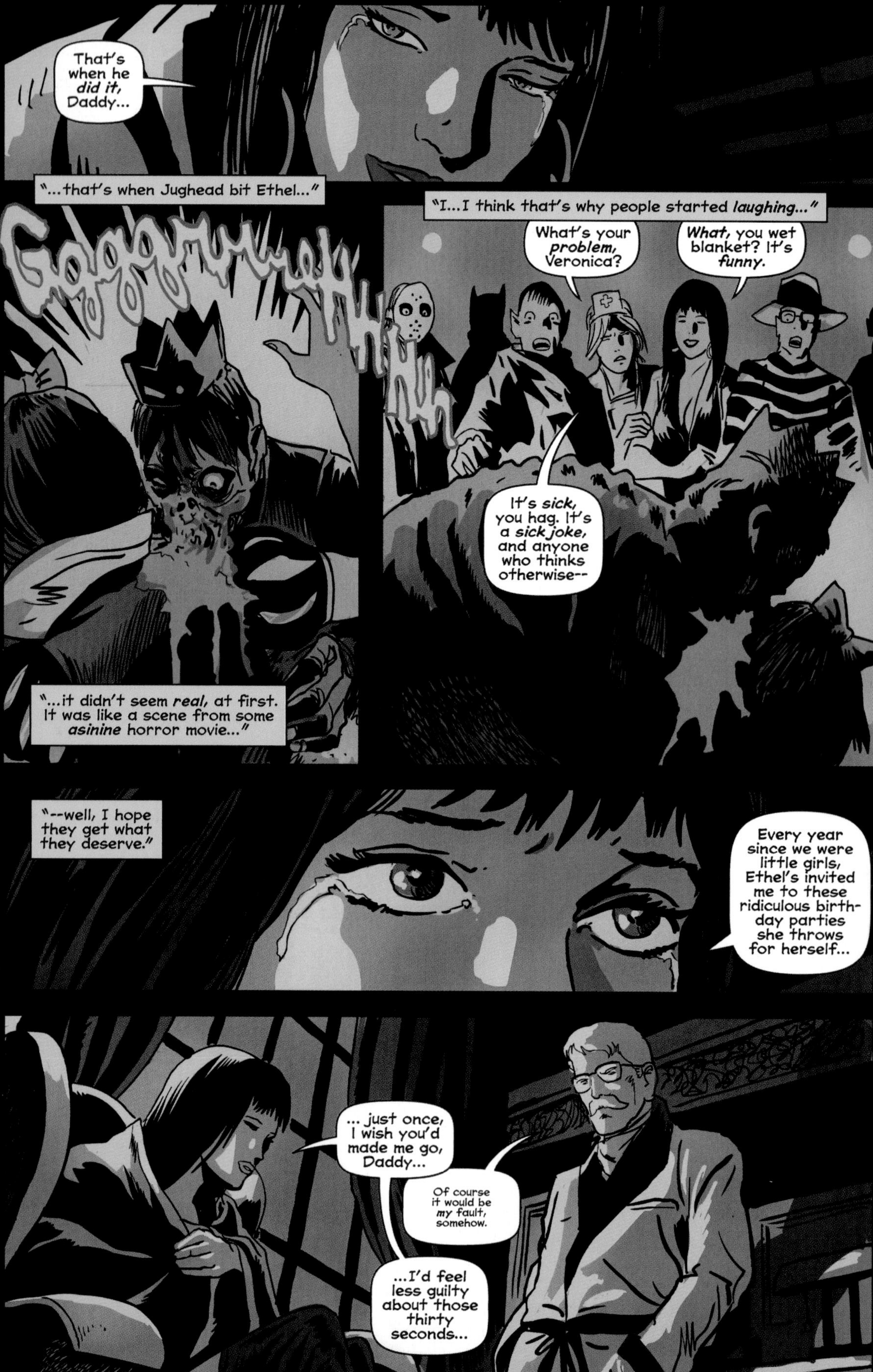
That's when he *did it,* Daddy...
"...that's when Jughead bit Ethel..."
"...it didn't seem *real,* at first. It was like a scene from some *asinine* horror movie..."
"I...I think that's why people started *laughing...*"
What's your *problem,* Veronica?
What, you wet blanket? It's *funny.*
It's *sick,* you hag. It's a *sick joke,* and anyone who thinks otherwise--
"--well, I hope they get what they deserve."
Every year since we were little girls, Ethel's invited me to these ridiculous birth-day parties she throws for herself...
... just once, I wish you'd made me go, Daddy...
Of course it would be *my* fault, somehow.
...I'd feel less guilty about those thirty seconds...

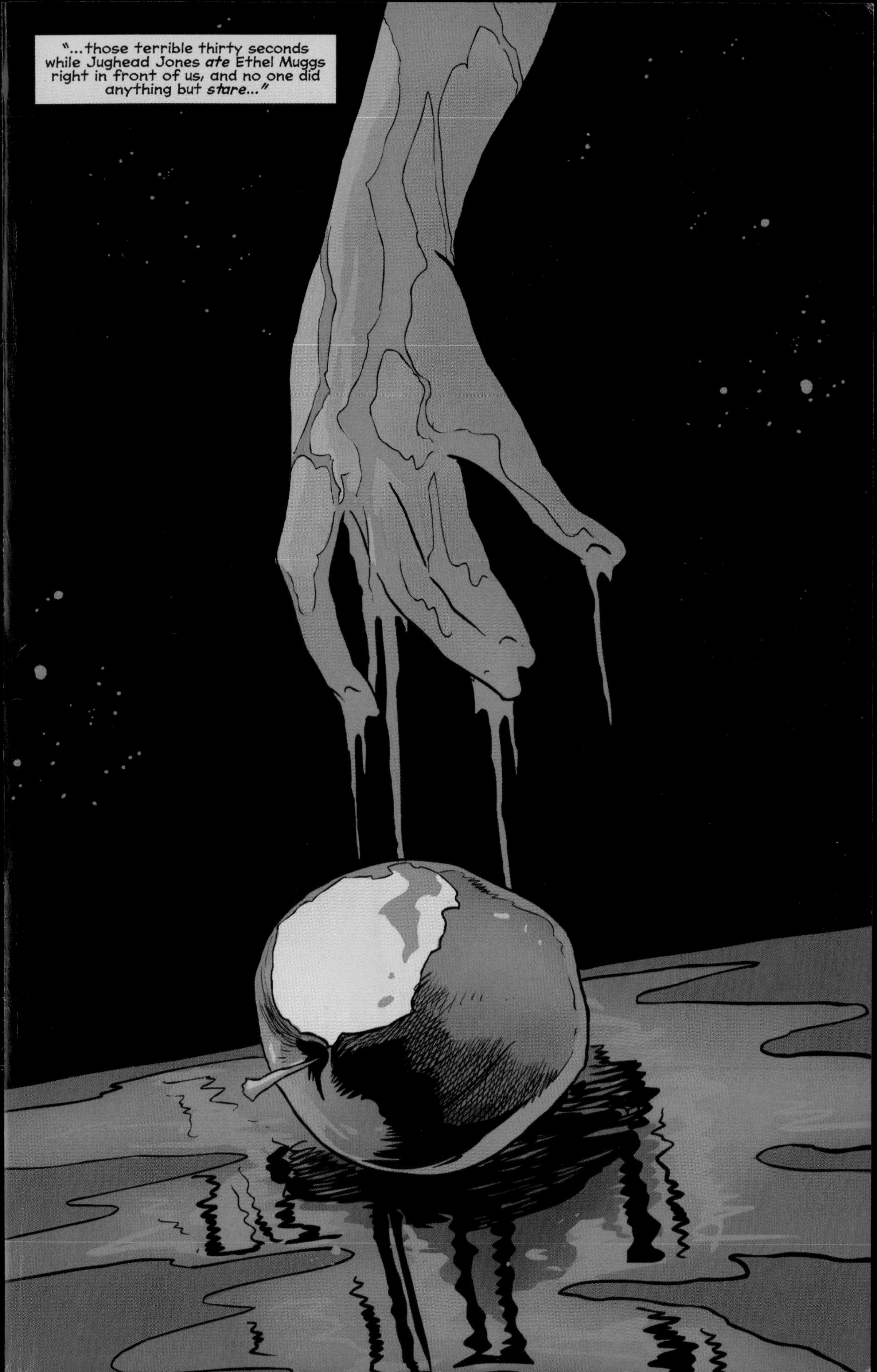
"...those terrible thirty seconds while Jughead Jones *ate* Ethel Muggs right in front of us, and no one did anything but *stare*..."

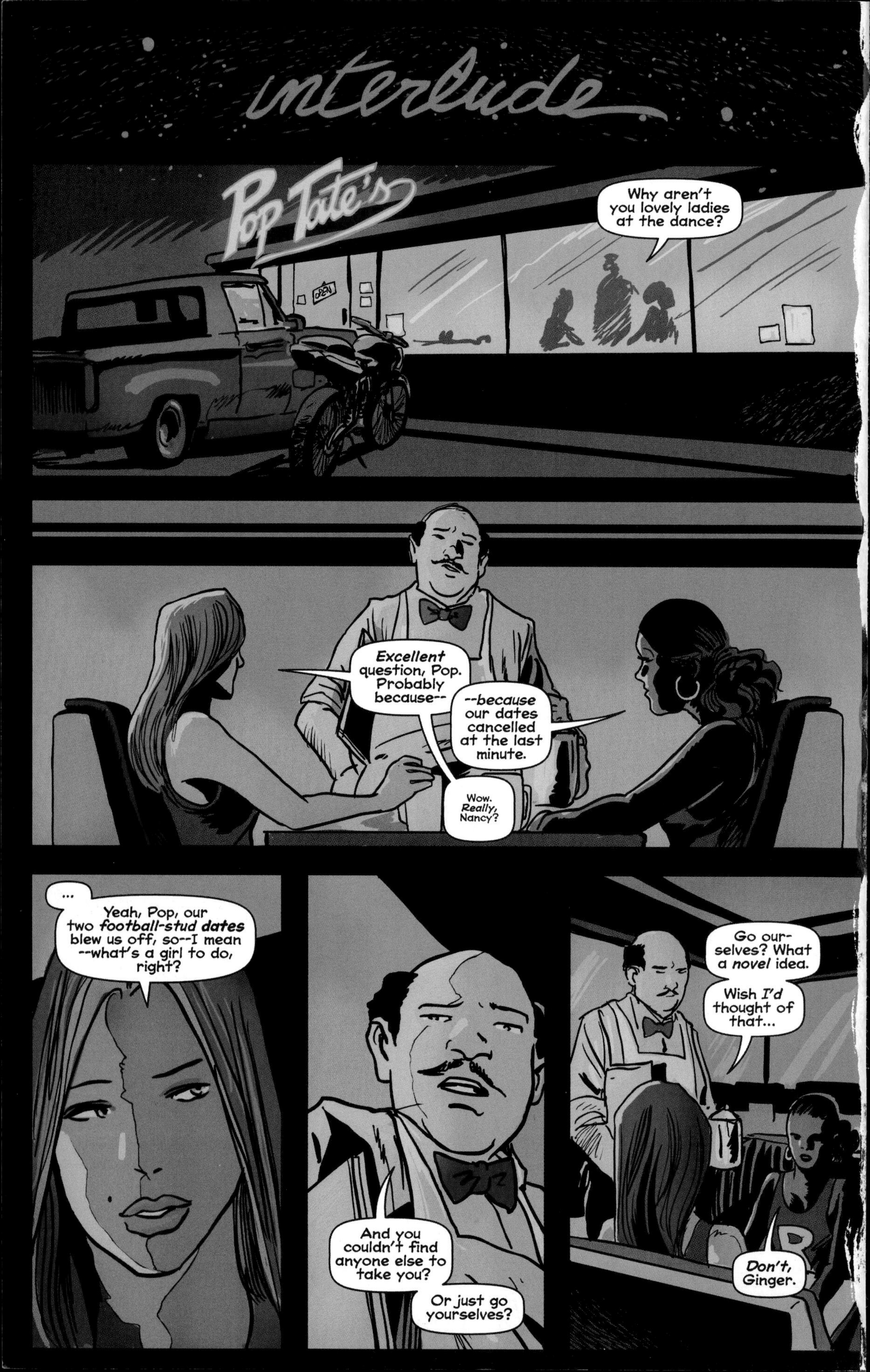
interlude
Pop Tate's
OPEN
Why aren't you lovely ladies at the dance?
Excellent question, Pop. Probably because--
--*because* our dates cancelled at the last minute.
Wow. *Really,* Nancy?
... Yeah, Pop, our two *football-stud dates* blew us off, so--I mean --what's a girl to do, right?
And you couldn't find anyone else to take you?
Or just go yourselves?
Go our-selves? What a *novel* idea.
Wish *I'd* thought of that...
Don't, Ginger.

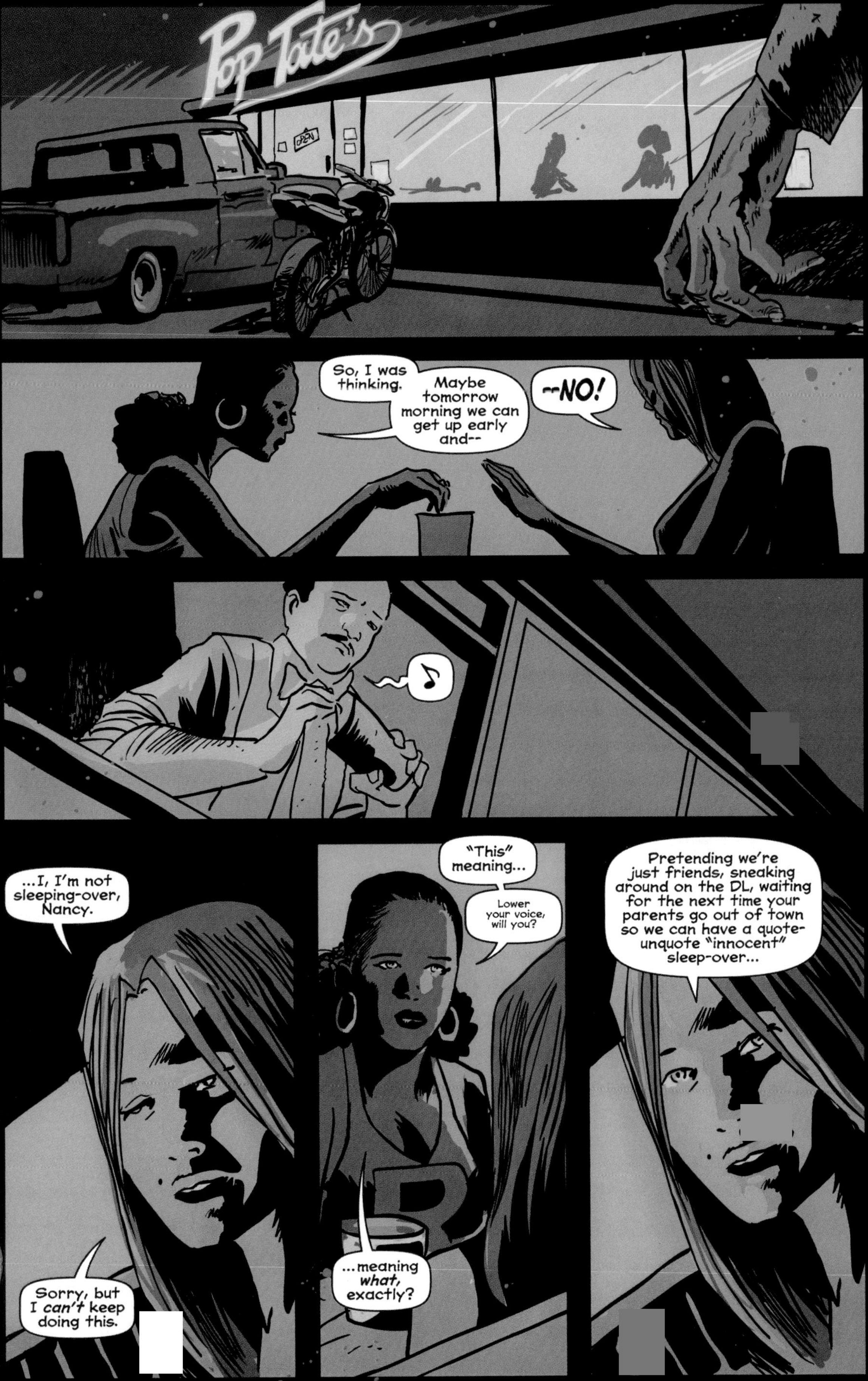
Pop Tate's
OPEN
So, I was thinking.
Maybe tomorrow morning we can get up early and--
--NO!
...I, I'm not sleeping-over, Nancy.
Sorry, but I *can't* keep doing this.
"This" meaning...
Lower your voice, will you?
...meaning *what,* exactly?
Pretending we're just friends, sneaking around on the DL, waiting for the next time your parents go out of town so we can have a quote-unquote "innocent" sleep-over...

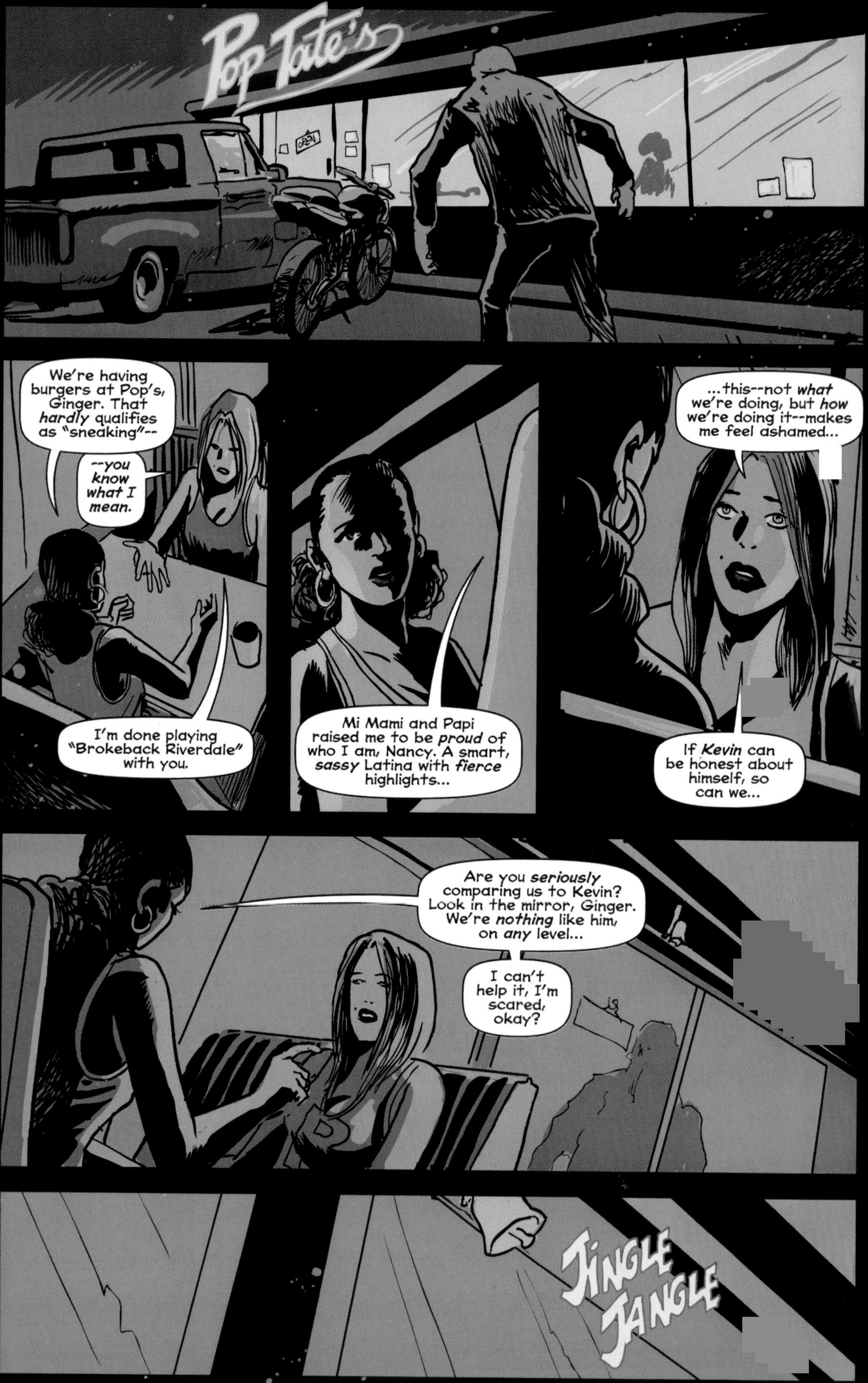
Pop Tate's
OPEN
We're having burgers at Pop's, Ginger. That hardly qualifies as "sneaking"--
--you know what I mean.
I'm done playing "Brokeback Riverdale" with you.
Mi Mami and Papi raised me to be proud of who I am, Nancy. A smart, sassy Latina with fierce highlights...
...this--not what we're doing, but how we're doing it--makes me feel ashamed...
If Kevin can be honest about himself, so can we...
Are you seriously comparing us to Kevin? Look in the mirror, Ginger. We're nothing like him, on any level...
I can't help it, I'm scared, okay?
JINGLE JANGLE

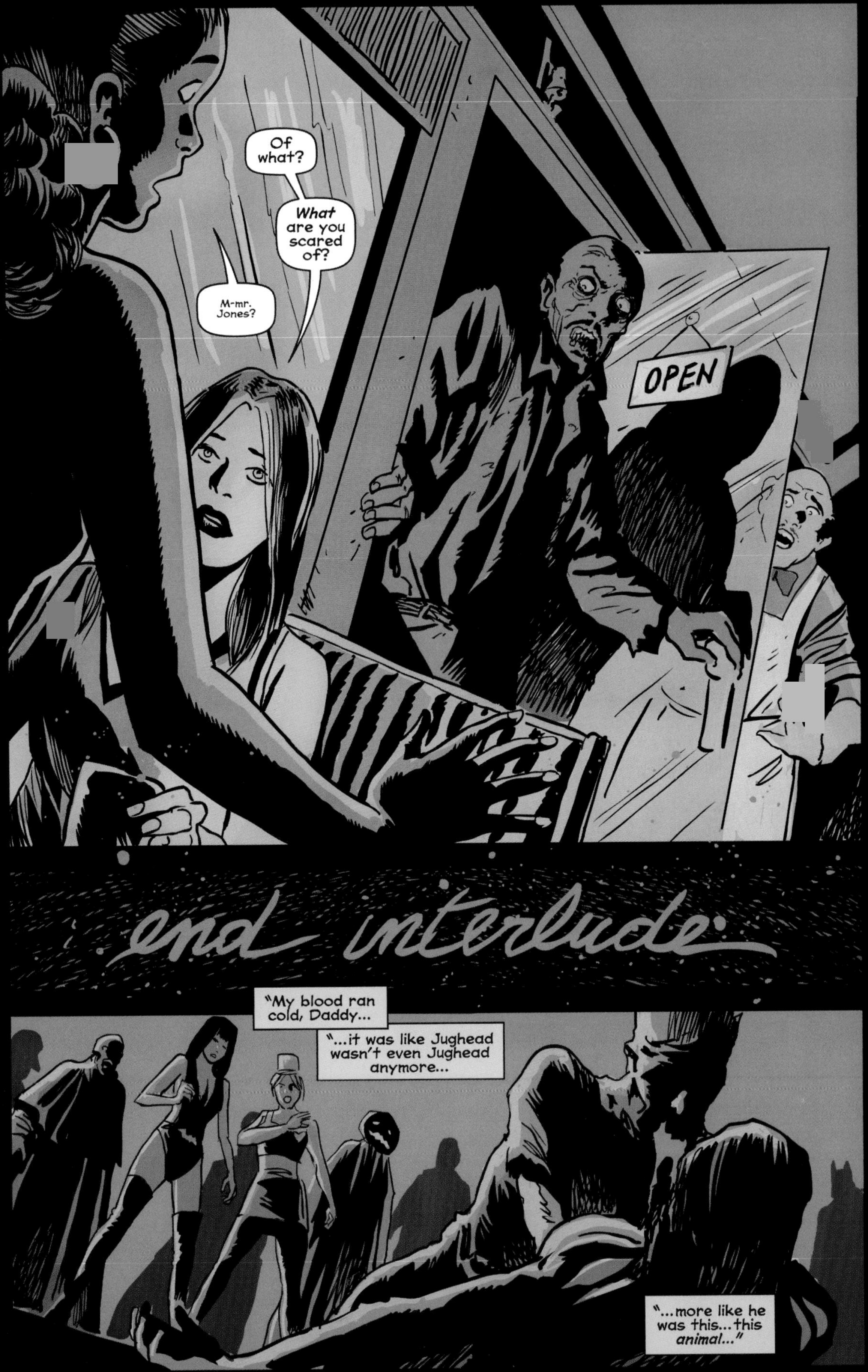
Of what?
What are you scared of?
M-mr. Jones?
OPEN
end interlude
"My blood ran cold, Daddy...
"...it was like Jughead wasn't even Jughead anymore...
"...more like he was this...this *animal*..."

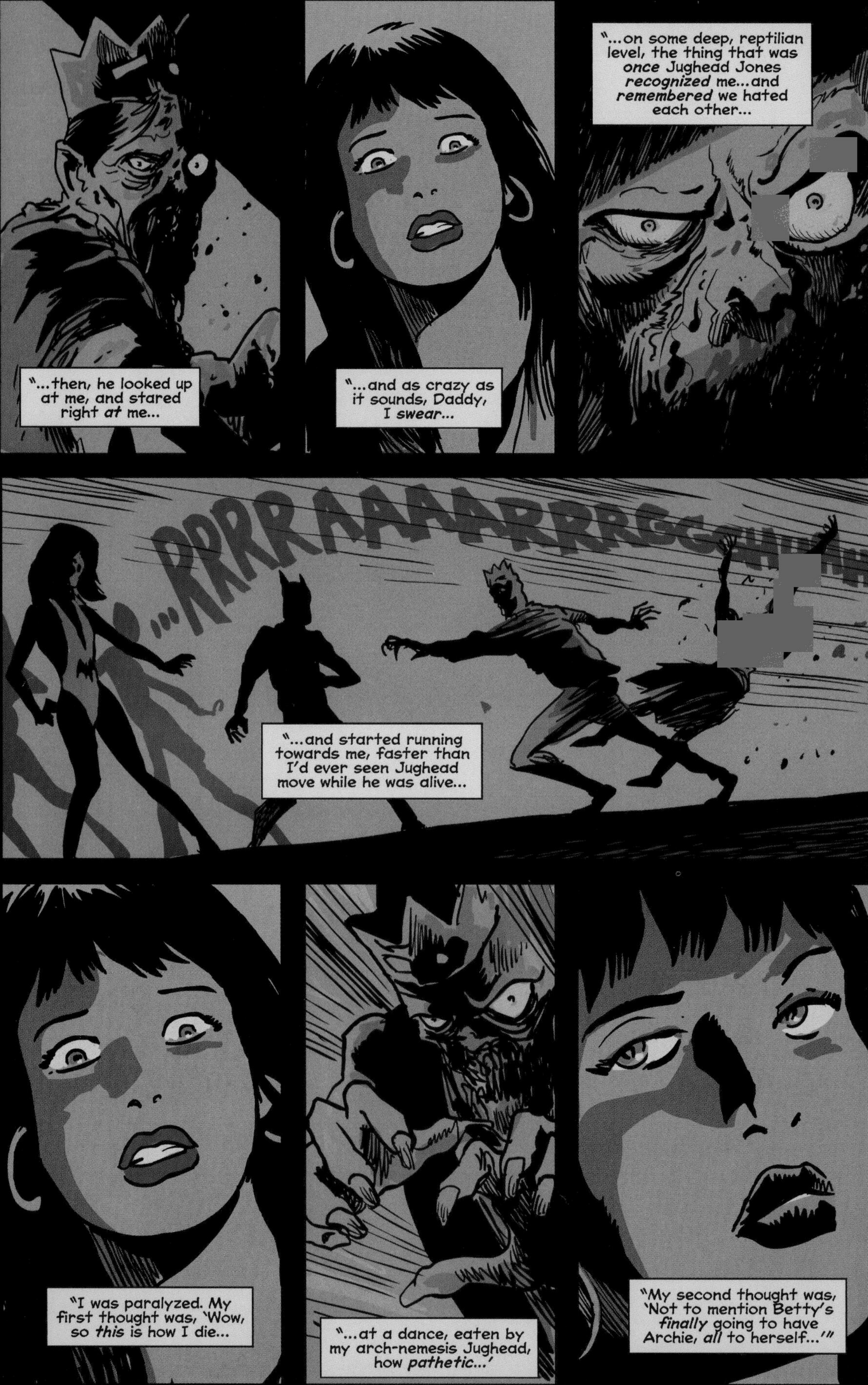
"...then, he looked up at me, and stared right *at* me...
"...and as crazy as it sounds, Daddy, I *swear*...
"...on some deep, reptilian level, the thing that was *once* Jughead Jones *recognized* me...and *remembered* we hated each other...
"...and started running towards me, faster than I'd ever seen Jughead move while he was alive...
"I was paralyzed. My first thought was, 'Wow, so *this* is how I die...
"...at a dance, eaten by my arch-nemesis Jughead, how *pathetic*...'
"My second thought was, 'Not to mention Betty's *finally* going to have Archie, *all* to herself...'"

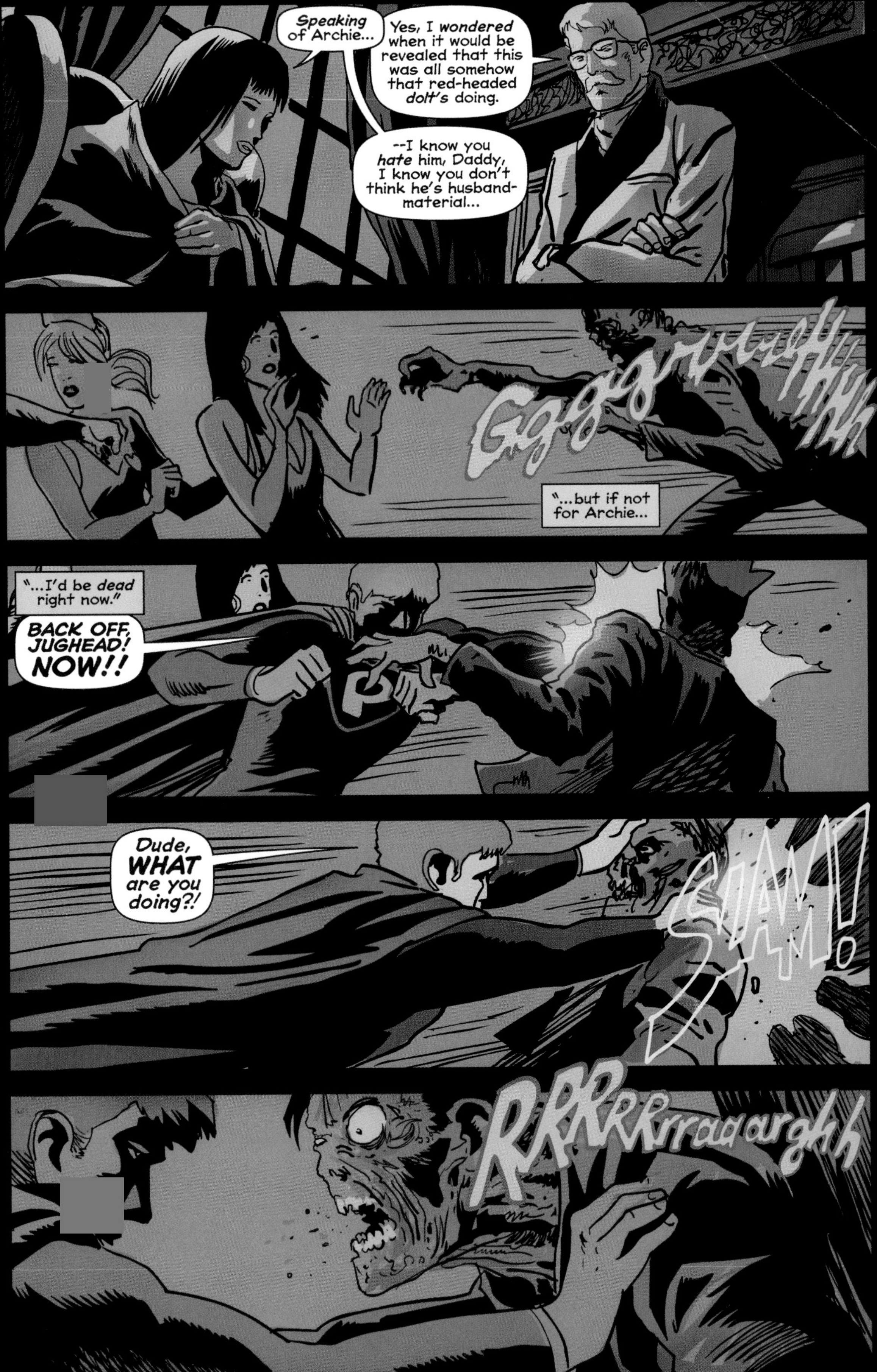
Speaking of Archie...
Yes, I wondered when it would be revealed that this was all somehow that red-headed dolt's doing.
--I know you hate him, Daddy, I know you don't think he's husband-material...
"...but if not for Archie...
"...I'd be dead right now."
BACK OFF, JUGHEAD! NOW!!
Dude, WHAT are you doing?!
SLAM!
RRRRRrraaarghh

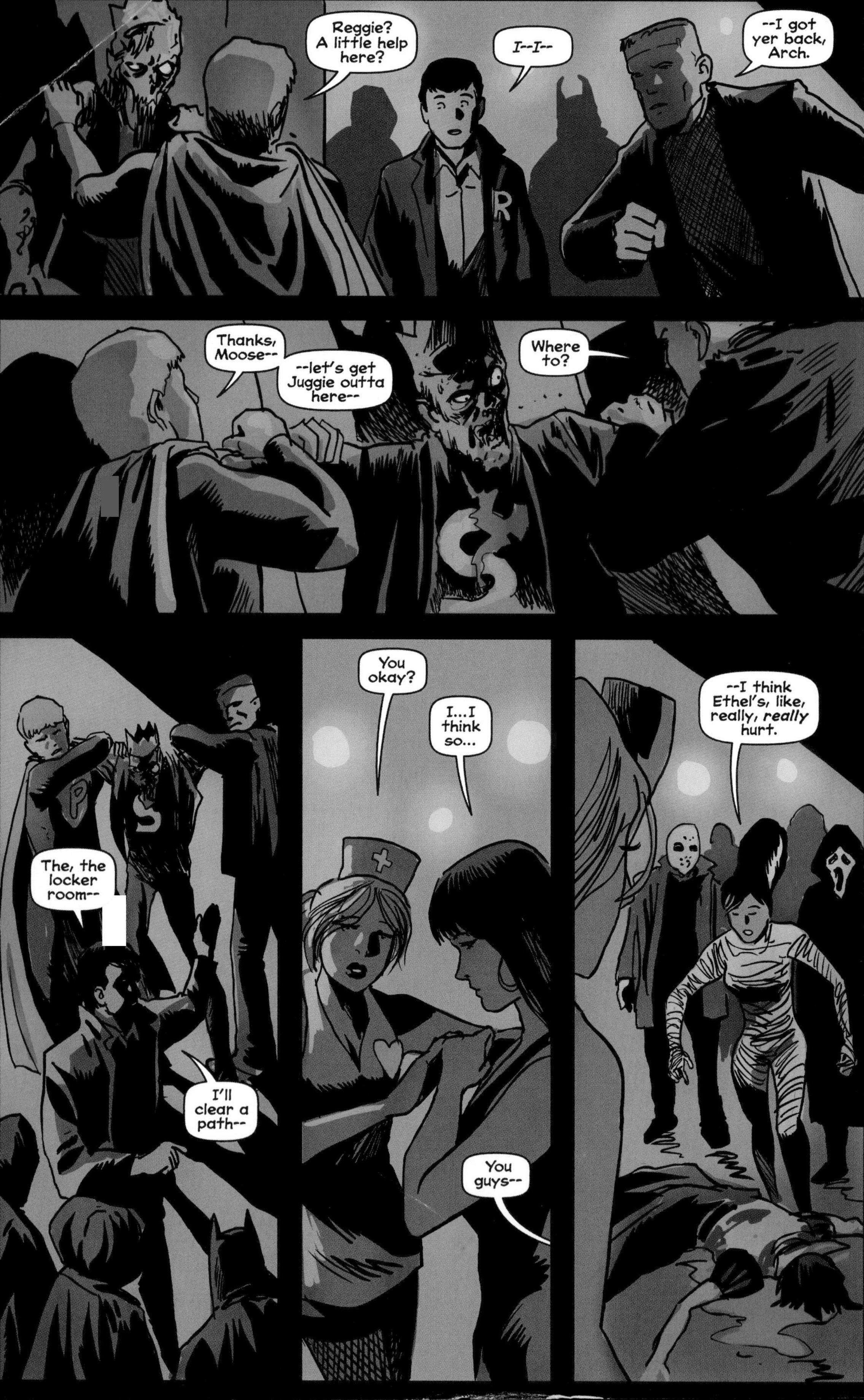
Reggie? A little help here?
I--I--
--I got yer back, Arch.
Thanks, Moose--
--let's get Juggie outta here--
Where to?
The, the locker room--
I'll clear a path--
You okay?
I...I think so...
You guys--
--I think Ethel's, like, really, *really* hurt.

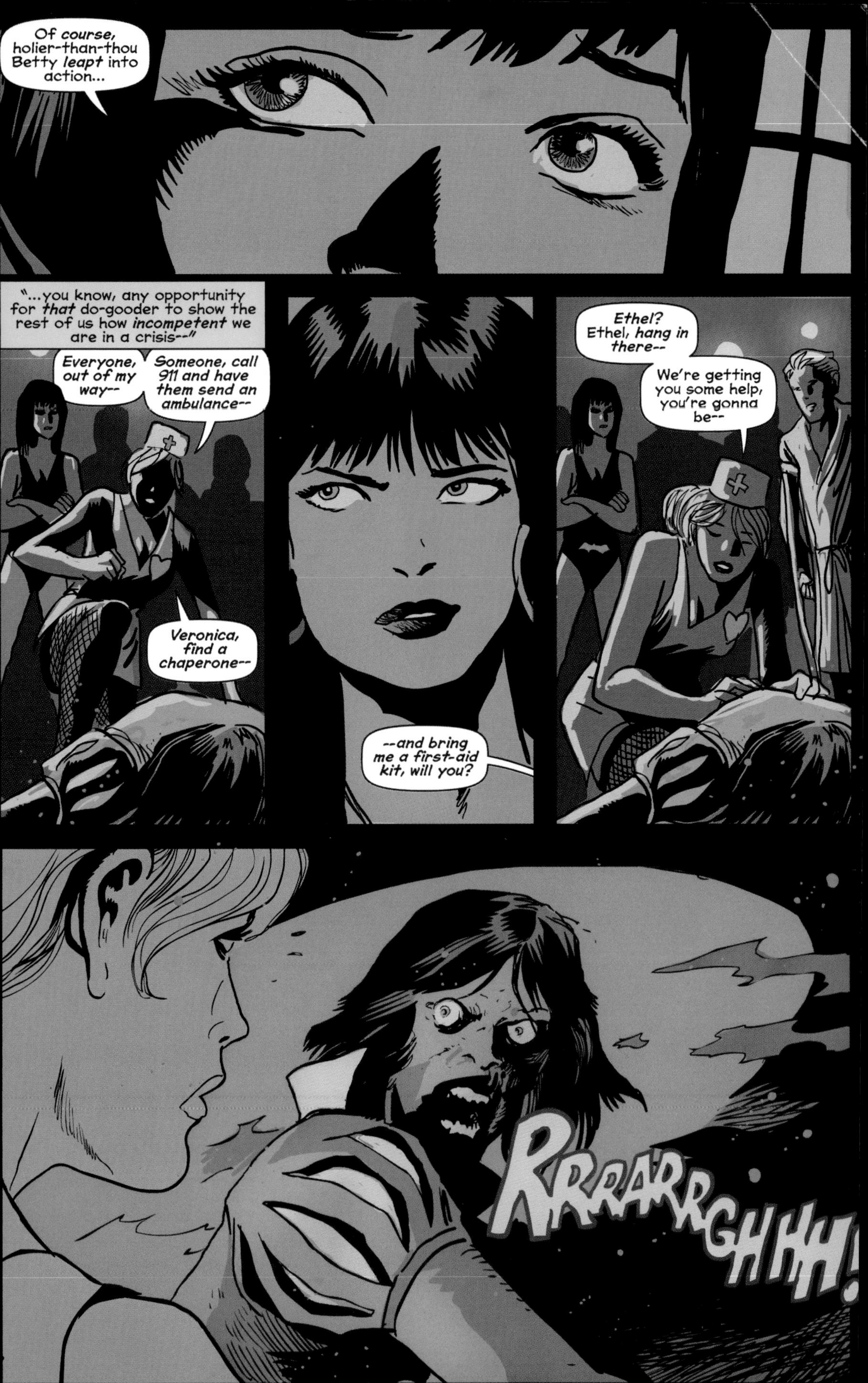
Of course, holier-than-thou Betty leapt into action...
"...you know, any opportunity for that do-gooder to show the rest of us how incompetent we are in a crisis--"
Everyone, out of my way--
Someone, call 911 and have them send an ambulance--
Veronica, find a chaperone--
--and bring me a first-aid kit, will you?
Ethel? Ethel, hang in there--
We're getting you some help, you're gonna be--
RRRARRRGHHH!

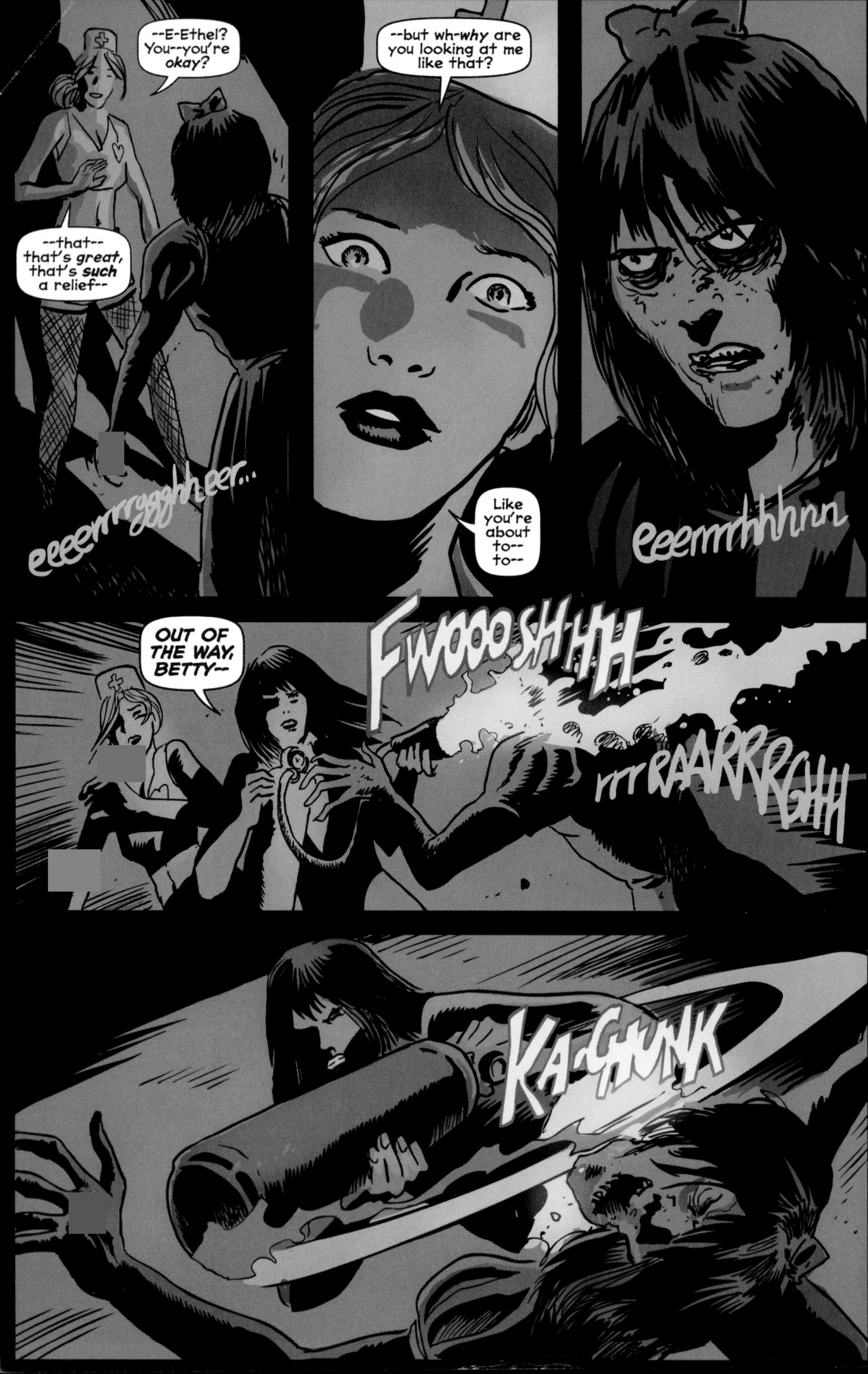
--E-Ethel? You--you're okay?
--that-- that's great, that's such a relief--
eeeerrrgggghheer...
--but wh-why are you looking at me like that?
Like you're about to-- to--
eeermhhhnn
OUT OF THE WAY, BETTY--
FWOOOSHHH
rrrRAARRRGHHH
KA-CHUNK

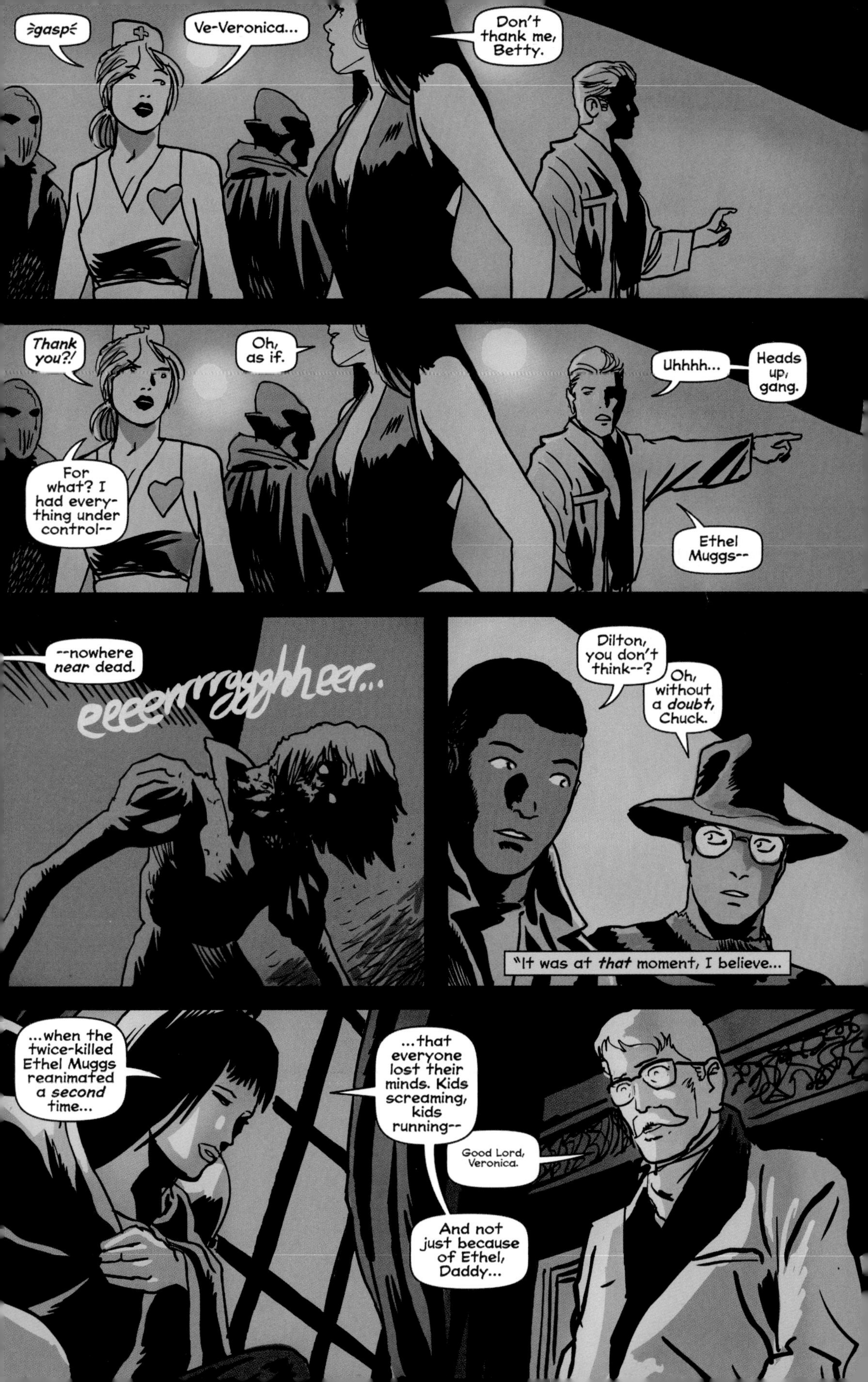
gasp
Ve-Veronica...
Don't thank me, Betty.
Thank you?!
Oh, as if.
For what? I had every-thing under control--
Uhhhh...
Heads up, gang.
Ethel Muggs--
--nowhere near dead.
eeeerrrrggghheer...
Dilton, you don't think--?
Oh, without a doubt, Chuck.
"It was at that moment, I believe...
...when the twice-killed Ethel Muggs reanimated a second time...
...that everyone lost their minds. Kids screaming, kids running--
Good Lord, Veronica.
And not just because of Ethel, Daddy...

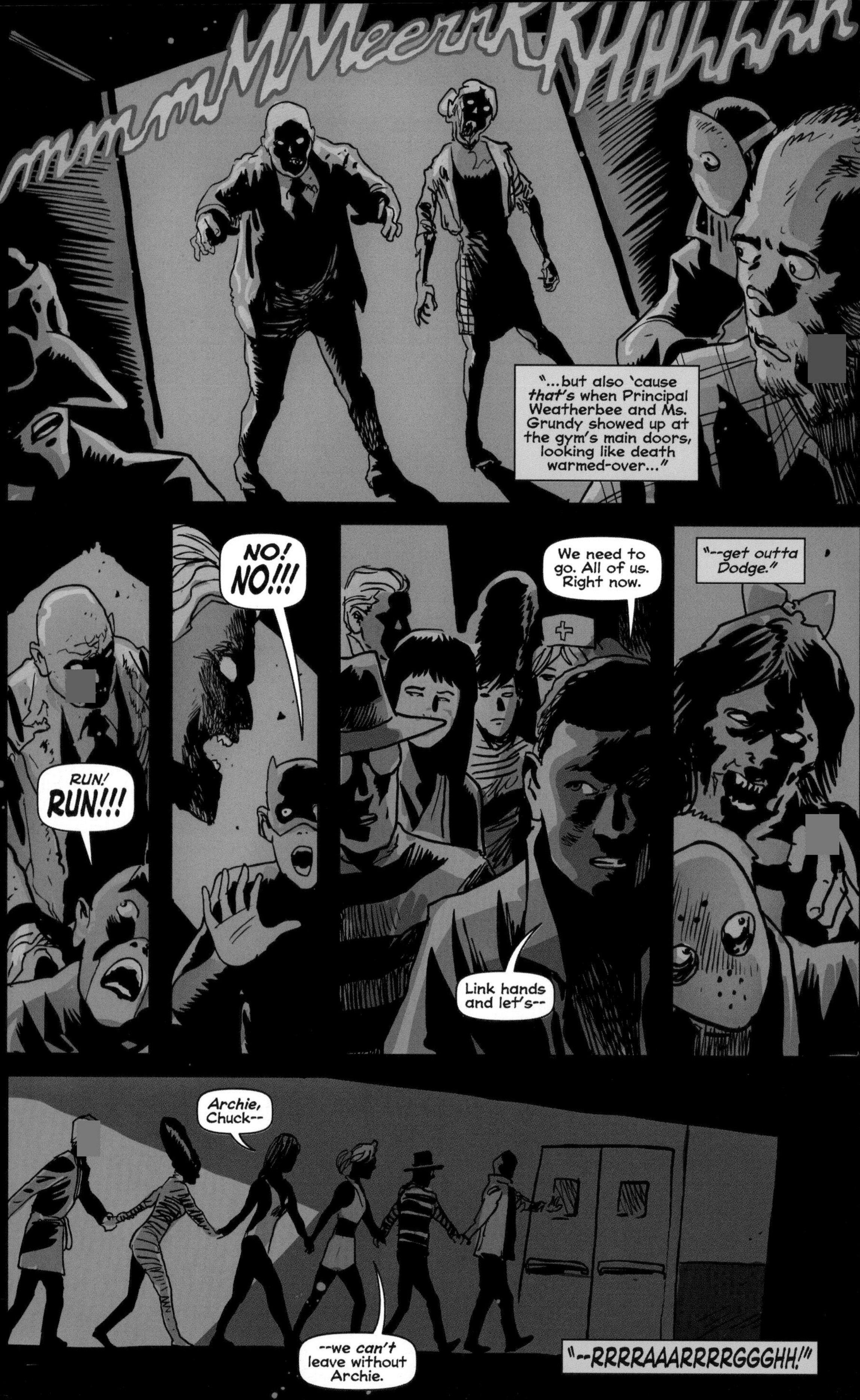
mmmmMMeerrRRHHhhhh
"...but also 'cause that's when Principal Weatherbee and Ms. Grundy showed up at the gym's main doors, looking like death warmed-over..."
RUN! RUN!!!
NO! NO!!!
We need to go. All of us. Right now.
Link hands and let's--
"--get outta Dodge."
Archie, Chuck--
--we can't leave without Archie.
"--RRRRAAARRRRGGGHH!"

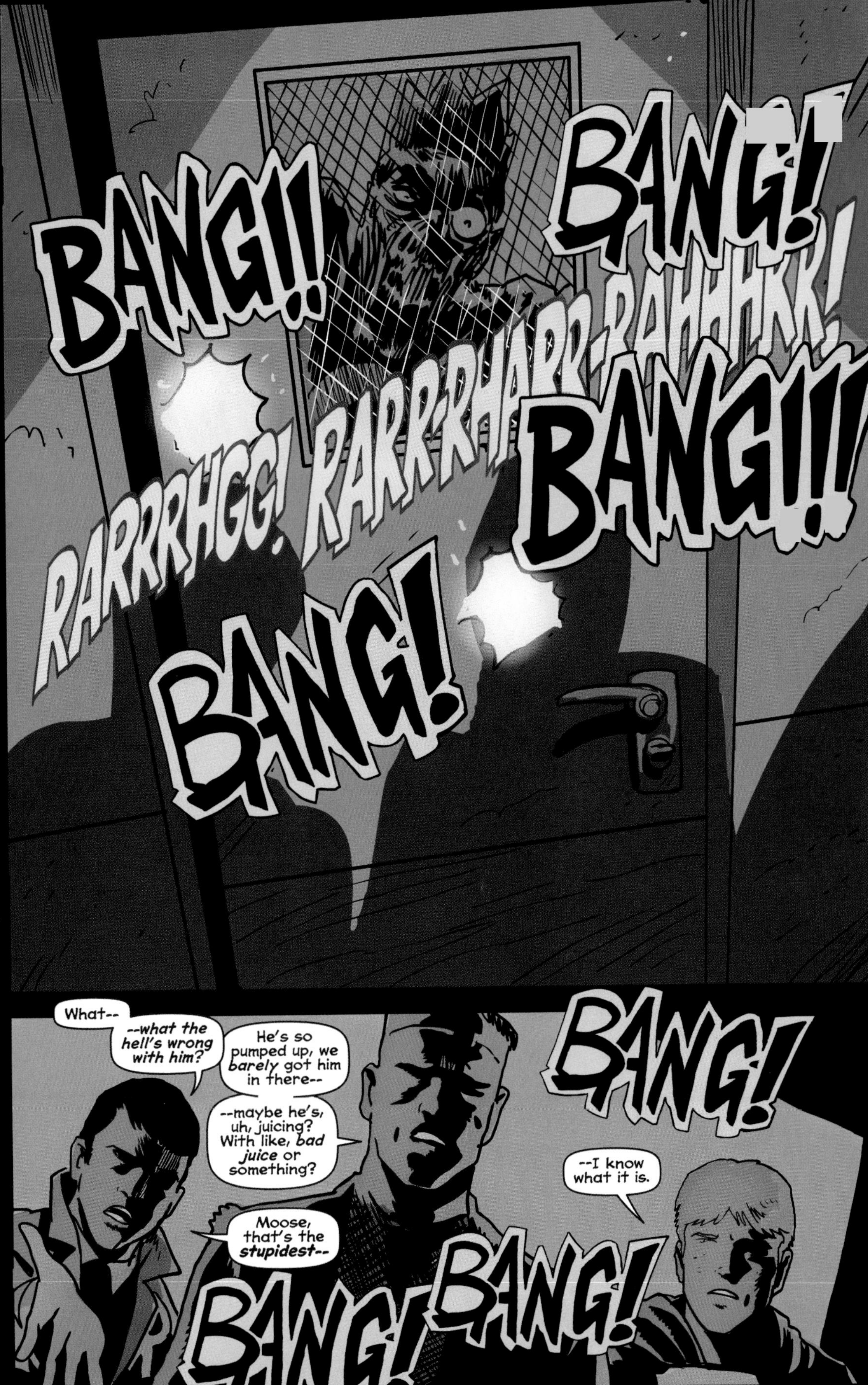
BANG!!
BANG!
RARRRHGG! RARR-RHARR-RAHHHRK!
BANG!!!
BANG!
What--
--*what the hell's wrong with him?*
He's so pumped up, we *barely* got him in there--
--maybe he's, uh, juicing? With like, *bad juice* or something?
BANG!
--I know what it is.
Moose, that's the ***stupidest--***
BANG! BANG!

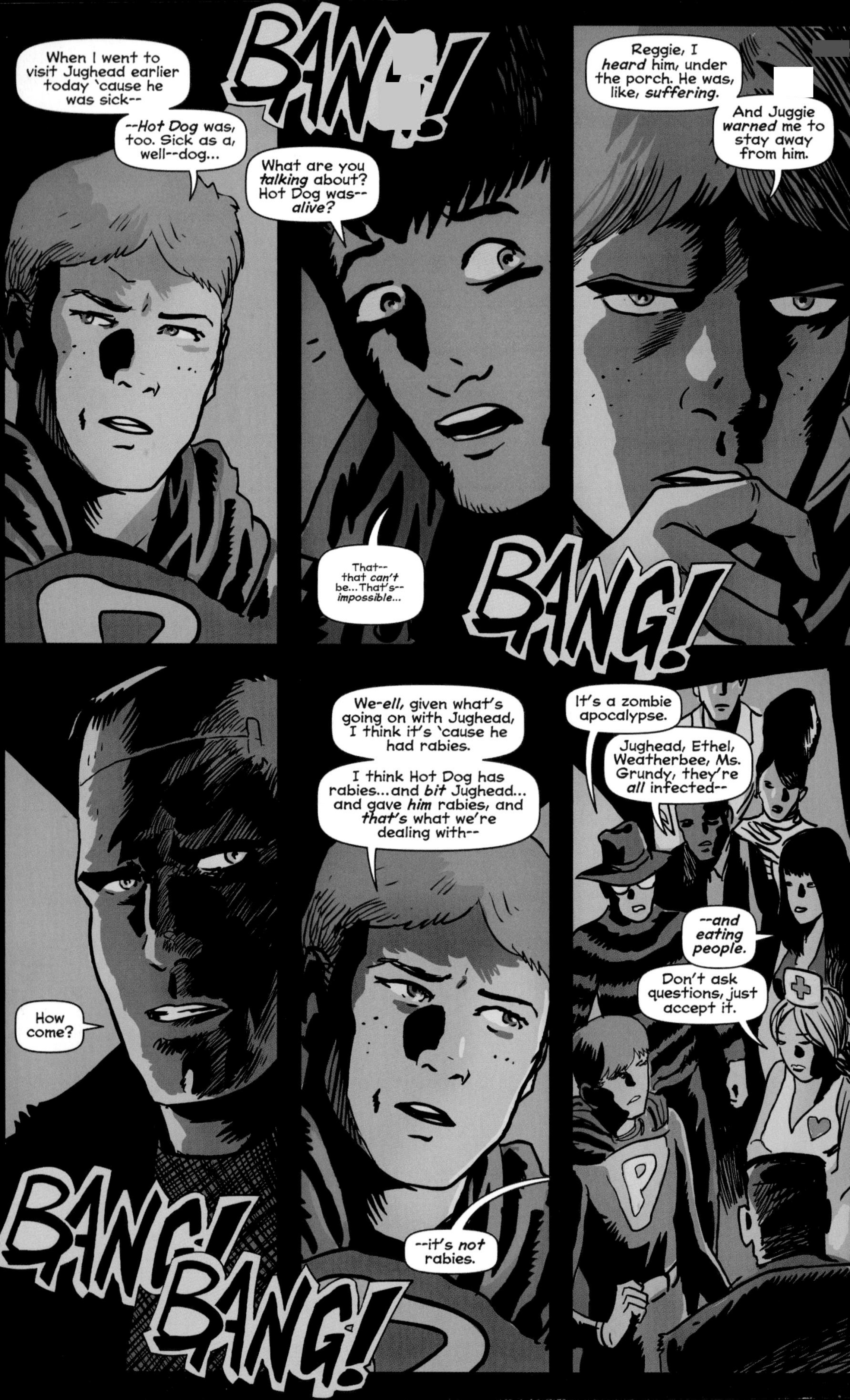
When I went to visit Jughead earlier today 'cause he was sick--
--Hot Dog was, too. Sick as a, well--dog...
BANG!
What are you talking about? Hot Dog was--alive?
That--that can't be...That's--impossible...
Reggie, I heard him, under the porch. He was, like, suffering.
And Juggie warned me to stay away from him.
BANG!
How come?
We-ell, given what's going on with Jughead, I think it's 'cause he had rabies.
I think Hot Dog has rabies...and bit Jughead...and gave him rabies, and that's what we're dealing with--
--it's not rabies.
BANG! BANG!
It's a zombie apocalypse.
Jughead, Ethel, Weatherbee, Ms. Grundy, they're all infected--
--and eating people.
Don't ask questions, just accept it.

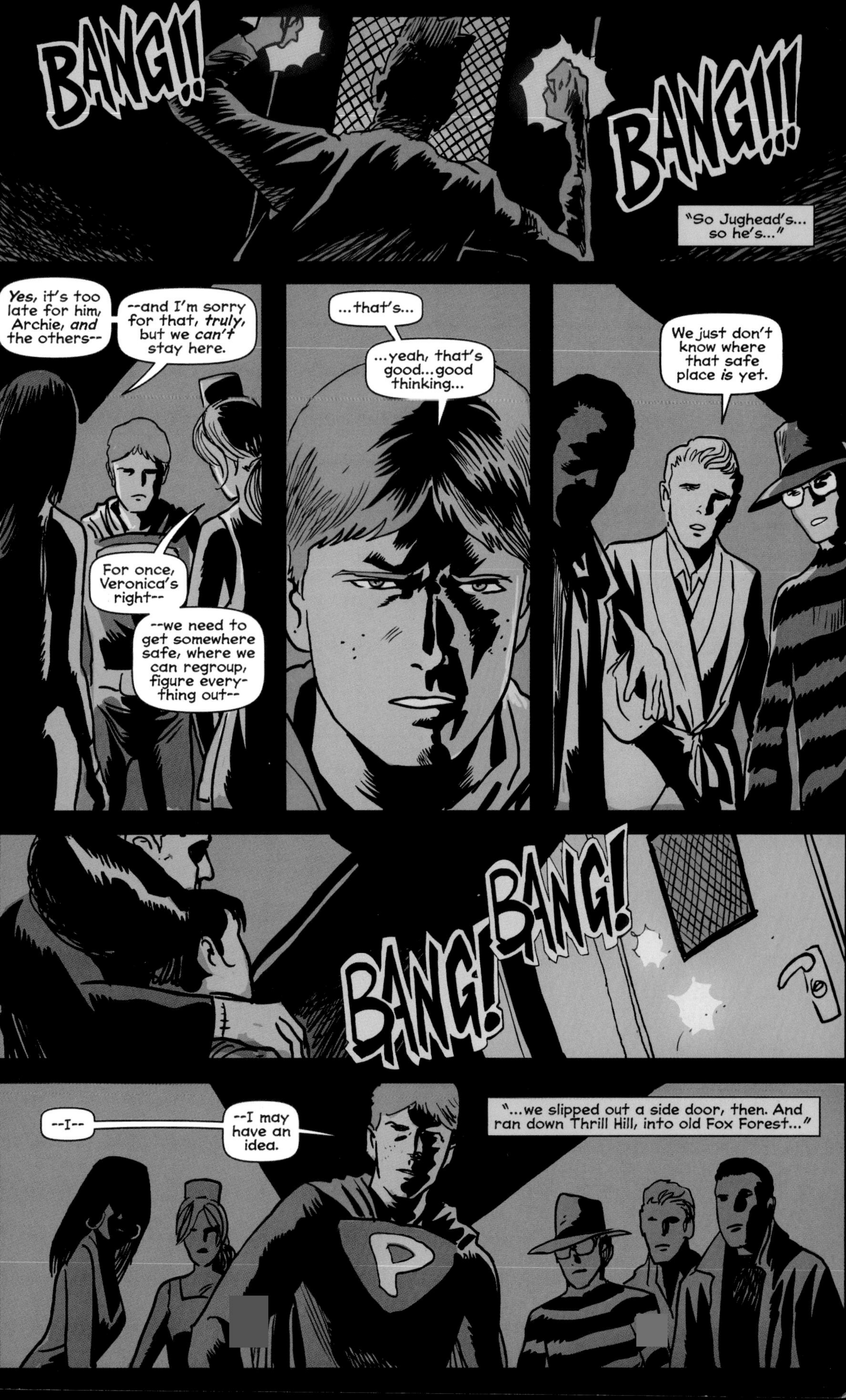
BANG!!
BANG!!!
"So Jughead's... so he's..."
Yes, it's too late for him, Archie, *and* the others--
--and I'm sorry for that, *truly,* but we *can't* stay here.
For once, Veronica's right--
--we need to get somewhere safe, where we can regroup, figure every-thing out--
...that's...
...yeah, that's good...good thinking...
We just don't know where that safe place *is* yet.
BANG!
BANG!
--I--
--I may have an idea.
"...we slipped out a side door, then. And ran down Thrill Hill, into old Fox Forest..."

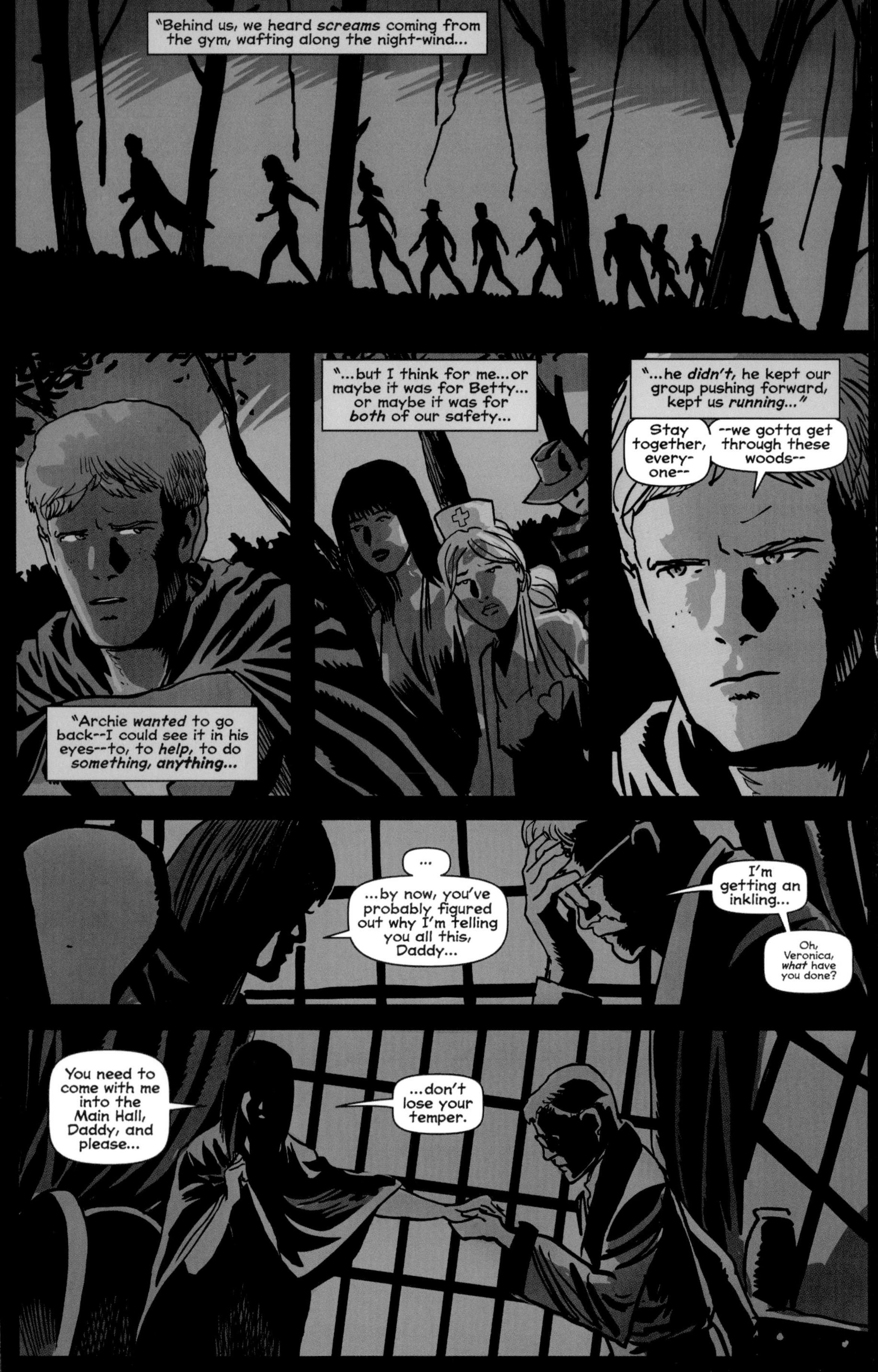
"Behind us, we heard screams coming from the gym, wafting along the night-wind...
"Archie wanted to go back--I could see it in his eyes--to, to help, to do something, anything...
"...but I think for me...or maybe it was for Betty... or maybe it was for both of our safety...
"...he didn't, he kept our group pushing forward, kept us running..."
Stay together, every-one--
--we gotta get through these woods--
...
...by now, you've probably figured out why I'm telling you all this, Daddy...
I'm getting an inkling...
Oh, Veronica, what have you done?
You need to come with me into the Main Hall, Daddy, and please...
...don't lose your temper.

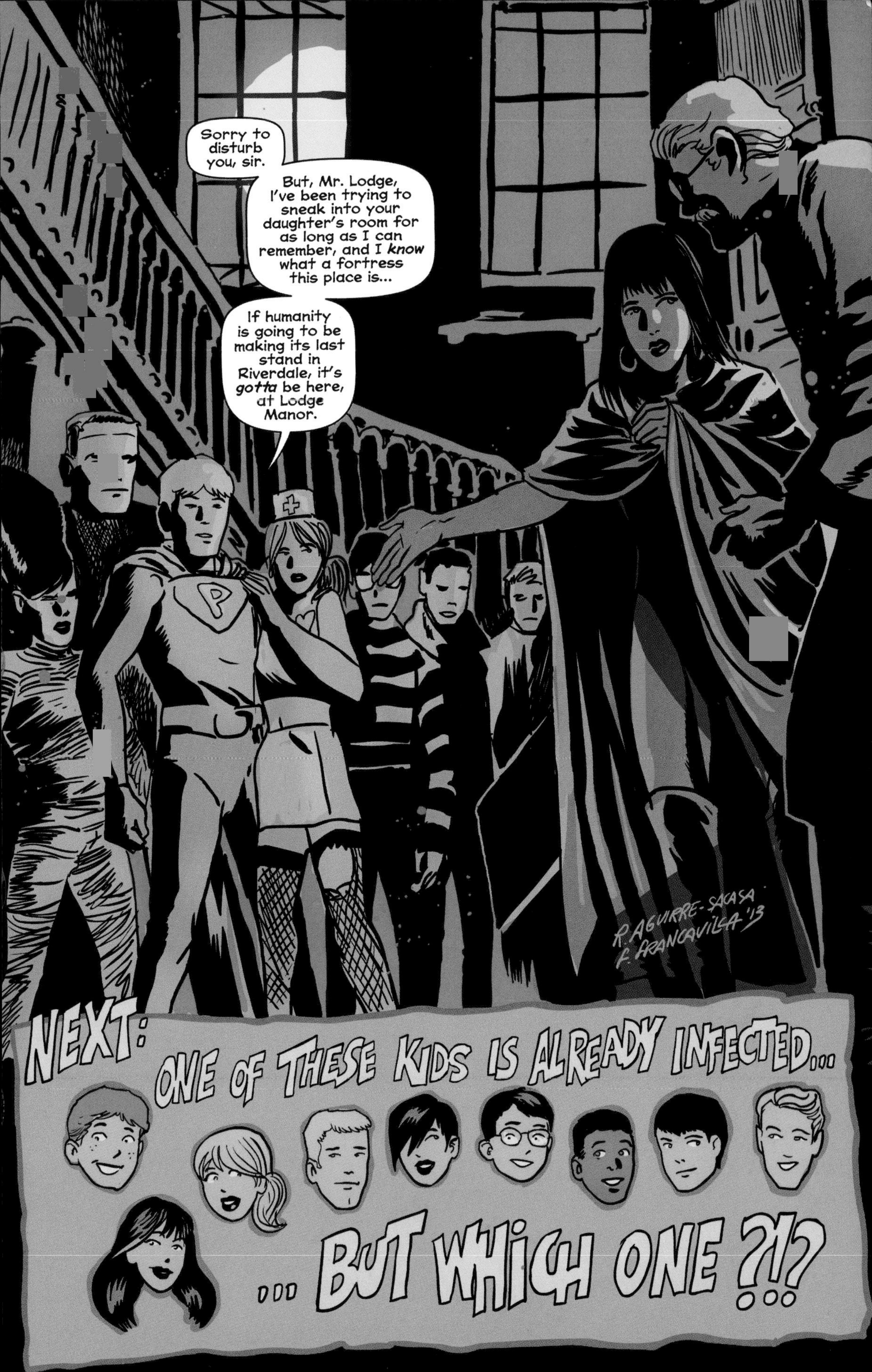
Sorry to disturb you, sir.
But, Mr. Lodge, I've been trying to sneak into your daughter's room for as long as I can remember, and I *know* what a fortress this place is...
If humanity is going to be making its last stand in Riverdale, it's *gotta* be here, at Lodge Manor.
R. AGUIRRE-SACASA F. FRANCAVILLA '13
NEXT: ONE OF THESE KIDS IS ALREADY INFECTED...
...BUT WHICH ONE ?!?

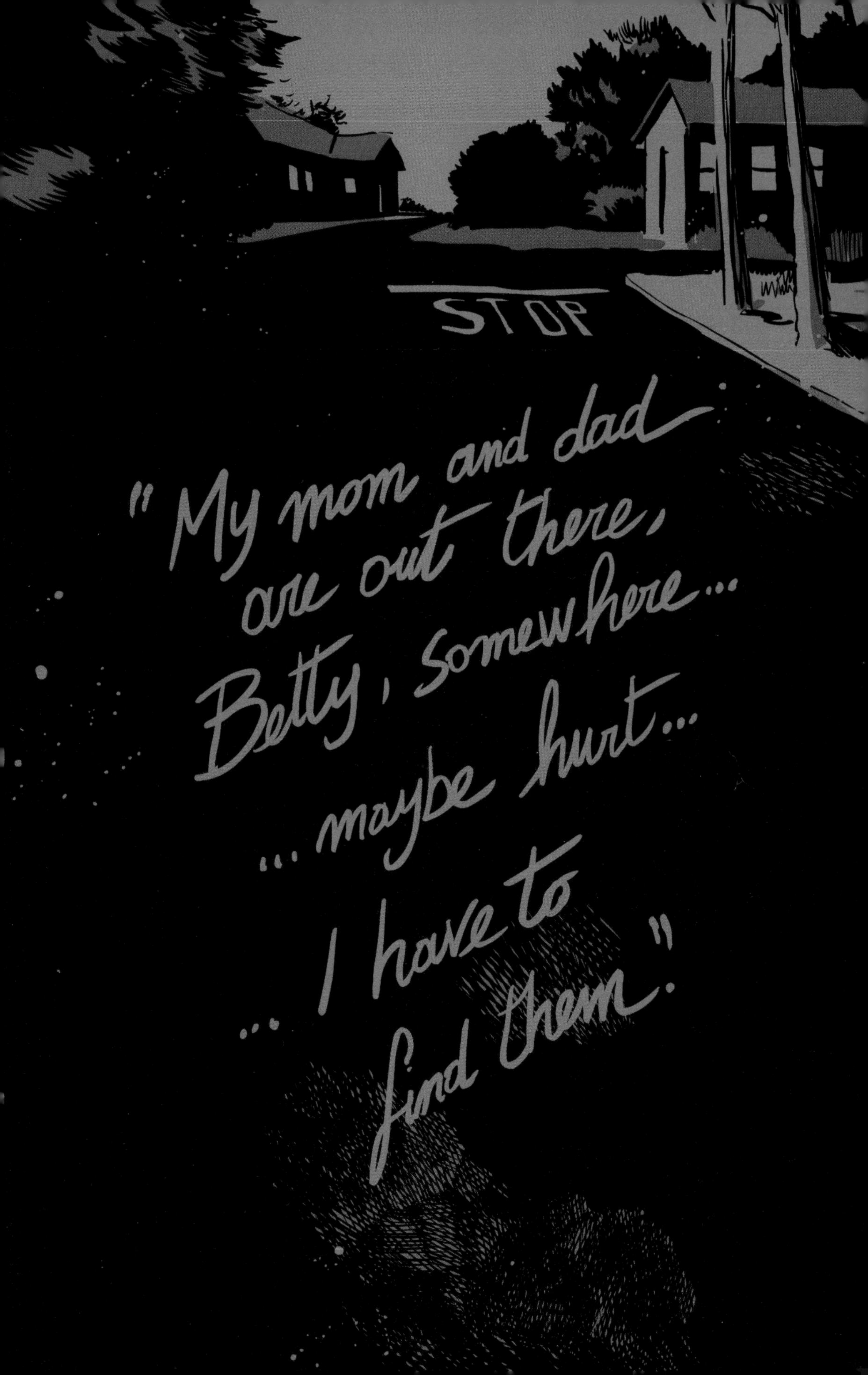
STOP
"My mom and dad are out there, Betty, somewhere...
...maybe hurt...
...I have to find them."

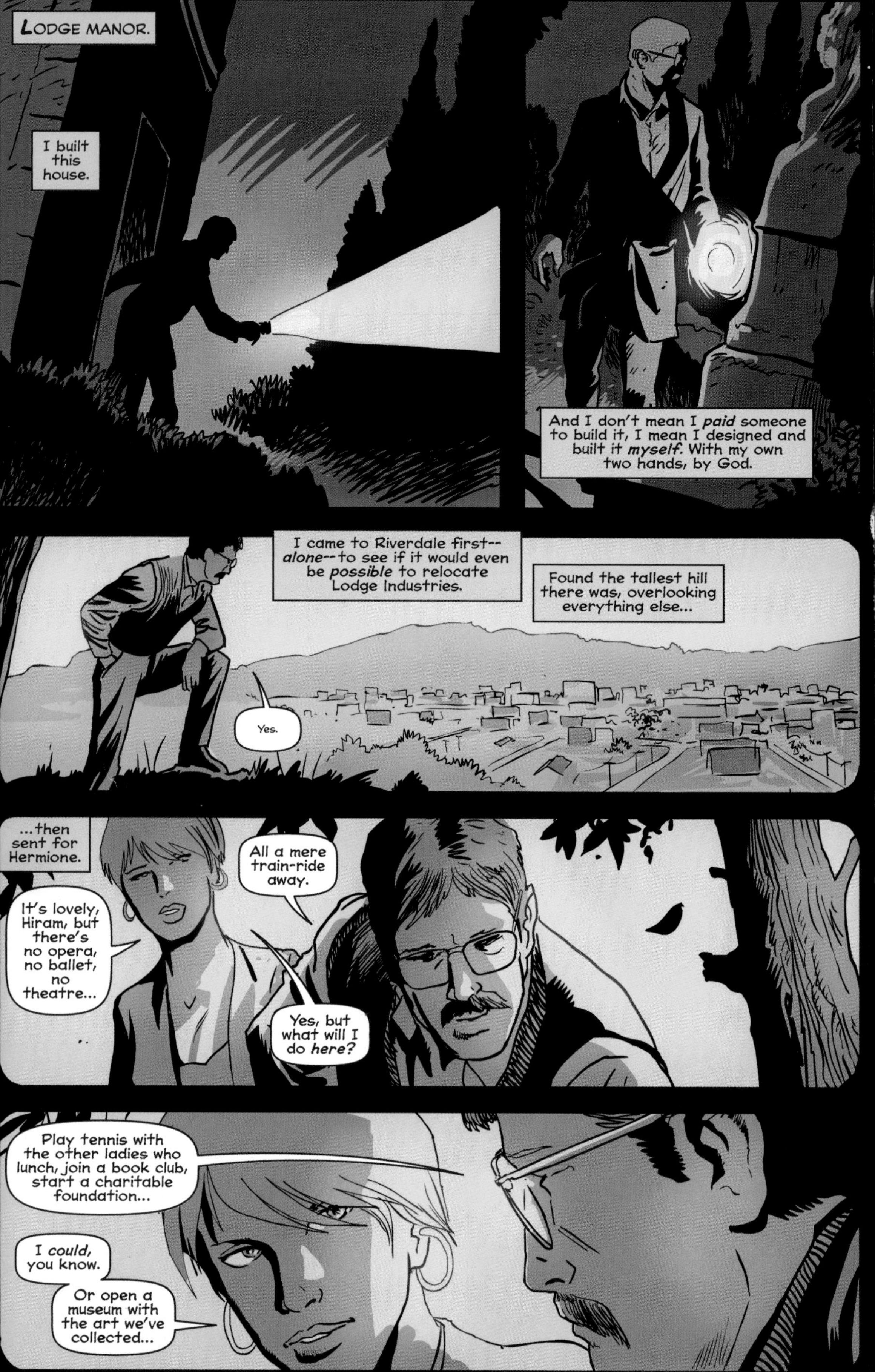

LODGE MANOR.
I built this house.
And I don't mean I *paid* someone to build it, I mean I designed and built it *myself*. With my own two hands, by God.
I came to Riverdale first--*alone*--to see if it would even be *possible* to relocate Lodge Industries.
Found the tallest hill there was, overlooking everything else...
Yes.
...then sent for Hermione.
It's lovely, Hiram, but there's no opera, no ballet, no theatre...
All a mere train-ride away.
Yes, but what will I do *here*?
Play tennis with the other ladies who lunch, join a book club, start a charitable foundation...
I *could*, you know.
Or open a museum with the art we've collected...

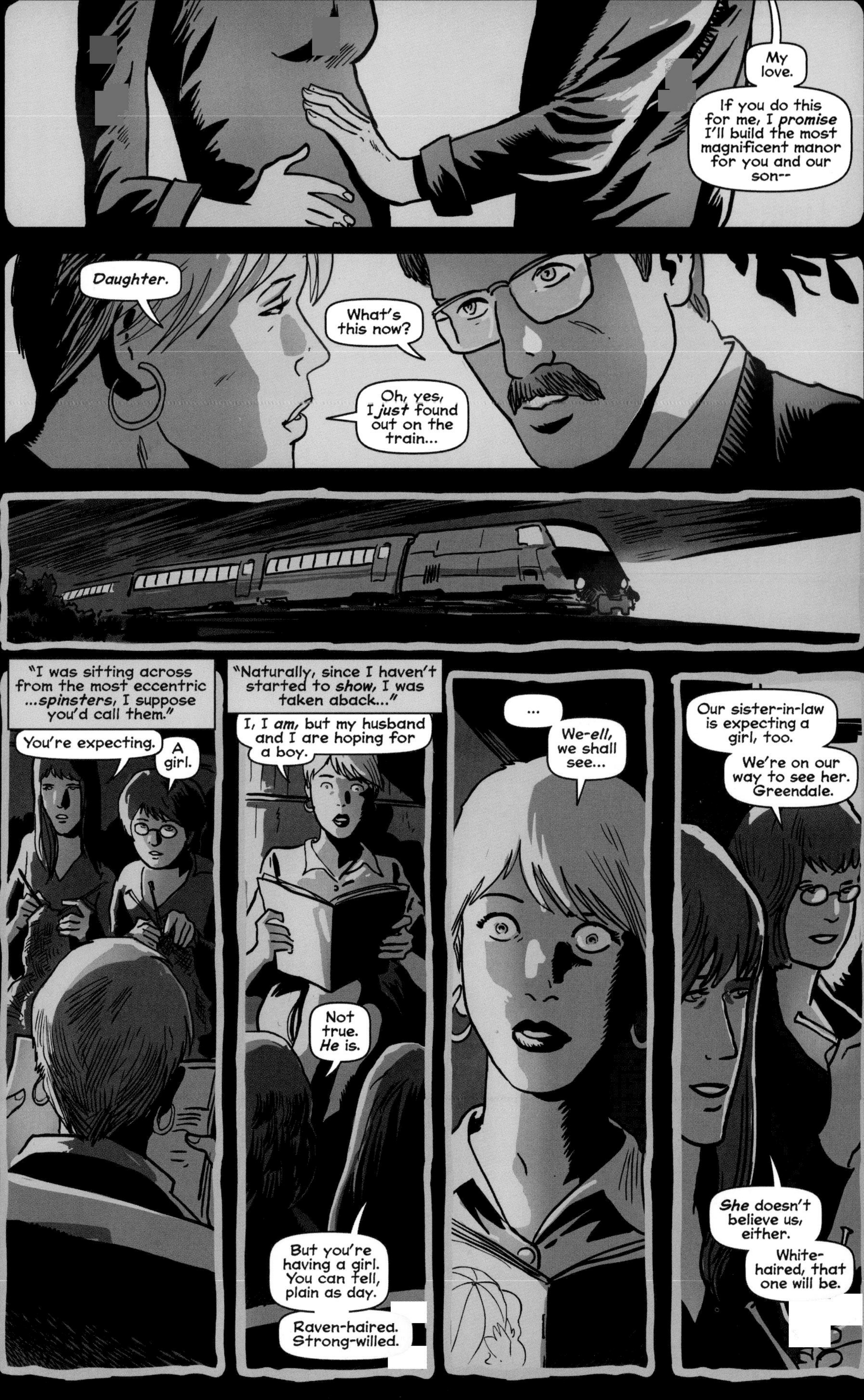
My love.
If you do this for me, I *promise* I'll build the most magnificent manor for you and our son--
Daughter.
What's this now?
Oh, yes, I *just* found out on the train...
"I was sitting across from the most eccentric ...*spinsters*, I suppose you'd call them."
You're expecting.
A girl.
"Naturally, since I haven't started to *show*, I was taken aback..."
I, I *am*, but my husband and I are hoping for a boy.
Not true. *He* is.
But you're having a girl. You can tell, plain as day.
Raven-haired. Strong-willed.
...
We-*ell*, we shall see...
Our sister-in-law is expecting a girl, too.
We're on our way to see her. Greendale.
She doesn't believe us, either.
White-haired, that one will be.

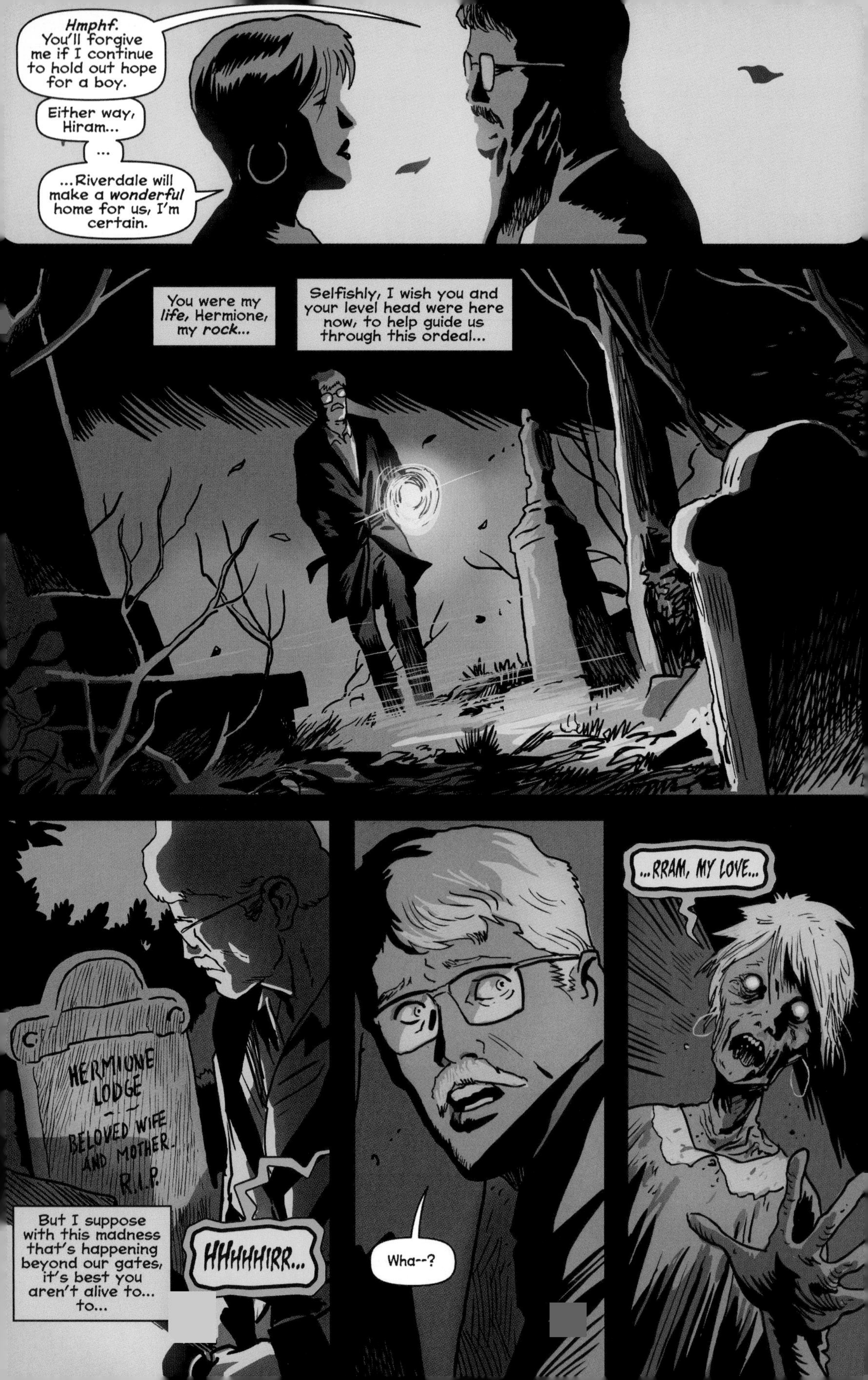
Hmphf. You'll forgive me if I continue to hold out hope for a boy.
Either way, Hiram...
...
...Riverdale will make a wonderful home for us, I'm certain.
You were my life, Hermione, my rock...
Selfishly, I wish you and your level head were here now, to help guide us through this ordeal...
HERMIONE LODGE
BELOVED WIFE AND MOTHER.
R.I.P.
But I suppose with this madness that's happening beyond our gates, it's best you aren't alive to... to...
HHHHHIRR...
Wha--?
...RRAM, MY LOVE...

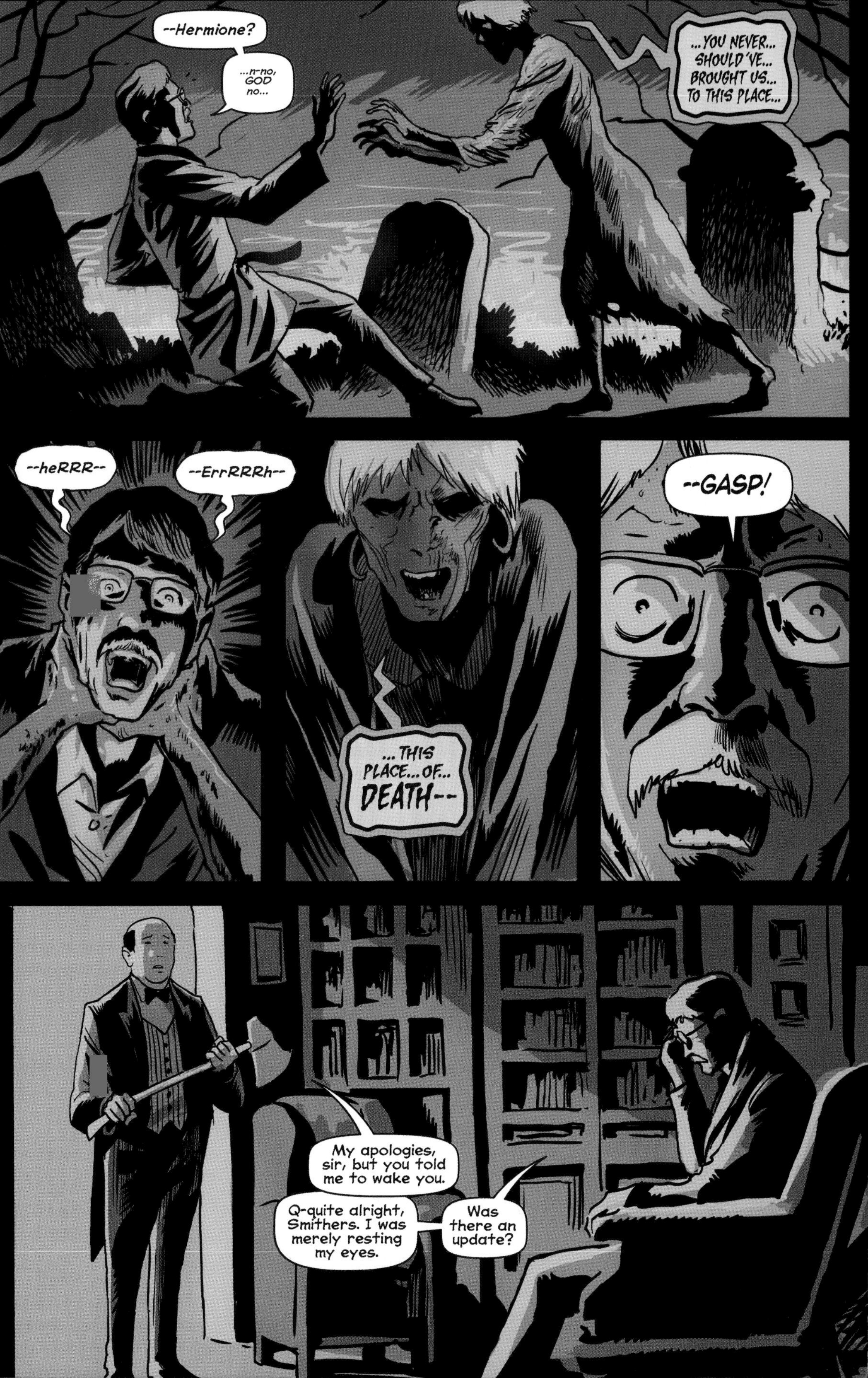
--Hermione?
...n-no, GOD no...
...YOU NEVER... SHOULD'VE... BROUGHT US... TO THIS PLACE...
--heRRR--
--ErrRRRh--
...THIS PLACE...OF... DEATH--
--GASP!
My apologies, sir, but you told me to wake you.
Q-quite alright, Smithers. I was merely resting my eyes.
Was there an update?

I've just finished a sweep of the perimeter; every point of egress and ingress is intact and secure. Additionally, I've turned on all the security cameras and activated the alarms.

"Operation: Lockdown" proceeds apace.

Good. Well done.

And the rest of town?

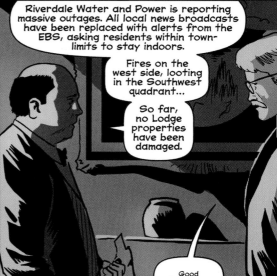

Riverdale Water and Power is reporting massive outages. All local news broadcasts have been replaced with alerts from the EBS, asking residents within town-limits to stay indoors.

Fires on the west side, looting in the Southwest quadrant...

So far, no Lodge properties have been damaged.

Good Lord, how did it fall apart so quickly...?

And beyond Riverdale?

Sporadic reporting, mostly rumors and speculation relayed through social media, twittering and the like, though that is decreasing, with each passing hour...

Most significantly, sir: Lodge satellite intercepted a transmission sent from the White House to the National Guard...

...the words "quarantine" and "extermination" were uttered, in connection to something being described as "that situation in Riverdale."

...

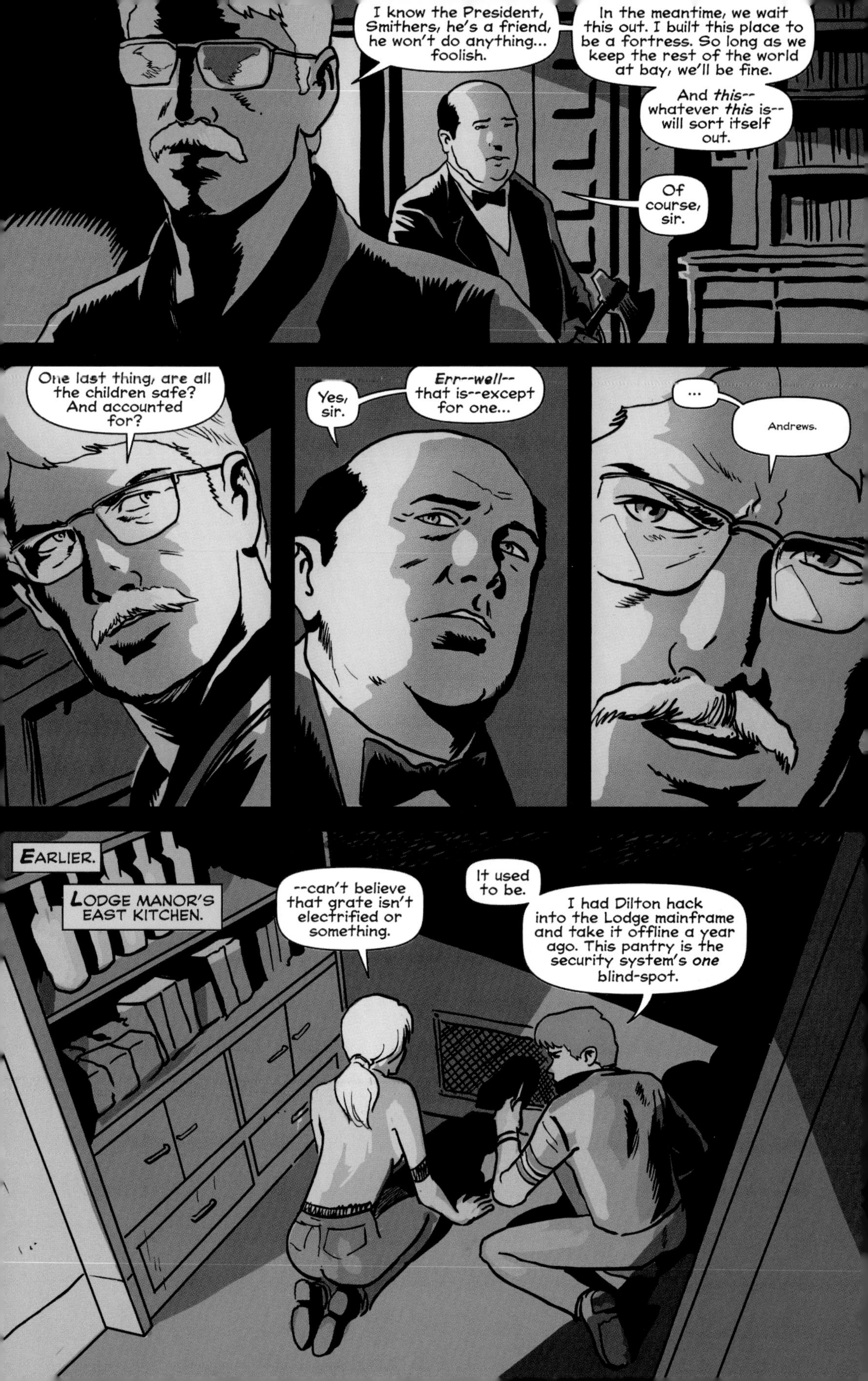
I know the President, Smithers, he's a friend, he won't do anything... foolish.
In the meantime, we wait this out. I built this place to be a fortress. So long as we keep the rest of the world at bay, we'll be fine.
And *this*-- whatever *this* is-- will sort itself out.
Of course, sir.
One last thing, are all the children safe? And accounted for?
Yes, sir.
Err--well-- that is--except for one...
...
Andrews.
EARLIER.
LODGE MANOR'S EAST KITCHEN.
--can't believe that grate isn't electrified or something.
It used to be.
I had Dilton hack into the Lodge mainframe and take it offline a year ago. This pantry is the security system's *one* blind-spot.

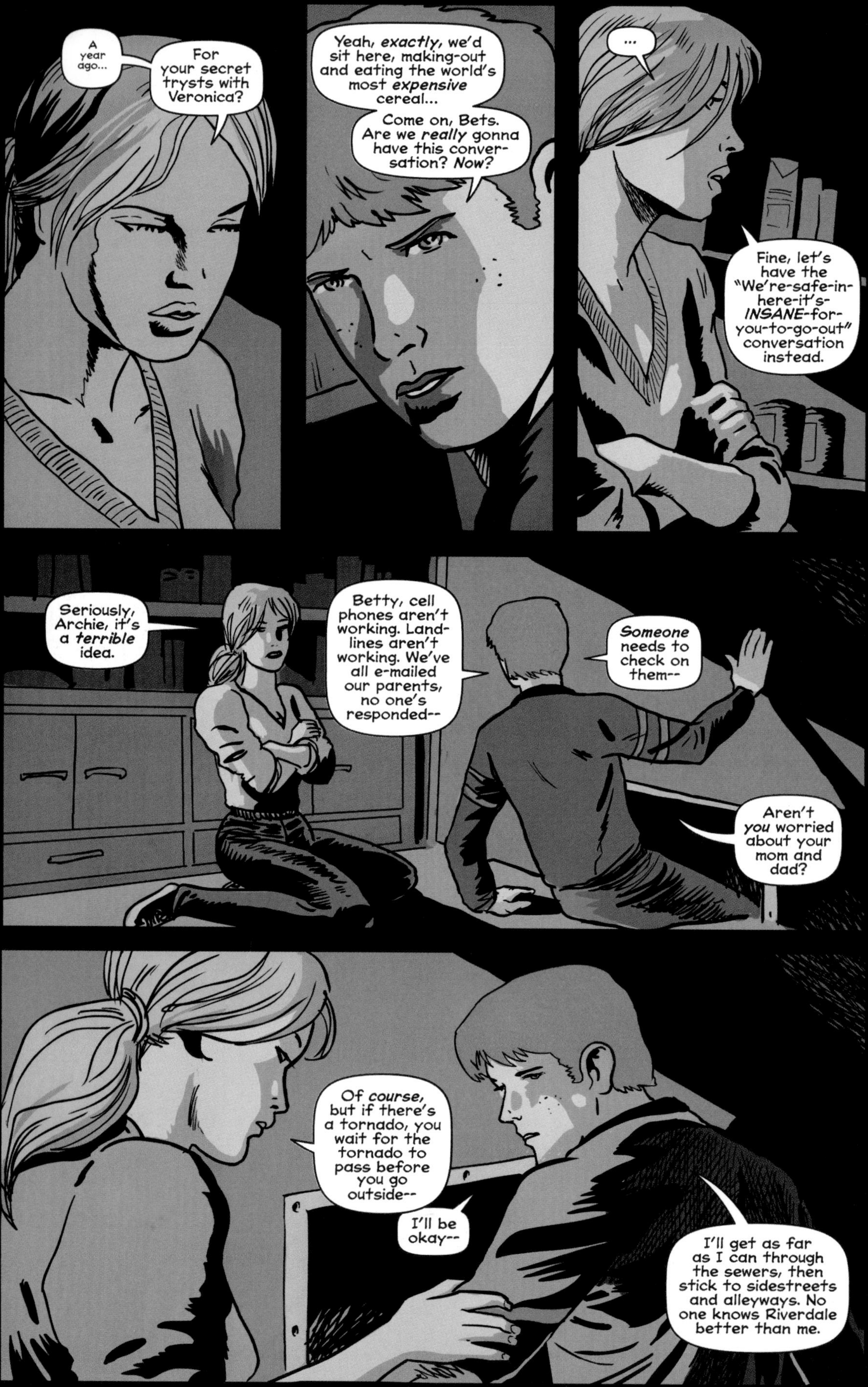
A year ago...
For your secret trysts with Veronica?
Yeah, *exactly*, we'd sit here, making-out and eating the world's most *expensive* cereal...
Come on, Bets. Are we *really* gonna have this conver-sation? *Now*?
...
Fine, let's have the "We're-safe-in-here-it's-*INSANE*-for-you-to-go-out" conversation instead.
Seriously, Archie, it's a *terrible* idea.
Betty, cell phones aren't working. Land-lines aren't working. We've all e-mailed our parents, no one's responded--
Someone needs to check on them--
Aren't *you* worried about your mom and dad?
Of *course*, but if there's a tornado, you wait for the tornado to pass before you go outside--
I'll be okay--
I'll get as far as I can through the sewers, then stick to sidestreets and alleyways. No one knows Riverdale better than me.

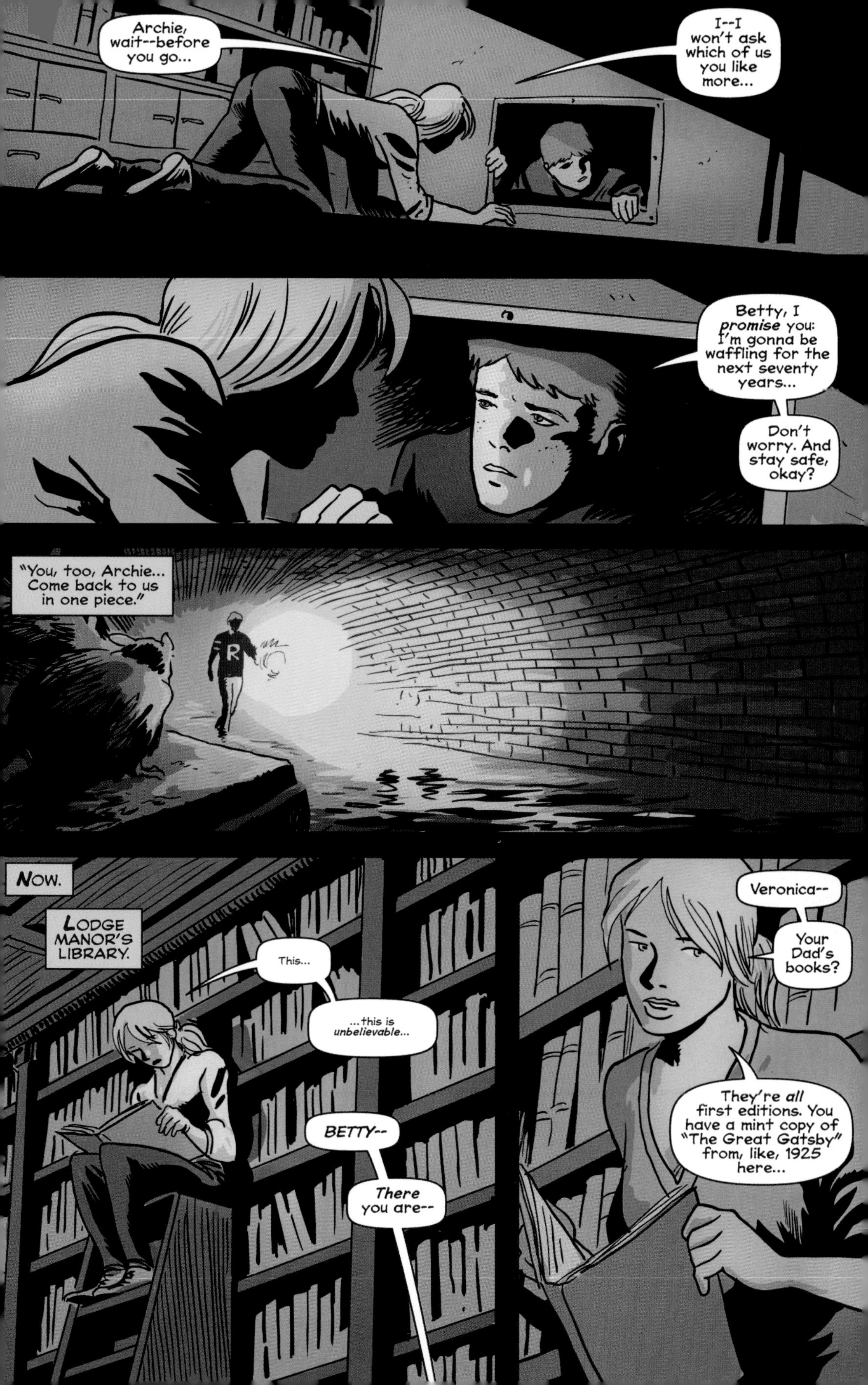
Archie, wait--before you go...
I--I won't ask which of us you like more...
Betty, I *promise* you: I'm gonna be waffling for the next seventy years...
Don't worry. And stay safe, okay?
"You, too, Archie... Come back to us in one piece."
NOW.
LODGE MANOR'S LIBRARY.
This...
...this is *unbelievable*...
Veronica--
Your Dad's books?
They're *all* first editions. You have a mint copy of "The Great Gatsby" from, like, 1925 here...
BETTY--
There you are--

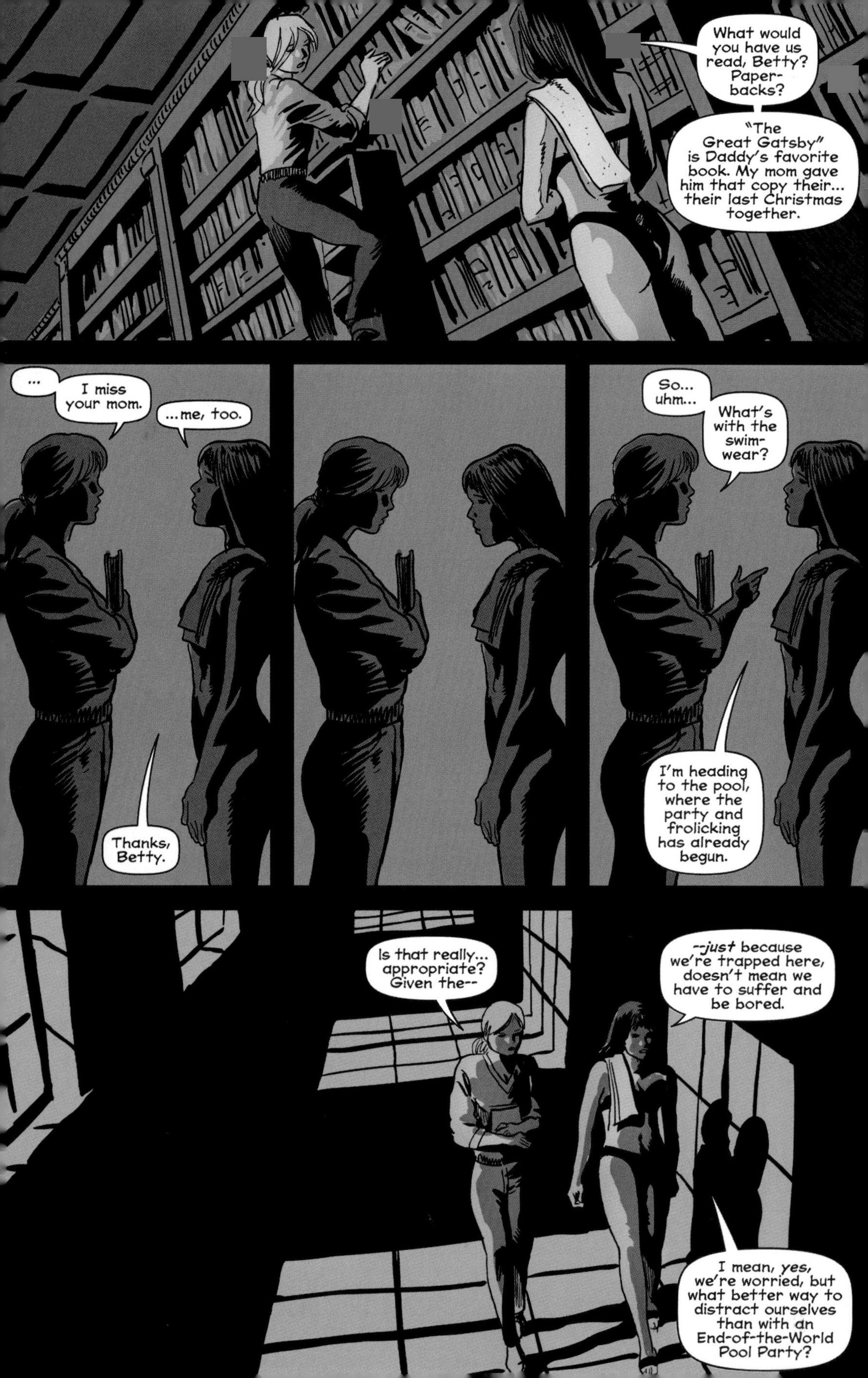
What would you have us read, Betty? Paper-backs?
"The Great Gatsby" is Daddy's favorite book. My mom gave him that copy their... their last Christmas together.
...
I miss your mom.
...me, too.
Thanks, Betty.
So... uhm...
What's with the swim-wear?
I'm heading to the pool, where the party and frolicking has already begun.
Is that really... appropriate? Given the--
--*just* because we're trapped here, doesn't mean we have to suffer and be bored.
I mean, *yes*, we're worried, but what better way to distract ourselves than with an End-of-the-World Pool Party?

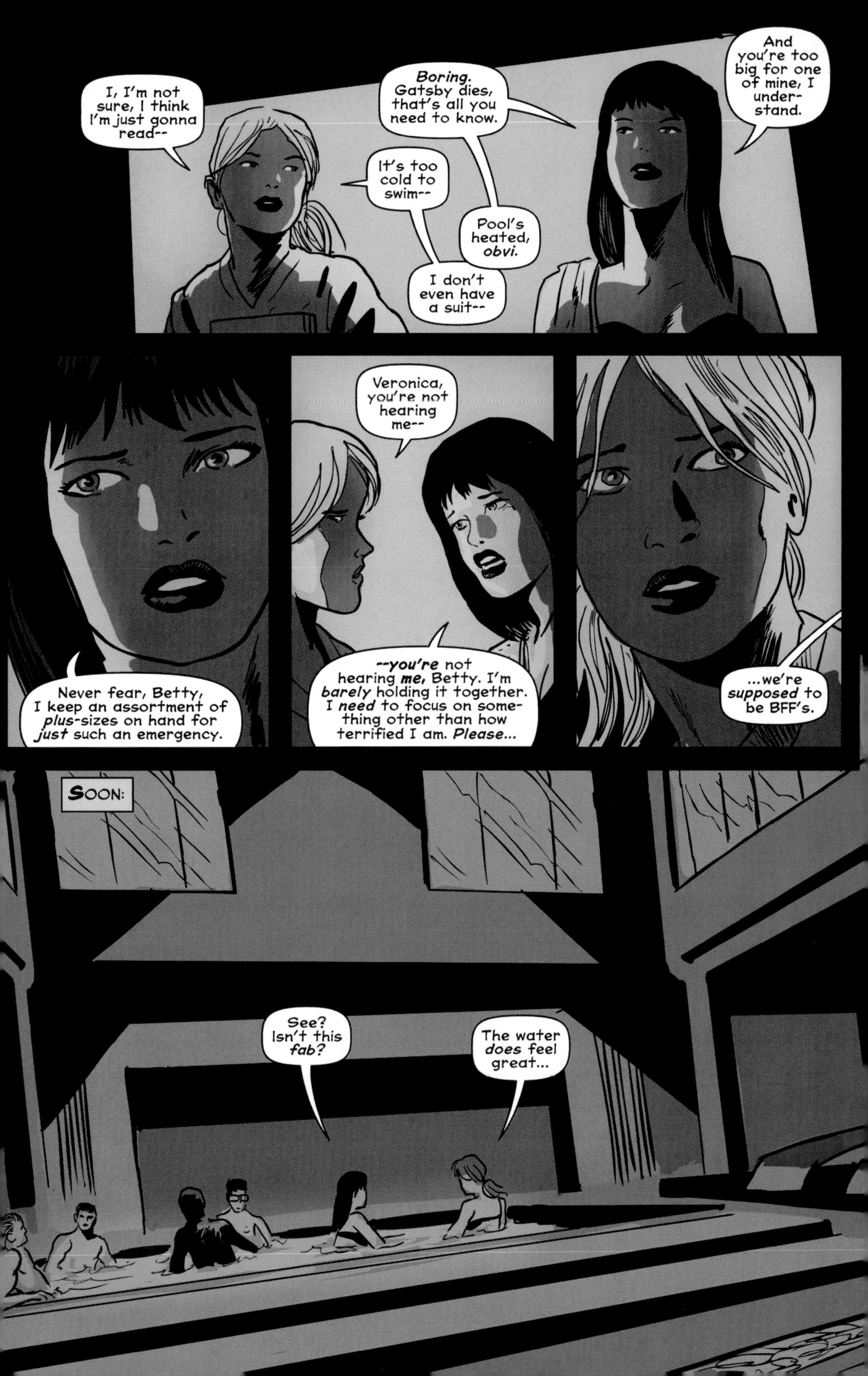
I, I'm not sure, I think I'm just gonna read--
Boring. Gatsby dies, that's all you need to know.
And you're too big for one of mine, I under-stand.
It's too cold to swim--
Pool's heated, obvi.
I don't even have a suit--
Never fear, Betty, I keep an assortment of plus-sizes on hand for just such an emergency.
Veronica, you're not hearing me--
--you're not hearing me, Betty. I'm barely holding it together. I need to focus on some-thing other than how terrified I am. Please...
...we're supposed to be BFF's.
SOON:
See? Isn't this fab?
The water does feel great...

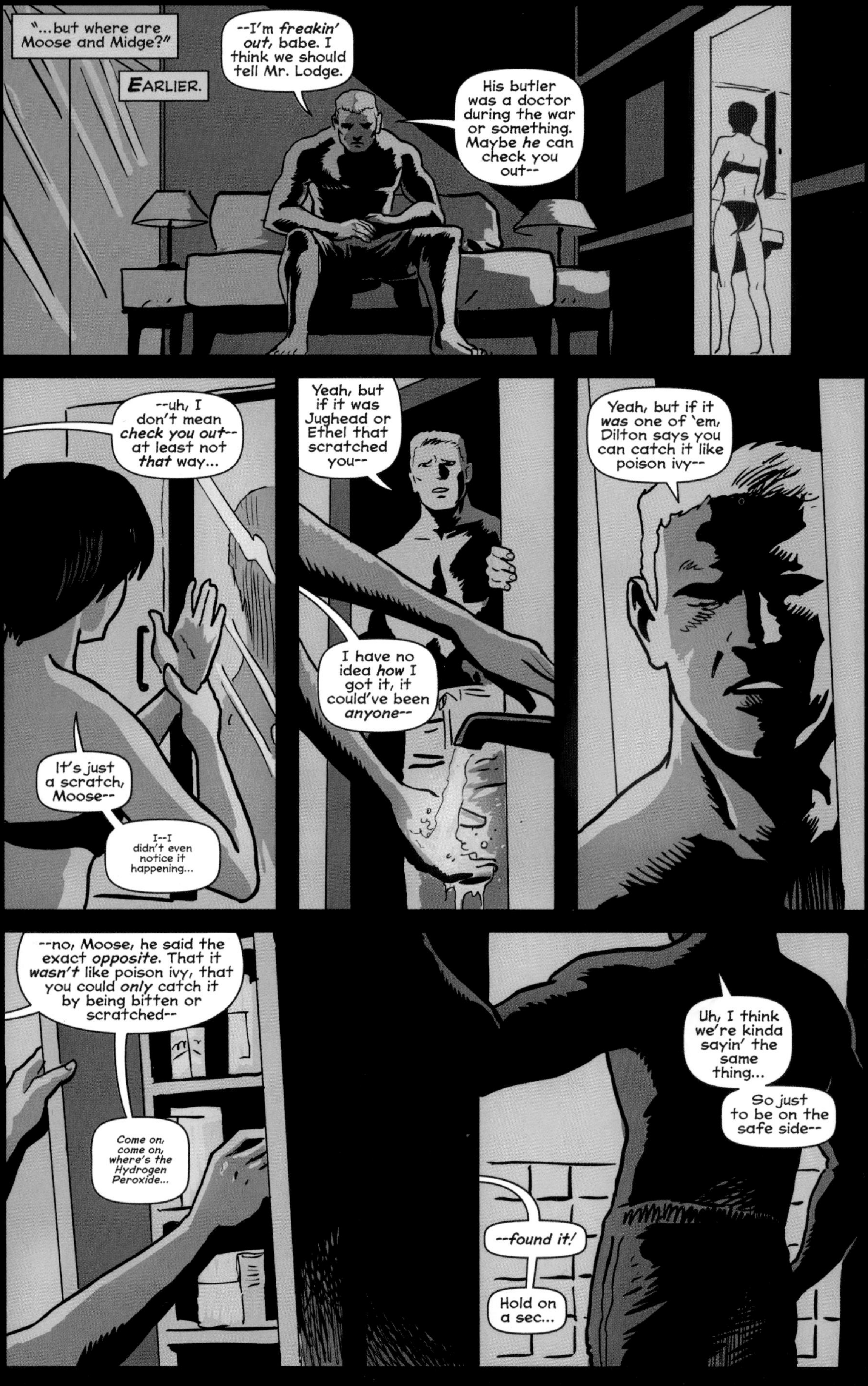
"...but where are Moose and Midge?"
EARLIER.
--I'm freakin' out, babe. I think we should tell Mr. Lodge.
His butler was a doctor during the war or something. Maybe he can check you out--
--uh, I don't mean check you out-- at least not that way...
It's just a scratch, Moose--
I--I didn't even notice it happening...
Yeah, but if it was Jughead or Ethel that scratched you--
I have no idea how I got it, it could've been anyone--
Yeah, but if it was one of 'em, Dilton says you can catch it like poison ivy--
--no, Moose, he said the exact opposite. That it wasn't like poison ivy, that you could only catch it by being bitten or scratched--
Come on, come on, where's the Hydrogen Peroxide...
Uh, I think we're kinda sayin' the same thing...
So just to be on the safe side--
--found it!
Hold on a sec...

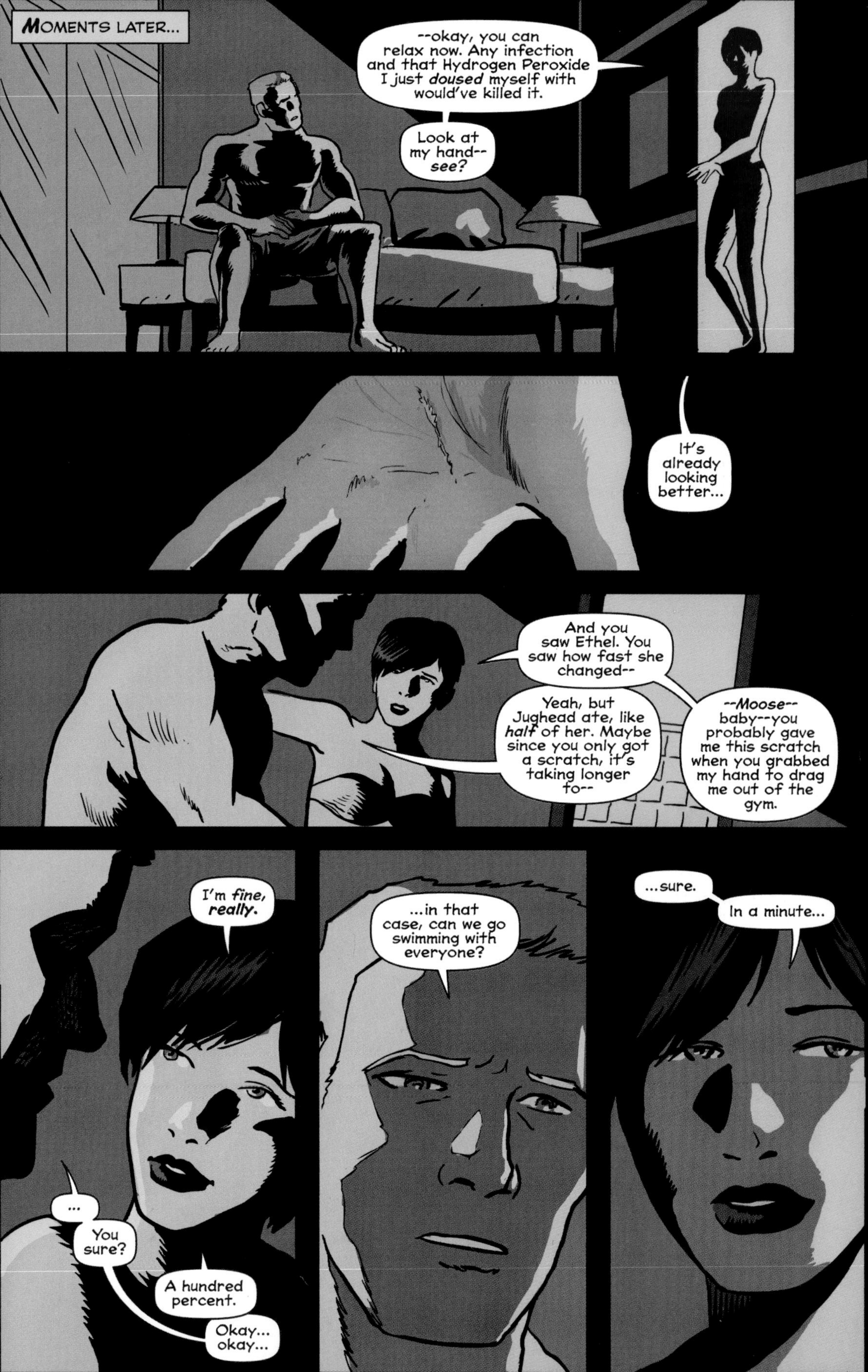
Moments later...
--okay, you can relax now. Any infection and that Hydrogen Peroxide I just *doused* myself with would've killed it.
Look at my hand-- *see?*
It's already looking better...
And you saw Ethel. You saw how fast she changed--
--*Moose*-- baby--you probably gave me this scratch when you grabbed my hand to drag me out of the gym.
Yeah, but Jughead ate, like *half* of her. Maybe since you only got a scratch, it's taking longer to--
I'm *fine, really.*
...
You sure?
A hundred percent.
Okay... okay...
...in that case, can we go swimming with everyone?
...sure.
In a minute...

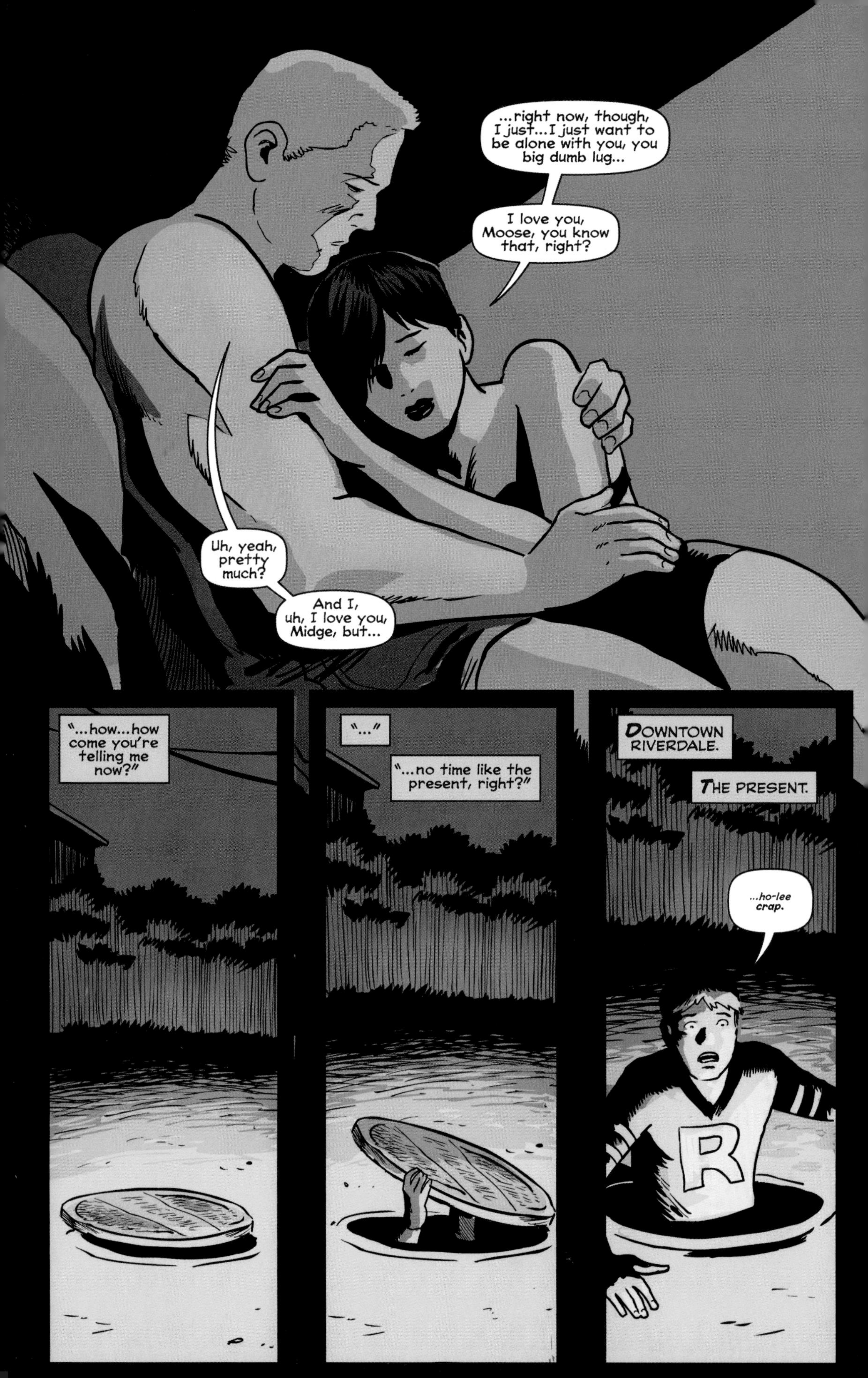
...right now, though, I just...I just want to be alone with you, you big dumb lug...
I love you, Moose, you know that, right?
Uh, yeah, pretty much?
And I, uh, I love you, Midge, but...
"...how...how come you're telling me now?"
"..."
"...no time like the present, right?"
DOWNTOWN RIVERDALE.
THE PRESENT.
...ho-lee crap.

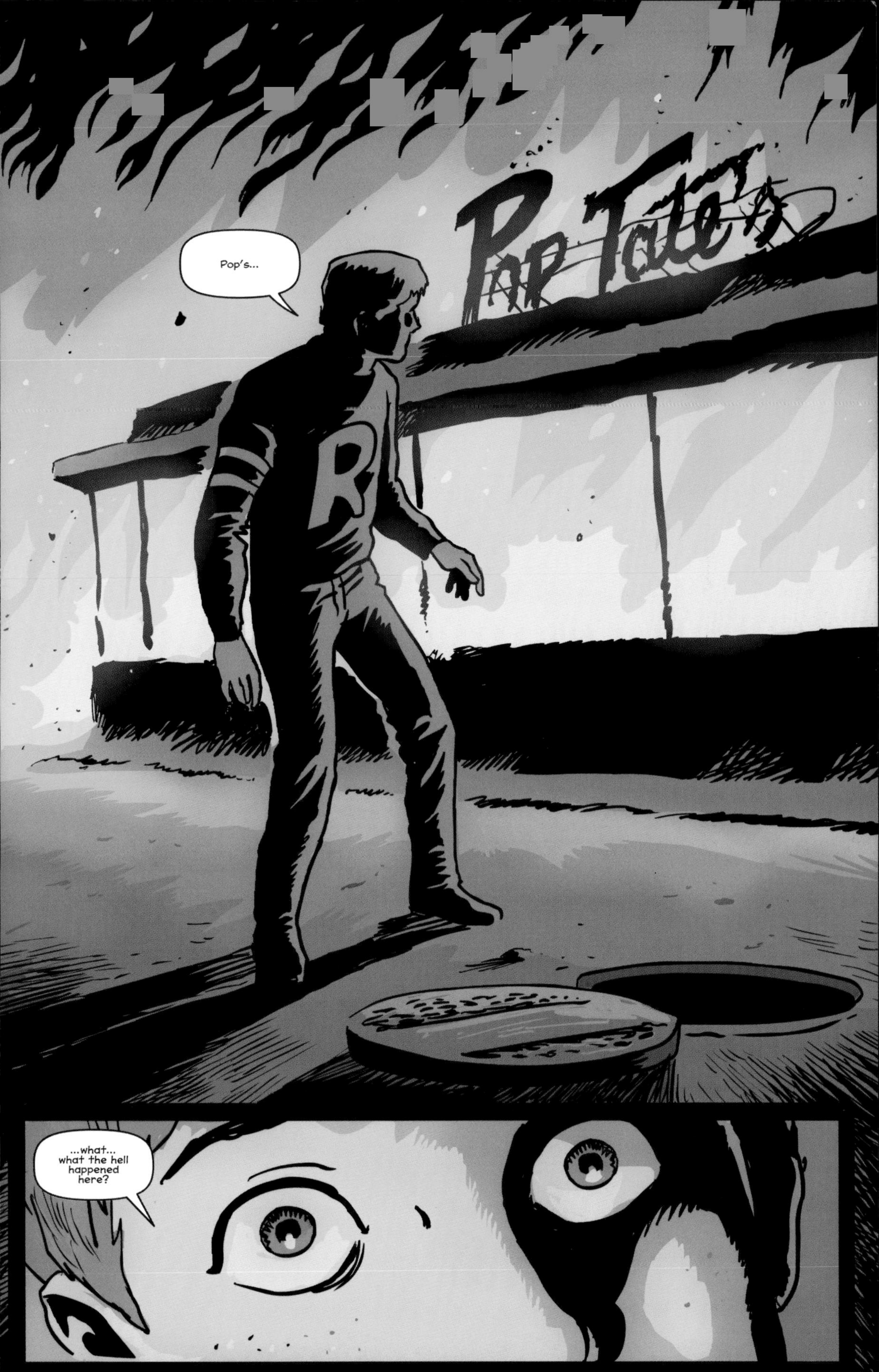
Pop Tate's
Pop's...
...what... what the hell happened here?

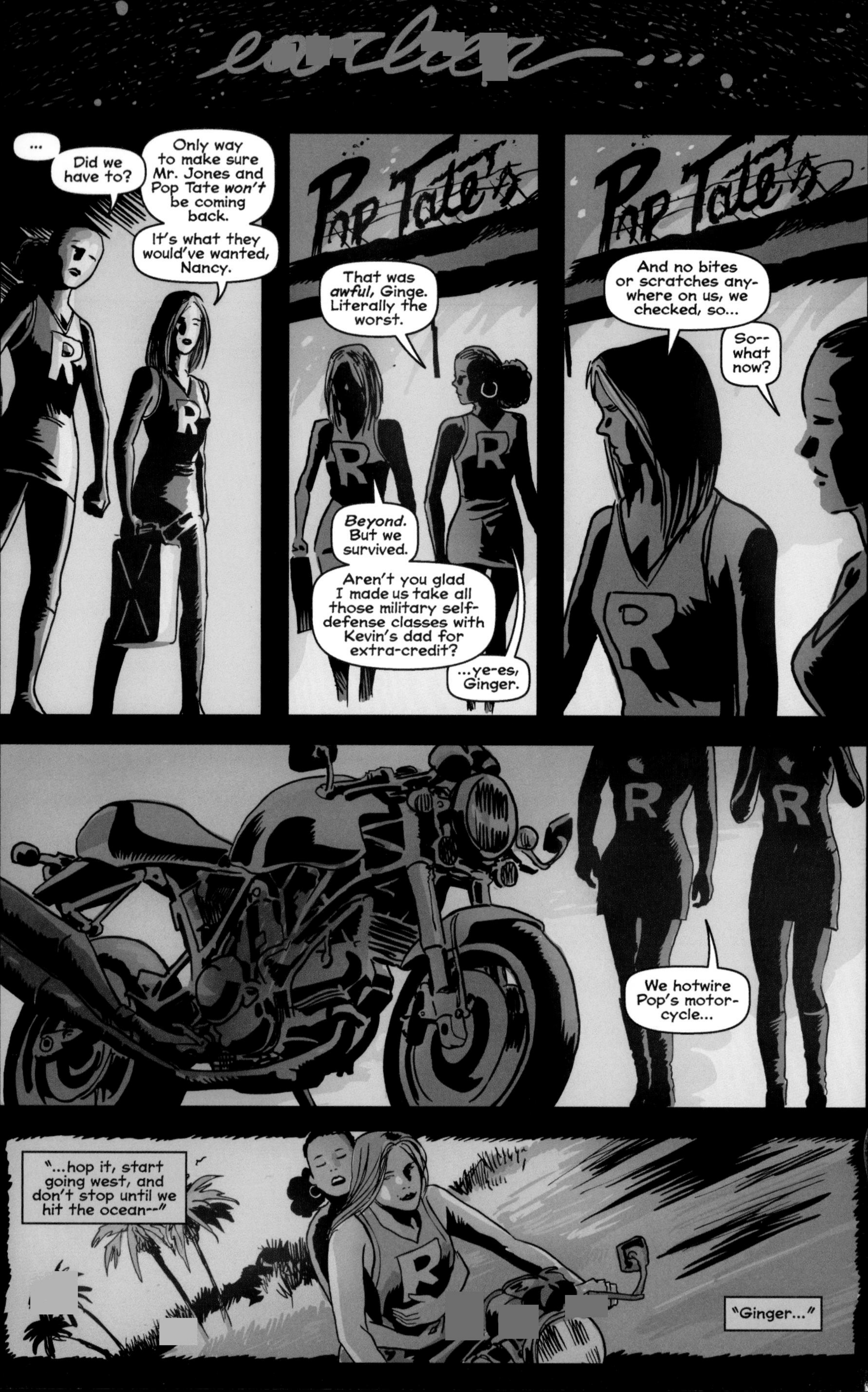

...
Did we have to?
Only way to make sure Mr. Jones and Pop Tate *won't* be coming back.
It's what they would've wanted, Nancy.
Pop Tate's
That was *awful*, Ginge. Literally the worst.
Beyond. But we survived.
Aren't you glad I made us take all those military self-defense classes with Kevin's dad for extra-credit?
...ye-es, Ginger.
Pop Tate's
And no bites or scratches anywhere on us, we checked, so...
So-- what now?
We hotwire Pop's motorcycle...
"...hop it, start going west, and don't stop until we hit the ocean--"
"Ginger..."

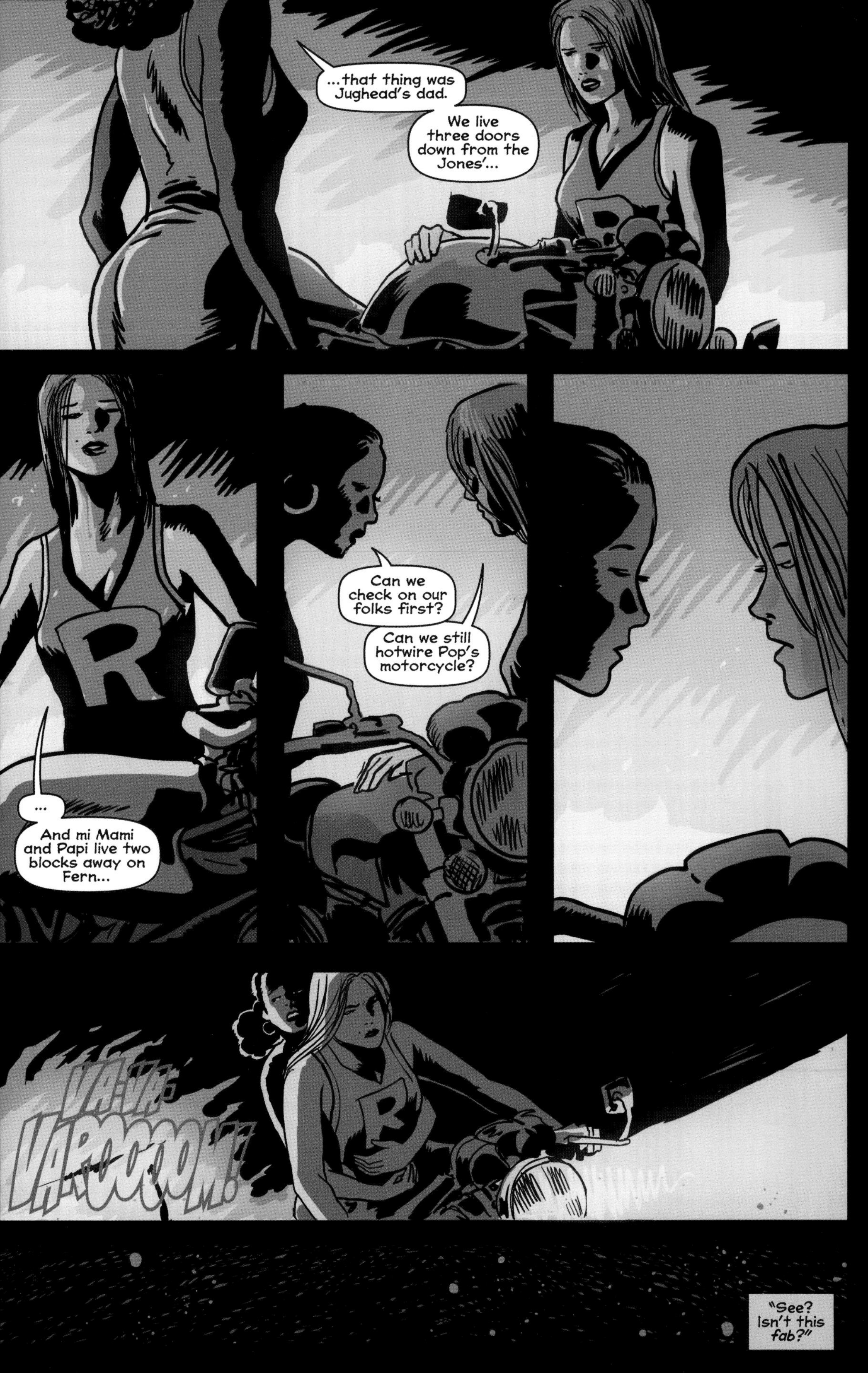

...that thing was Jughead's dad.
We live three doors down from the Jones'...
...
And mi Mami and Papi live two blocks away on Fern...
Can we check on our folks first?
Can we still hotwire Pop's motorcycle?
VA-VA-VAROOOOM!
"See? Isn't this fab?"

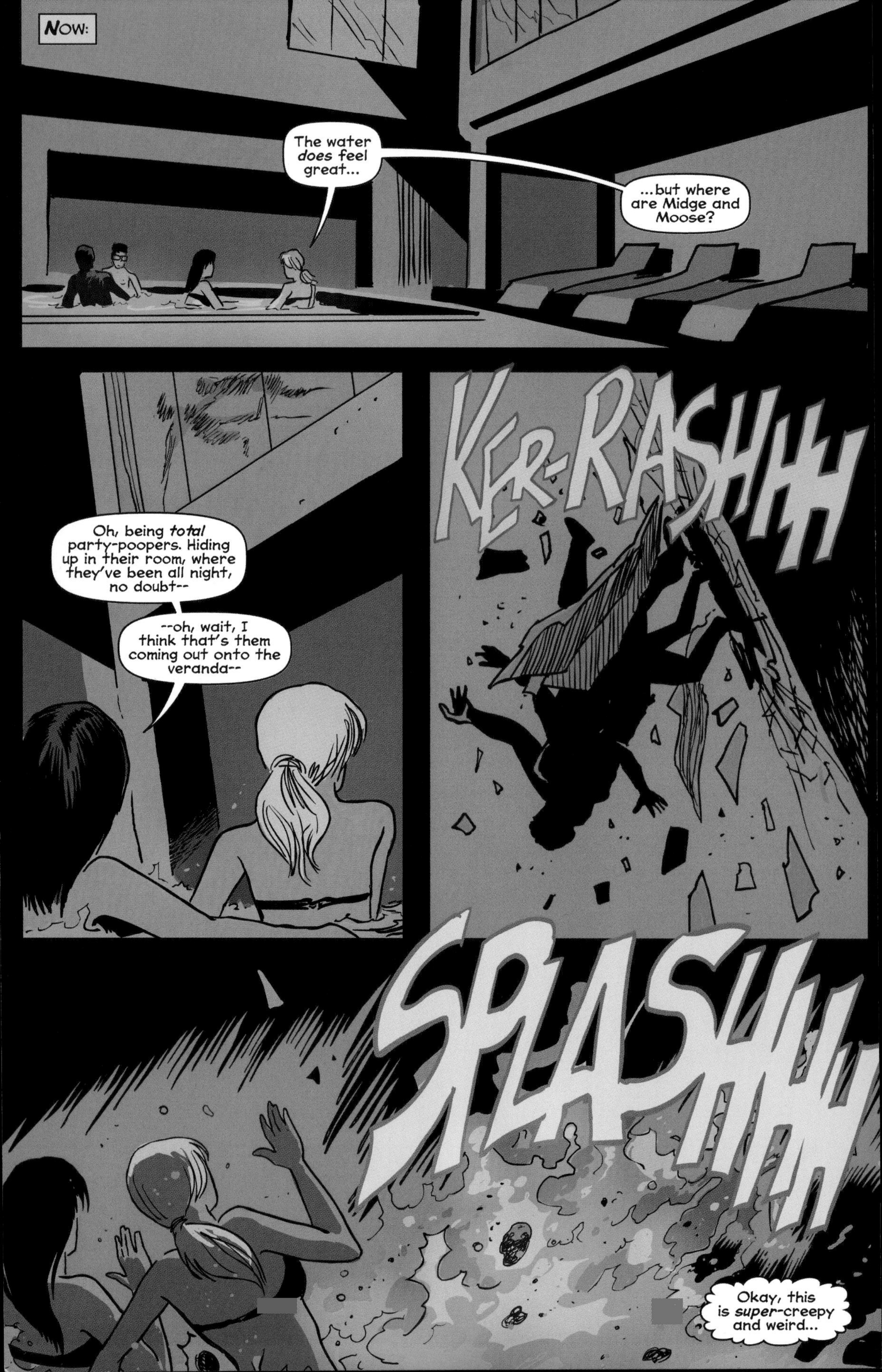
NOW:
The water does feel great...
...but where are Midge and Moose?
Oh, being total party-poopers. Hiding up in their room, where they've been all night, no doubt--
--oh, wait, I think that's them coming out onto the veranda--
KER-RASHHH
SPLASHHH
Okay, this is super-creepy and weird...

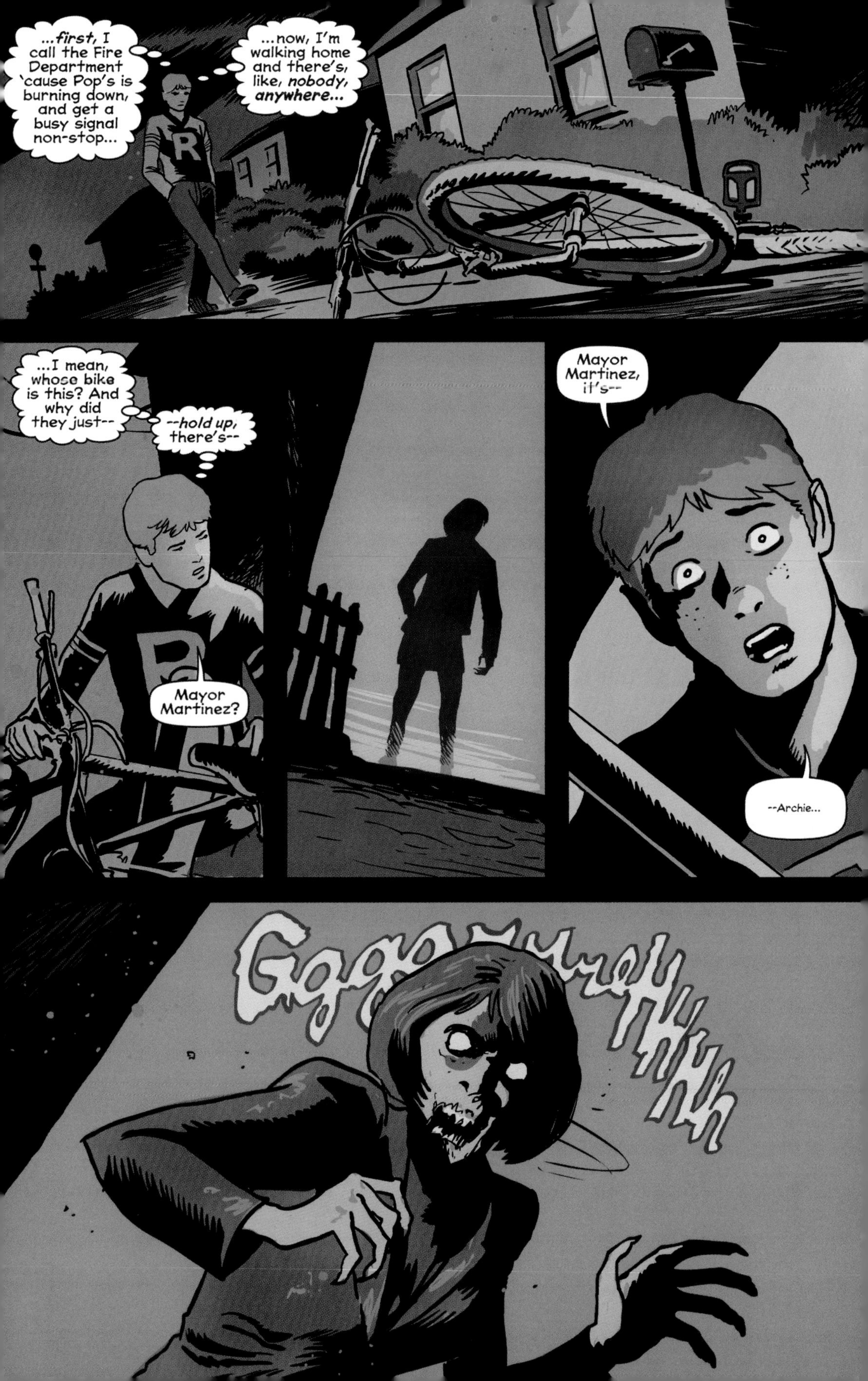
...first, I call the Fire Department 'cause Pop's is burning down, and get a busy signal non-stop...
...now, I'm walking home and there's, like, nobody, anywhere...
...I mean, whose bike is this? And why did they just--
--hold up, there's--
Mayor Martinez?
Mayor Martinez, it's--
--Archie...

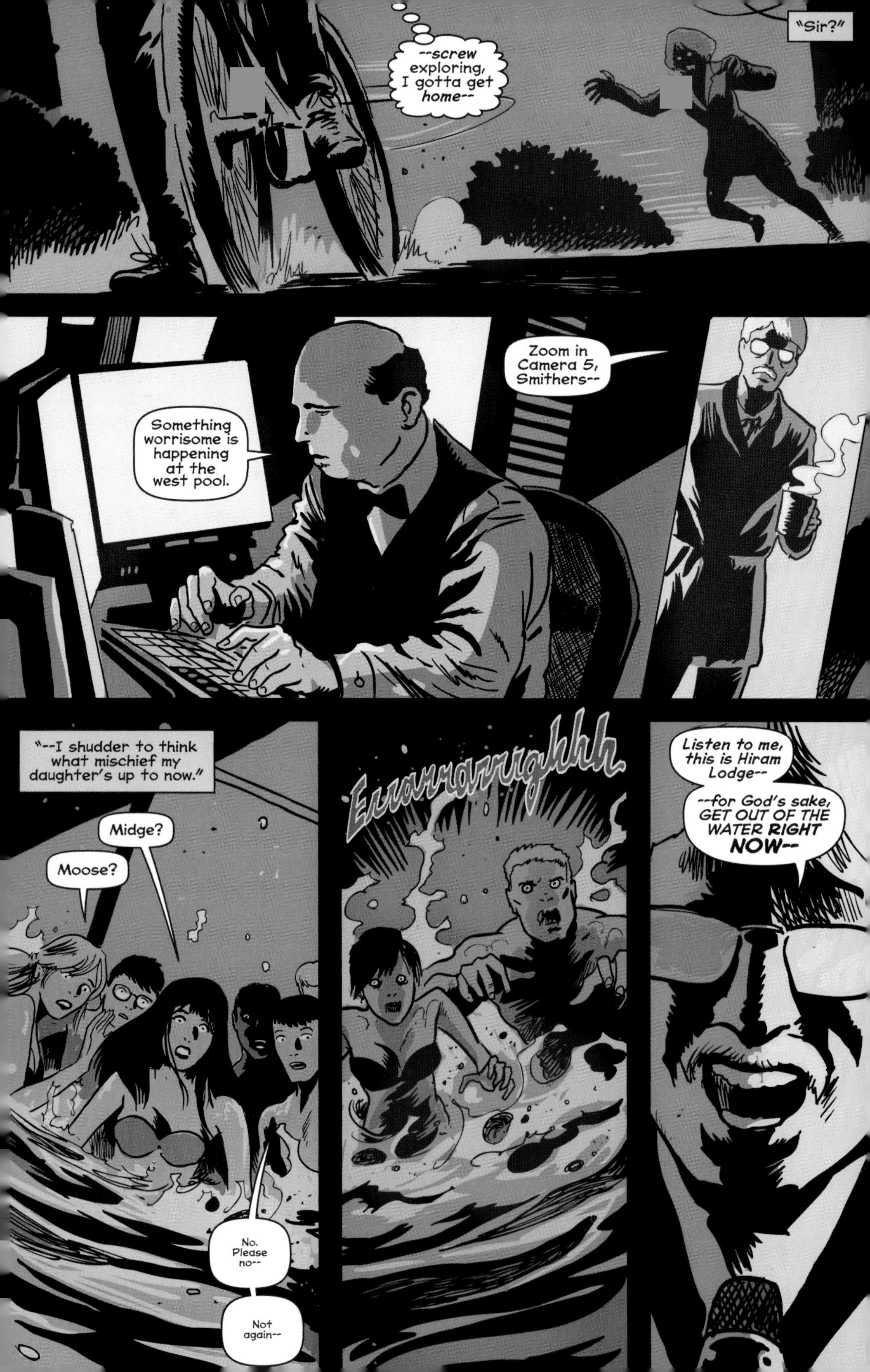
--screw exploring, I gotta get home--
"Sir?"
Zoom in Camera 5, Smithers--
Something worrisome is happening at the west pool.
"--I shudder to think what mischief my daughter's up to now."
Midge?
Moose?
No. Please no--
Not again--
Errarrarrrghhh
Listen to me, this is Hiram Lodge--
--for God's sake, GET OUT OF THE WATER RIGHT NOW--

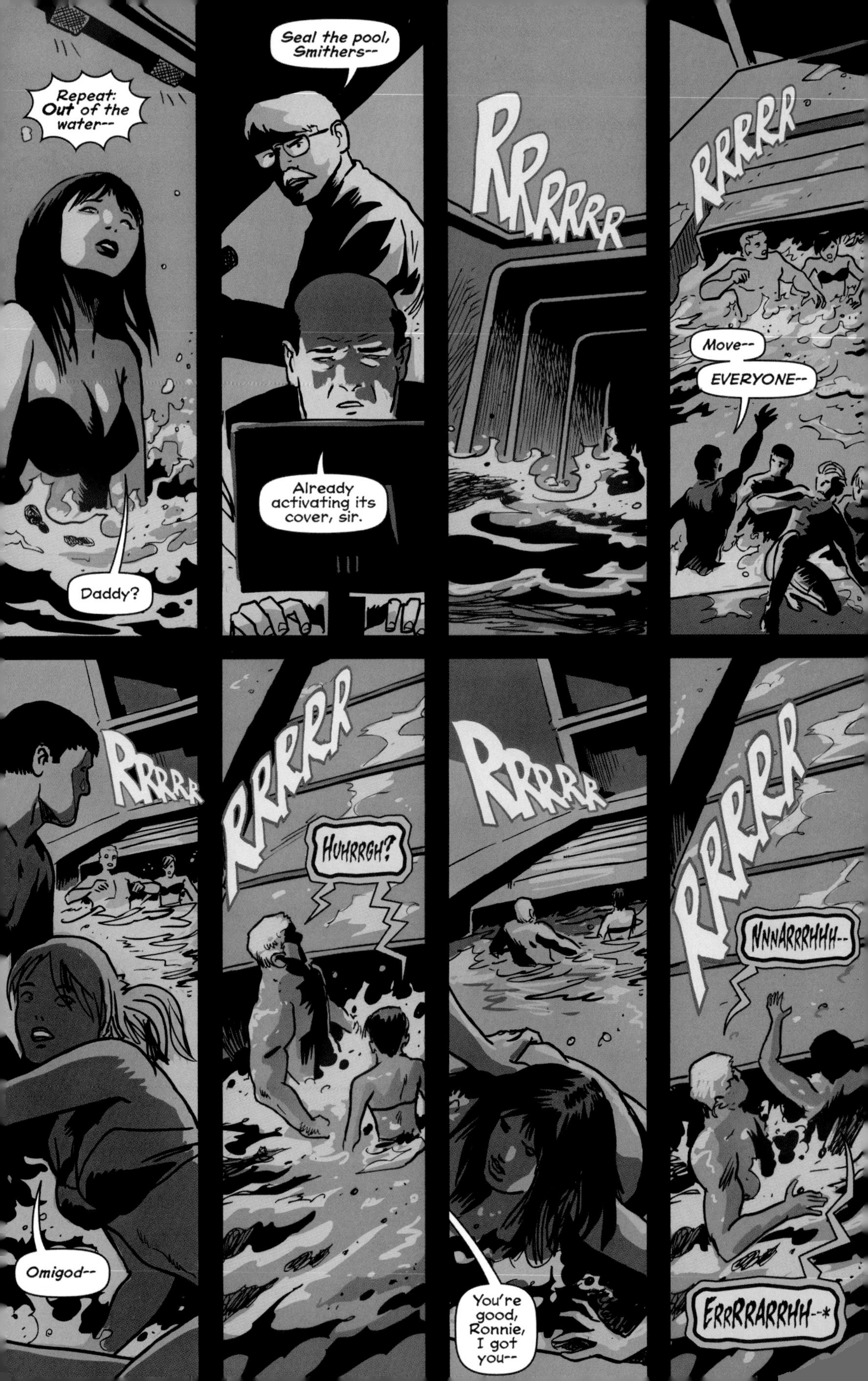
Repeat: Out of the water--
Daddy?
Seal the pool, Smithers--
Already activating its cover, sir.
RRRRRRR
RRRRR
Move--
EVERYONE--
RRRRR
Omigod--
RRRRR
HUHRRGH?
RRRRR
You're good, Ronnie, I got you--
RRRRR
NNNARRRHHH--
ERRRRARRHH--*

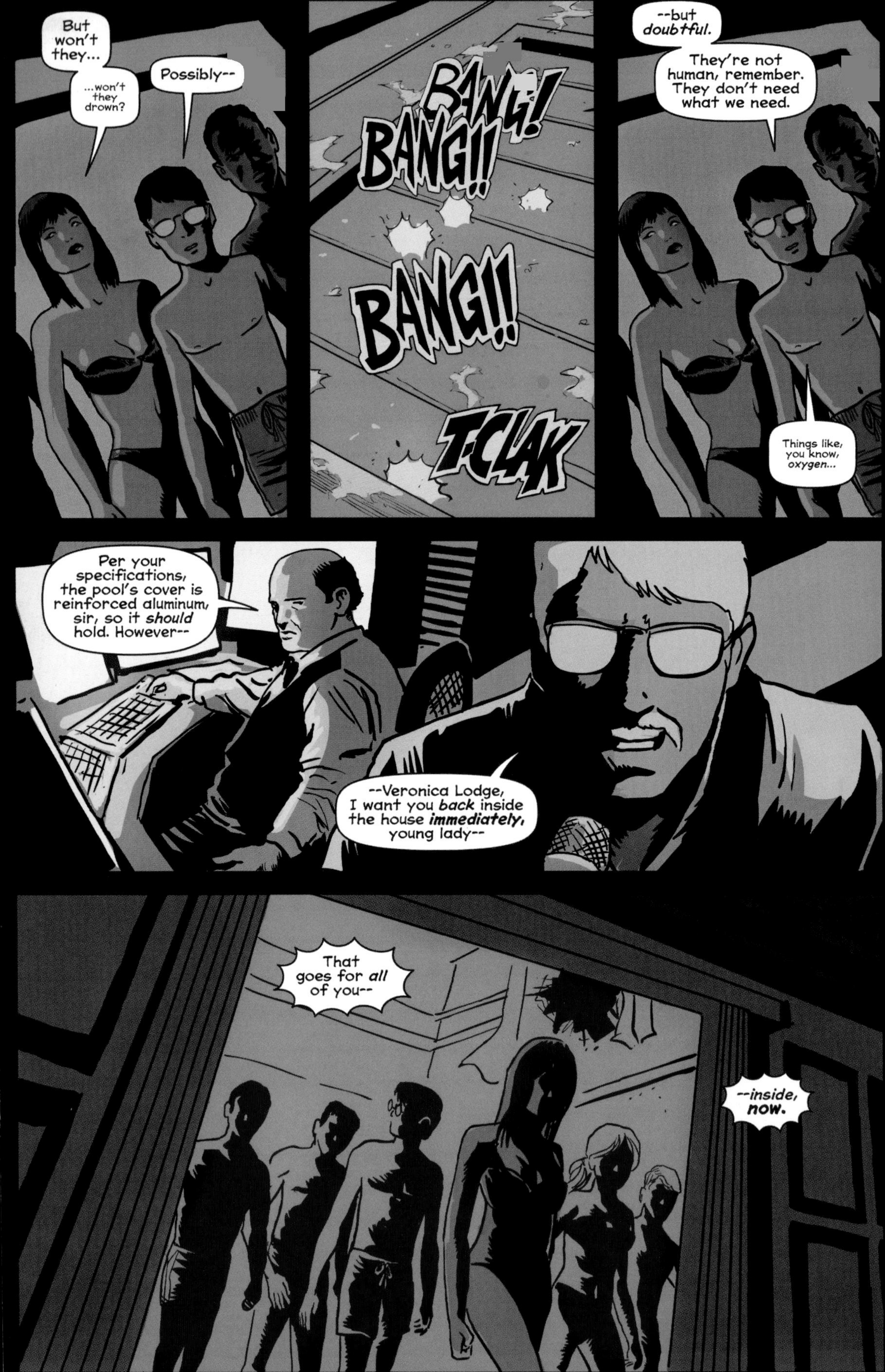

But won't they...
...won't they drown?
Possibly--
BANG!
BANG!!
BANG!!
T-CLAK
--but *doubtful.*
They're not human, remember. They don't need what we need.
Things like, you know, *oxygen...*
Per your specifications, the pool's cover is reinforced aluminum, sir, so it *should* hold. However--
--Veronica Lodge, I want you *back* inside the house ***immediately,*** young lady--
That goes for *all* of you--
--inside, ***now.***

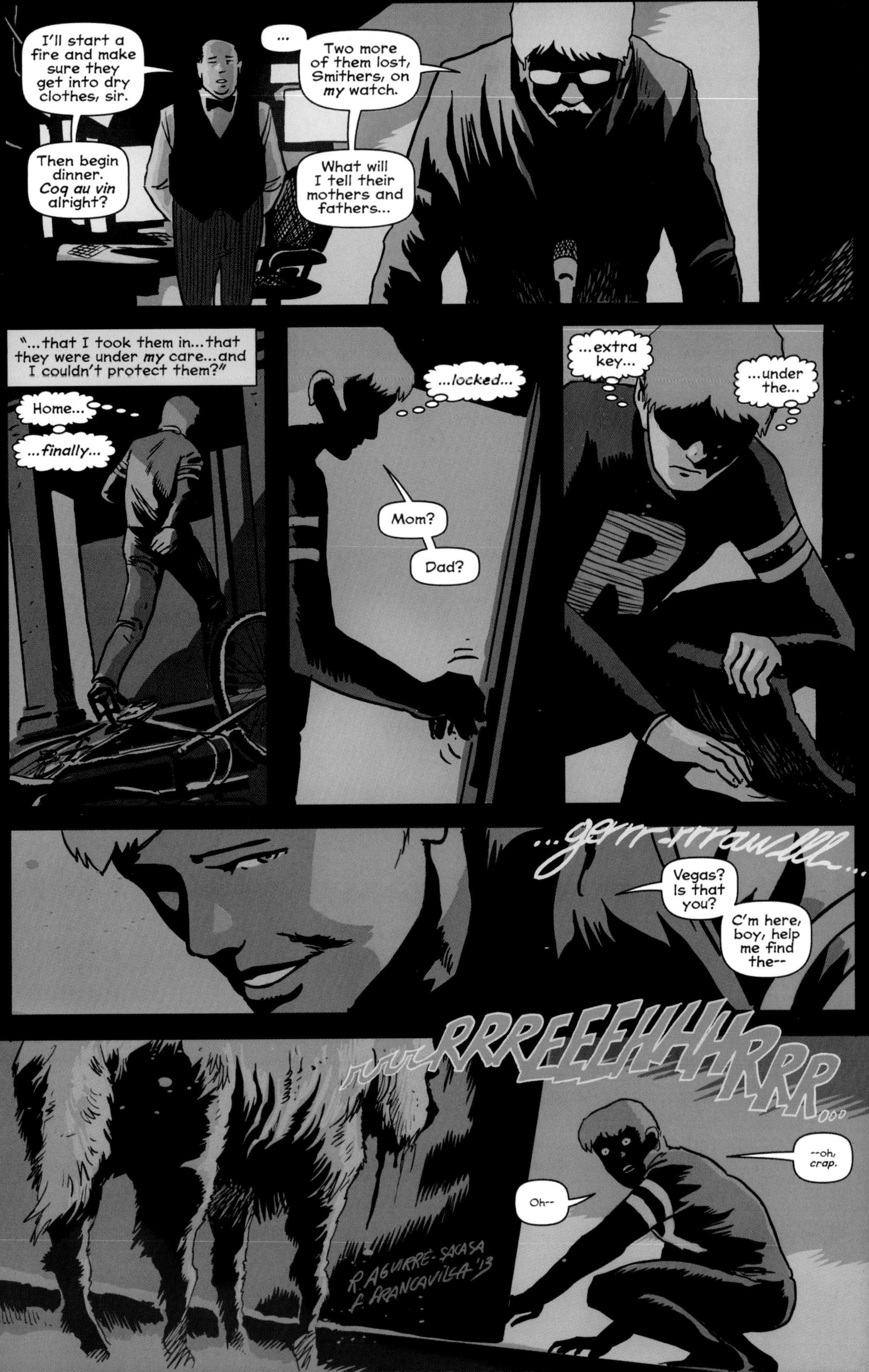
I'll start a fire and make sure they get into dry clothes, sir.
Then begin dinner. Coq au vin alright?
...
Two more of them lost, Smithers, on my watch.
What will I tell their mothers and fathers...
"...that I took them in...that they were under my care...and I couldn't protect them?"
Home...
...finally...
...locked...
Mom?
Dad?
...extra key...
...under the...
...grrr-rrrawlll...
Vegas? Is that you?
C'm here, boy, help me find the--
rrrRRREEEHHRRR...
--oh, crap.
Oh--
R. AGUIRRE-SACASA
F. FRANCAVILLA '13

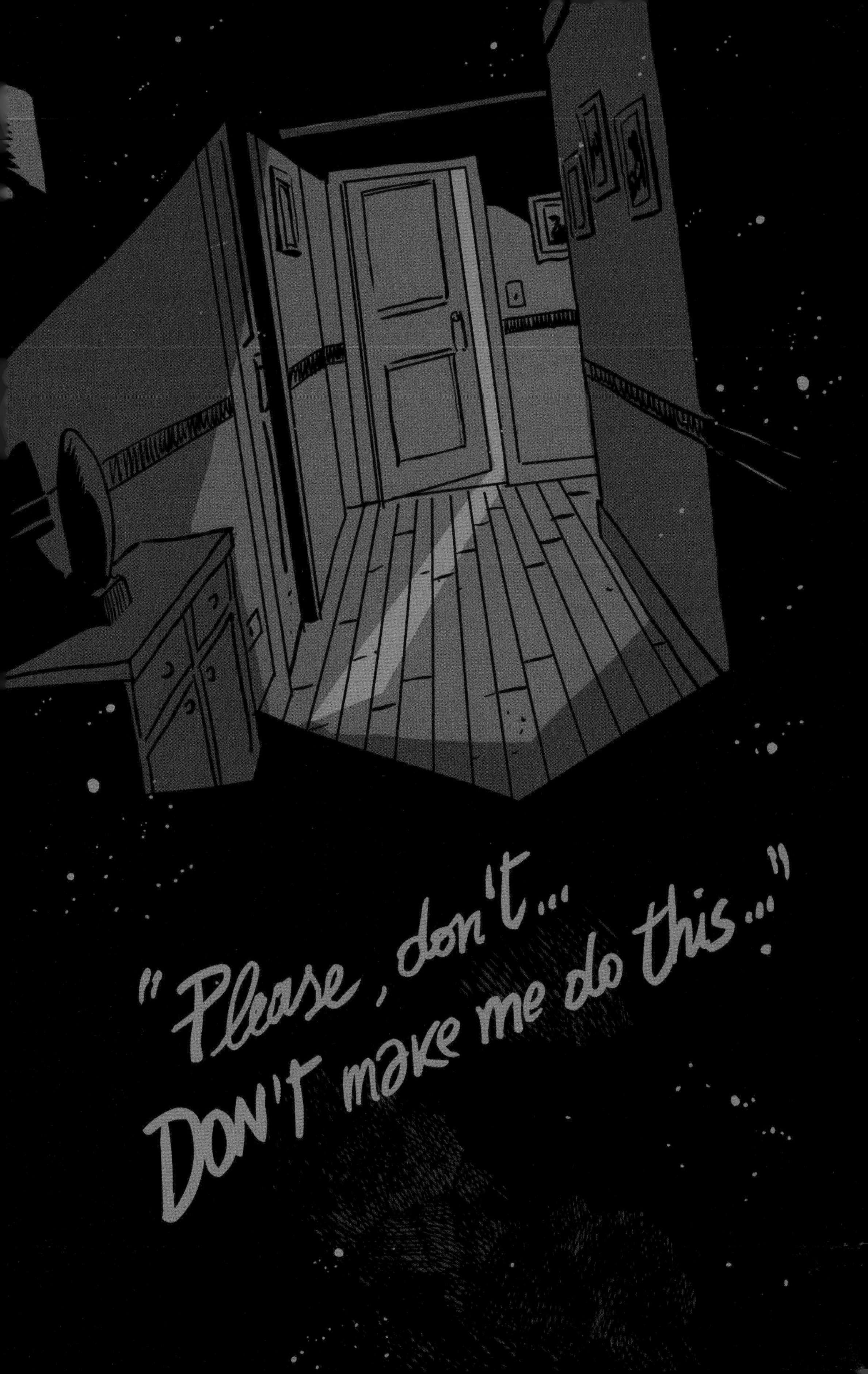
"Please, don't...
Don't make me do this..."

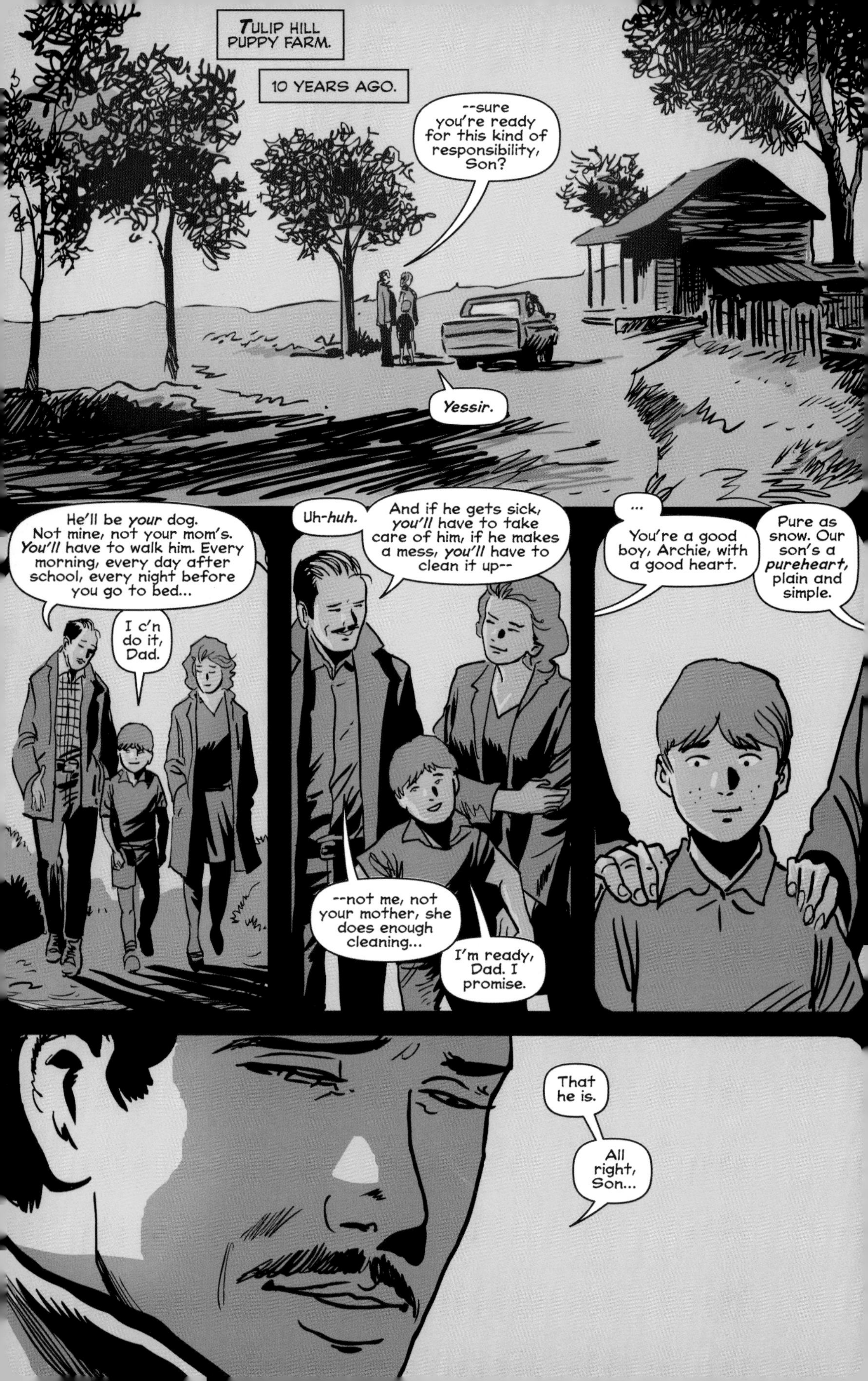
TULIP HILL PUPPY FARM.
10 YEARS AGO.
--sure you're ready for this kind of responsibility, Son?
Yessir.
He'll be your dog. Not mine, not your mom's. You'll have to walk him. Every morning, every day after school, every night before you go to bed...
I c'n do it, Dad.
Uh-huh.
And if he gets sick, you'll have to take care of him, if he makes a mess, you'll have to clean it up--
--not me, not your mother, she does enough cleaning...
I'm ready, Dad. I promise.
...
You're a good boy, Archie, with a good heart.
Pure as snow. Our son's a pureheart, plain and simple.
That he is.
All right, Son...

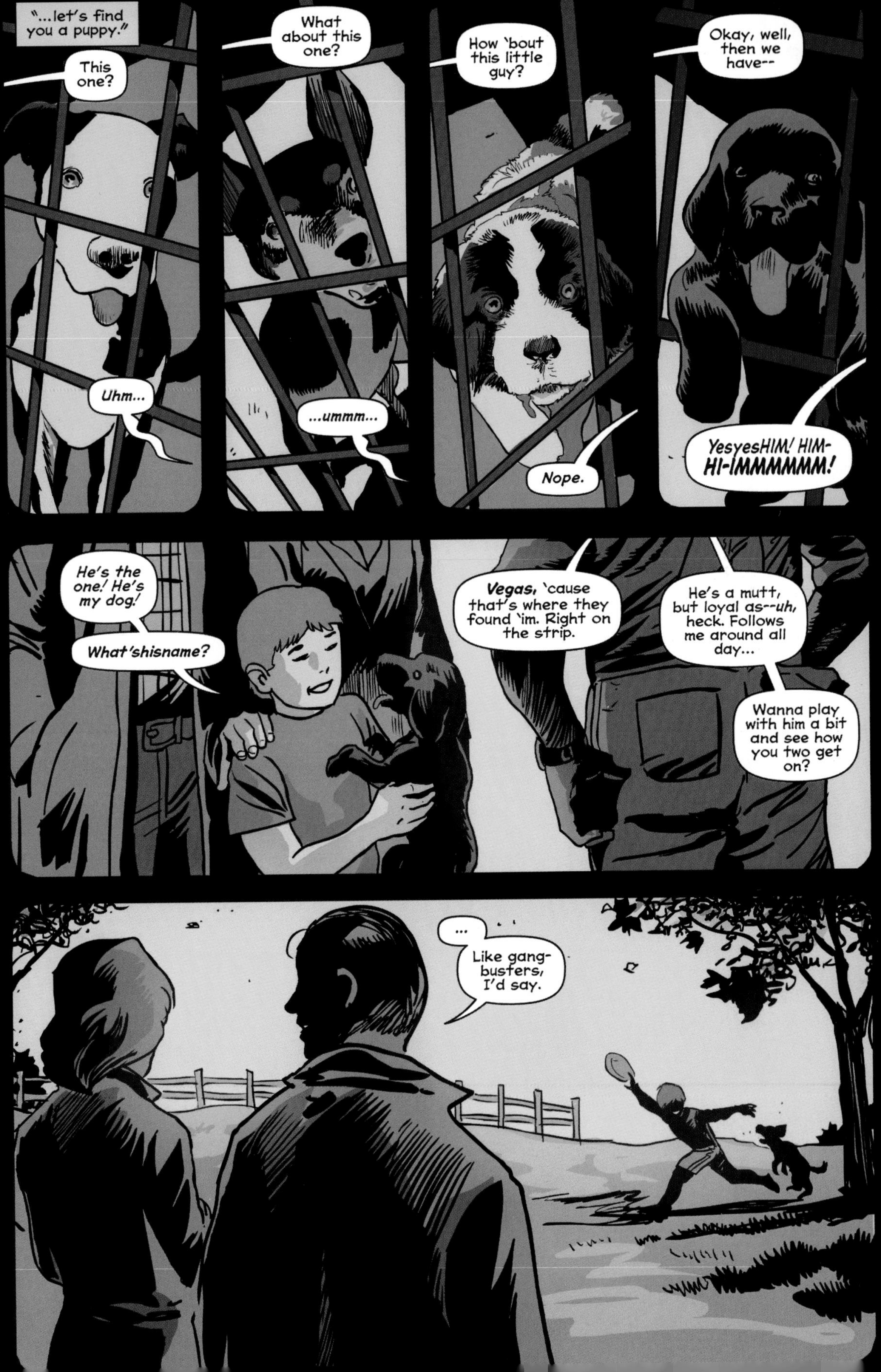
"...let's find you a puppy."
This one?
Uhm...
What about this one?
...ummm...
How 'bout this little guy?
Nope.
Okay, well, then we have--
YesyesHIM! HIM-HI-IMMMMMM!
He's the one! He's my dog!
What'shisname?
Vegas, 'cause that's where they found 'im. Right on the strip.
He's a mutt, but loyal as--uh, heck. Follows me around all day...
Wanna play with him a bit and see how you two get on?
... Like gang-busters, I'd say.

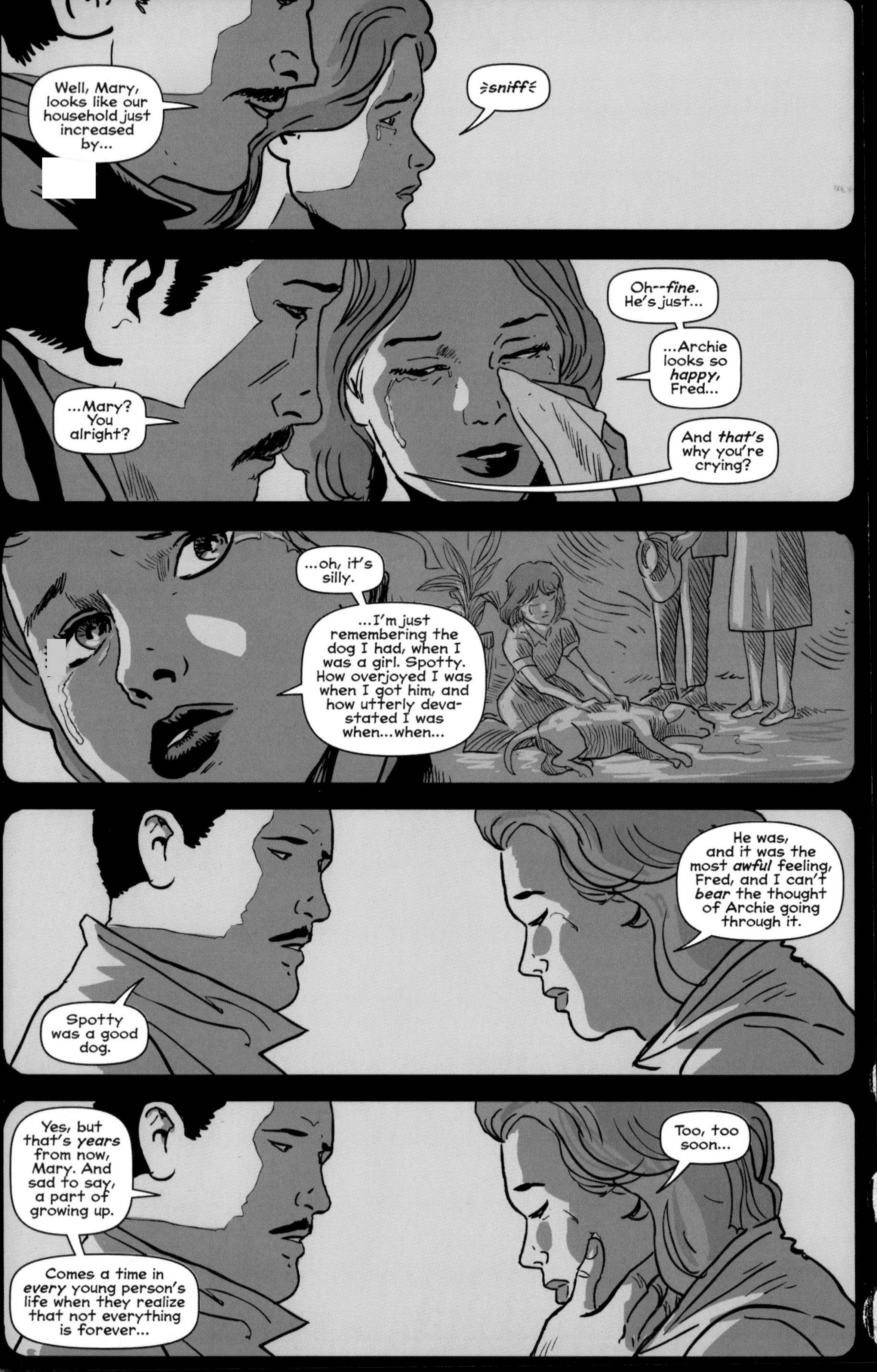
Well, Mary, looks like our household just increased by...
≥sniff≤
...Mary? You alright?
Oh--*fine*. He's just...
...Archie looks so *happy*, Fred...
And *that's* why you're crying?
...oh, it's silly.
...I'm just remembering the dog I had, when I was a girl. Spotty. How overjoyed I was when I got him, and how utterly devastated I was when...when...
Spotty was a good dog.
He was, and it was the most *awful* feeling, Fred, and I can't *bear* the thought of Archie going through it.
Yes, but that's *years* from now, Mary. And sad to say, a part of growing up.
Too, too soon...
Comes a time in *every* young person's life when they realize that not everything is forever...

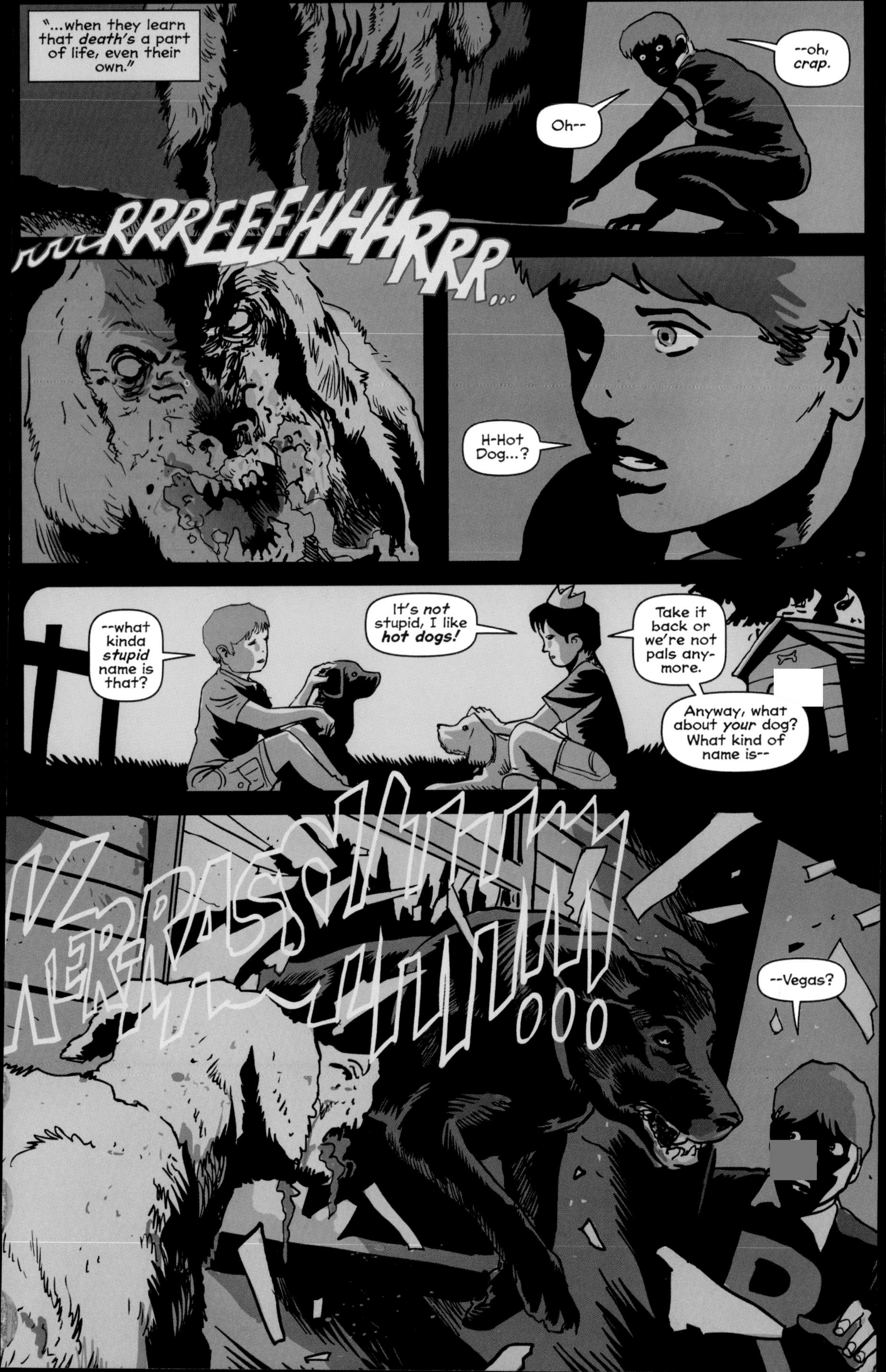
"...when they learn that *death's* a part of life, even their own."
Oh--
--oh, *crap.*
rrrRRRREEEHHHRRR...
H-Hot Dog...?
--what kinda *stupid* name is that?
It's *not* stupid, I like ***hot dogs!***
Take it back or we're not pals any-more.
Anyway, what about *your* dog? What kind of name is--
KERRASSHHHHHH
--Vegas?

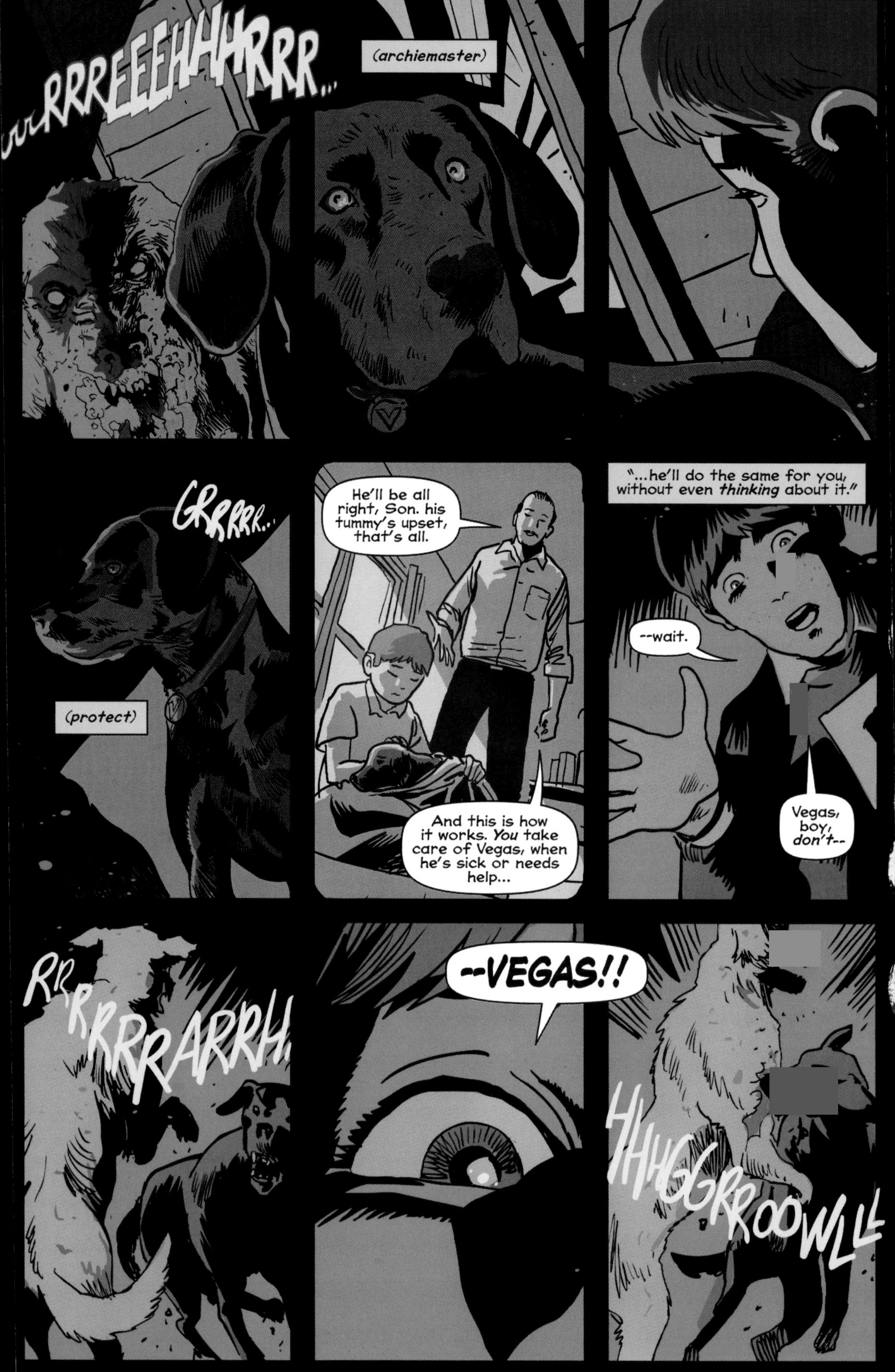
rrrRRREEEHHHRRR...
(archiemaster)
GRRRRR...
(protect)
He'll be all right, Son. his tummy's upset, that's all.
And this is how it works. *You* take care of Vegas, when he's sick or needs help...
"...he'll do the same for you, without even *thinking* about it."
--wait.
Vegas, boy, *don't*--
RRRRRRARRH
--VEGAS!!
HHHGGRROOWLLL

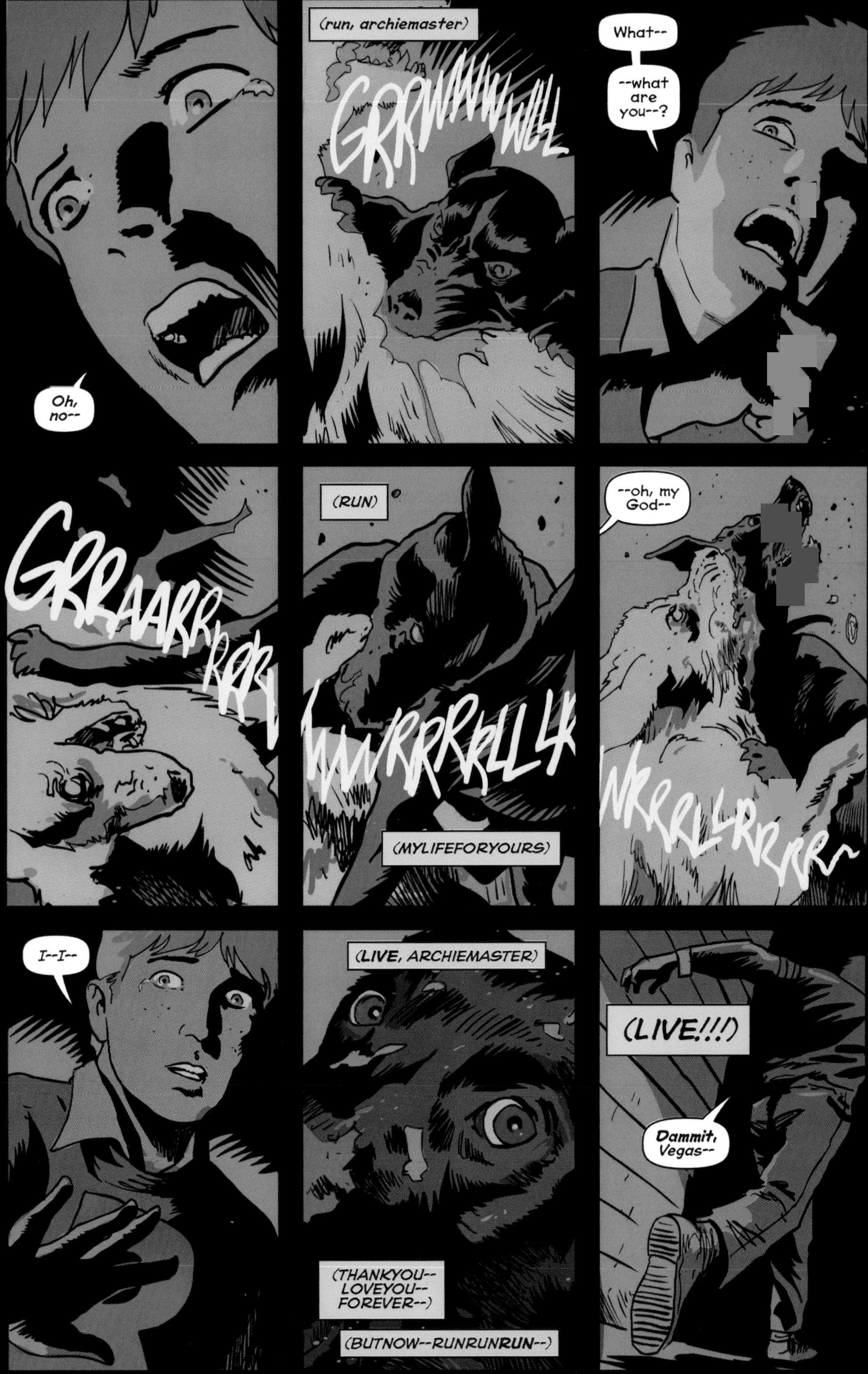
Oh, no--
(run, archiemaster)
GRRWWWWLL
What--
--what are you--?
GRRAARRRRRWWRRRRLLLK
(RUN)
(MYLIFEFORYOURS)
--oh, my God--
NRRRLLRRRRR
I--I--
(LIVE, ARCHIEMASTER)
(THANKYOU--LOVEYOU--FOREVER--)
(BUTNOW--RUNRUNRUN--)
(LIVE!!!)
Dammit, Vegas--

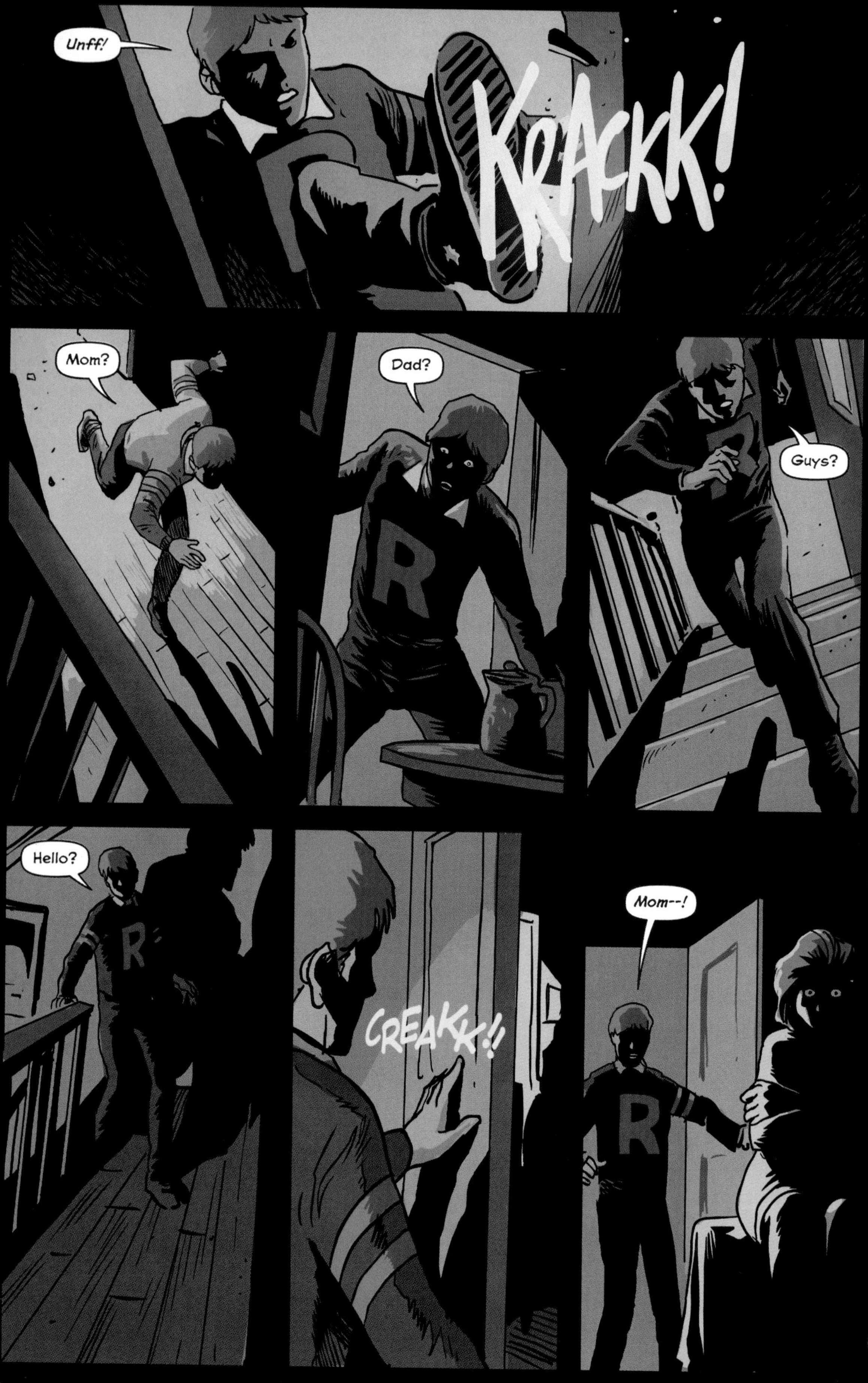
Unff!
KRACKK!
Mom?
Dad?
Guys?
Hello?
CREAKK!!
Mom--!

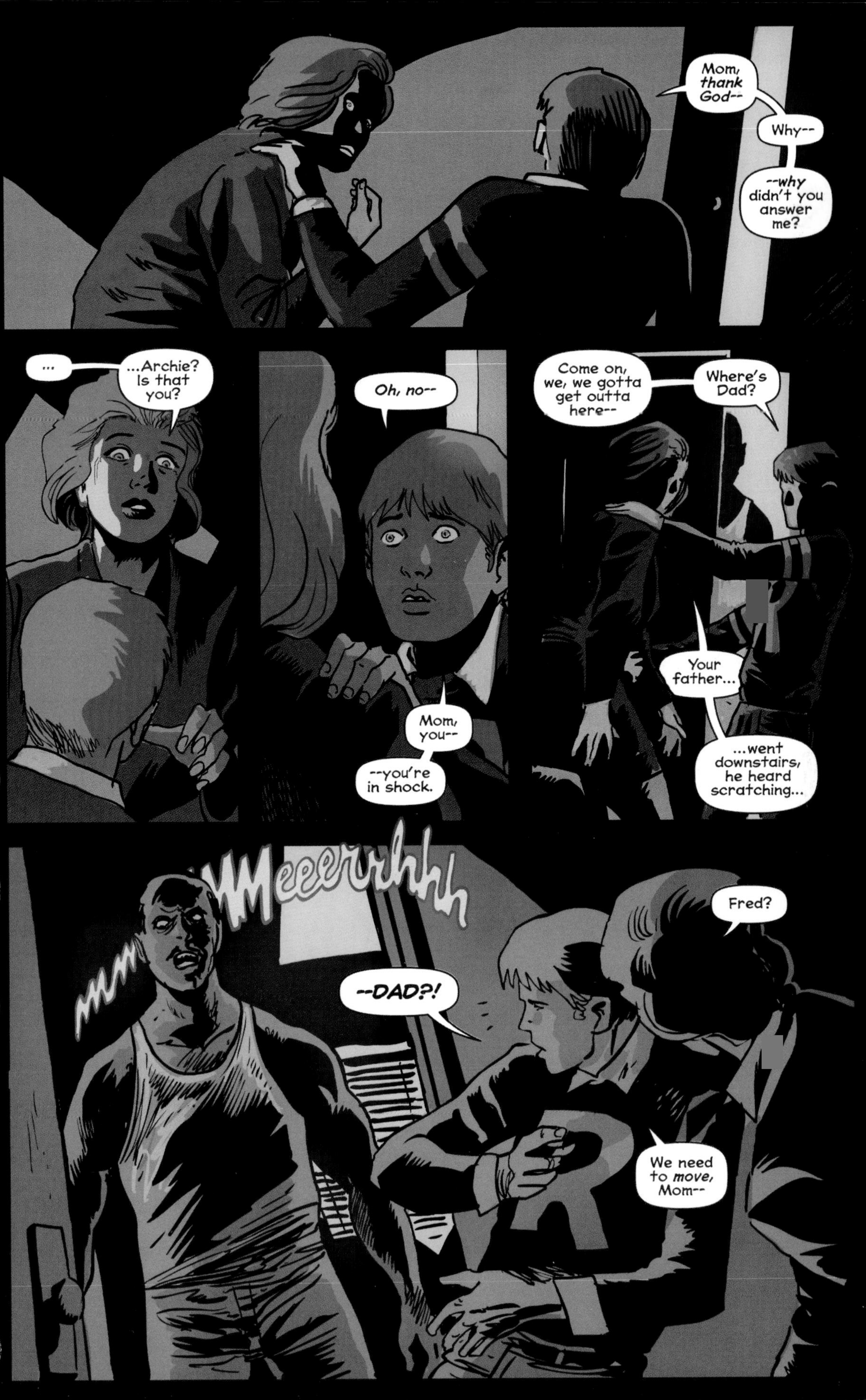
Mom, thank God--
Why--
--why didn't you answer me?
...
...Archie? Is that you?
Oh, no--
Mom, you--
--you're in shock.
Come on, we, we gotta get outta here--
Where's Dad?
Your father...
...went downstairs, he heard scratching...
MMeeerrhhh
--DAD?!
Fred?
We need to move, Mom--

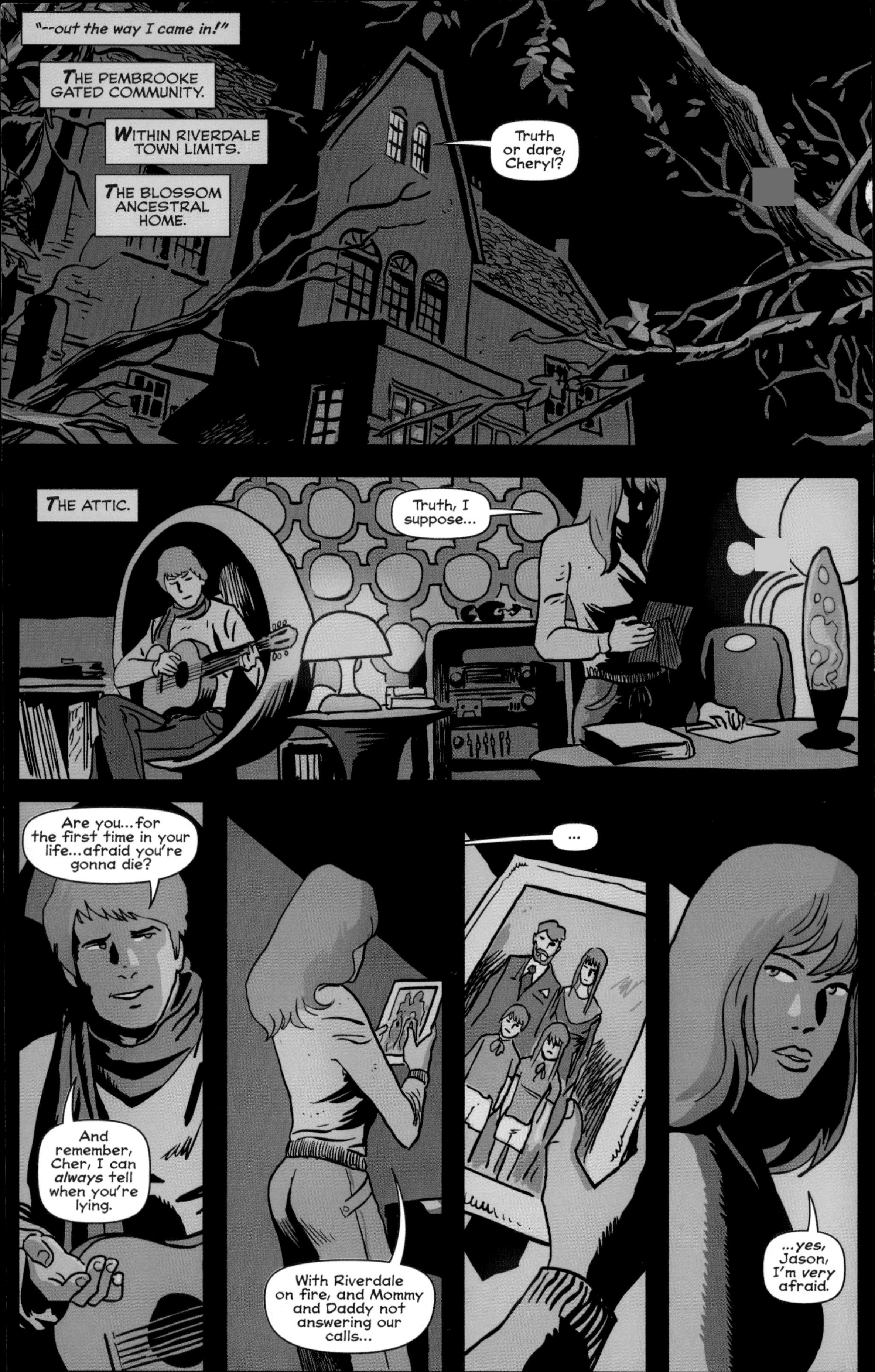
"--out the way I came in!"
THE PEMBROOKE GATED COMMUNITY.
WITHIN RIVERDALE TOWN LIMITS.
THE BLOSSOM ANCESTRAL HOME.
Truth or dare, Cheryl?
THE ATTIC.
Truth, I suppose...
Are you...for the first time in your life...afraid you're gonna die?
And remember, Cher, I can *always* tell when you're lying.
With Riverdale on fire, and Mommy and Daddy not answering our calls...
...
...yes, Jason, I'm *very* afraid.

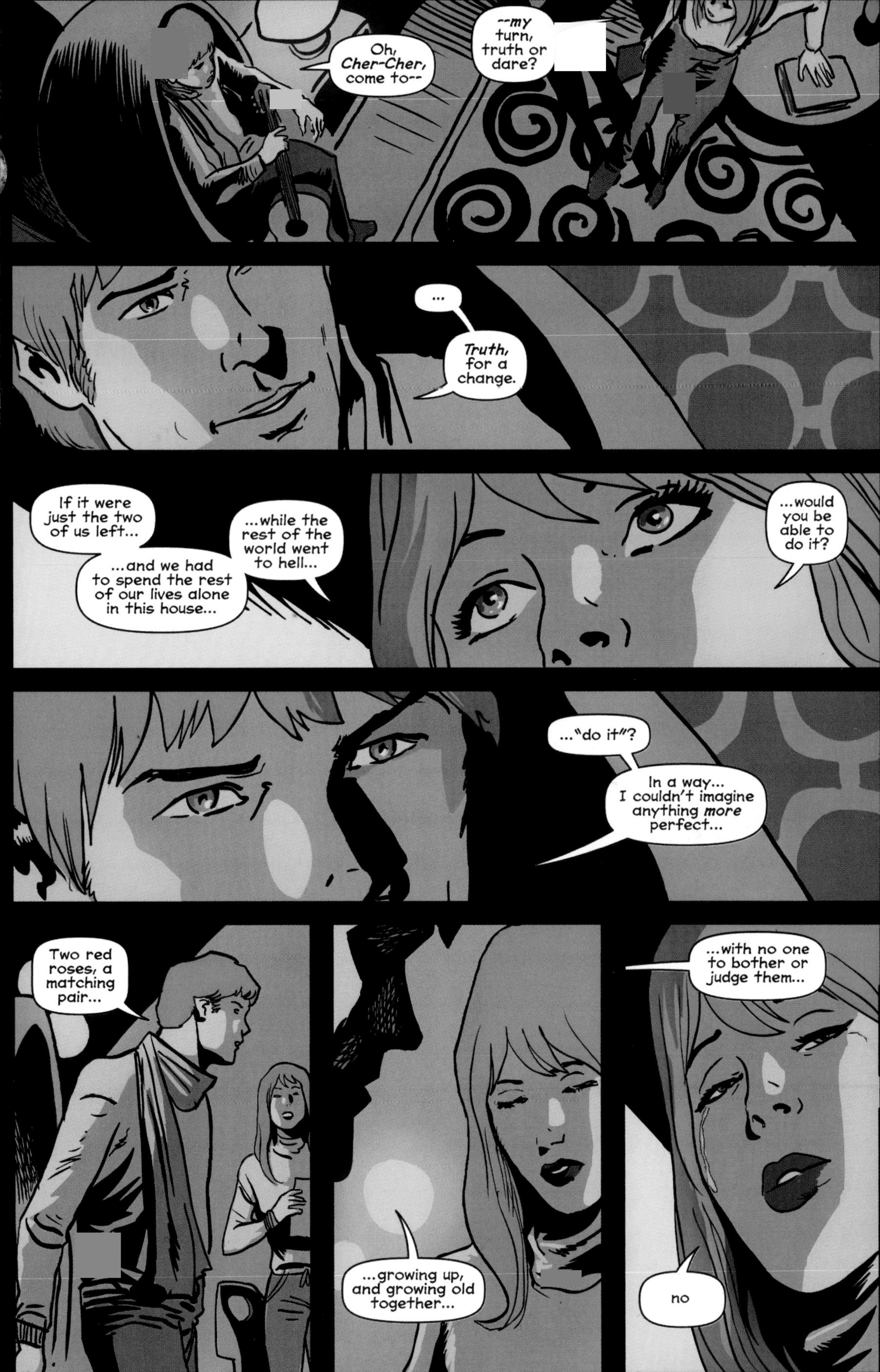
Oh, *Cher-Cher*, come to--
--*my* turn, truth or dare?
...
Truth, for a change.
If it were just the two of us left...
...and we had to spend the rest of our lives alone in this house...
...while the rest of the world went to hell...
...would you be able to do it?
..."do it"?
In a way... I couldn't imagine anything *more* perfect...
Two red roses, a matching pair...
...growing up, and growing old together...
...with no one to bother or judge them...
no

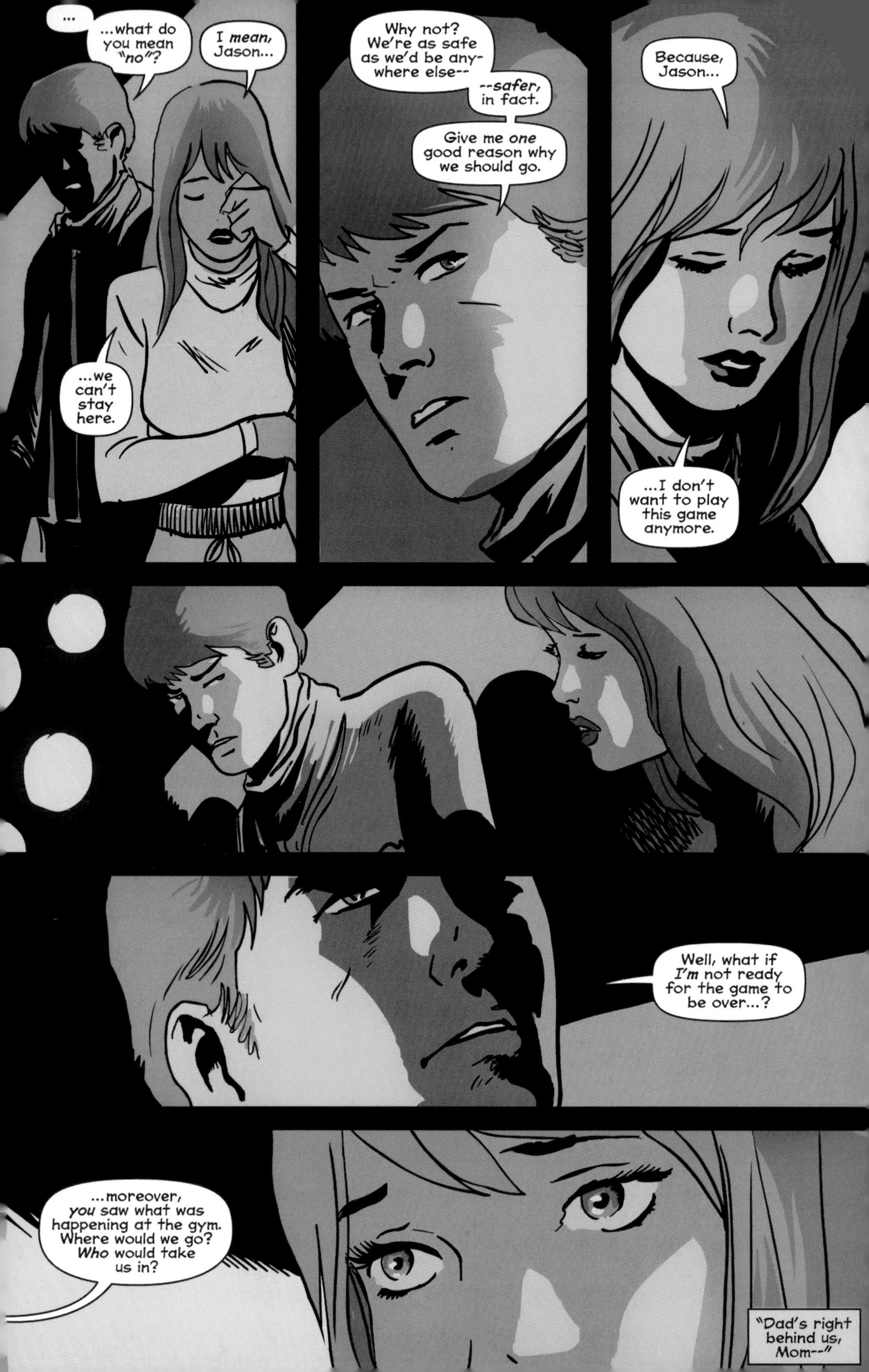
...
...what do you mean "no"?
I mean, Jason...
...we can't stay here.
Why not? We're as safe as we'd be anywhere else--
--safer, in fact.
Give me one good reason why we should go.
Because, Jason...
...I don't want to play this game anymore.
Well, what if I'm not ready for the game to be over...?
...moreover, you saw what was happening at the gym. Where would we go? Who would take us in?
"Dad's right behind us, Mom--"

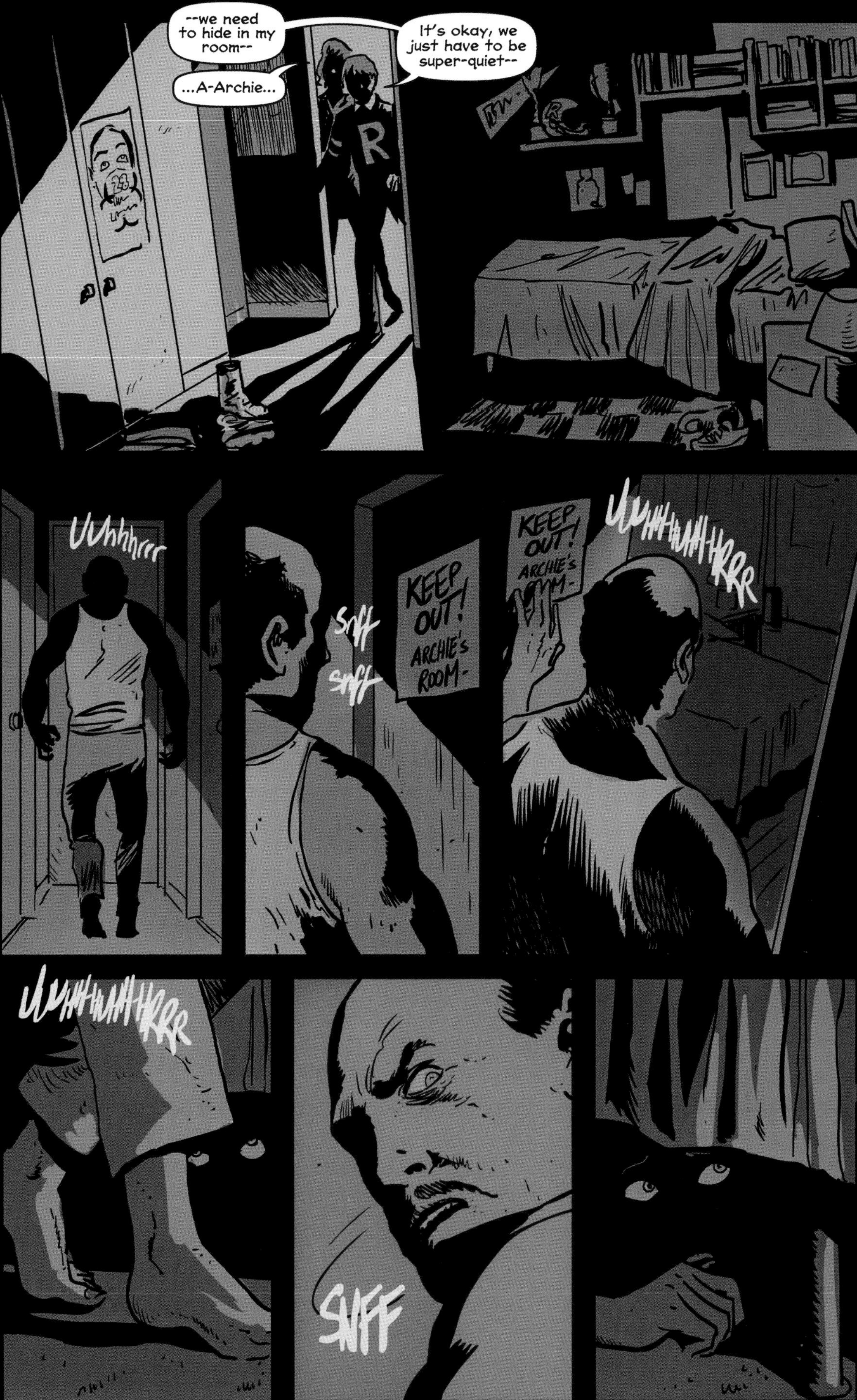
--we need to hide in my room--
It's okay, we just have to be super-quiet--
...A-Archie...
Uuhhhrrr
SNFF
SNFF
KEEP OUT! ARCHIE's ROOM-
KEEP OUT! ARCHIE's ROOM-
UUHHHUHHHRRR
UUHHHUHHHRRR
SNFF

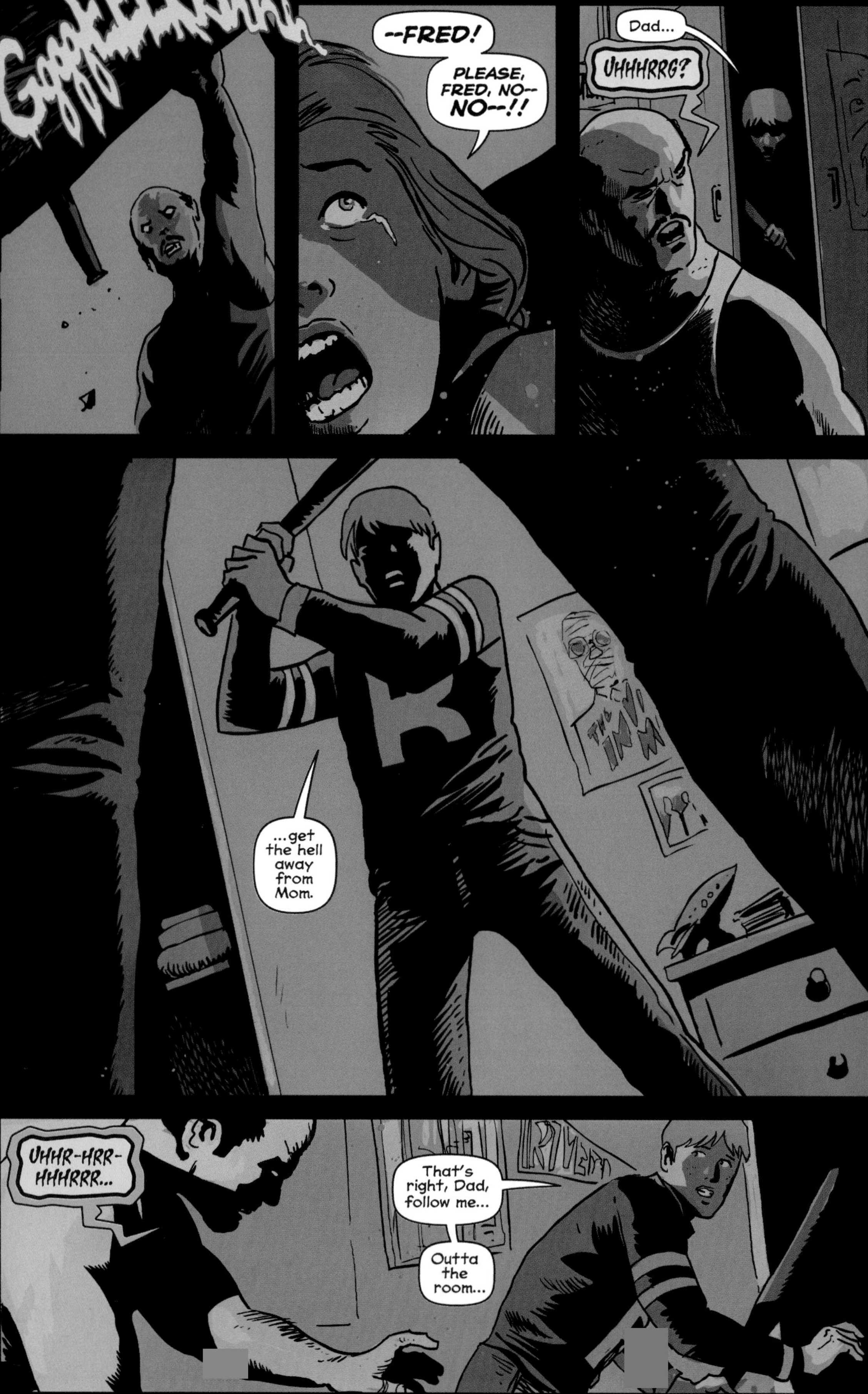
GggEEERRhhh
--FRED!
PLEASE, FRED, NO-- NO--!!
Dad...
UHHHRRG?
...get the hell away from Mom.
UHHR-HRR-HHHRRR...
That's right, Dad, follow me...
Outta the room...

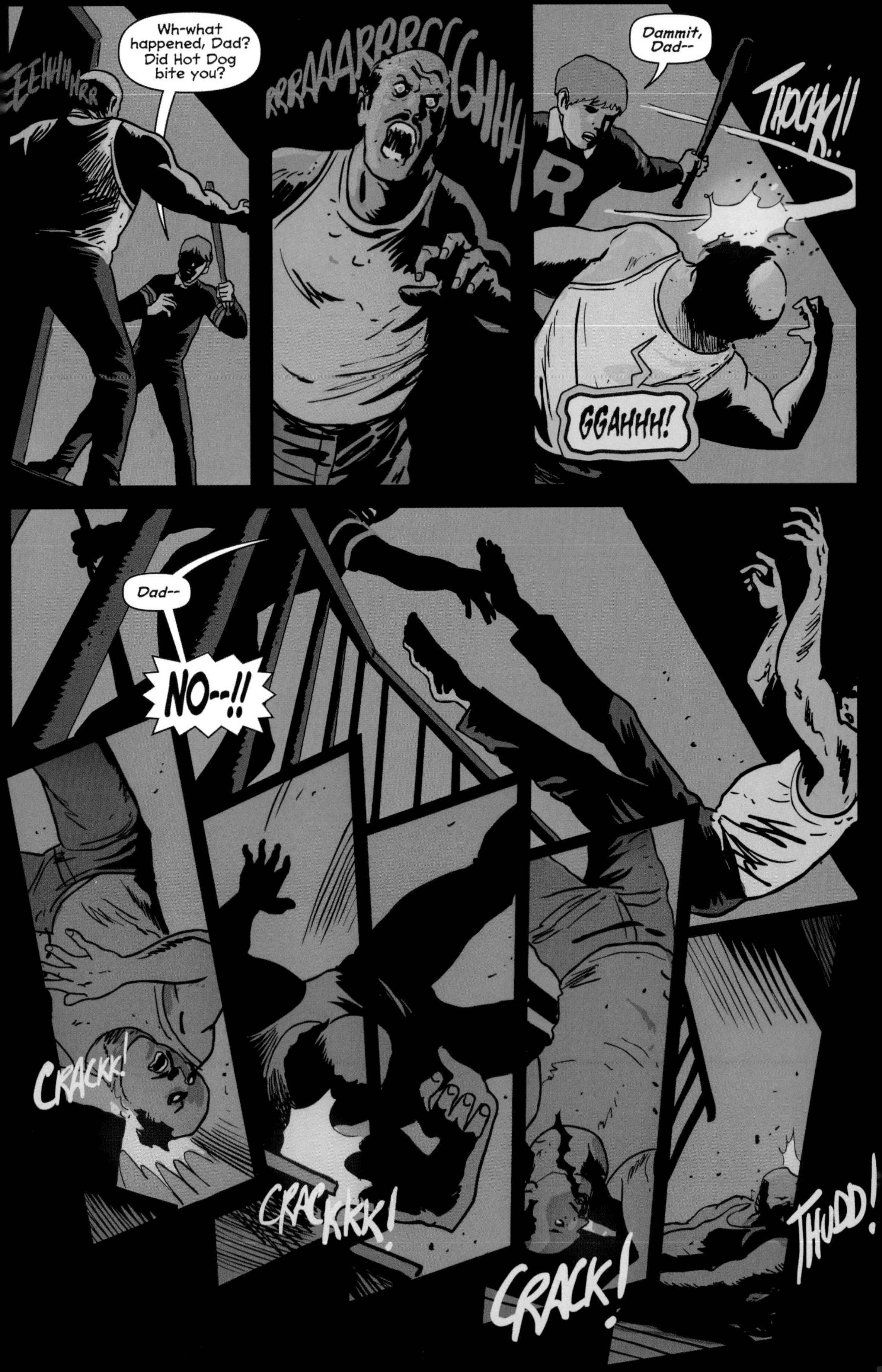
EEEHHHHRR
Wh-what happened, Dad? Did Hot Dog bite you?
RRRAAARRRGGGHHH
Dammit, Dad--
THOCK!!
GGAHHH!
Dad--
NO--!!
CRACKK!
CRACKKK!
CRACK!
THUDD!

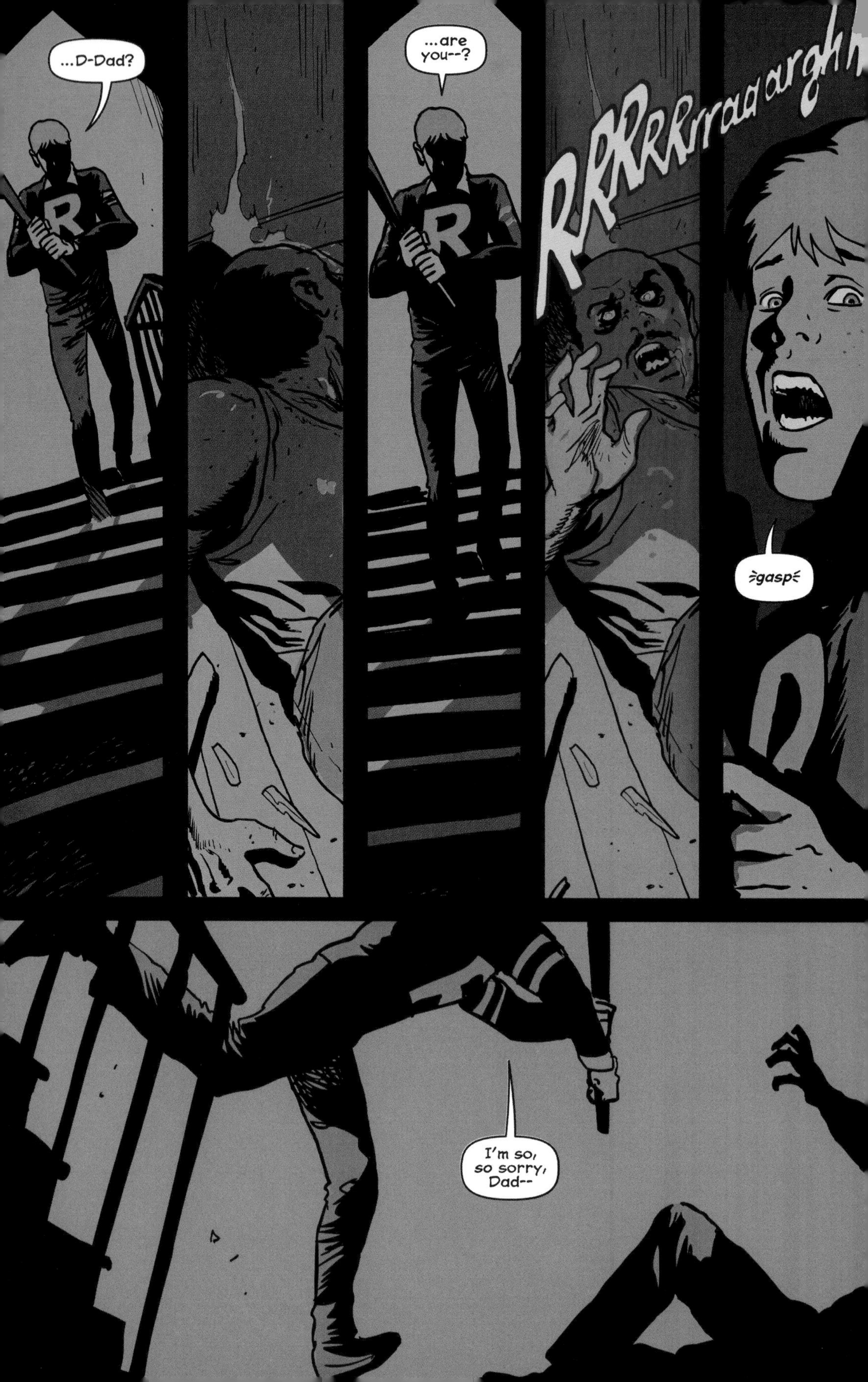
...D-Dad?
...are you--?
RRRRRrraaarghh
gasp
I'm so, so sorry, Dad--

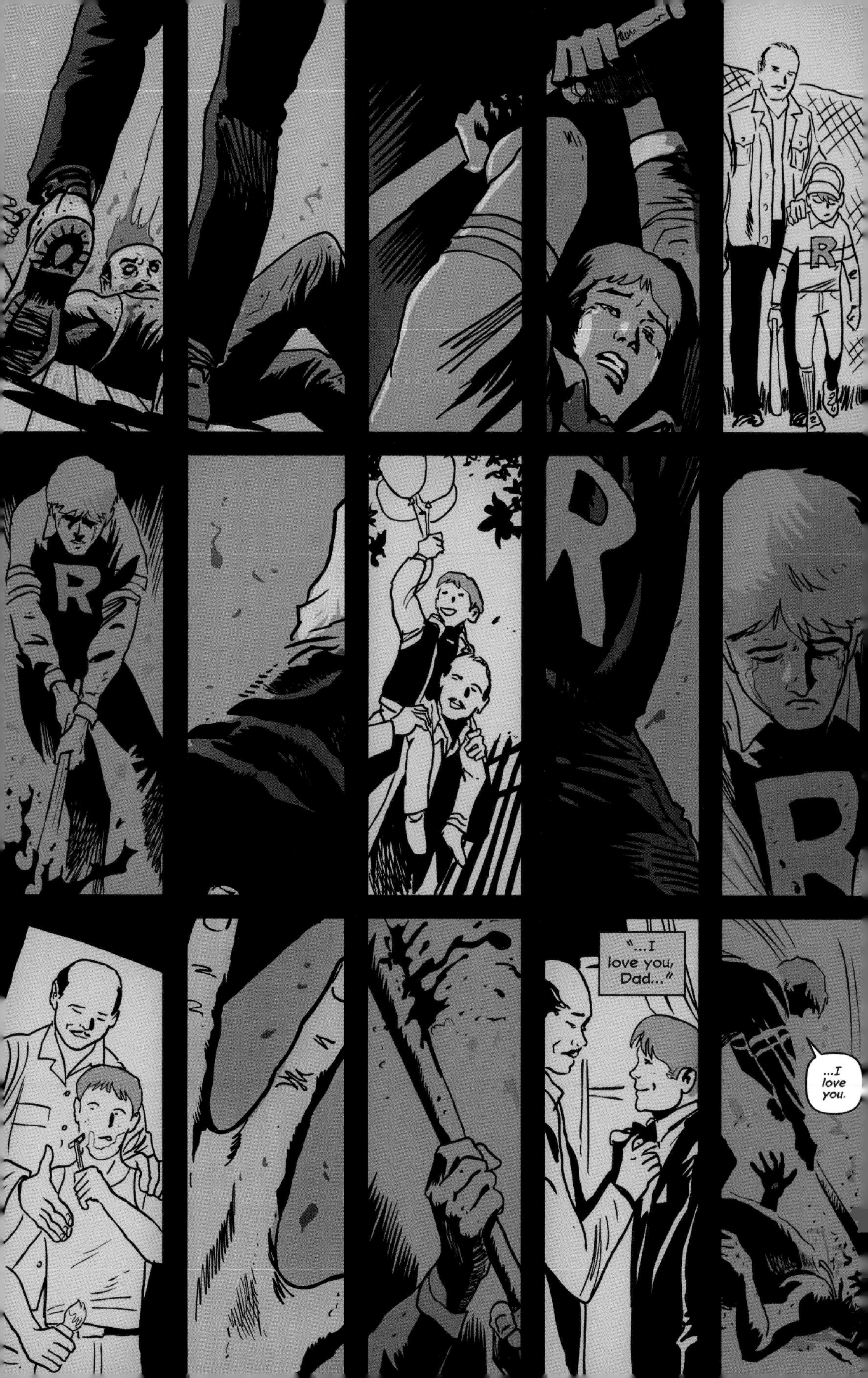
"...I love you, Dad..."
...I love you.

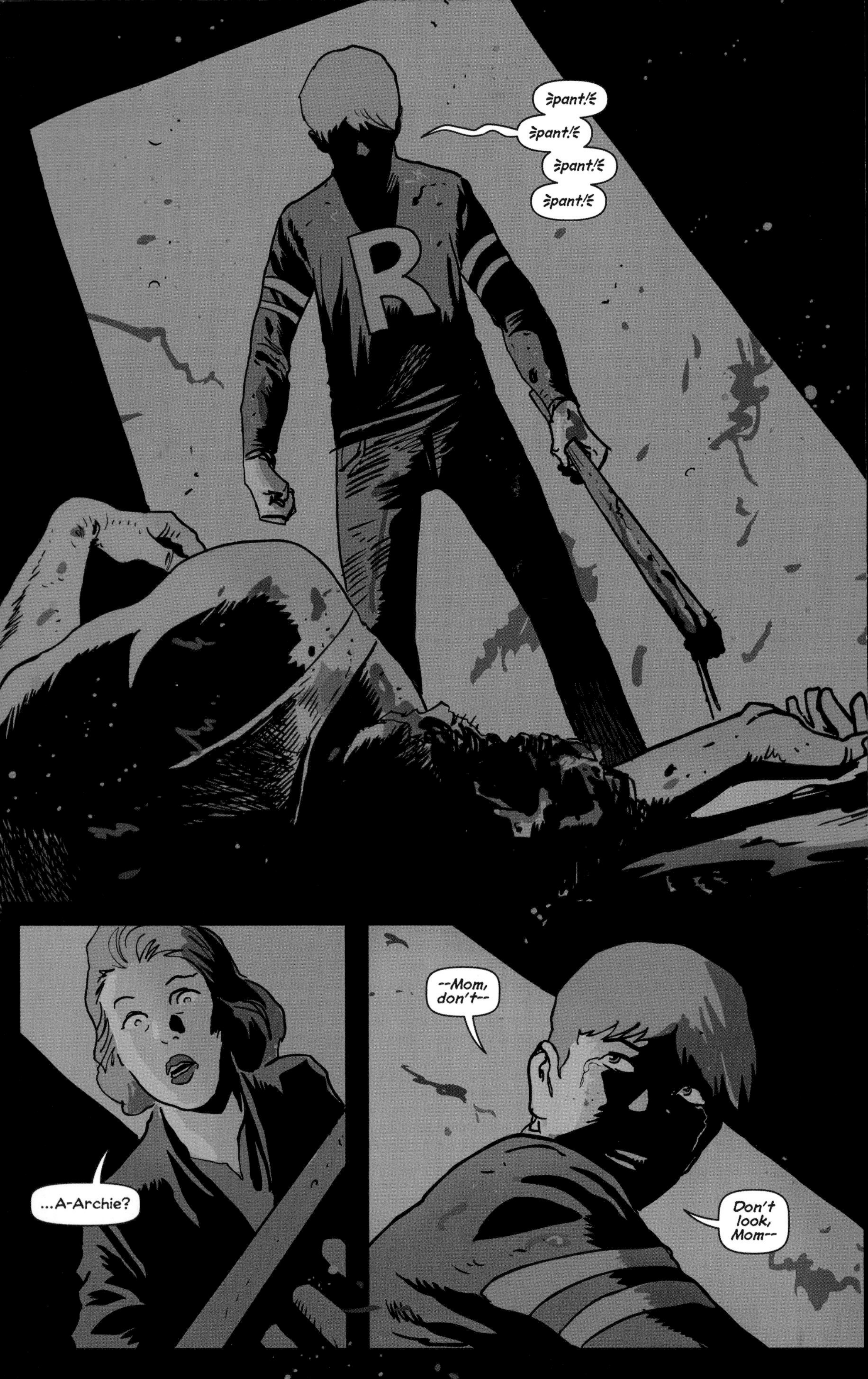

pant!
pant!
pant!
pant!
...A-Archie?
--Mom, don't--
Don't look, Mom--

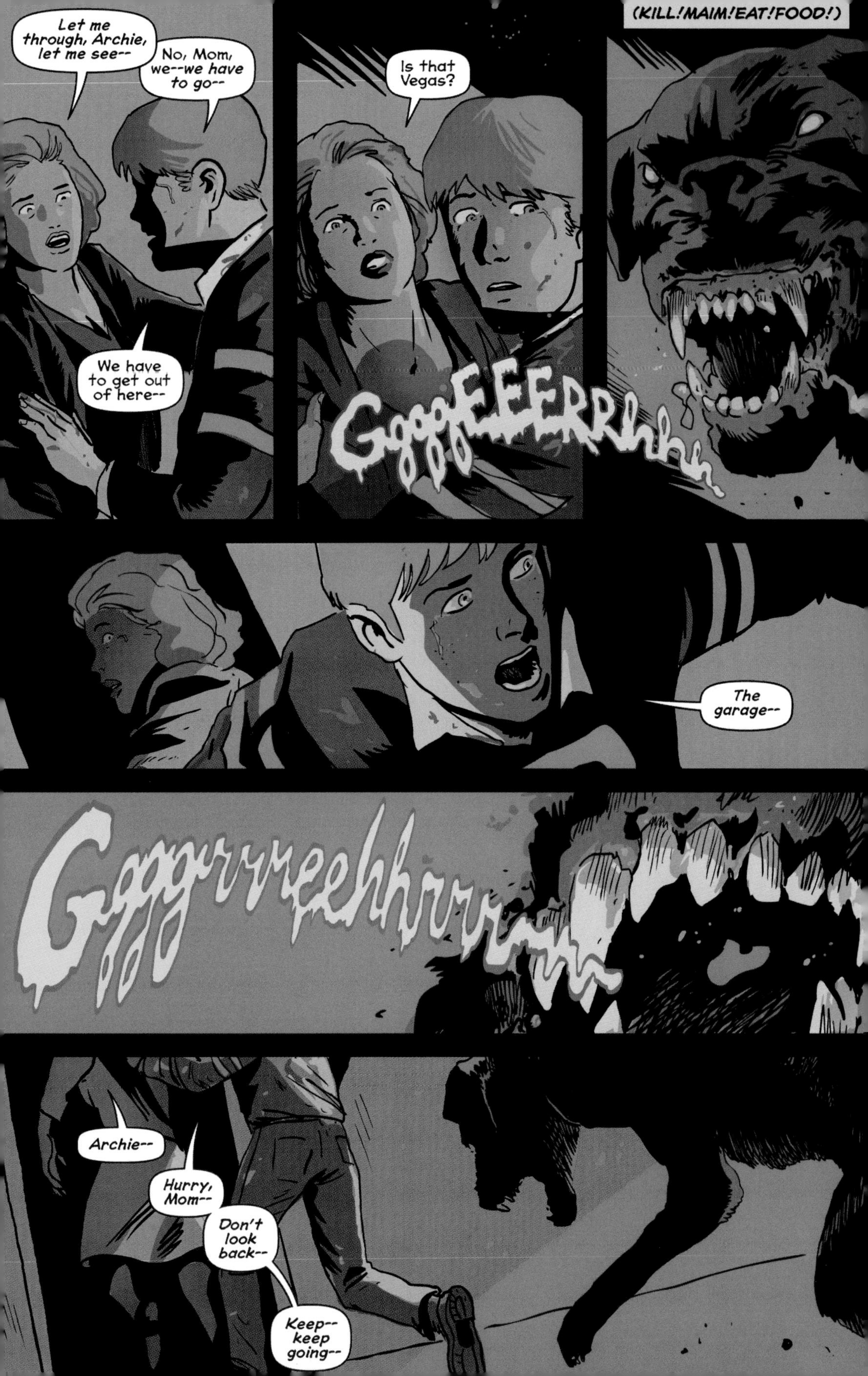
Let me through, Archie, let me see--
No, Mom, we--we have to go--
We have to get out of here--
Is that Vegas?
GgggEEERRhhhh
(KILL!MAIM!EAT!FOOD!)
The garage--
Gggrrreehhrrrnn
Archie--
Hurry, Mom--
Don't look back--
Keep--keep going--

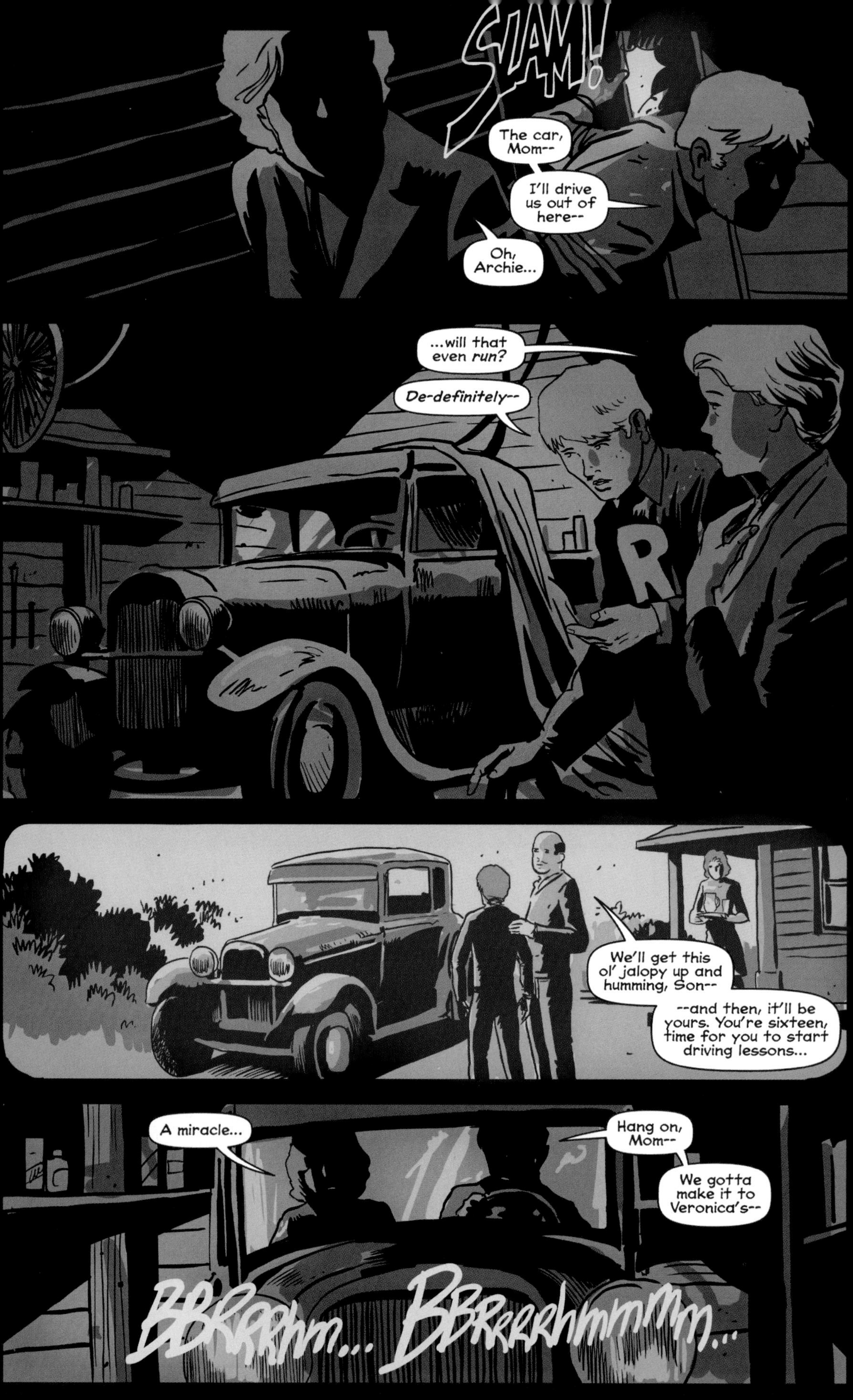
SLAM!
The car, Mom--
I'll drive us out of here--
Oh, Archie...
...will that even *run*?
De-definitely--
We'll get this ol' jalopy up and humming, Son--
--and then, it'll be yours. You're sixteen, time for you to start driving lessons...
A miracle...
Hang on, Mom--
We gotta make it to Veronica's--
BBRRRhm... BBRRRRhmmmm...

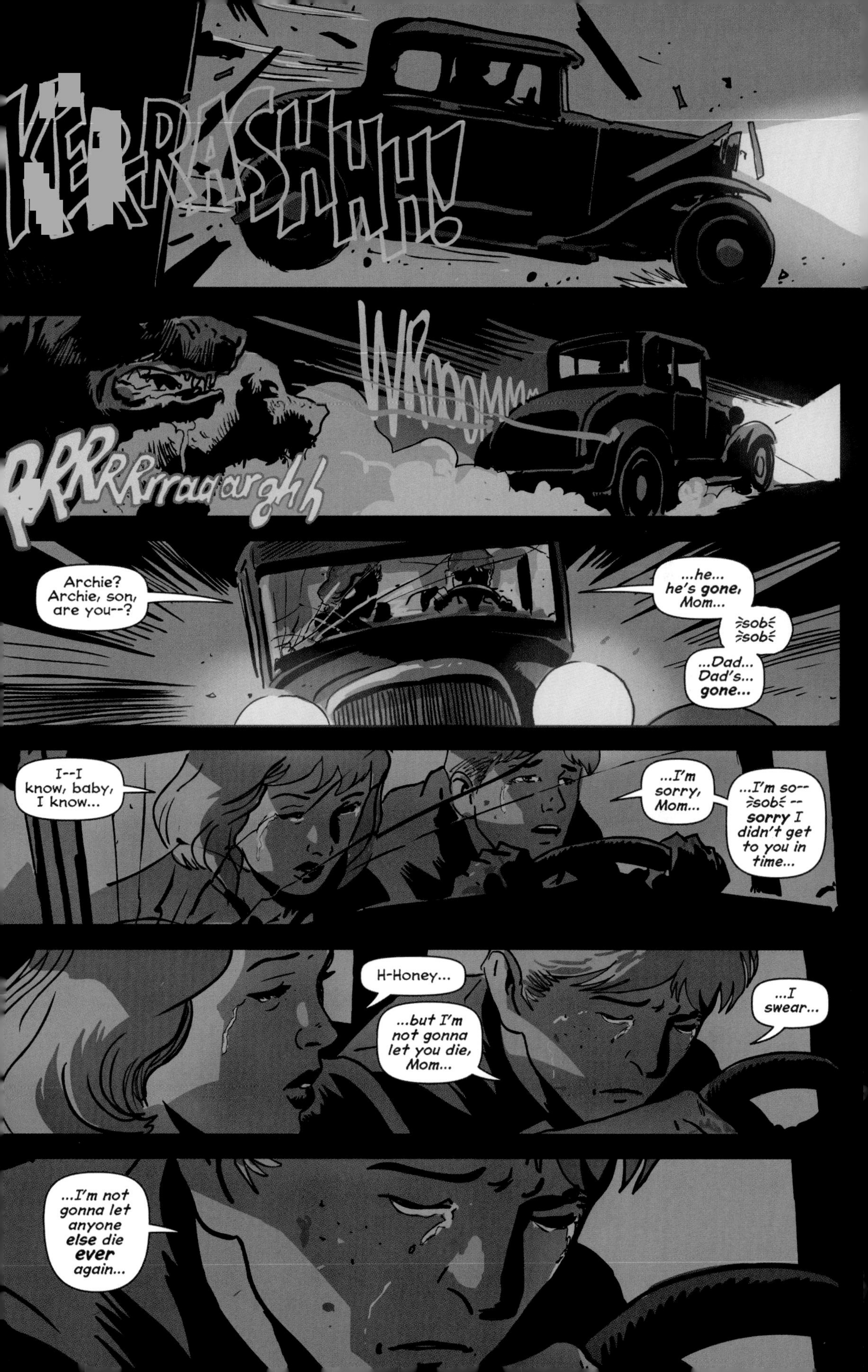
KERRASHHH!
WRoooMM..
RRRRrrraaaarghh
Archie? Archie, son, are you--?
...he... he's gone, Mom...
≷sob≶ ≷sob≶
...Dad... Dad's... gone...
I--I know, baby, I know...
...I'm sorry, Mom...
...I'm so-- ≷sob≶ -- sorry I didn't get to you in time...
H-Honey...
...but I'm not gonna let you die, Mom...
...I swear...
...I'm not gonna let anyone else die ever again...

epilogue

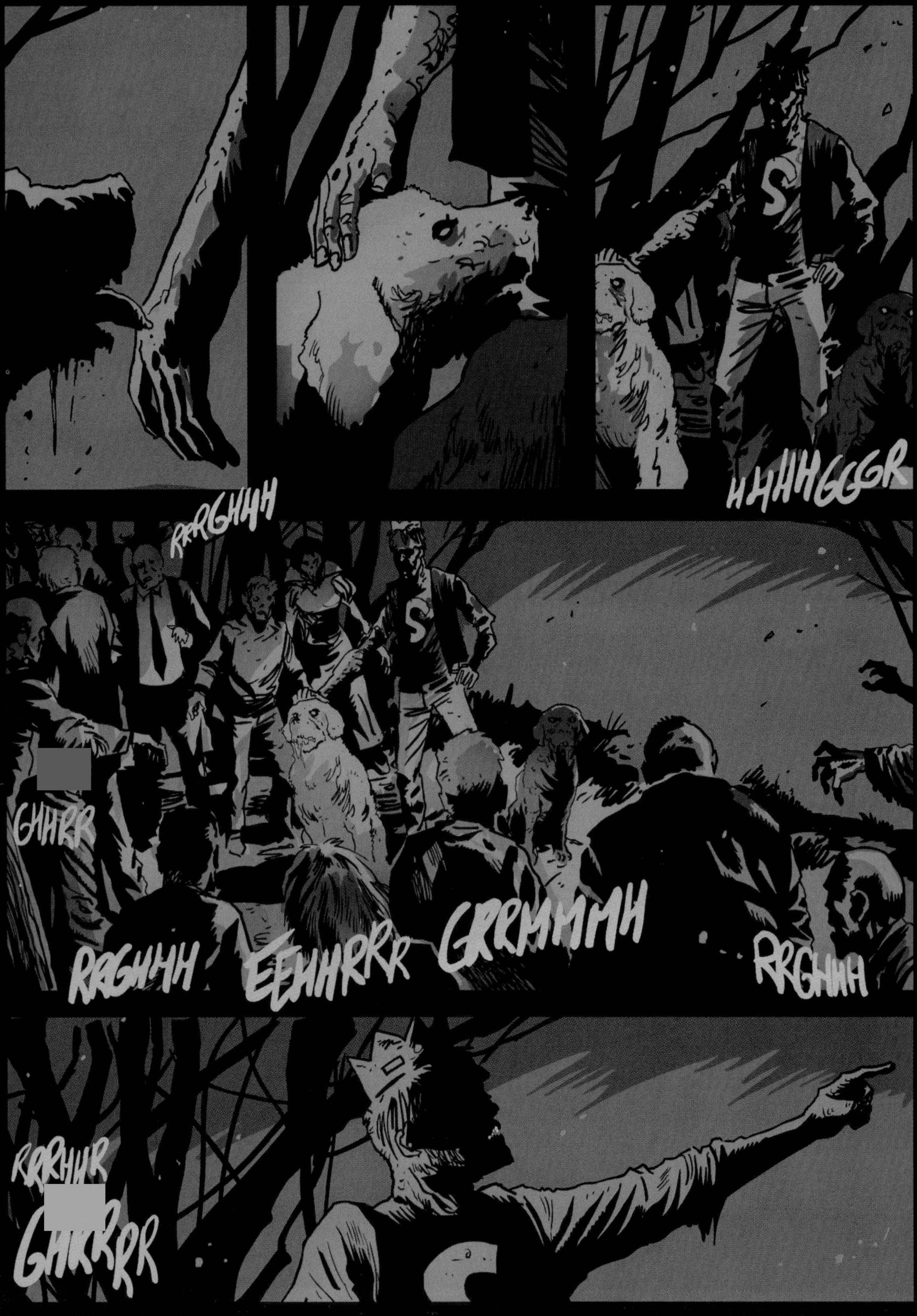
HHHHGGGR
RRRGHHH
GHHRR
RRGHHH
EEHHRRR
GRRMMMH
RRGHHH
RRRHHR
GHRRRR

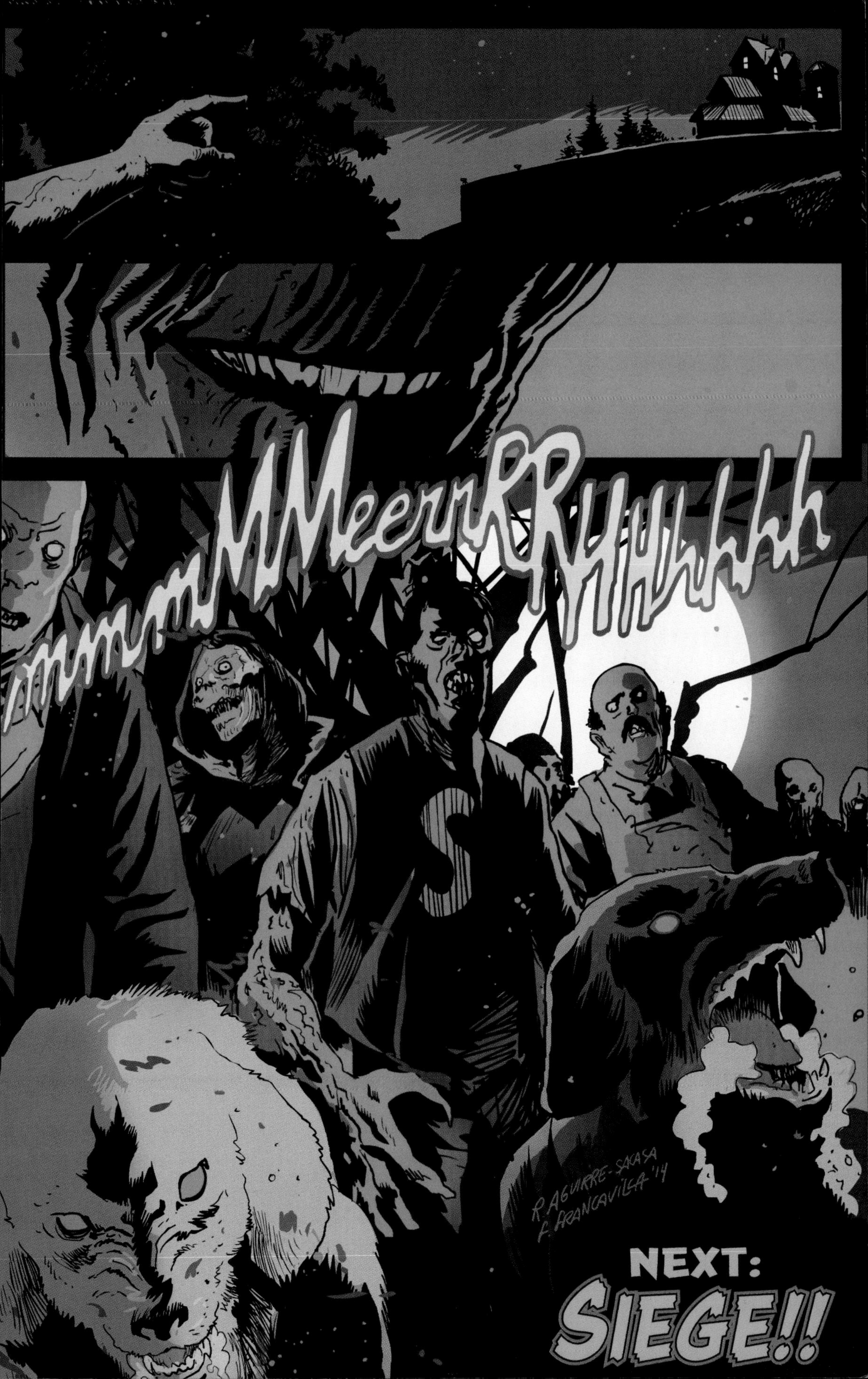
mmmmMMeerrrRRUHhhhh
R. AGUIRRE-SACASA
F. FRANCAVILLA '14
NEXT:
SIEGE!!

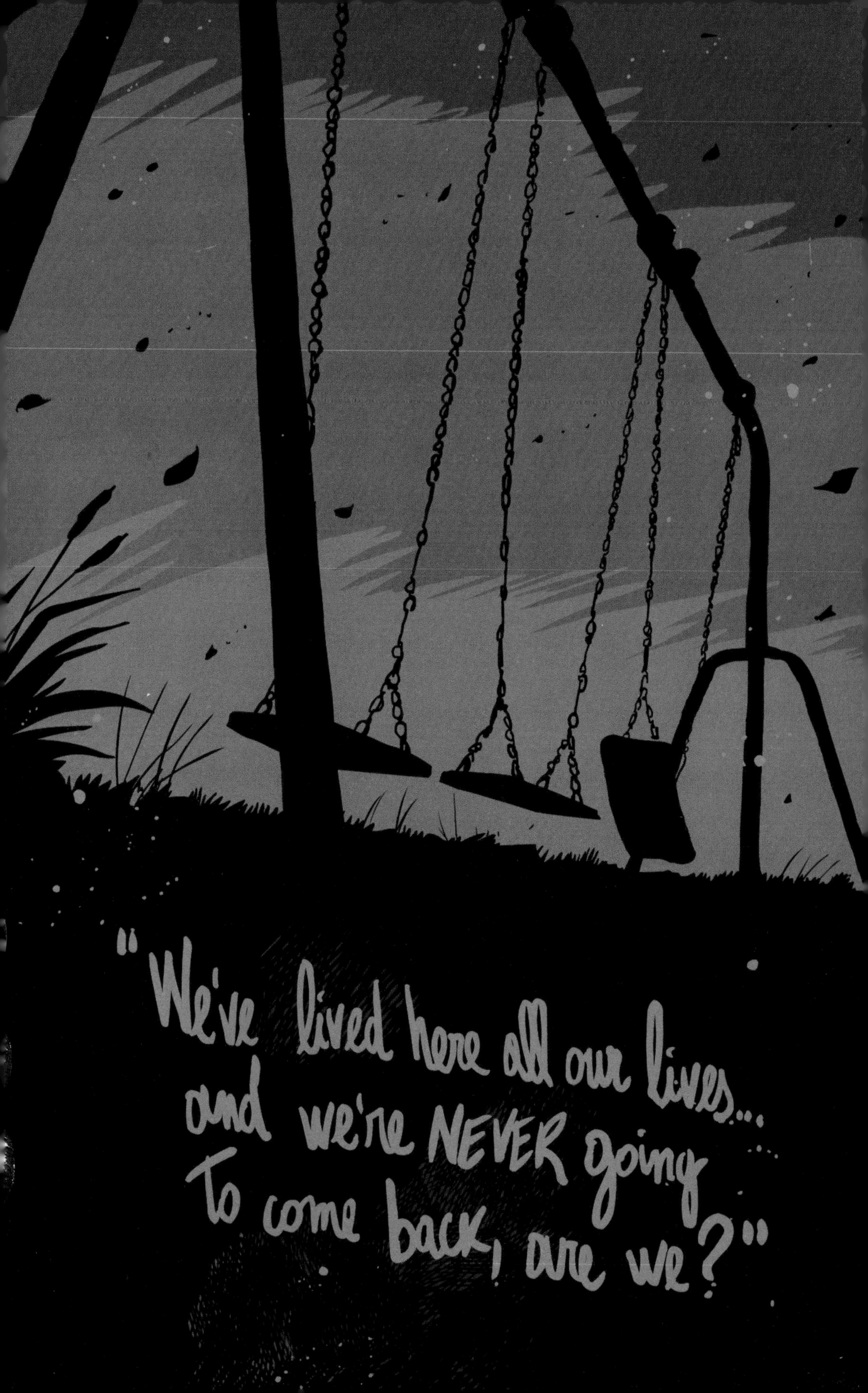
"We've lived here all our lives... and we're NEVER going to come back, are we?"

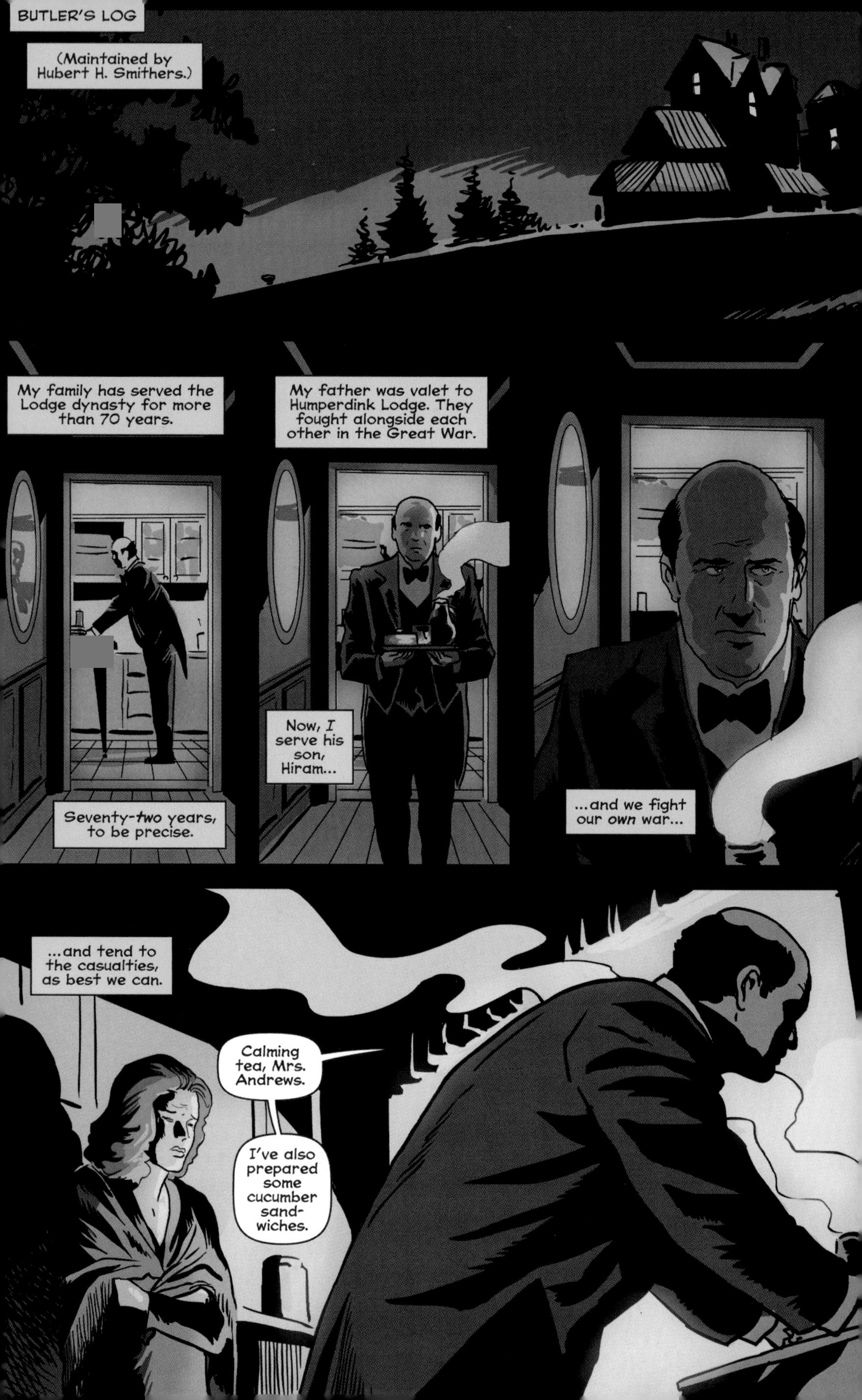

BUTLER'S LOG
(Maintained by Hubert H. Smithers.)
My family has served the Lodge dynasty for more than 70 years.
Seventy-*two* years, to be precise.
My father was valet to Humperdink Lodge. They fought alongside each other in the Great War.
Now, *I* serve his son, Hiram...
...and we fight our *own* war...
...and tend to the casualties, as best we can.
Calming tea, Mrs. Andrews.
I've also prepared some cucumber sand-wiches.

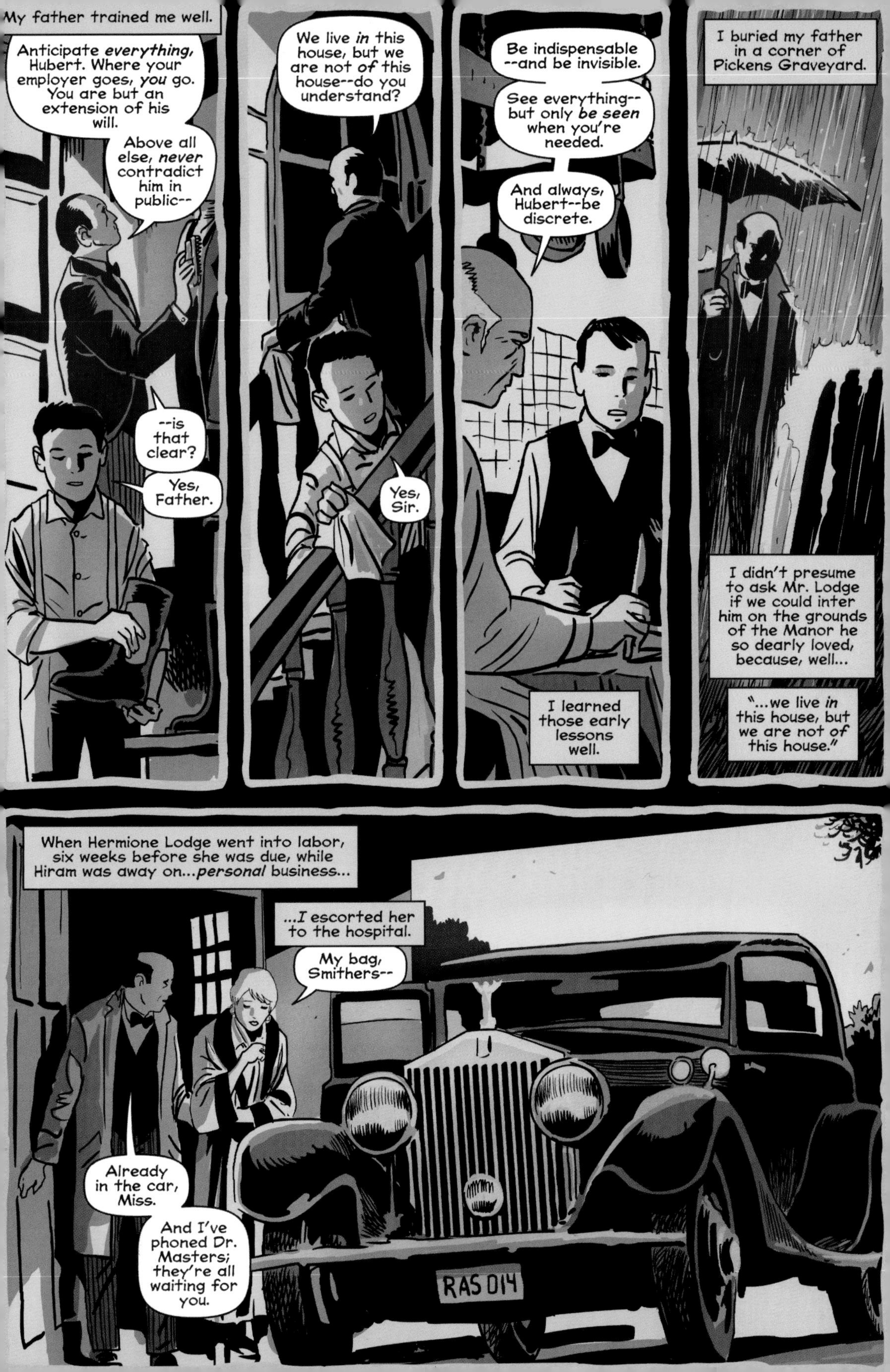

My father trained me well.
Anticipate *everything,* Hubert. Where your employer goes, *you* go. You are but an extension of his will.
Above all else, *never* contradict him in public--
--is that clear?
Yes, Father.
We live *in* this house, but we are not *of* this house--do you understand?
Yes, Sir.
Be indispensable --and be invisible.
See everything-- but only *be seen* when you're needed.
And always, Hubert--be discrete.
I learned those early lessons well.
I buried my father in a corner of Pickens Graveyard.
I didn't presume to ask Mr. Lodge if we could inter him on the grounds of the Manor he so dearly loved, because, well...
"...we live *in* this house, but we are not *of* this house."
When Hermione Lodge went into labor, six weeks before she was due, while Hiram was away on...*personal* business...
...*I* escorted her to the hospital.
My bag, Smithers--
Already in the car, Miss.
And I've phoned Dr. Masters; they're all waiting for you.
RAS 014

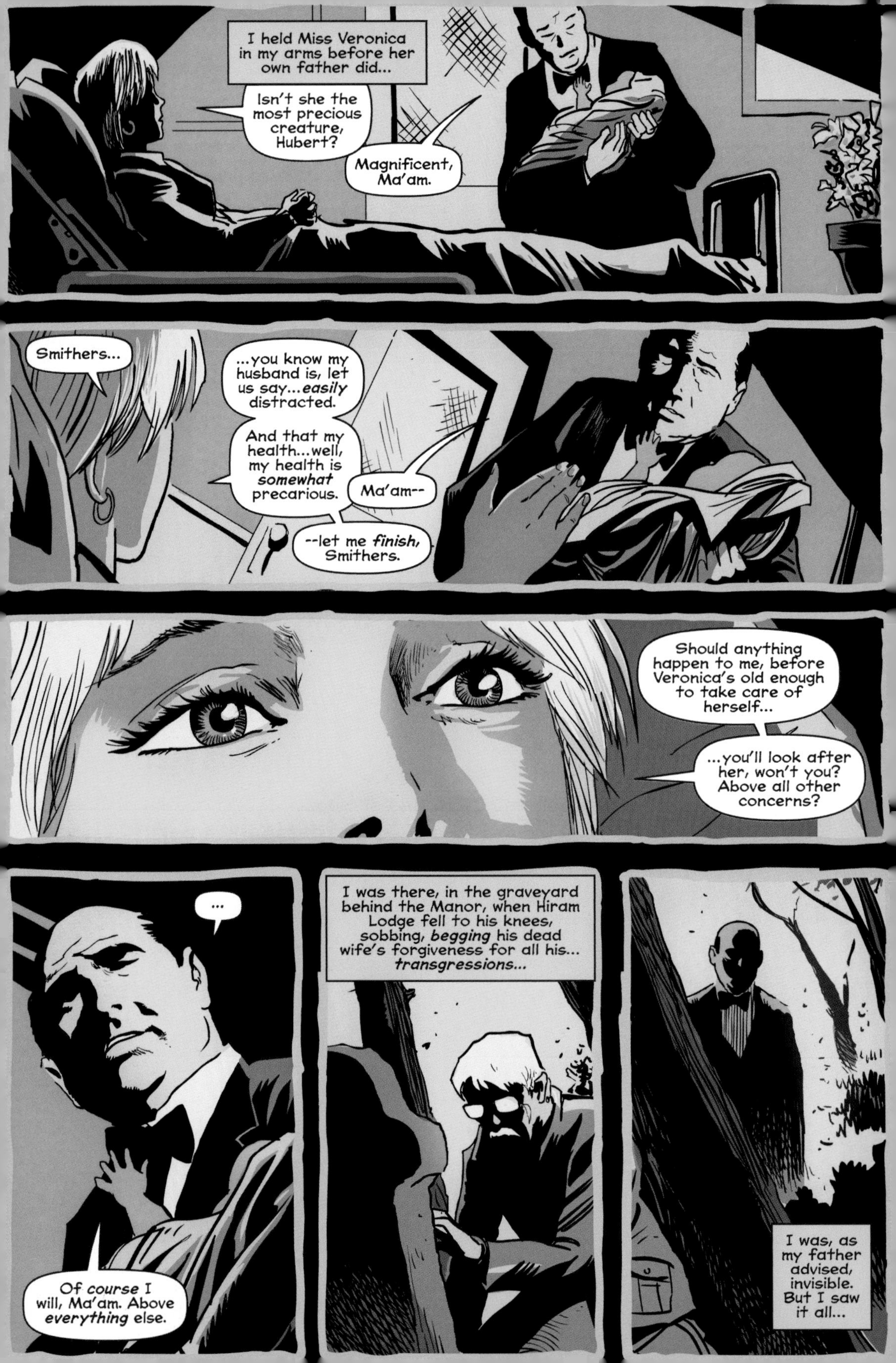
I held Miss Veronica in my arms before her own father did...
Isn't she the most precious creature, Hubert?
Magnificent, Ma'am.
Smithers...
...you know my husband is, let us say...*easily* distracted.
And that my health...well, my health is *somewhat* precarious.
Ma'am--
--let me *finish*, Smithers.
Should anything happen to me, before Veronica's old enough to take care of herself...
...you'll look after her, won't you? Above all other concerns?
...
Of *course* I will, Ma'am. Above *everything* else.
I was there, in the graveyard behind the Manor, when Hiram Lodge fell to his knees, sobbing, *begging* his dead wife's forgiveness for all his... *transgressions*...
I was, as my father advised, invisible. But I saw it all...

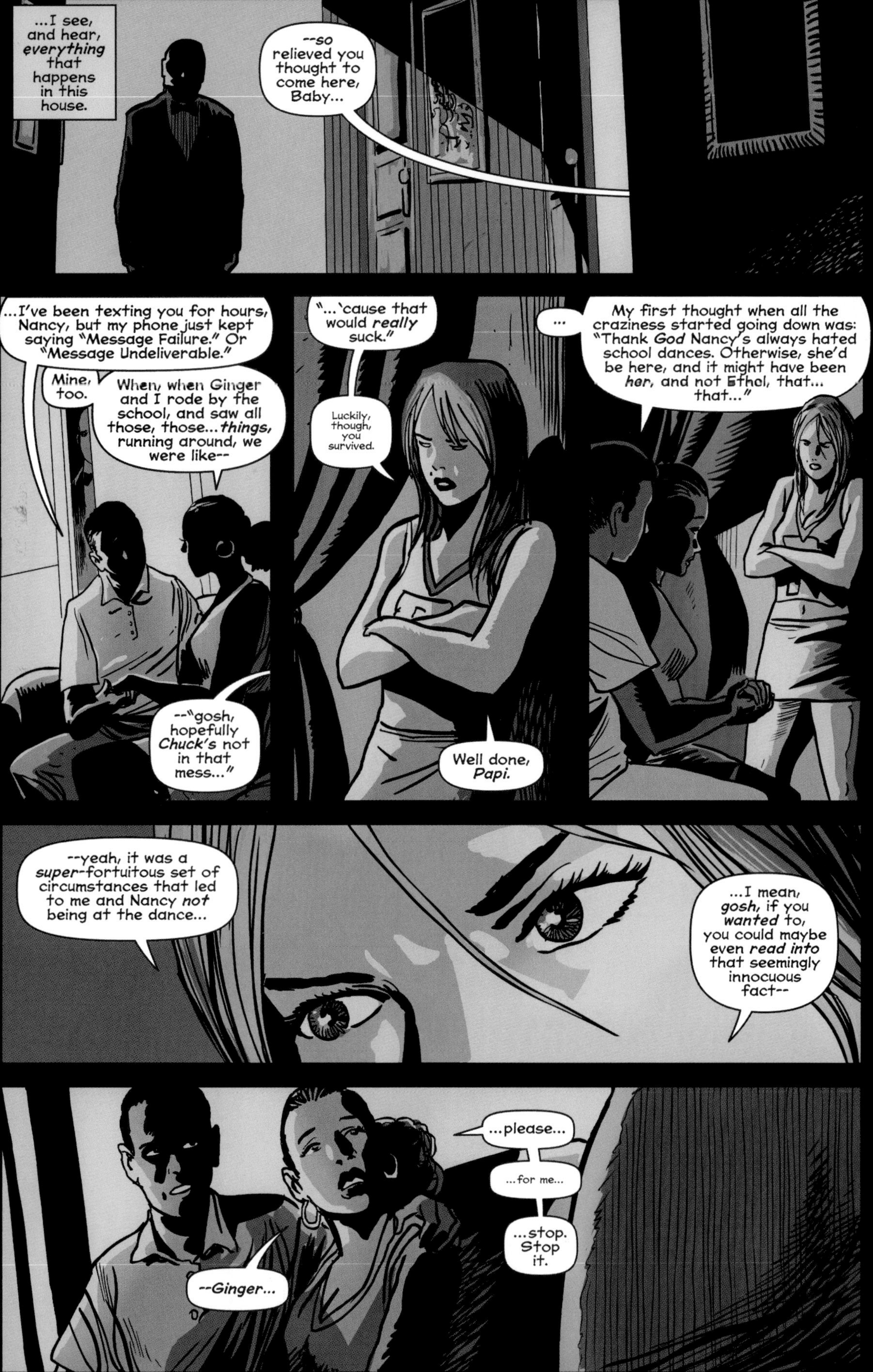
...I see, and hear, everything that happens in this house.
--so relieved you thought to come here, Baby...
...I've been texting you for hours, Nancy, but my phone just kept saying "Message Failure." Or "Message Undeliverable."
Mine, too.
When, when Ginger and I rode by the school, and saw all those, those...things, running around, we were like--
--"gosh, hopefully Chuck's not in that mess..."
"...'cause that would really suck."
Luckily, though, you survived.
Well done, Papi.
...
My first thought when all the craziness started going down was: "Thank God Nancy's always hated school dances. Otherwise, she'd be here, and it might have been her, and not Ethel, that... that..."
--yeah, it was a super-fortuitous set of circumstances that led to me and Nancy not being at the dance...
...I mean, gosh, if you wanted to, you could maybe even read into that seemingly innocuous fact--
...please...
...for me...
...stop. Stop it.
--Ginger...

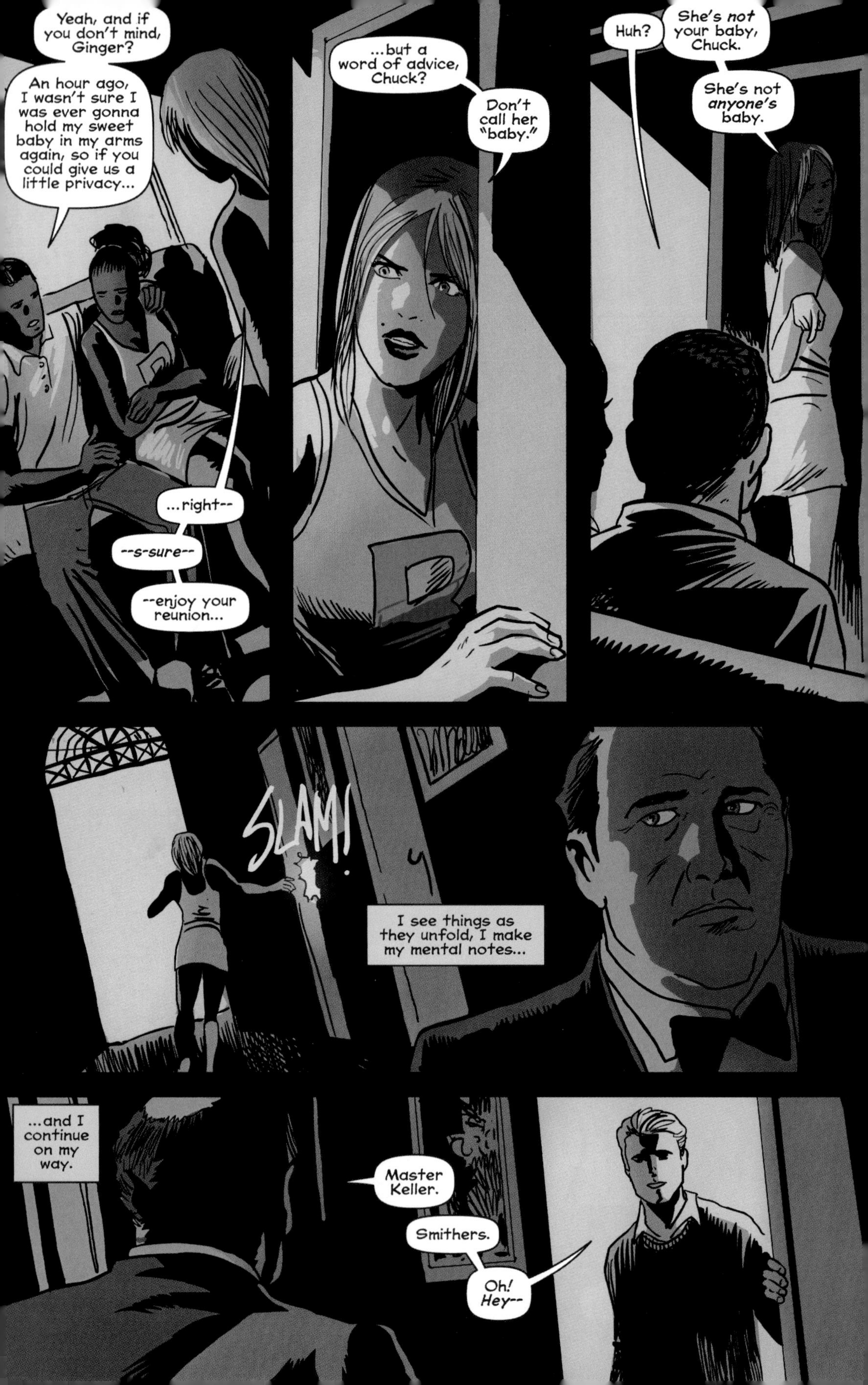

Yeah, and if you don't mind, Ginger?
An hour ago, I wasn't sure I was ever gonna hold my sweet baby in my arms again, so if you could give us a little privacy...
...right--
--s-sure--
--enjoy your reunion...
...but a word of advice, Chuck?
Don't call her "baby."
Huh?
She's *not* your baby, Chuck.
She's not *anyone's* baby.
SLAM!
I see things as they unfold, I make my mental notes...
...and I continue on my way.
Master Keller.
Smithers.
Oh! Hey--

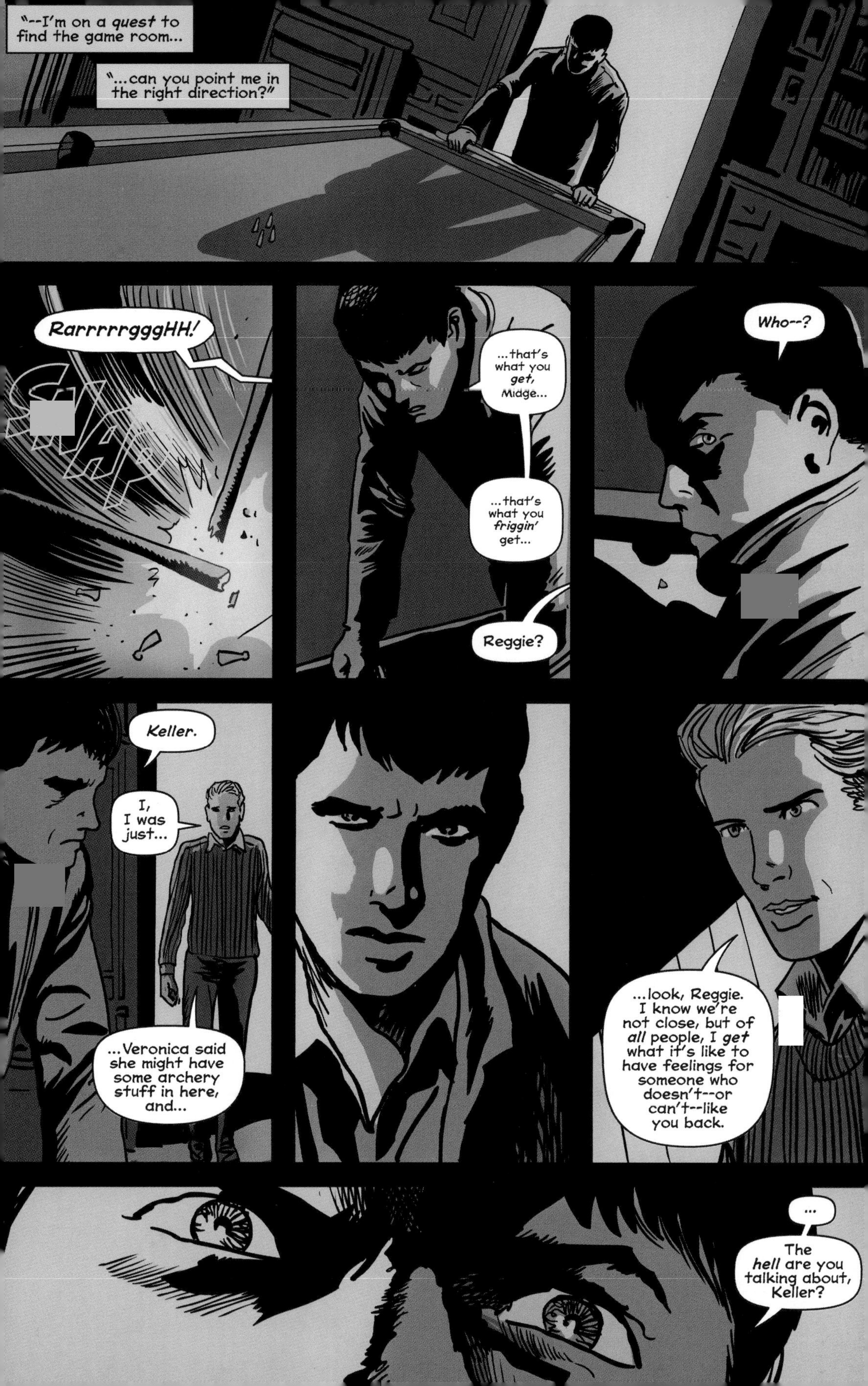
"--I'm on a *quest* to find the game room...
"...can you point me in the right direction?"
RarrrrrgggHH!
...that's what you *get*, Midge...
...that's what you *friggin'* get...
Reggie?
Who--?
Keller.
I, I was just...
...Veronica said she might have some archery stuff in here, and...
...look, Reggie. I know we're not close, but of *all* people, I *get* what it's like to have feelings for someone who doesn't--or can't--like you back.
...
The *hell* are you talking about, Keller?

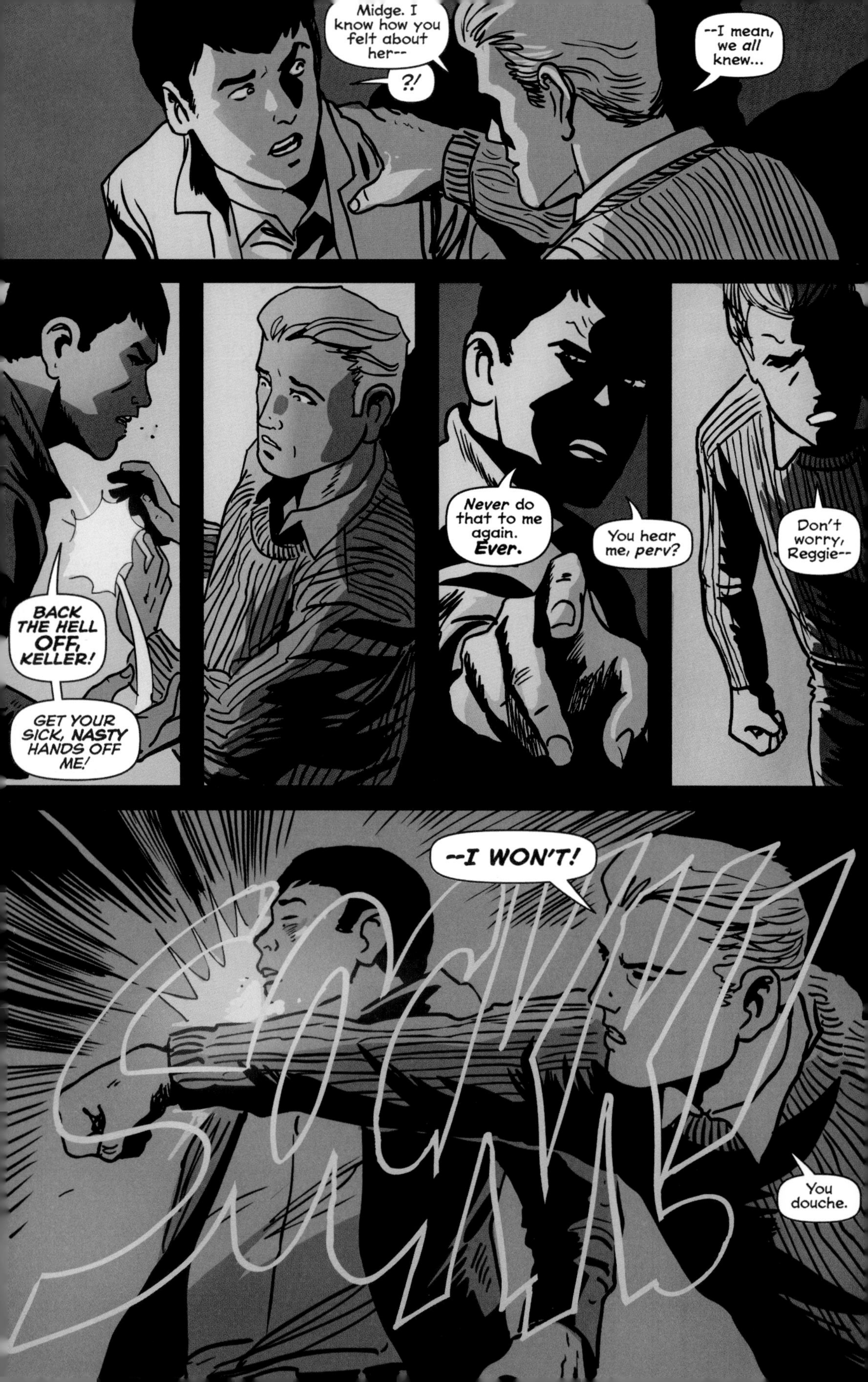
Midge. I know how you felt about her--
?!
--I mean, we all knew...
BACK THE HELL OFF, KELLER!
GET YOUR SICK, NASTY HANDS OFF ME!
Never do that to me again. Ever.
You hear me, perv?
Don't worry, Reggie--
--I WON'T!
SOCK
You douche.

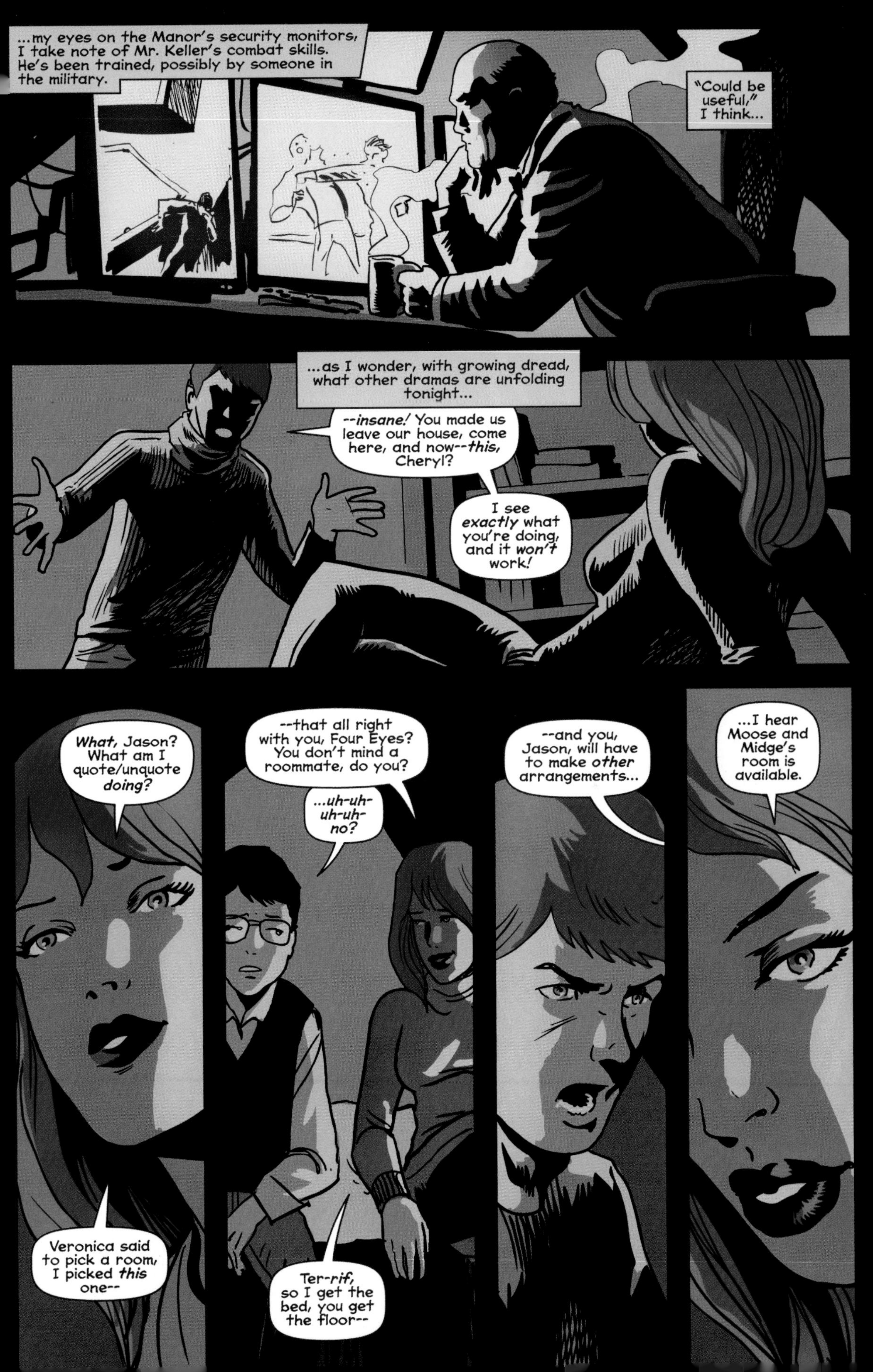

...my eyes on the Manor's security monitors, I take note of Mr. Keller's combat skills. He's been trained, possibly by someone in the military.
"Could be useful," I think...
...as I wonder, with growing dread, what other dramas are unfolding tonight...
--insane! You made us leave our house, come here, and now--this, Cheryl?
I see exactly what you're doing, and it won't work!
What, Jason? What am I quote/unquote doing?
Veronica said to pick a room, I picked this one--
--that all right with you, Four Eyes? You don't mind a roommate, do you?
...uh-uh-uh-uh-no?
Ter-rif, so I get the bed, you get the floor--
--and you, Jason, will have to make other arrangements...
...I hear Moose and Midge's room is available.

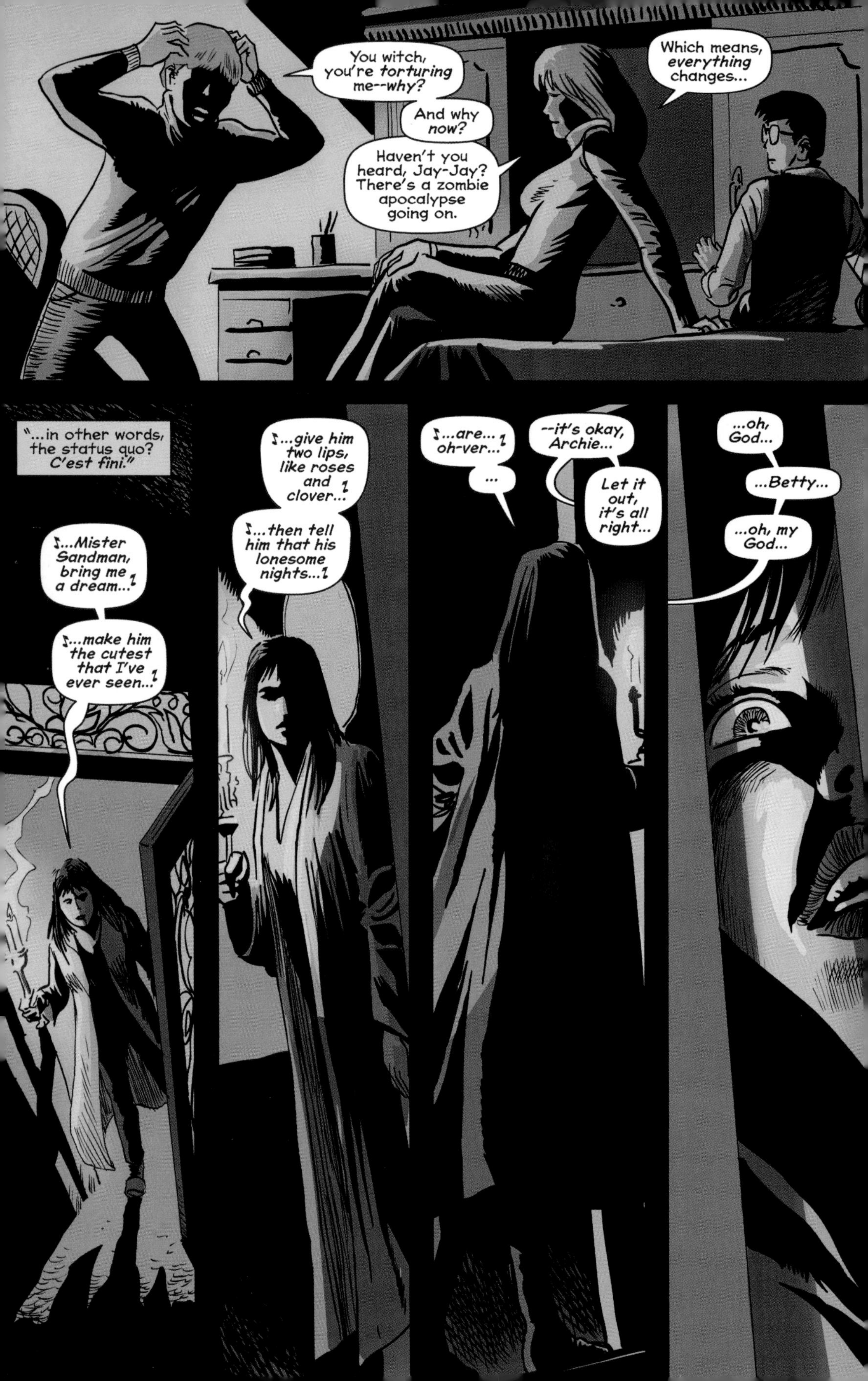
You witch, you're *torturing* me--*why?*
And why *now?*
Haven't you heard, Jay-Jay? There's a zombie apocalypse going on.
Which means, *everything* changes...
"...in other words, the status quo? *C'est fini.*"
♪...Mister Sandman, bring me a dream...♪
♪...make him the cutest that I've ever seen...♪
♪...give him two lips, like roses and clover...♪
♪...then tell him that his lonesome nights...♪
♪...are... oh-ver...♪
...
--it's okay, Archie...
Let it out, it's all right...
...oh, God...
...Betty...
...oh, my God...

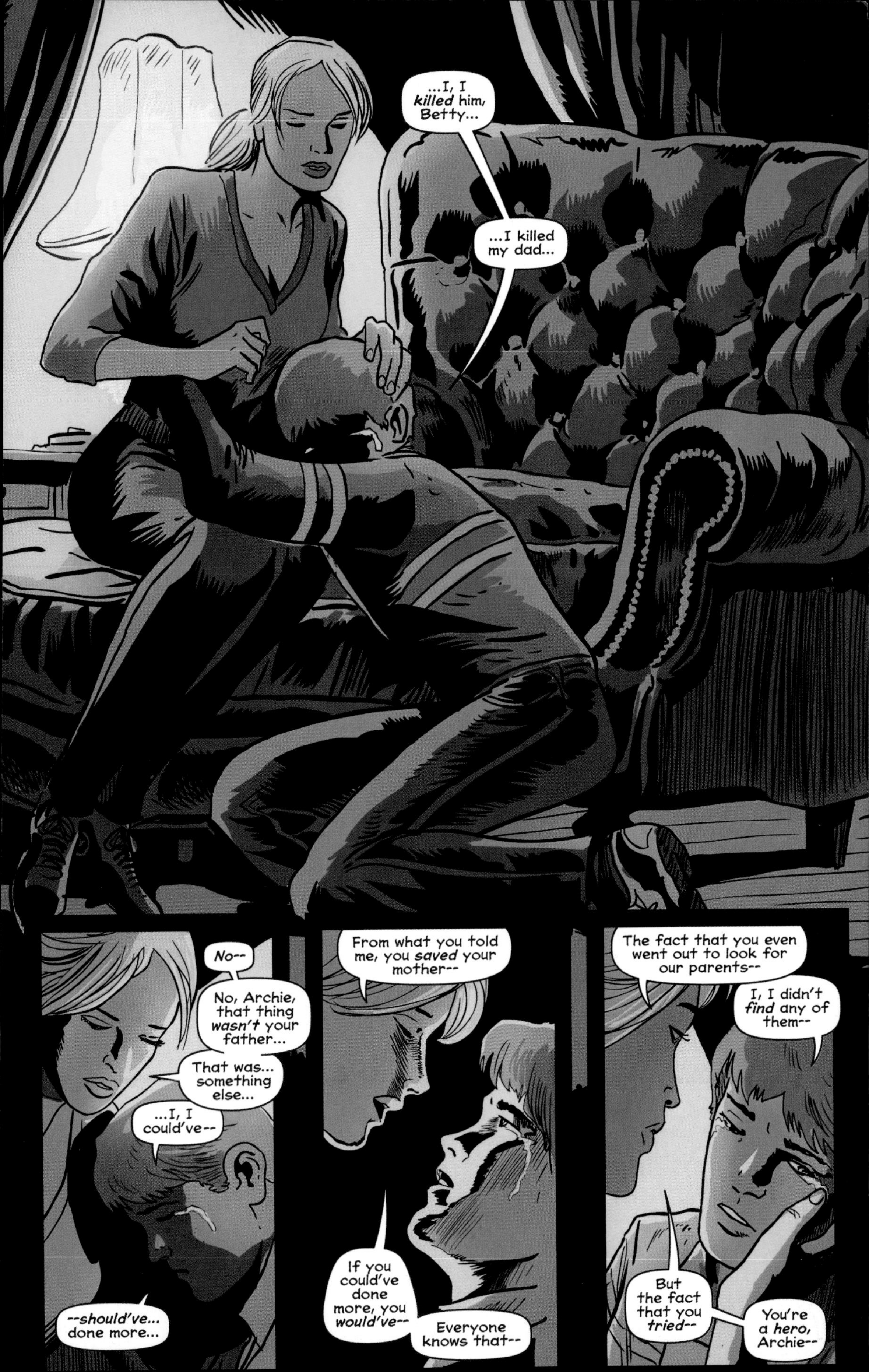
...I, I *killed* him, Betty...
...I killed my dad...
No--
No, Archie, that thing *wasn't* your father...
That was... something else...
...I, I could've--
--*should've*... done more...
From what you told me, you *saved* your mother--
If you could've done more, you *would've*--
Everyone knows that--
The fact that you even went out to look for our parents--
I, I didn't *find* any of them--
But the fact that you *tried*--
You're a *hero*, Archie--

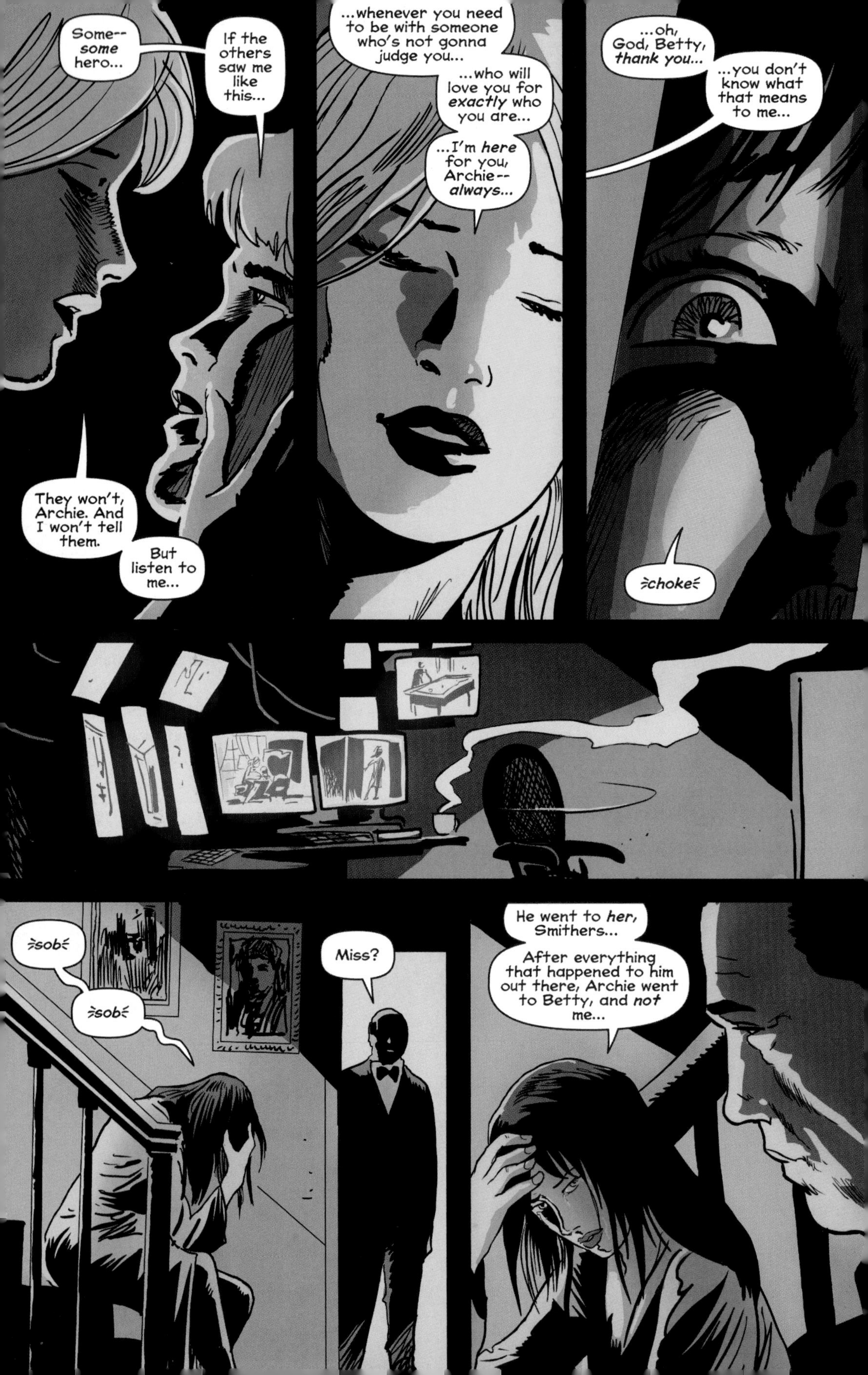
Some--
some
hero...
If the others saw me like this...
They won't, Archie. And I won't tell them.
But listen to me...
...whenever you need to be with someone who's not gonna judge you...
...who will love you for *exactly* who you are...
...I'm *here* for you, Archie-- *always*...
...oh, God, Betty, *thank you*...
...you don't know what that means to me...
choke
sob
sob
Miss?
He went to *her*, Smithers...
After everything that happened to him out there, Archie went to Betty, and *not* me...

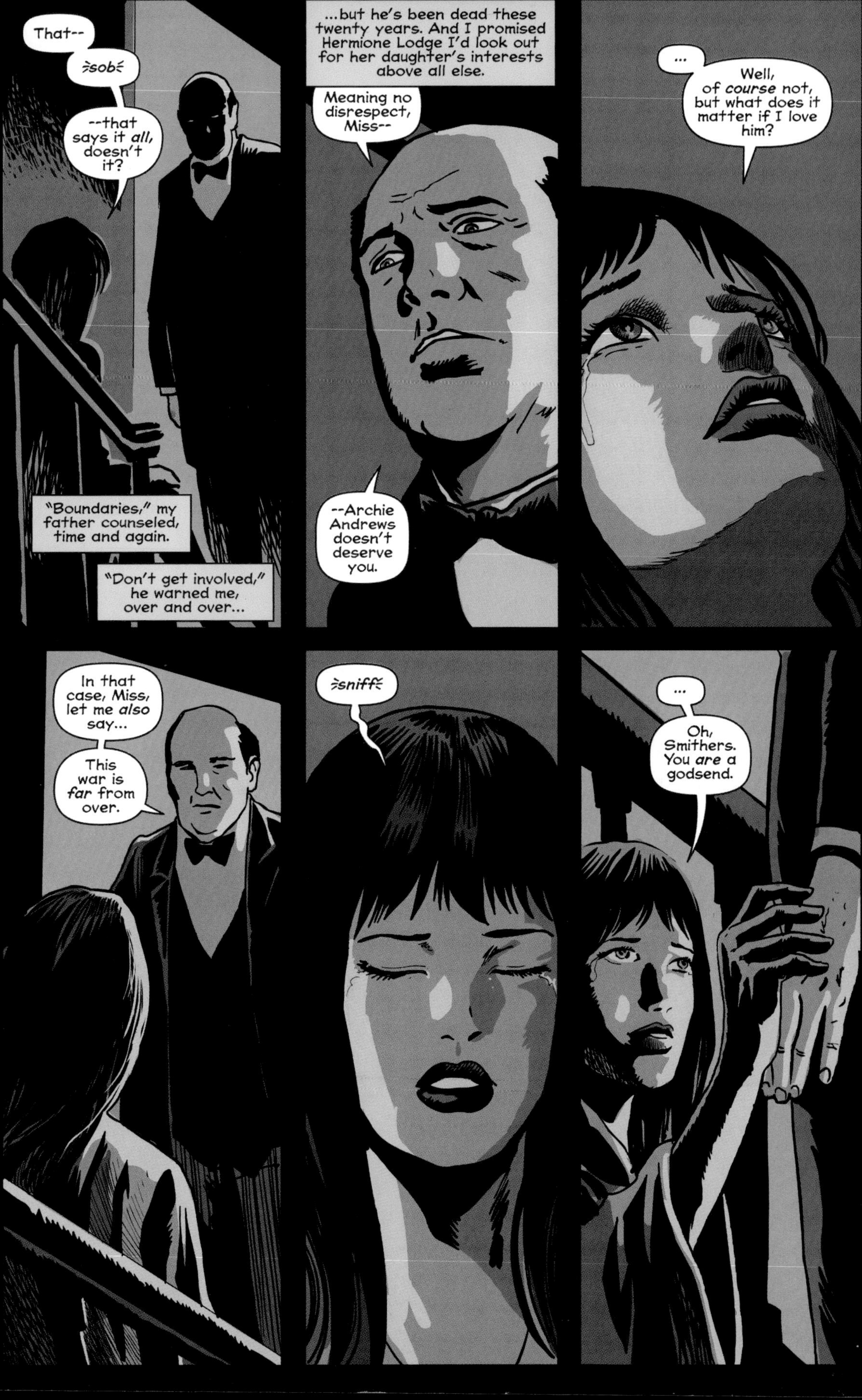
That--
sob
--that says it *all*, doesn't it?
"Boundaries," my father counseled, time and again.
"Don't get involved," he warned me, over and over...
...but he's been dead these twenty years. And I promised Hermione Lodge I'd look out for her daughter's interests above all else.
Meaning no disrespect, Miss--
--Archie Andrews doesn't deserve you.
...
Well, of *course* not, but what does it matter if I love him?
In that case, Miss, let me *also* say...
This war is *far* from over.
sniff
...
Oh, Smithers. You *are* a godsend.

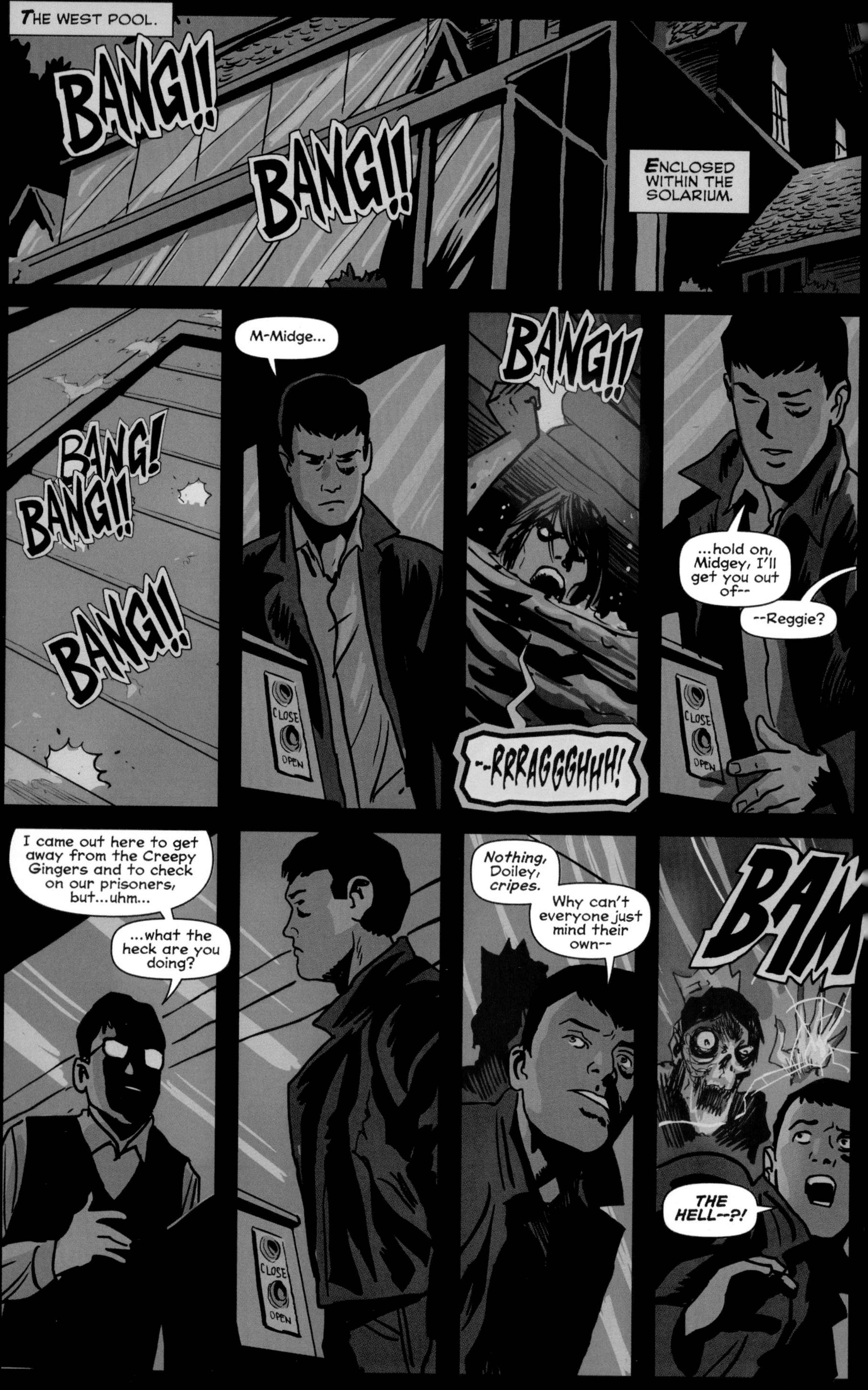
THE WEST POOL.
BANG!!
BANG!!
ENCLOSED WITHIN THE SOLARIUM.
BANG!
BANG!!
BANG!!
M-Midge...
BANG!!
--RRRAGGGHHH!
...hold on, Midgey, I'll get you out of--
--Reggie?
I came out here to get away from the Creepy Gingers and to check on our prisoners, but...uhm...
...what the heck are you doing?
Nothing, Doiley, cripes.
Why can't everyone just mind their own--
BAM
THE HELL--?!
CLOSE
OPEN

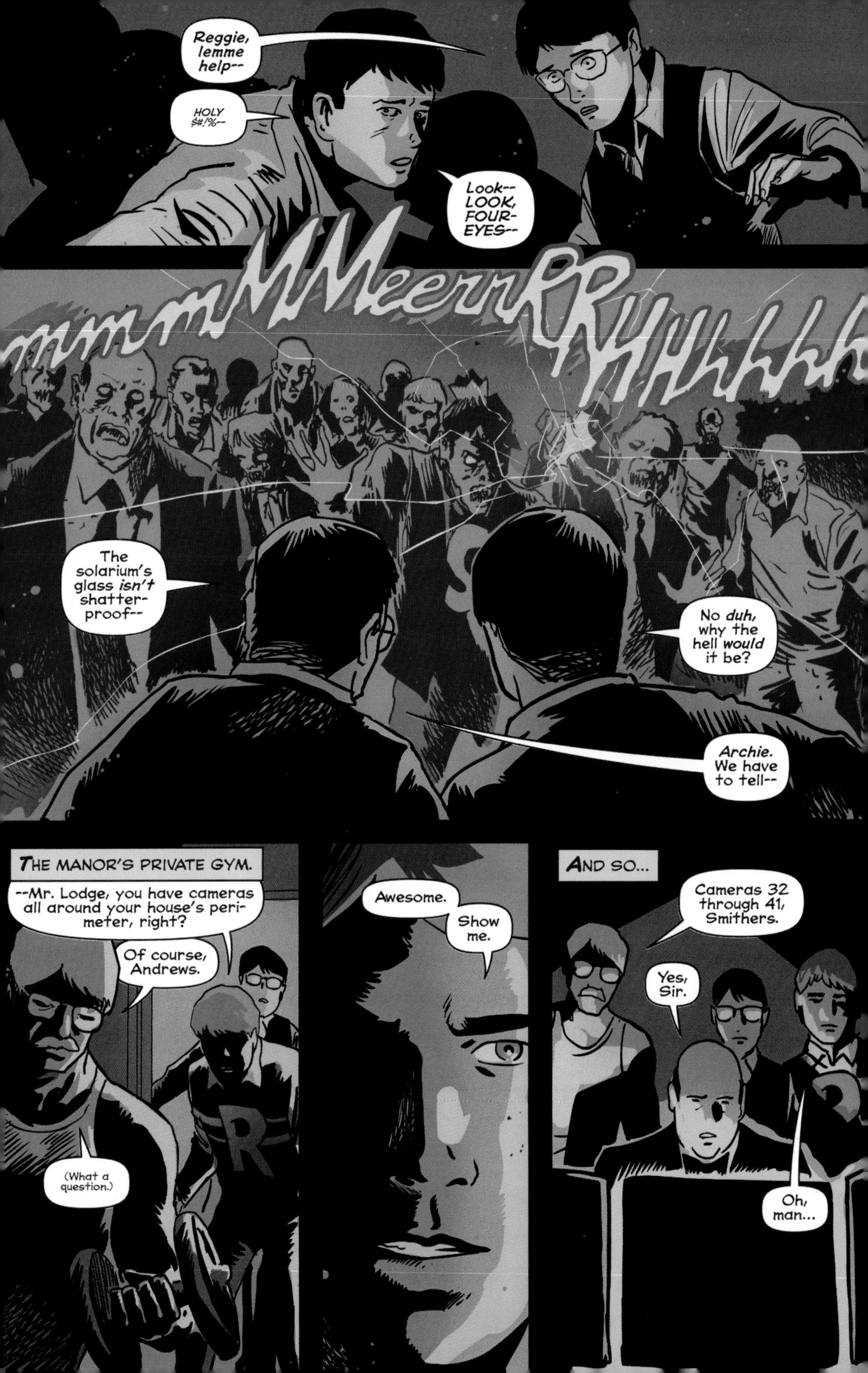
Reggie, lemme help--
HOLY $#!%--
Look-- LOOK, FOUR-EYES--
mmmMMeerrrRRYHHhhhh
The solarium's glass *isn't* shatter-proof--
No *duh*, why the hell *would* it be?
Archie. We have to tell--
THE MANOR'S PRIVATE GYM.
--Mr. Lodge, you have cameras all around your house's perimeter, right?
Of course, Andrews.
(What a question.)
Awesome.
Show me.
AND SO...
Cameras 32 through 41, Smithers.
Yes, Sir.
Oh, man...

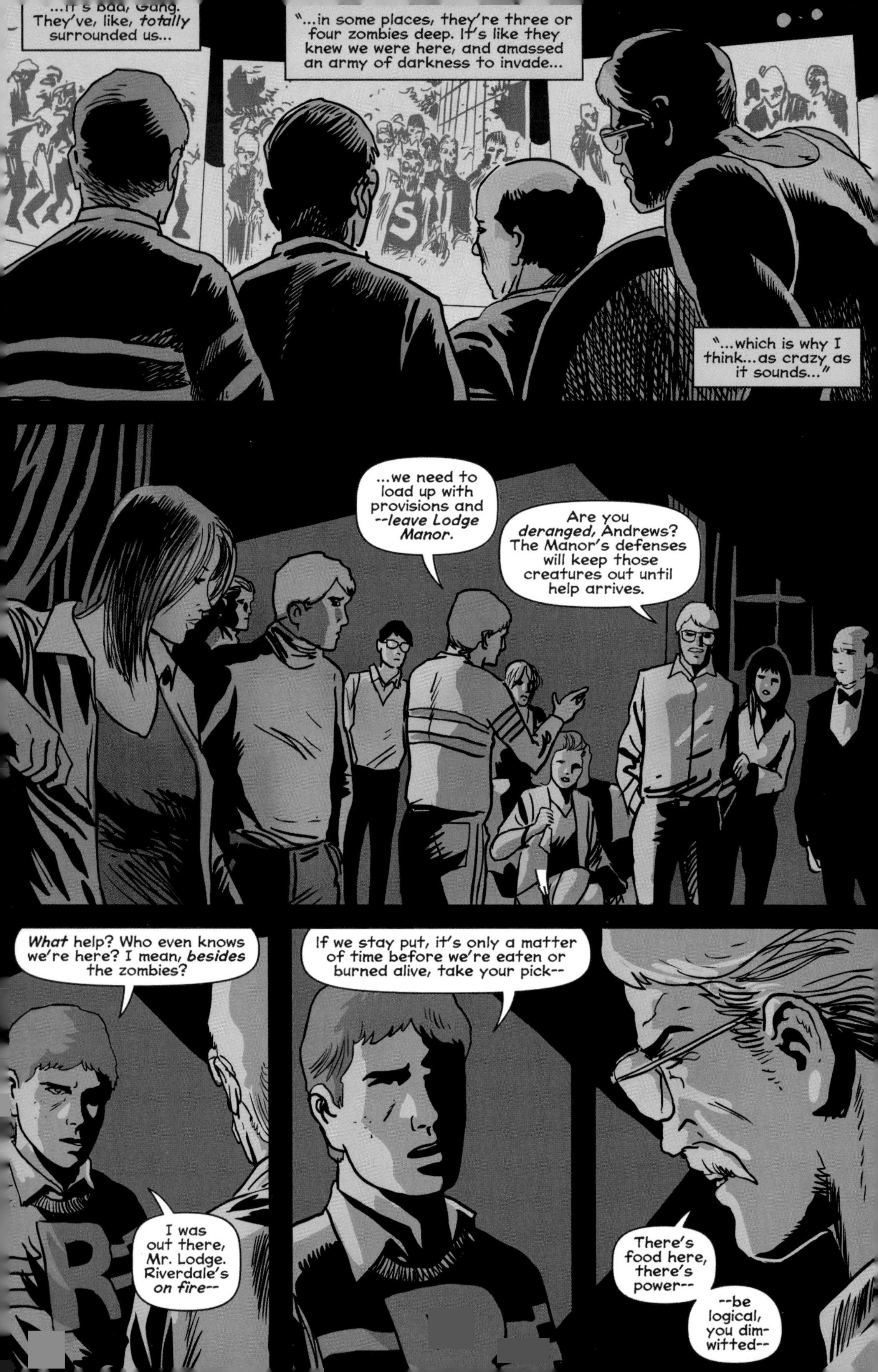

...it's bad, Gang. They've, like, *totally* surrounded us...
"...in some places, they're three or four zombies deep. It's like they knew we were here, and amassed an army of darkness to invade...
"...which is why I think...as crazy as it sounds..."
...we need to load up with provisions and *--leave Lodge Manor.*
Are you *deranged,* Andrews? The Manor's defenses will keep those creatures out until help arrives.
What help? Who even knows we're here? I mean, *besides* the zombies?
I was out there, Mr. Lodge. Riverdale's *on fire--*
If we stay put, it's only a matter of time before we're eaten or burned alive, take your pick--
There's food here, there's power--
--be logical, you dim-witted--

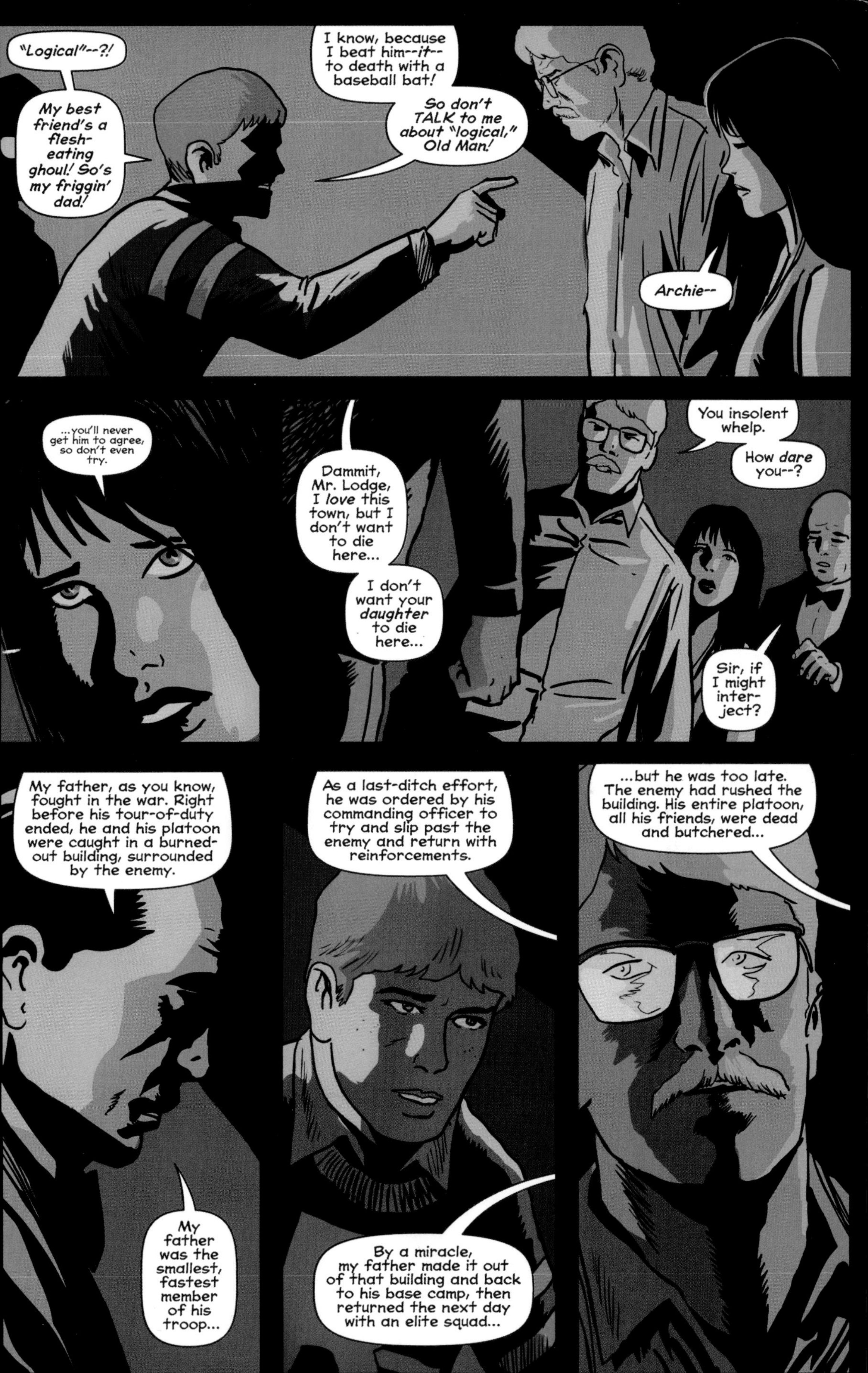
"Logical"--?!
My best friend's a flesh-eating ghoul! So's my friggin' dad!
I know, because I beat him--it--to death with a baseball bat!
So don't TALK to me about "logical," Old Man!
Archie--
...you'll never get him to agree, so don't even try.
Dammit, Mr. Lodge, I love this town, but I don't want to die here...
I don't want your daughter to die here...
You insolent whelp.
How dare you--?
Sir, if I might interject?
My father, as you know, fought in the war. Right before his tour-of-duty ended, he and his platoon were caught in a burned-out building, surrounded by the enemy.
My father was the smallest, fastest member of his troop...
As a last-ditch effort, he was ordered by his commanding officer to try and slip past the enemy and return with reinforcements.
By a miracle, my father made it out of that building and back to his base camp, then returned the next day with an elite squad...
...but he was too late. The enemy had rushed the building. His entire platoon, all his friends, were dead and butchered...

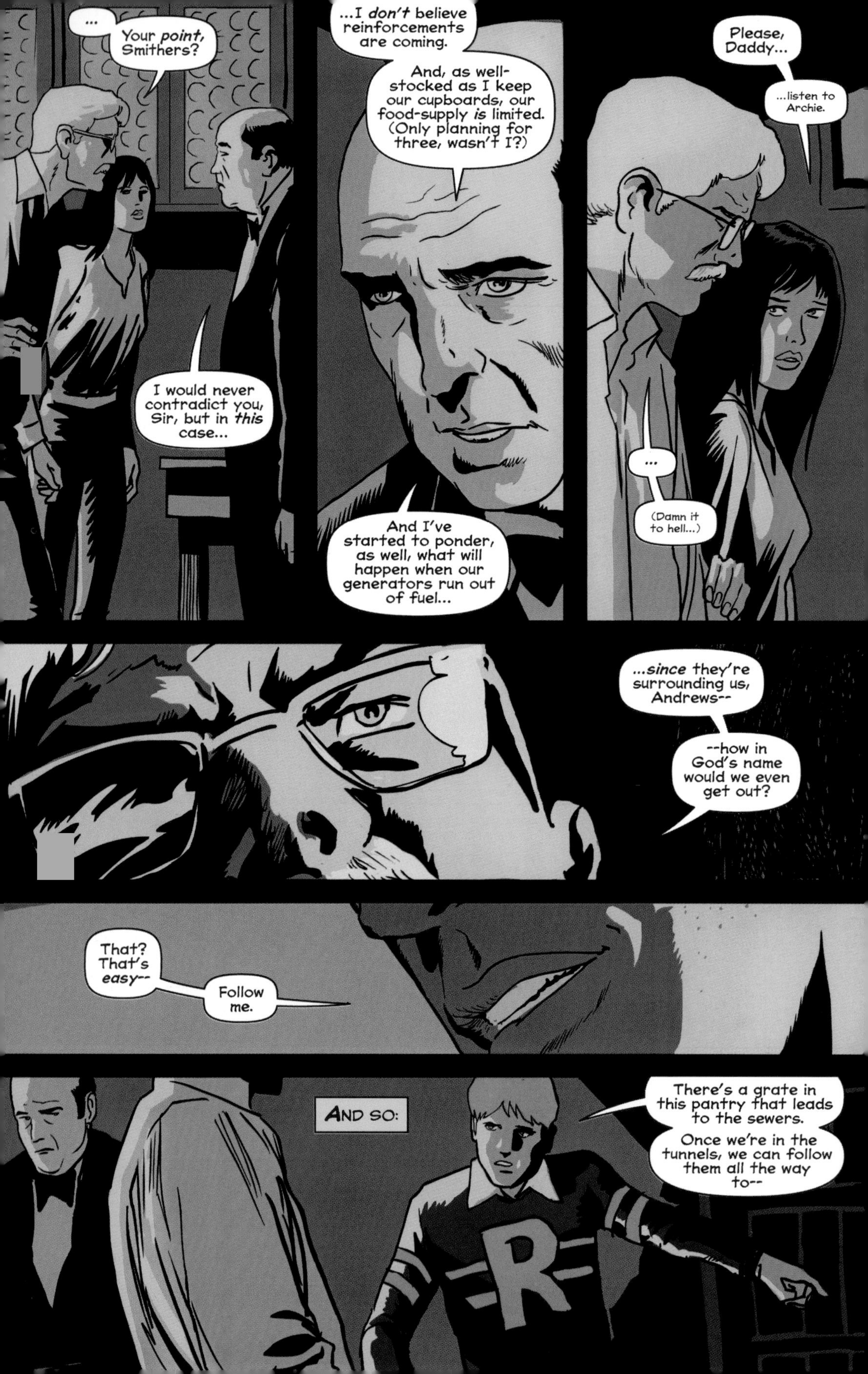
...
Your *point*, Smithers?
I would never contradict you, Sir, but in *this* case...
...I *don't* believe reinforcements are coming.
And, as well-stocked as I keep our cupboards, our food-supply *is* limited. (Only planning for three, wasn't I?)
And I've started to ponder, as well, what will happen when our generators run out of fuel...
Please, Daddy...
...listen to Archie.
...
(Damn it to hell...)
...*since* they're surrounding us, Andrews--
--how in God's name would we even get out?
That? That's *easy*--
Follow me.
AND SO:
There's a grate in this pantry that leads to the sewers.
Once we're in the tunnels, we can follow them all the way to--

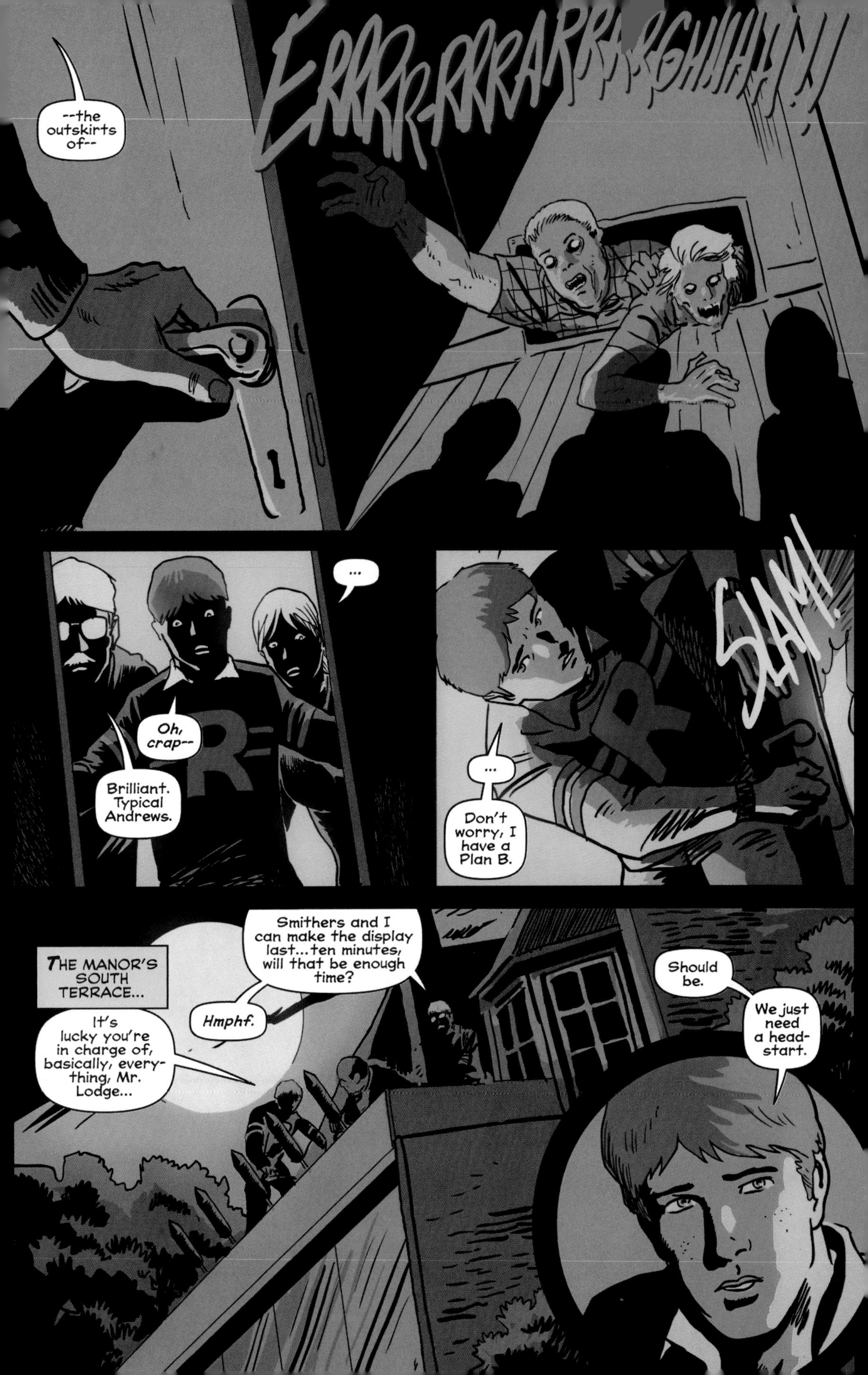
--the outskirts of--
ERRRR-RRRARRR-RGHIIIAH!!
...
Oh, crap--
Brilliant. Typical Andrews.
SLAM!
...
Don't worry, I have a Plan B.
THE MANOR'S SOUTH TERRACE...
It's lucky you're in charge of, basically, everything, Mr. Lodge...
Hmphf.
Smithers and I can make the display last...ten minutes, will that be enough time?
Should be.
We just need a head-start.

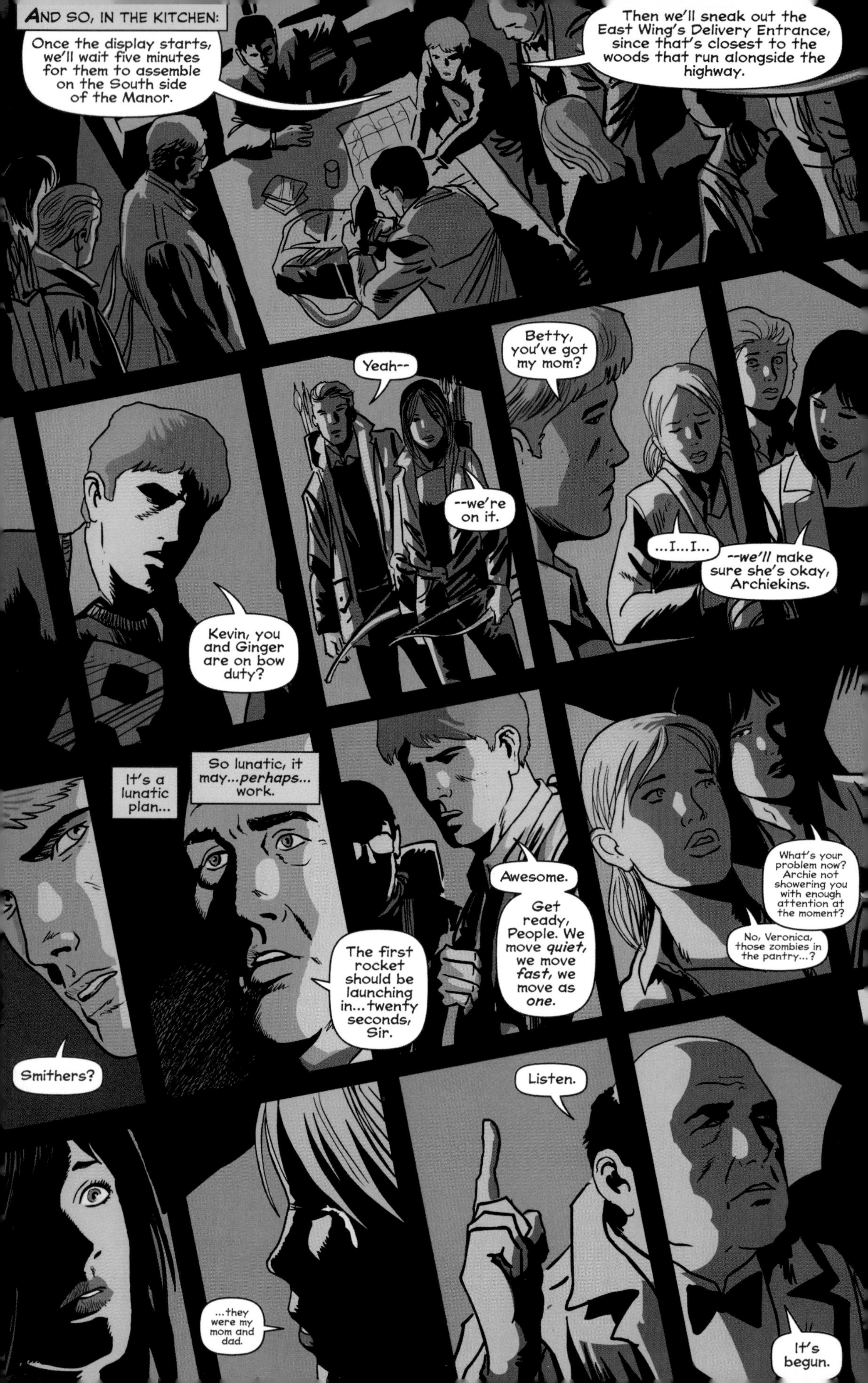
AND SO, IN THE KITCHEN:
Once the display starts, we'll wait five minutes for them to assemble on the South side of the Manor.
Then we'll sneak out the East Wing's Delivery Entrance, since that's closest to the woods that run alongside the highway.
Kevin, you and Ginger are on bow duty?
Yeah--
--we're on it.
Betty, you've got my mom?
...I...I...
--we'll make sure she's okay, Archiekins.
Smithers?
It's a lunatic plan...
So lunatic, it may...perhaps... work.
The first rocket should be launching in...twenty seconds, Sir.
Awesome.
Get ready, People. We move quiet, we move fast, we move as one.
What's your problem now? Archie not showering you with enough attention at the moment?
No, Veronica, those zombies in the pantry...?
...they were my mom and dad.
Listen.
It's begun.

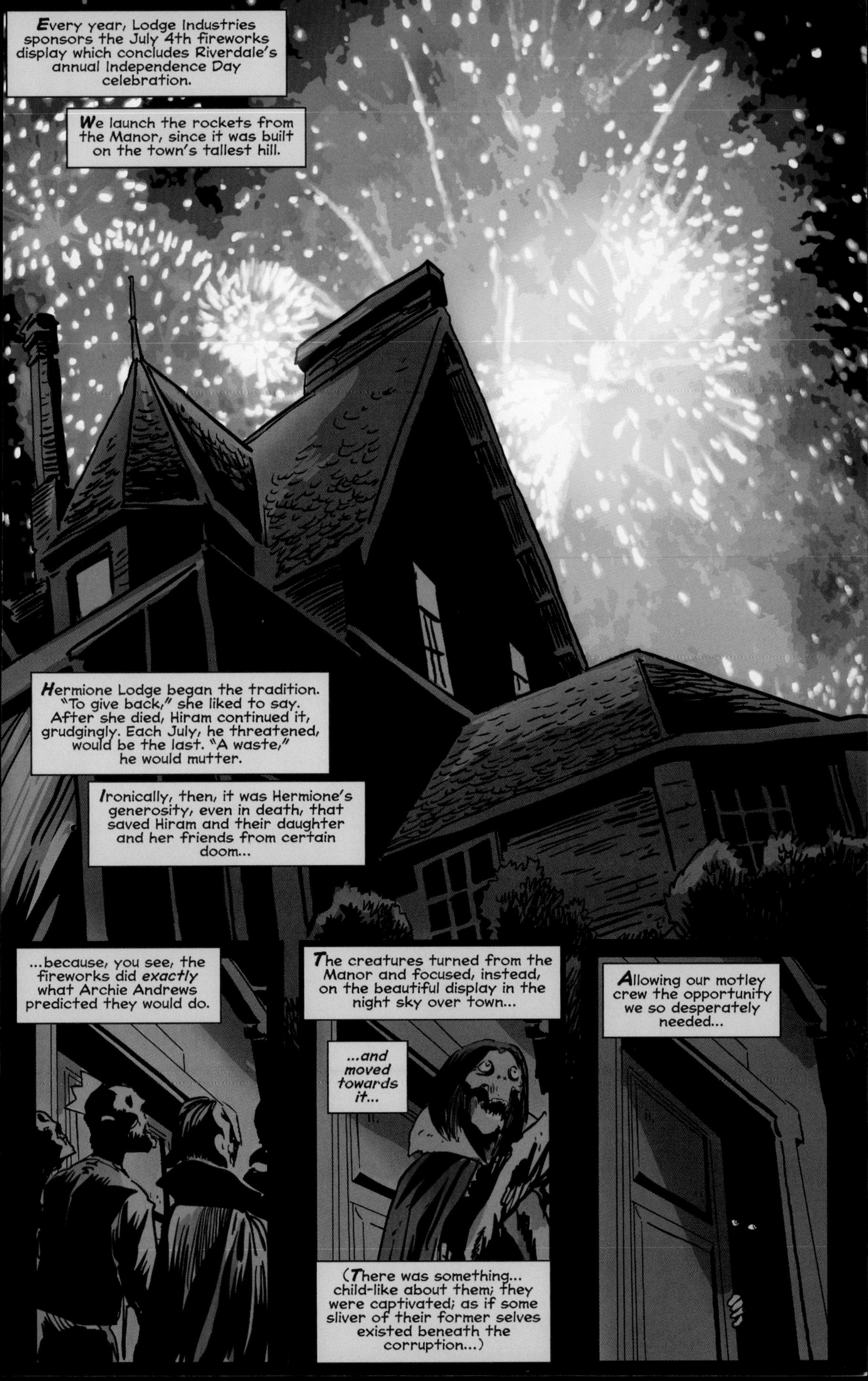
Every year, Lodge Industries sponsors the July 4th fireworks display which concludes Riverdale's annual Independence Day celebration.
We launch the rockets from the Manor, since it was built on the town's tallest hill.
Hermione Lodge began the tradition. "To give back," she liked to say. After she died, Hiram continued it, grudgingly. Each July, he threatened, would be the last. "A waste," he would mutter.
Ironically, then, it was Hermione's generosity, even in death, that saved Hiram and their daughter and her friends from certain doom...
...because, you see, the fireworks did *exactly* what Archie Andrews predicted they would do.
The creatures turned from the Manor and focused, instead, on the beautiful display in the night sky over town...
...and moved towards it...
(There was something... child-like about them; they were captivated; as if some sliver of their former selves existed beneath the corruption...)
Allowing our motley crew the opportunity we so desperately needed...

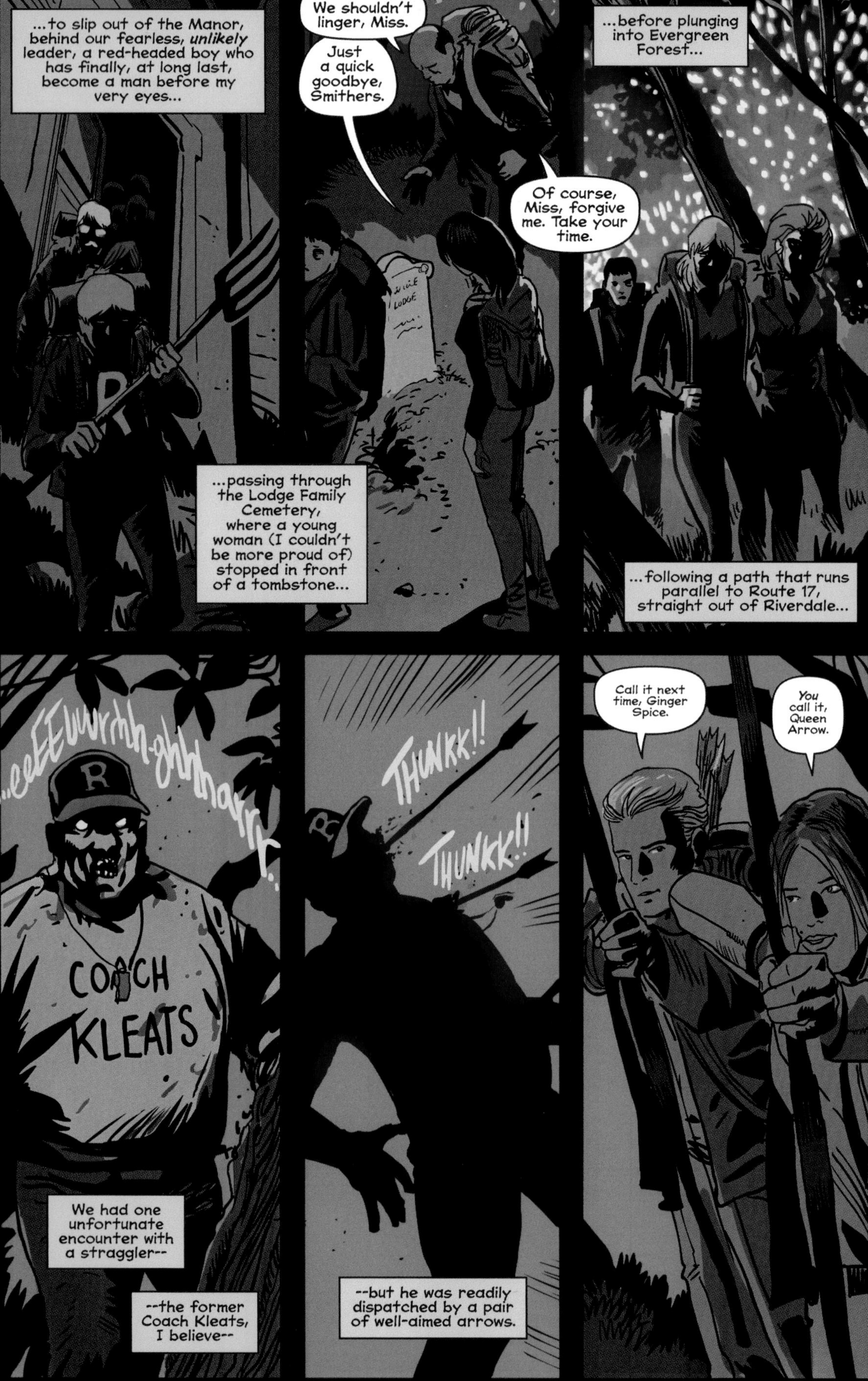

...to slip out of the Manor, behind our fearless, *unlikely* leader, a red-headed boy who has finally, at long last, become a man before my very eyes...
We shouldn't linger, Miss.
Just a quick goodbye, Smithers.
Of course, Miss, forgive me. Take your time.
...passing through the Lodge Family Cemetery, where a young woman (I couldn't be more proud of) stopped in front of a tombstone...
...before plunging into Evergreen Forest...
...following a path that runs parallel to Route 17, straight out of Riverdale...
...eeEEuuwrhh-ghhnarrr...
COACH KLEATS
We had one unfortunate encounter with a straggler--
--the former Coach Kleats, I believe--
THUNKK!!
THUNKK!!
--but he was readily dispatched by a pair of well-aimed arrows.
Call it next time, Ginger Spice.
You call it, Queen Arrow.

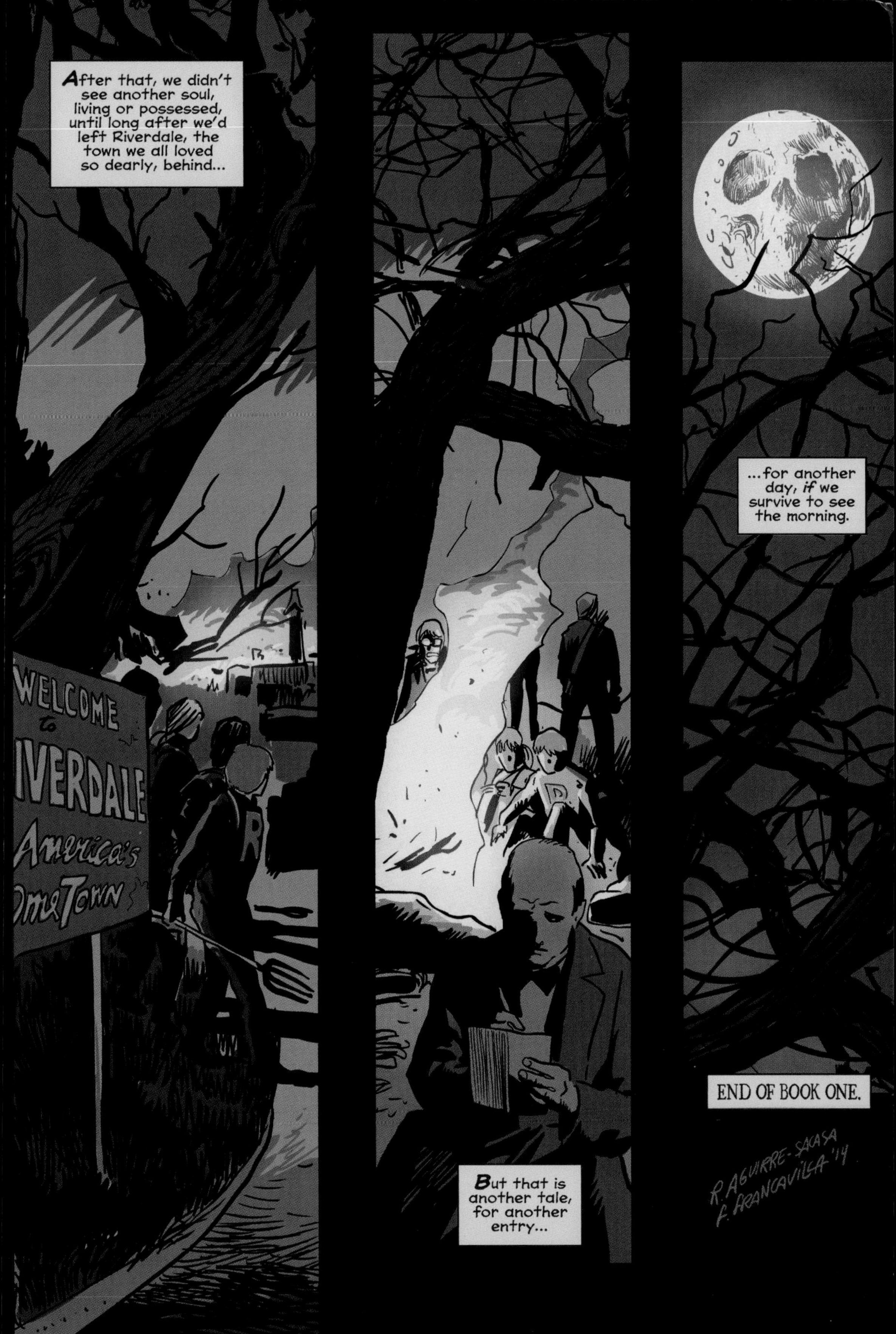
After that, we didn't see another soul, living or possessed, until long after we'd left Riverdale, the town we all loved so dearly, behind...
WELCOME to RIVERDALE America's HomeTown
But that is another tale, for another entry...
...for another day, if we survive to see the morning.
END OF BOOK ONE.
R. AGUIRRE-SACASA F. FRANCAVILLA '14

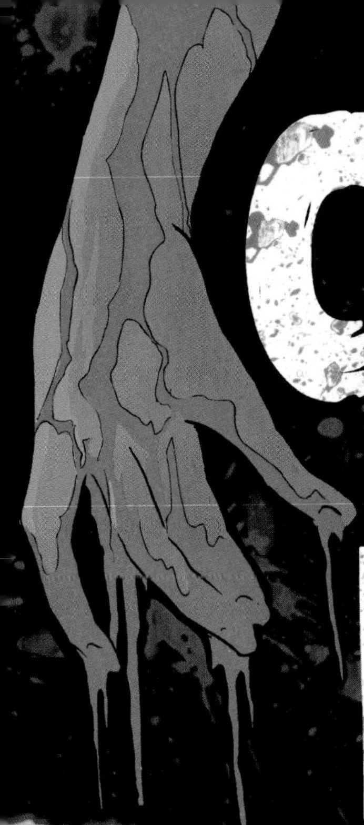

COVERS FROM THE DARKSIDE

It all started with a cover. Specifically, Francesco Francavilla's beautiful, scary, retro-horror variant cover to "Life with Archie" Magazine #23. Depicting Classic Archie (complete with his Riverdale "R" sweater) recoiling from Zombie Jughead, staggering amongst tombstones, Zombie Betty and Zombie Veronica not far behind. It was an instant classic. After a breakfast meeting, I told Jon Goldwater and his son Jesse that I wanted Archie to print posters of that cover so I could hang one up in my apartment. I also said that as much as I loved "Life with Archie," the kid inside me was a little disappointed that the comic underneath Francesco's cover didn't have any zombies in it. A few seconds of silence; then, three comic book light bulbs appeared over our heads, at precisely the same moment. *"This should be a comic book!"* Later that afternoon, I got an e-mail from Jon that read, simply: "Let's do this." I wholeheartedly agreed, wondering if the book should be called "Crypt of Archie." Since then, "Afterlife with Archie" (of course that *had* to be its title, *duh*—another instant classic) has become so much more than a zombie book, but since it began with a cover, it's only fitting to honor *all* of the covers that have graced our first five issues. And, of course, the inspiration for it all.

Roberto
aguirri
Sacasa—

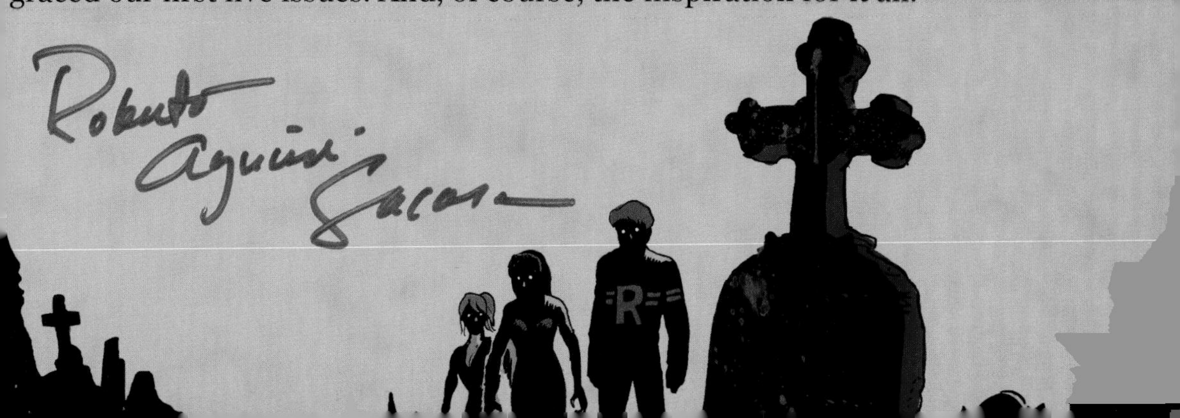

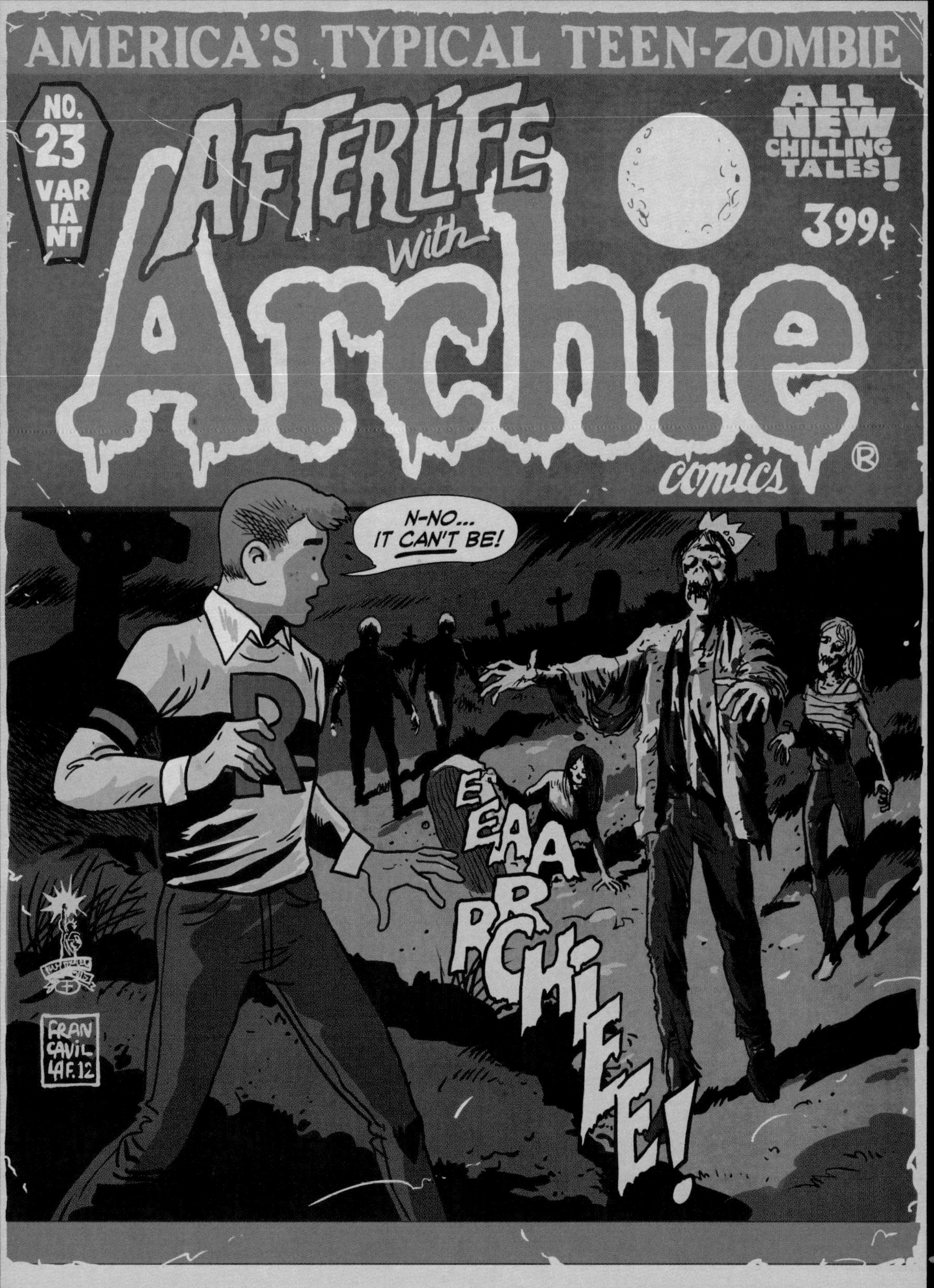
AMERICA'S TYPICAL TEEN-ZOMBIE
NO. 23 VARIANT
AFTERLIFE with Archie
comics ®
ALL NEW CHILLING TALES!
399¢
N-NO... IT CAN'T BE!
EEAAA R RCHIEEE!
FRAN CAVIL LA F.12

Originally published in 2013, this variant cover for "Life with Archie" Magazine #23 served as the inspiration for what was to become the most successful new brand in the history of Archie Comics.

Artwork by **FRANCESCO FRANCAVILLA**

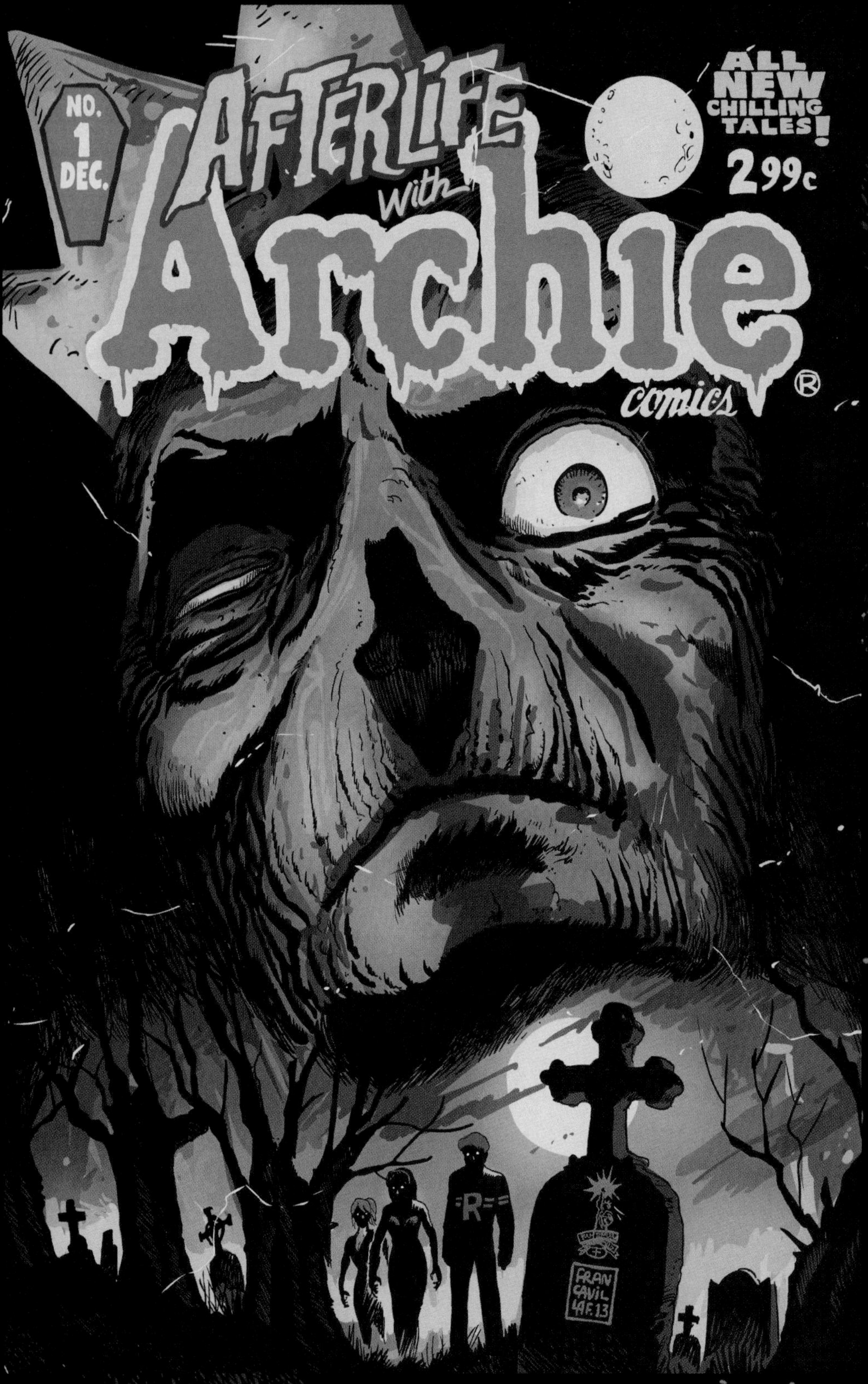
NO. 1 DEC.
AFTERLIFE with Archie
comics
ALL NEW CHILLING TALES!
299c

The main cover for "Afterlife with Archie" #1.
One of four covers released for the initial launch, the artwork for this cover was used to heavily promote the ground-breaking new series.

Artwork by **FRANCESCO FRANCAVILLA**

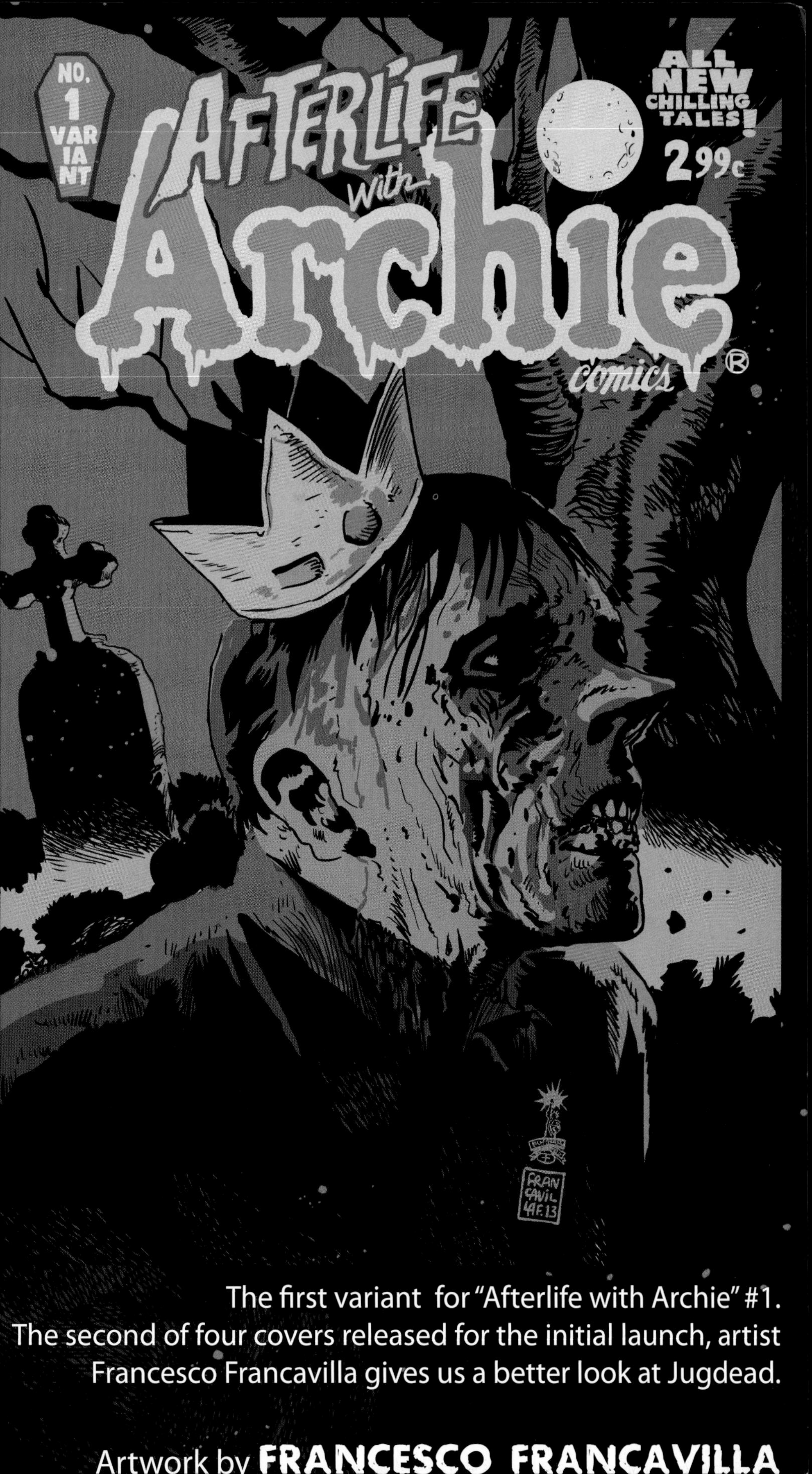
NO. 1 VARIANT
AFTERLIFE with Archie
comics
ALL NEW CHILLING TALES!
2 99c

The first variant for "Afterlife with Archie" #1.
The second of four covers released for the initial launch, artist Francesco Francavilla gives us a better look at Jugdead.

Artwork by **FRANCESCO FRANCAVILLA**

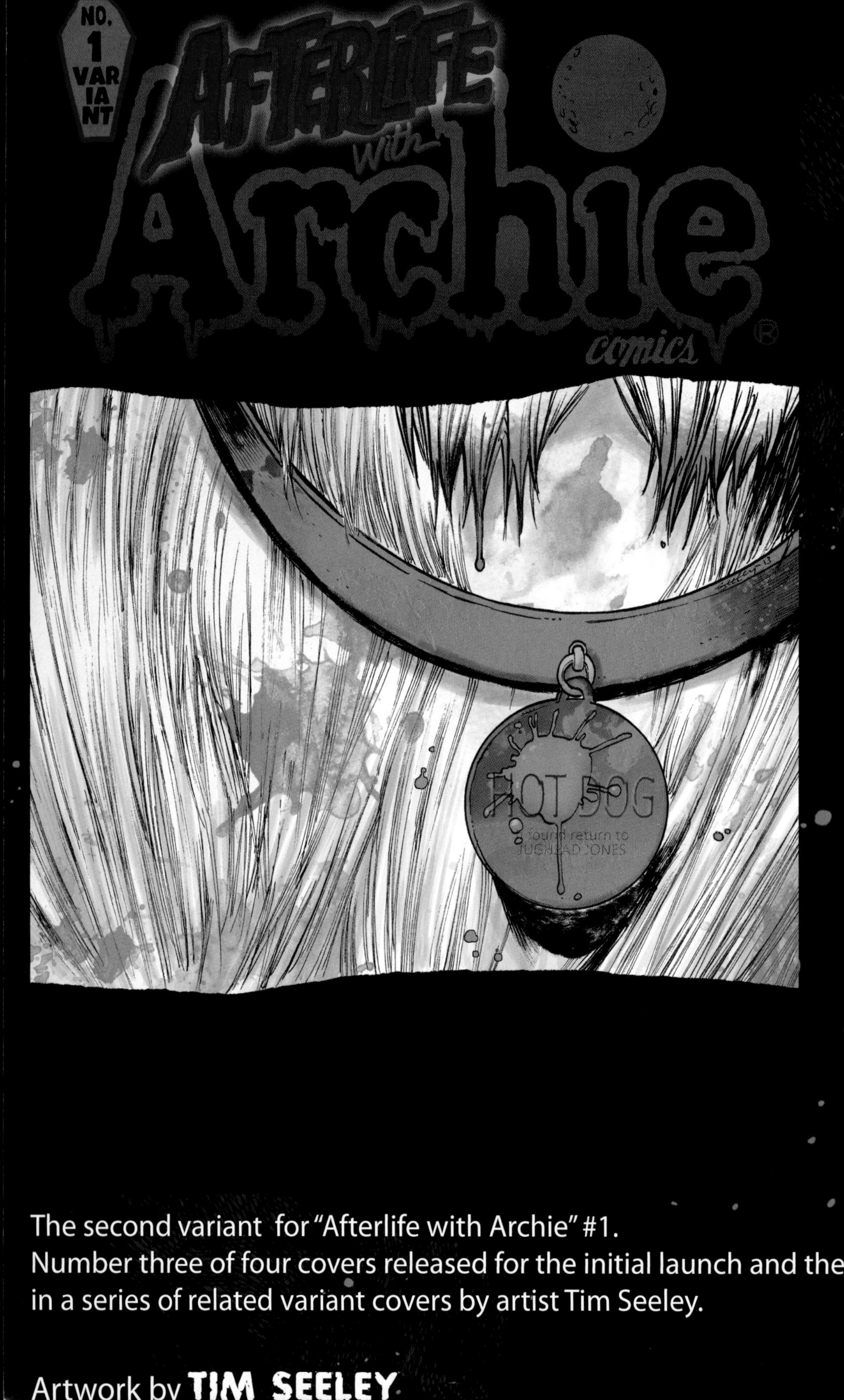
NO. 1 VARIANT
AFTERLIFE
with
Archie
comics
HOT DOG
If found return to
JUGHEAD JONES

The second variant for "Afterlife with Archie" #1.
Number three of four covers released for the initial launch and the
in a series of related variant covers by artist Tim Seeley.

Artwork by **TIM SEELEY**

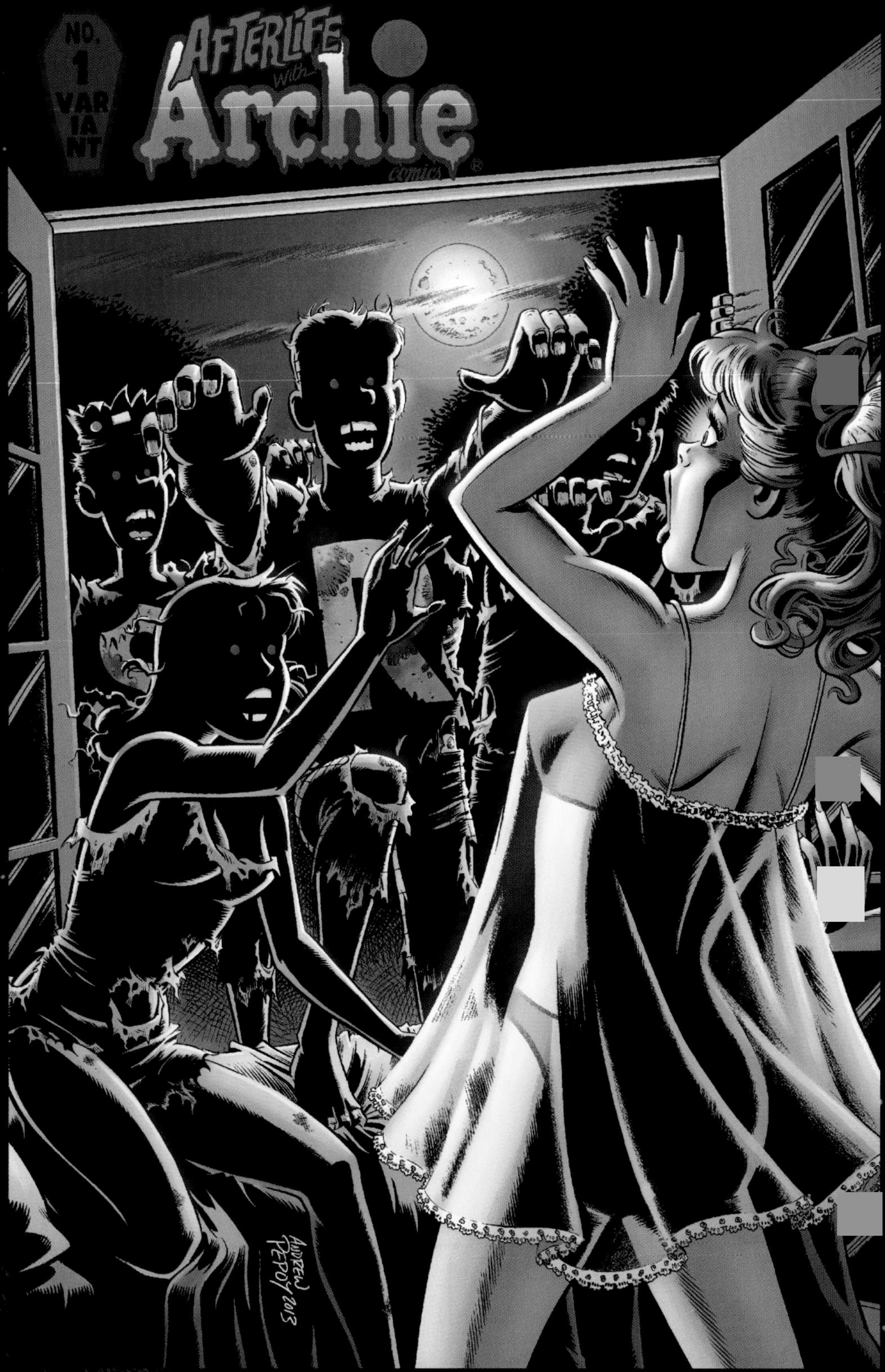
NO. 1 VARIANT
AFTERLIFE with Archie
comics
ANDREW PEPOY 2013

The third variant for "Afterlife with Archie" #1.
This cover proved to be one of our most popular variants, ranking second in overall sales of the initial print run of the first issue.

Artwork by **ANDREW PEPOY** AND **TITO PEÑA**

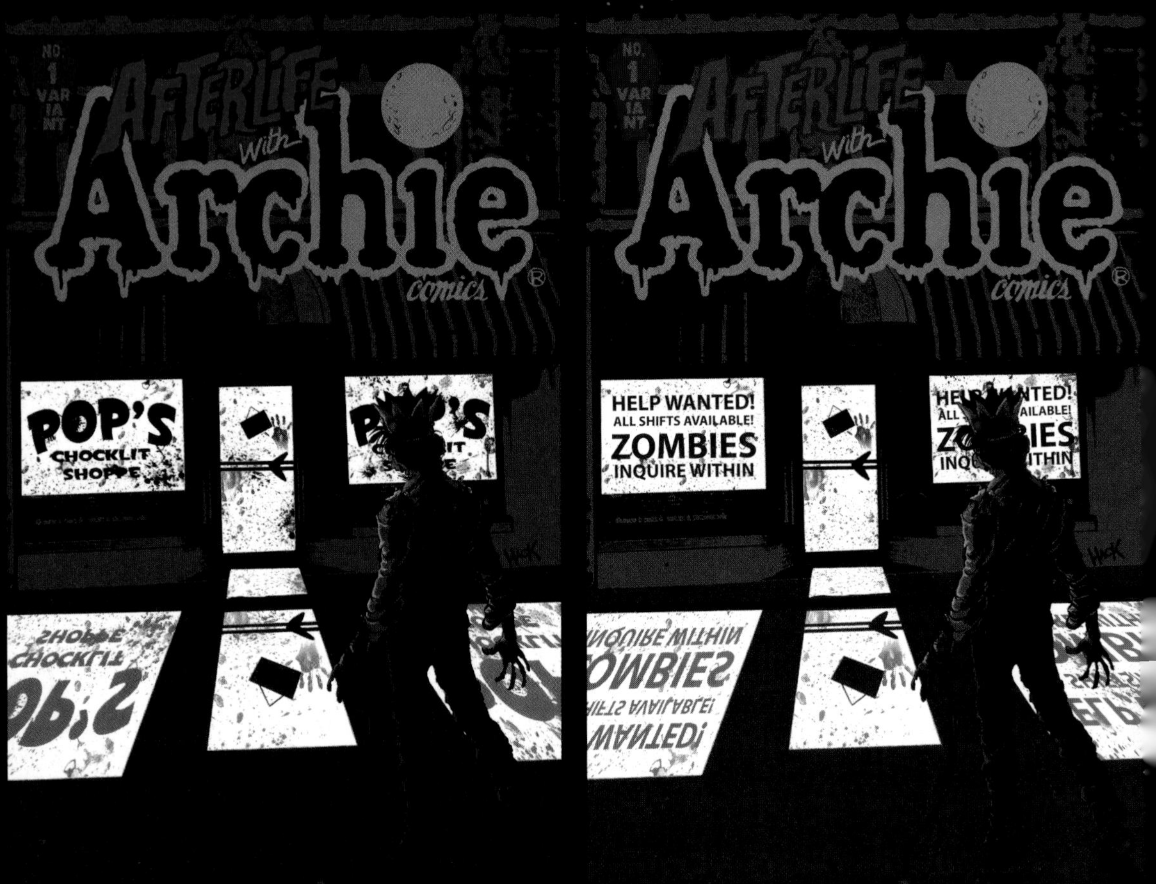
NO. 1 VARIANT
AFTERLIFE with Archie comics
POP'S CHOCKLIT SHOPPE
HELP WANTED! ALL SHIFTS AVAILABLE! ZOMBIES INQUIRE WITHIN

Limited Edition NY Comic Con variants for "Afterlife with Archie" #1.

Finding a single copy of the first print run of "Afterlife with Archie" #1 is difficult enough, these two variant covers are quite possibly the most elusive of the bunch.

Limited to only 400 copies, the "Bloody Pop's" variant cover, only available at the Archie Comics booth during the New York Comic Con, sold out within hours of the doors opening.

Initially only offered as an incentive to fans for showing their Archie love by attending the convention as an Archie-inspired zombie, the demand to sell was too great and only when every other copy of "Afterlife with Archie" #1 was sold, the "Help Wanted" variant was finally made available for purchase, selling out every issue of the 200 copy print run.

Artwork by **ROBERT HACK**

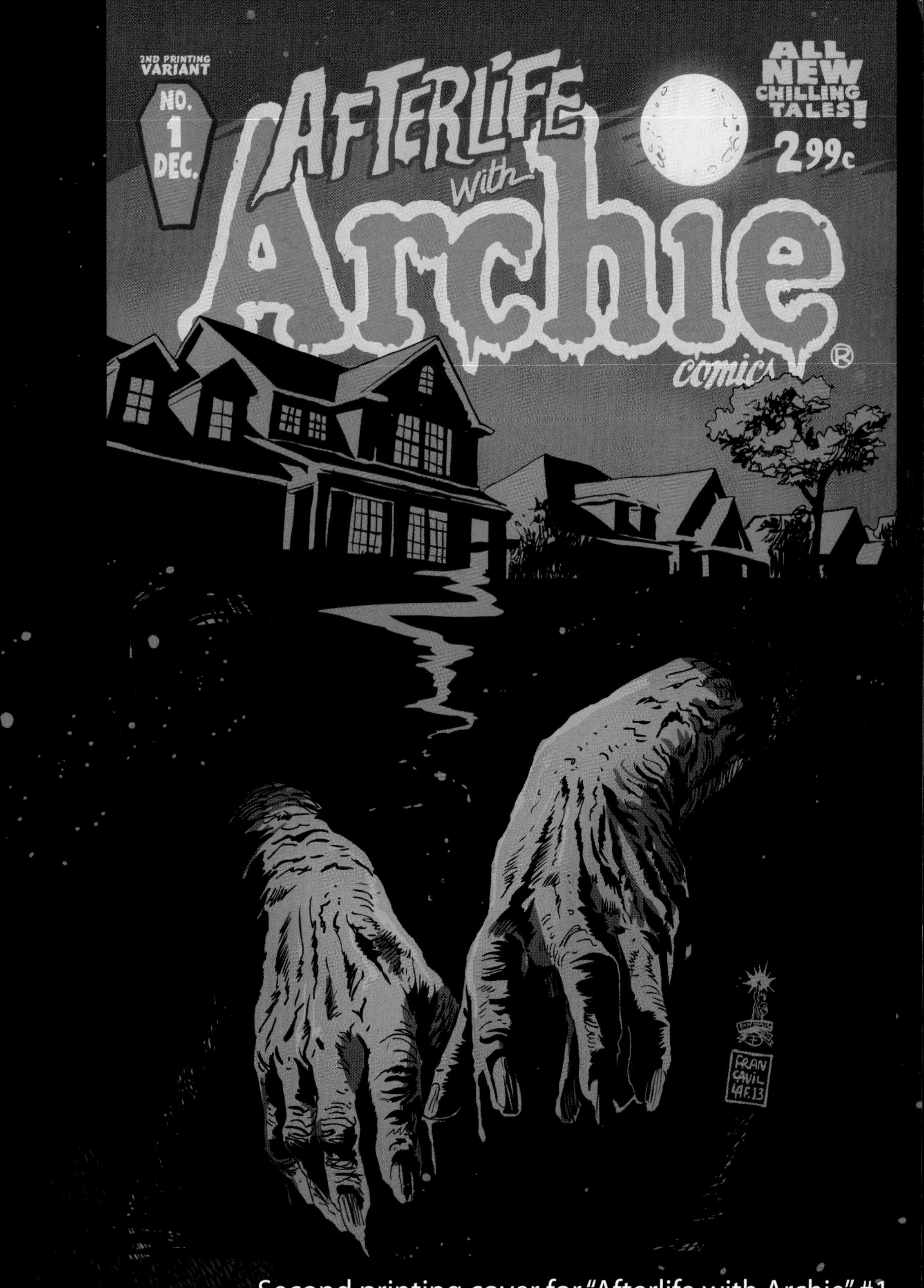
2ND PRINTING VARIANT
NO. 1 DEC.
AFTERLIFE with Archie comics
ALL NEW CHILLING TALES!
2.99c
FRAN CAVIL LAF.13

Second printing cover for "Afterlife with Archie" #1.
After the first print run of "Afterlife with Archie" #1 sold out across the country, artist Francesco Francavilla quickly responded with an all-new image for the second printing.

Artwork by **FRANCESCO FRANCAVILLA**

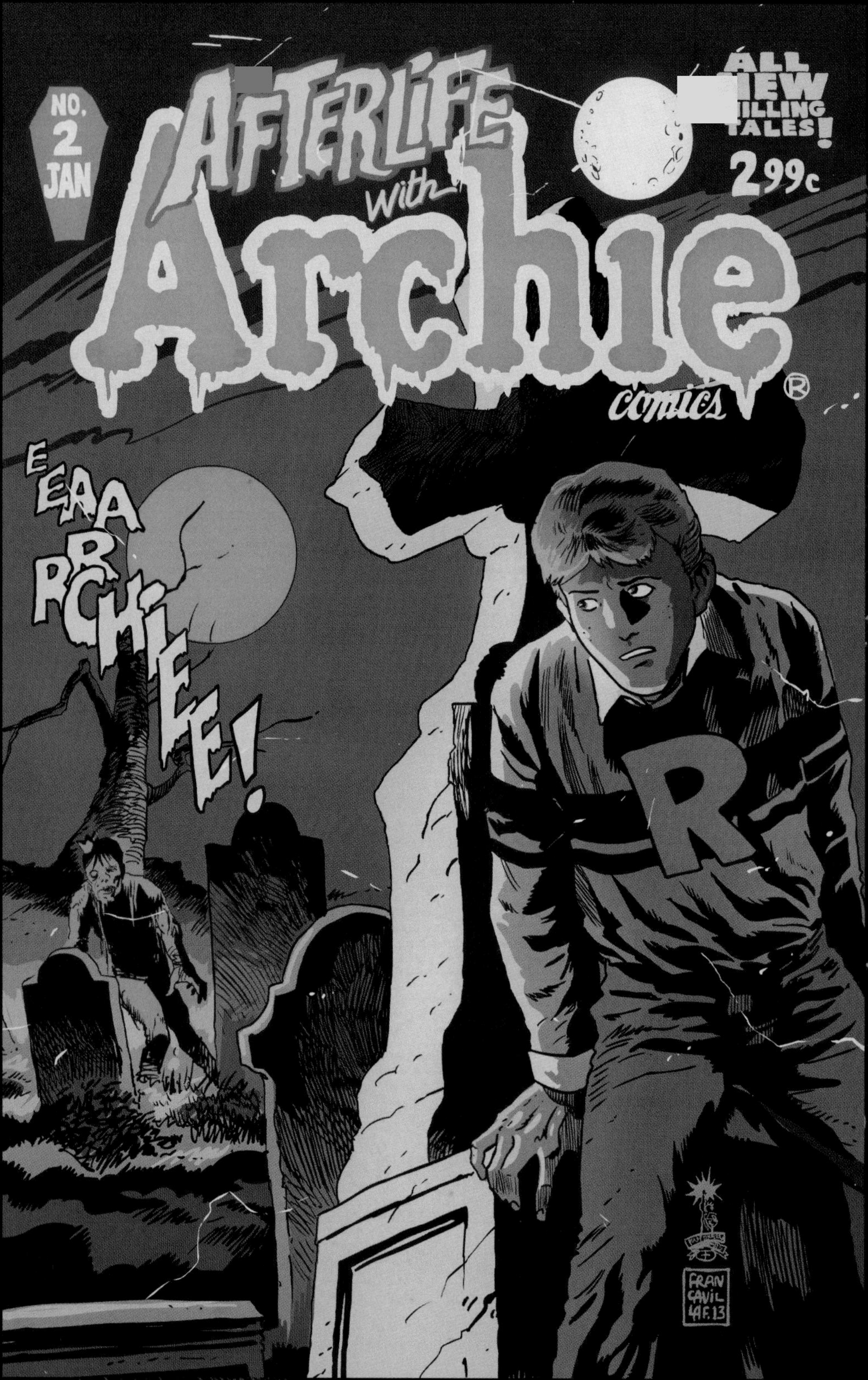
NO. 2 JAN
AFTERLIFE
with
Archie
comics
ALL
TALES!
2 99c
EEAAARRCHIEEE!

Cover for "Afterlife with Archie" #2.
While the original cover for issue #1 artfully gave fans a glimpse at what they could expect, artist Francesco Francavilla's cover for issue #2 intensified the terror and impending doom.

Artwork by **FRANCESCO FRANCAVILLA**

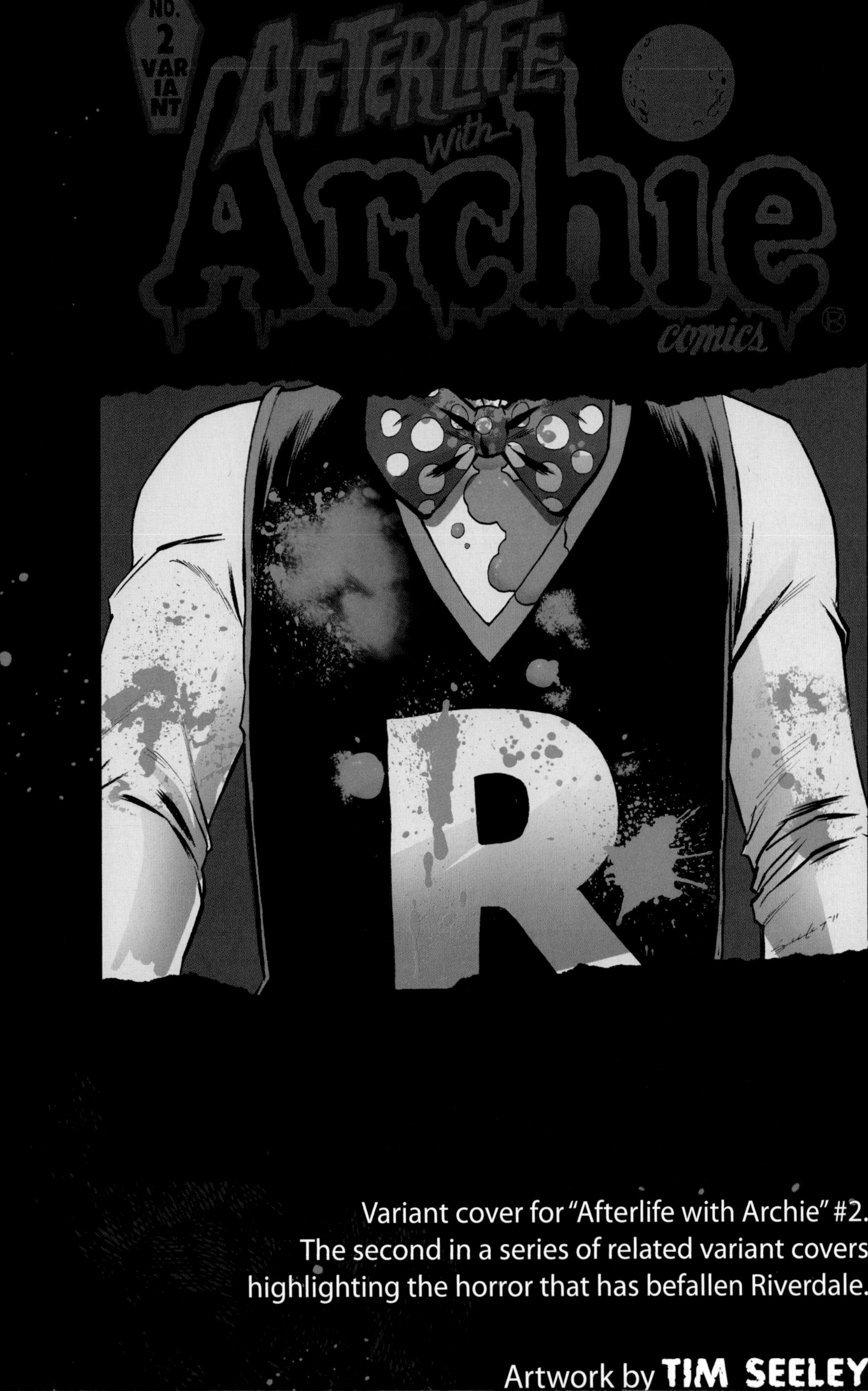
NO. 2 VARIANT
AFTERLIFE with Archie
comics

Variant cover for "Afterlife with Archie" #2.
The second in a series of related variant covers
highlighting the horror that has befallen Riverdale.

Artwork by **TIM SEELEY**

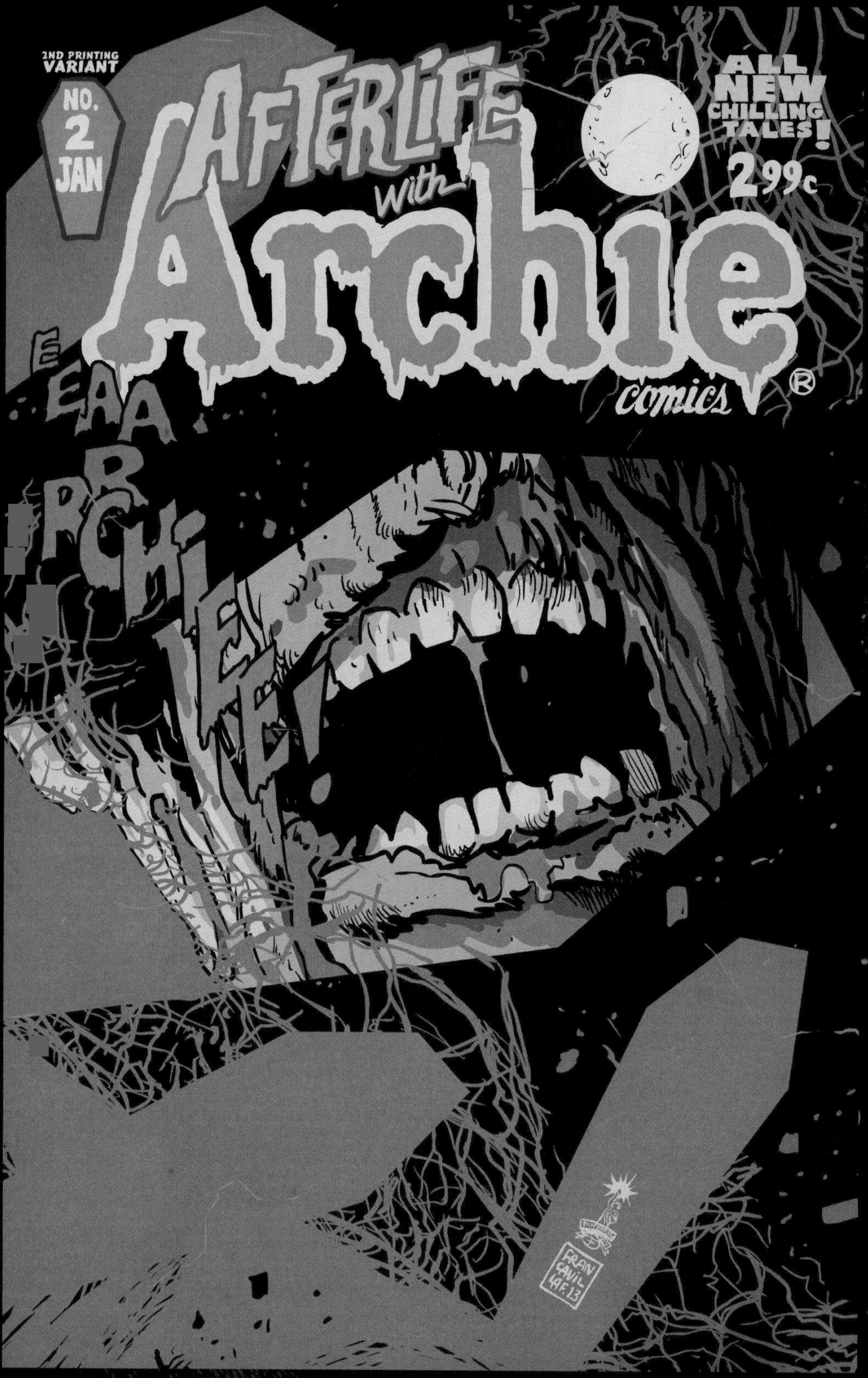
2ND PRINTING
VARIANT
NO. 2 JAN
AFTERLIFE
with
Archie
ALL NEW CHILLING TALES!
2.99c
comics

Second printing cover for "Afterlife with Archie" #2.
[redacted]nce again, "Afterlife with Archie" sold out across the country, so Francesco Francavilla provided an all-new cover for the second printing of the break-out series.

Artwork by **FRANCESCO FRANCAVILLA**

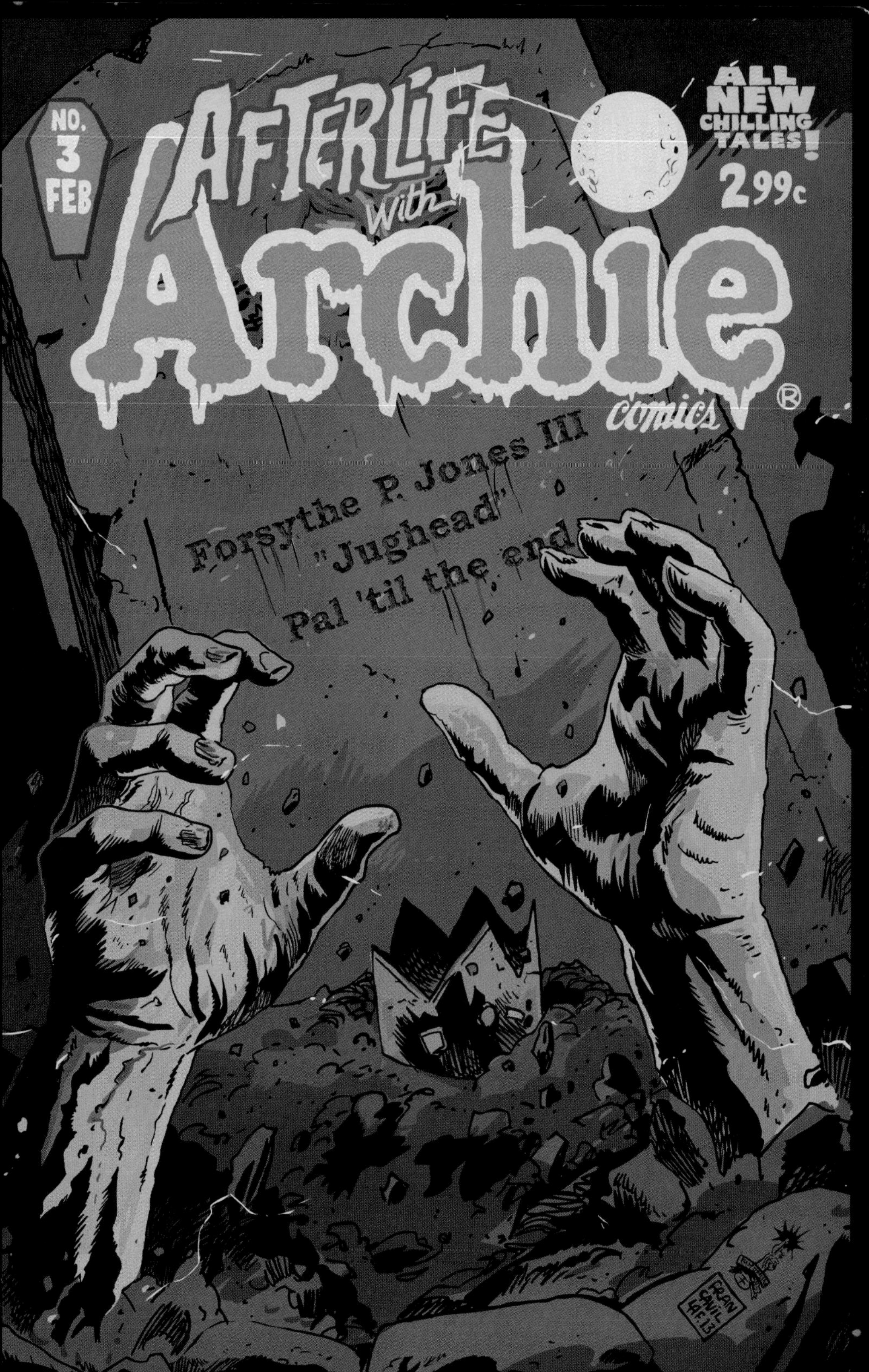
NO. 3 FEB
AFTERLIFE with Archie
comics
ALL NEW CHILLING TALES!
2.99c
Forsythe P. Jones III
"Jughead"
Pal 'til the end

Cover for "Afterlife with Archie" #3.
as the series broke new ground for Archie Comics, artist Francesco Francavilla has Jugdead breaking through his grave and rising to terrorize Riverdale.

Artwork by **FRANCESCO FRANCAVILLA**

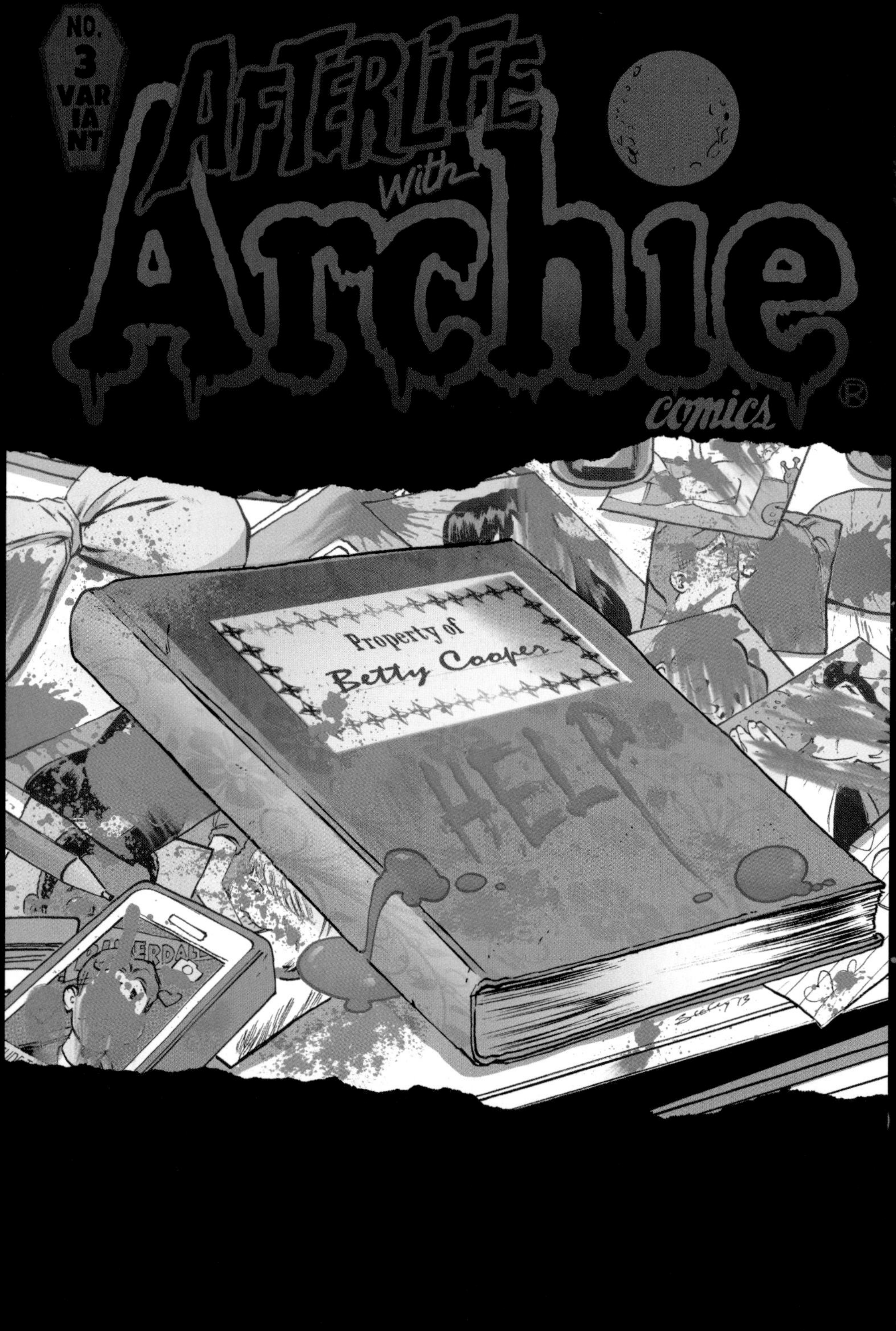
NO. 3 VARIANT
AFTERLIFE with Archie comics
Property of Betty Cooper
HELP
Seeley '13

Variant cover for "Afterlife with Archie" #3.
The third in a series of related variant covers, this time bringing the horror home, in a personal way, for Betty Cooper.

Artwork by **TIM SEELEY**

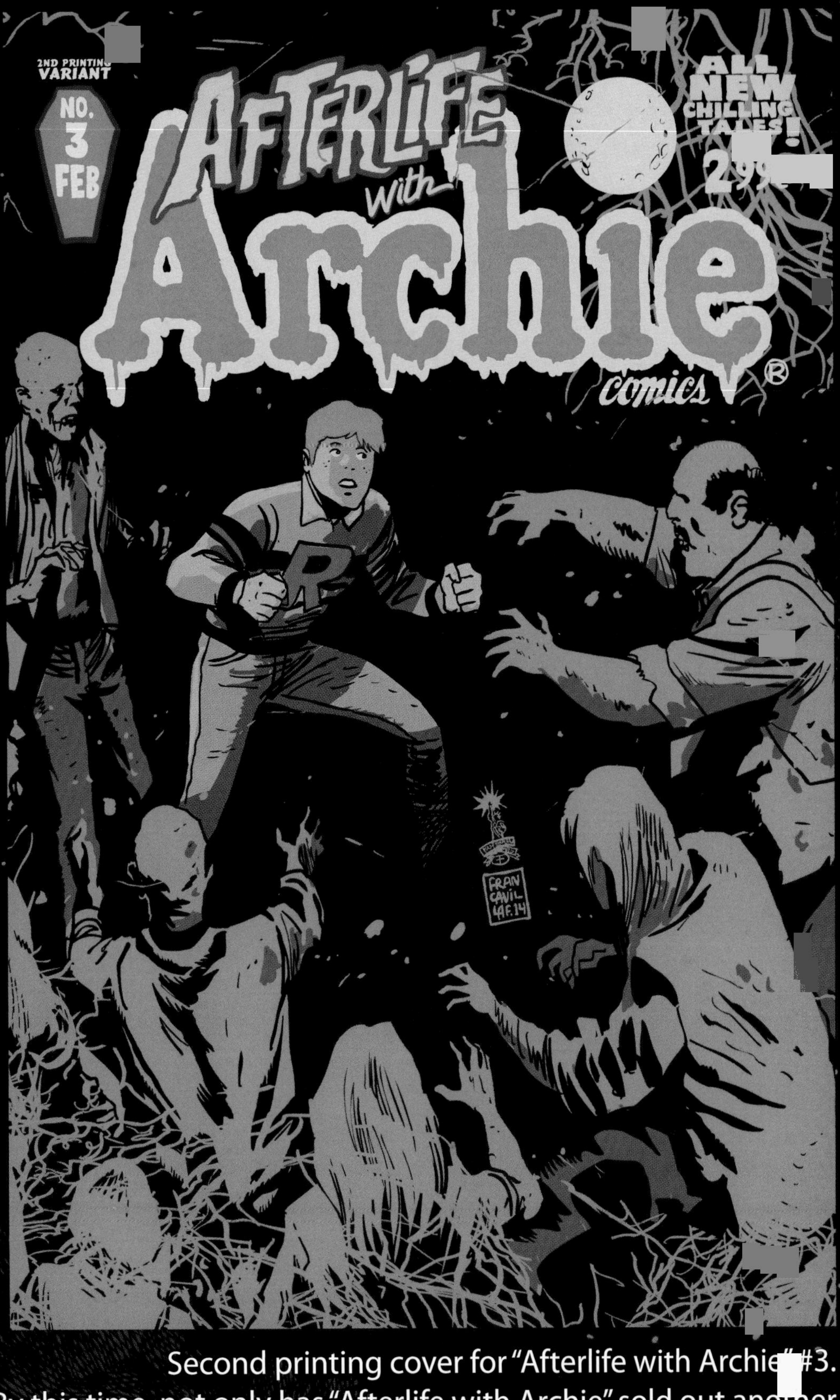
2ND PRINTING VARIANT
NO. 3 FEB
AFTERLIFE with Archie
ALL NEW CHILLING TALES!
comics

Second printing cover for "Afterlife with Archie" #3. By this time, not only has "Afterlife with Archie" sold out another printing of its latest issue, but it has become a multi-award winning series, garnering praise from reviewers and celebrities alike.

Artwork by **FRANCESCO FRANCAVILLA**

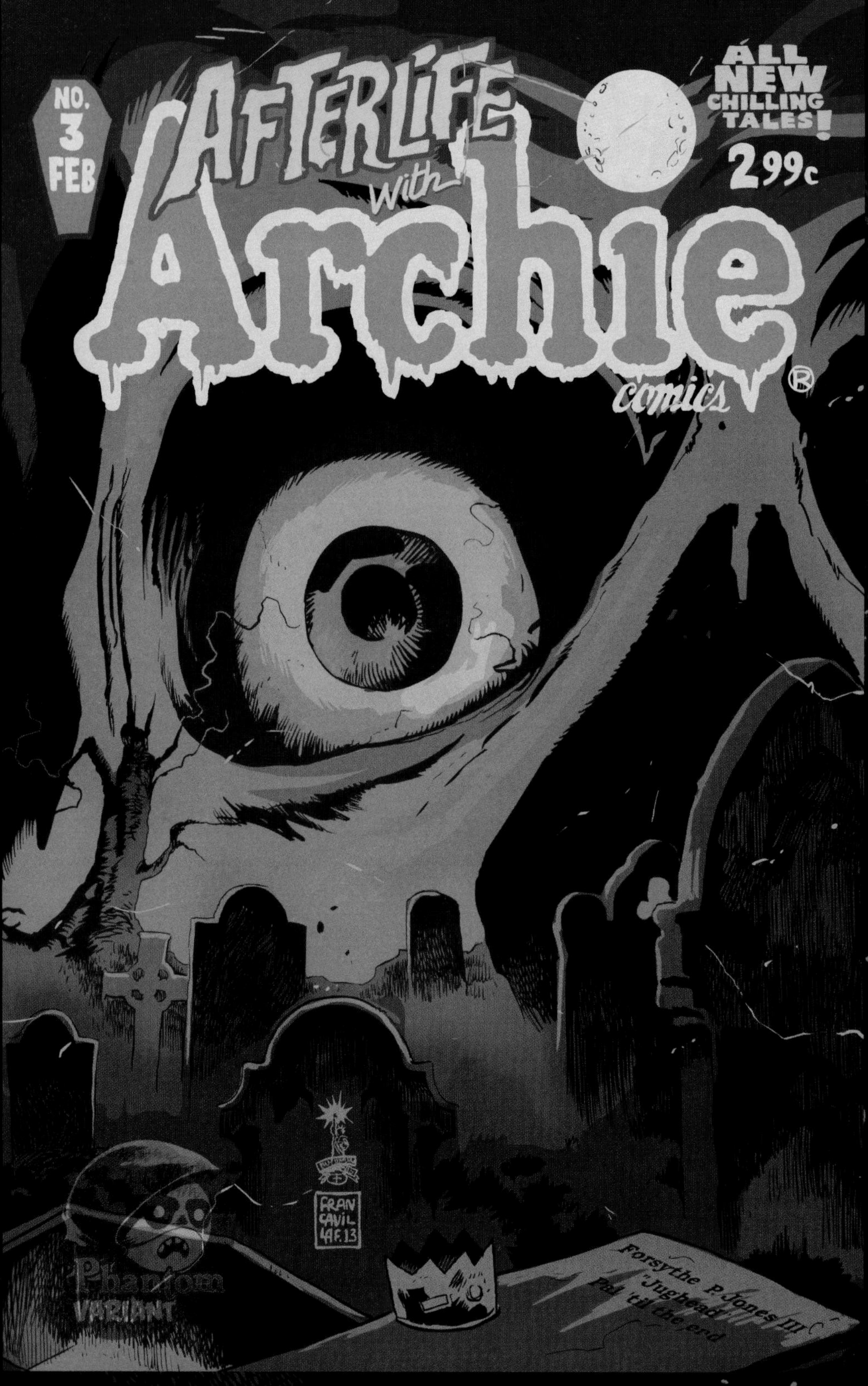
NO. 3 FEB
AFTERLIFE with Archie
comics
ALL NEW CHILLING TALES!
2.99c
FRAN CAVIL LAF.13
Phantom VARIANT
Forsythe P. Jones III
"Jughead"
Pal 'til the end

Phantom variant cover for "Afterlife with Archie" #3.
With the all of the positive reviews and praise pouring in, Archie Comics was approached by the Phantom Group, a collection of comics retailers, to provide an exclusive variant cover for issue #3.

Artwork by **FRANCESCO FRANCAVILLA**

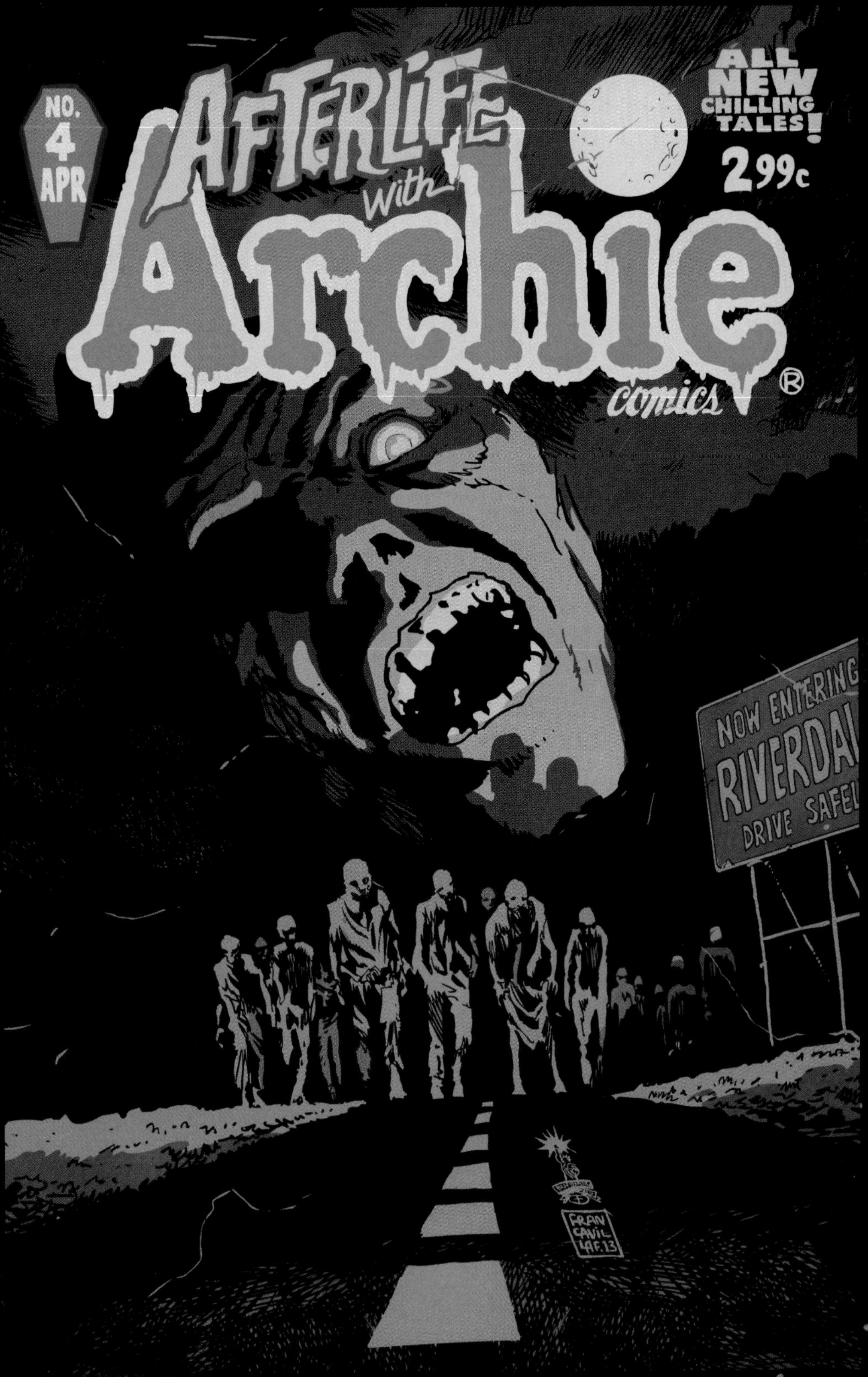
NO. 4 APR
AFTERLIFE with ARCHIE
comics ®
ALL NEW CHILLING TALES!
2.99c
NOW ENTERING RIVERDA
DRIVE SAFEL
FRAN CAVIL LAF.13

Cover for "Afterlife with Archie" #4
The horde has amassed and the end is near. Artist Francesco Francavilla brings the terror to the forefront as Jugdead oversees his army on the march.

Artwork by **FRANCESCO FRANCAVILLA**

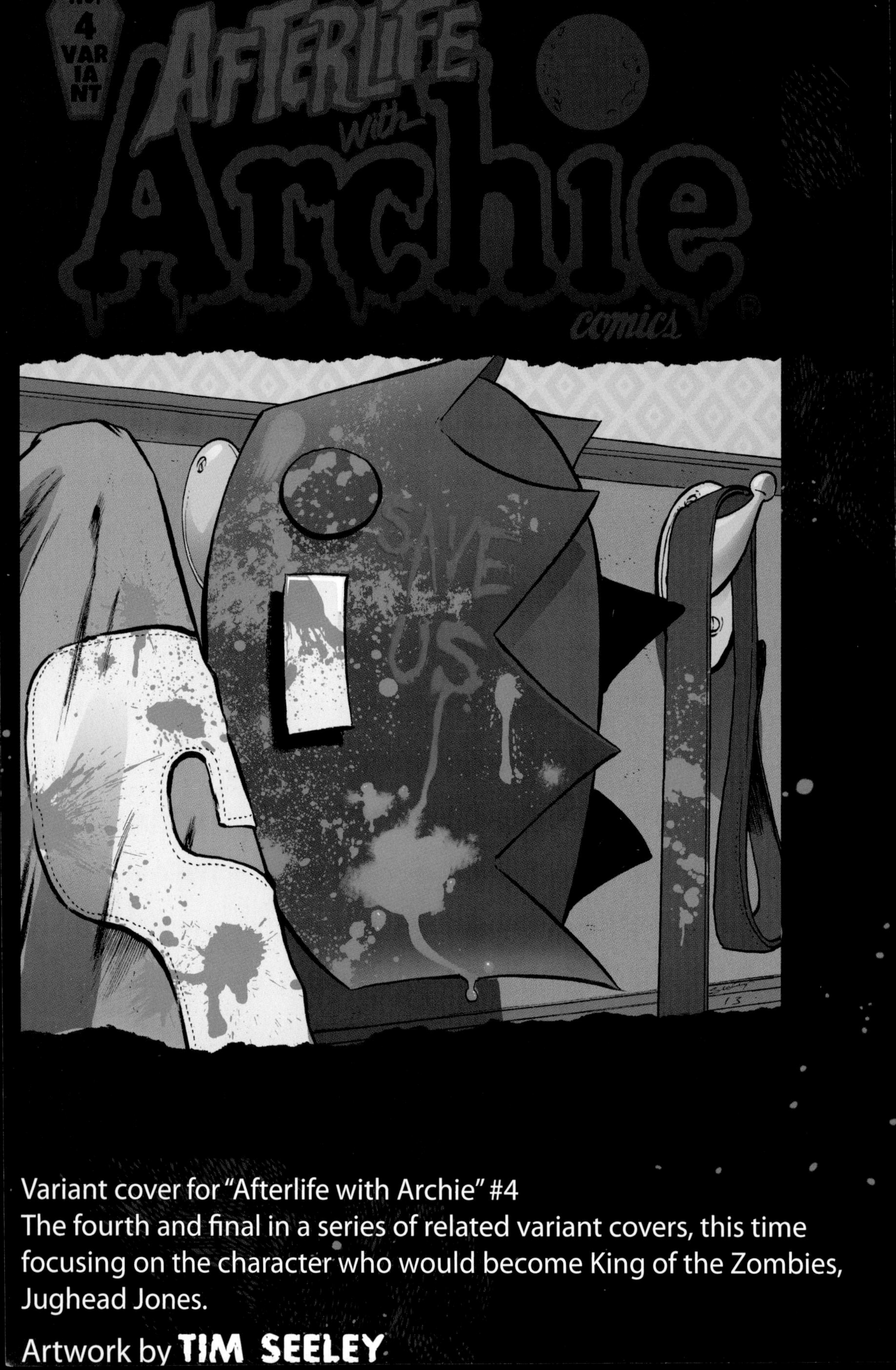
4
VARIANT
AFTERLIFE with Archie
comics
SAVE US

Variant cover for "Afterlife with Archie" #4
The fourth and final in a series of related variant covers, this time focusing on the character who would become King of the Zombies, Jughead Jones.

Artwork by **TIM SEELEY**

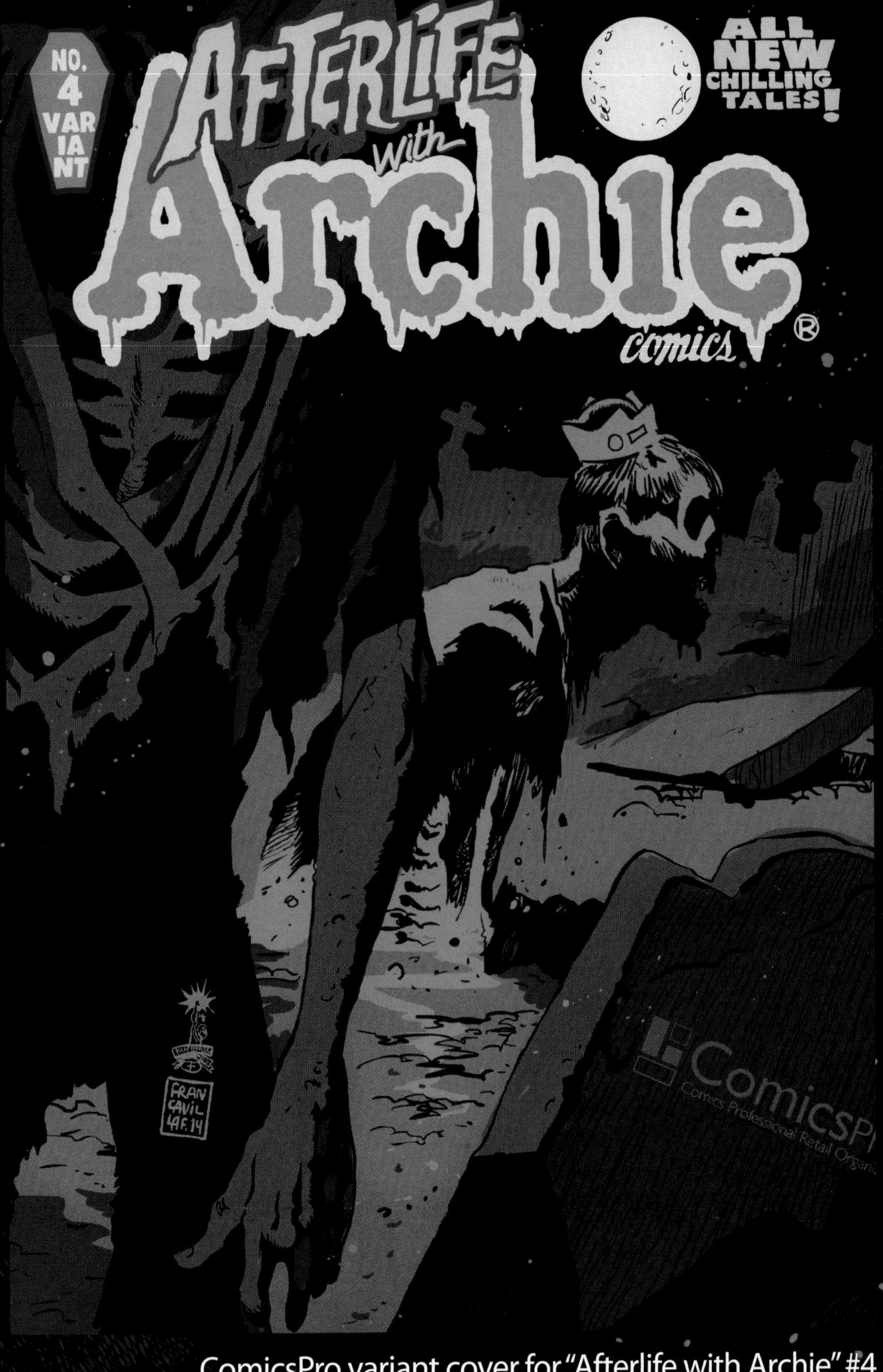
NO. 4 VARIANT
AFTERLIFE with Archie
comics®
ALL NEW CHILLING TALES!
FRAN CAVIL LAF.14
ComicsPro
Comics Professional Retail Organi

ComicsPro variant cover for "Afterlife with Archie" #4
When Archie Comics was approached to provide an exclusive cover for the Comics Professional Retailer Organization, artist Francesco Francavilla took it to the graveyard and delivered this spine-tingling image.

Artwork by **FRANCESCO FRANCAVILLA**

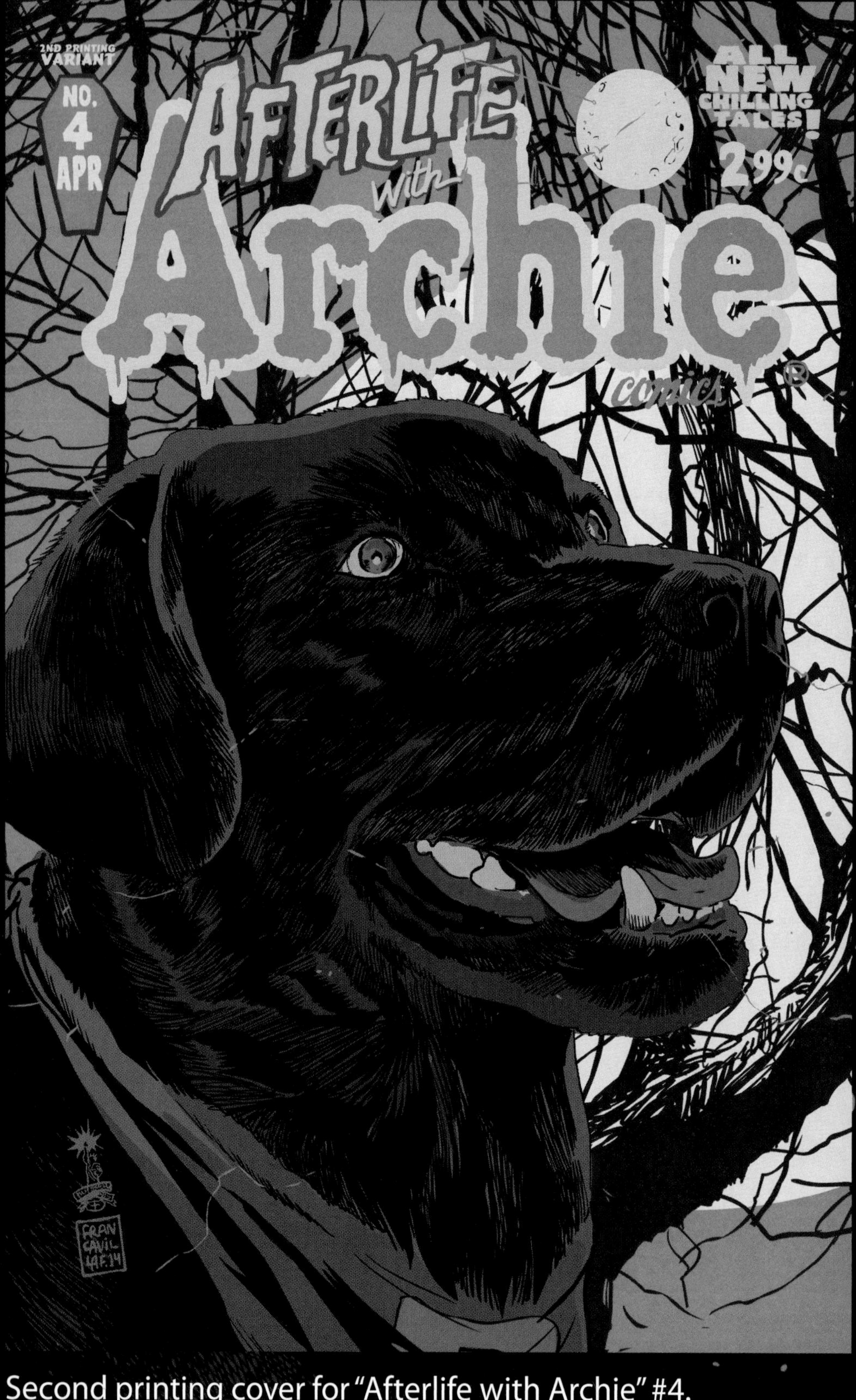
2ND PRINTING VARIANT
NO. 4 APR
AFTERLIFE with Archie comics
ALL NEW CHILLING TALES!
2.99¢
FRAN CAVIL LAF.14

Second printing cover for "Afterlife with Archie" #4.
Artist Francesco Francavilla takes a different approach to the second printing cover for issue #4, focusing upon a key hero from writer Roberto Aguirre-Sacasa's latest installment.

Artwork by **FRANCESCO FRANCAVILLA**

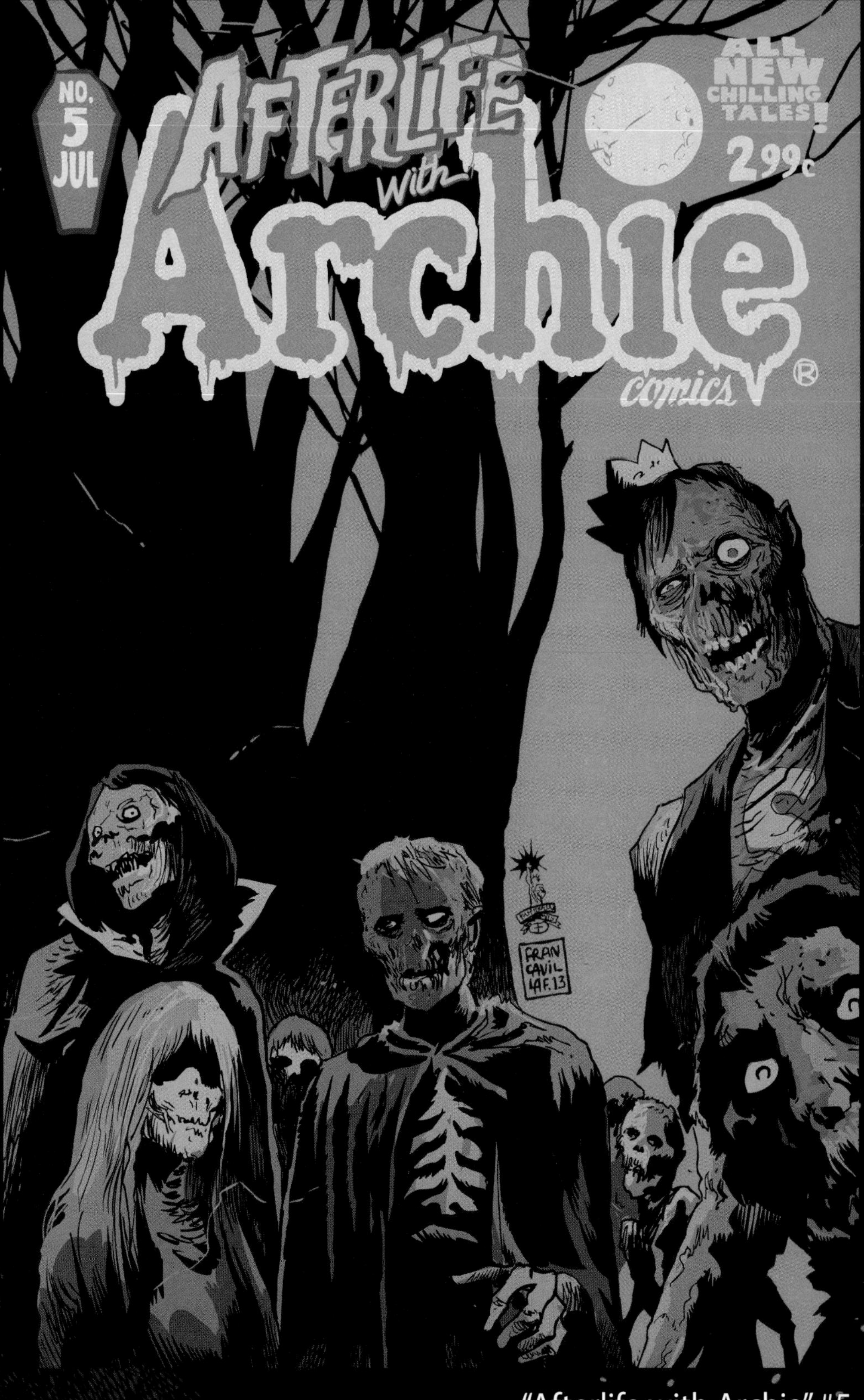
NO. 5 JUL
AFTERLIFE
with
Archie
comics
ALL NEW CHILLING TALES!

"Afterlife with Archie" #5.
Jugdead and his follows are coming to get you in this cover for this fifth and final issue of our first arc, "Escape from Riverdale."

Artwork by **FRANCESCO FRANCAVILLA**

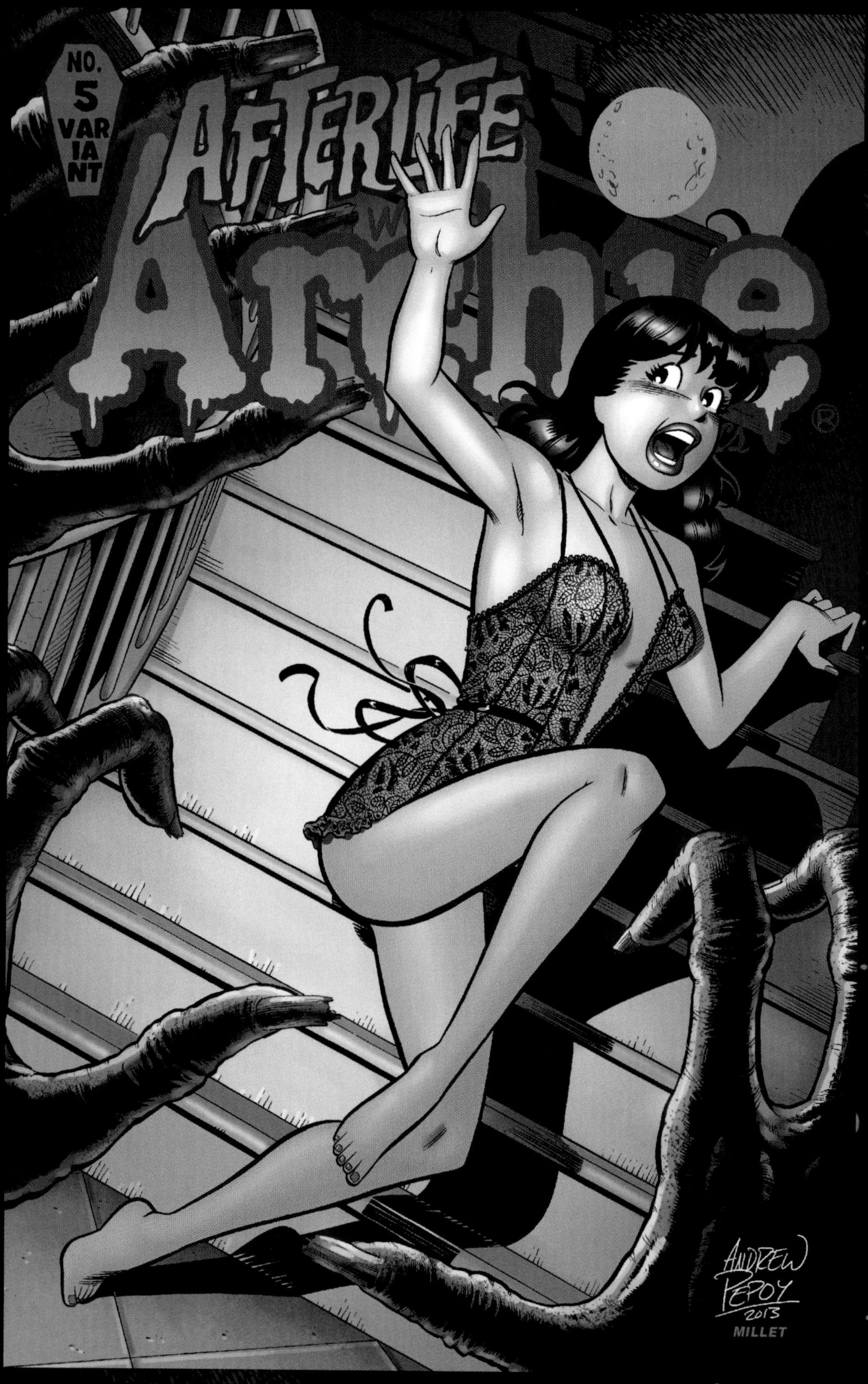
NO. 5 VARIANT
AFTERLIFE
Archie
ANDREW PEPOY 2013
MILLET

Variant cover for "Afterlife with Archie" #5.
Artist Andrew Pepoy brings a horror pin-up flair to this variant cover for issue #5.

Artwork by **ANDREW PEPOY AND JASON MILLET**

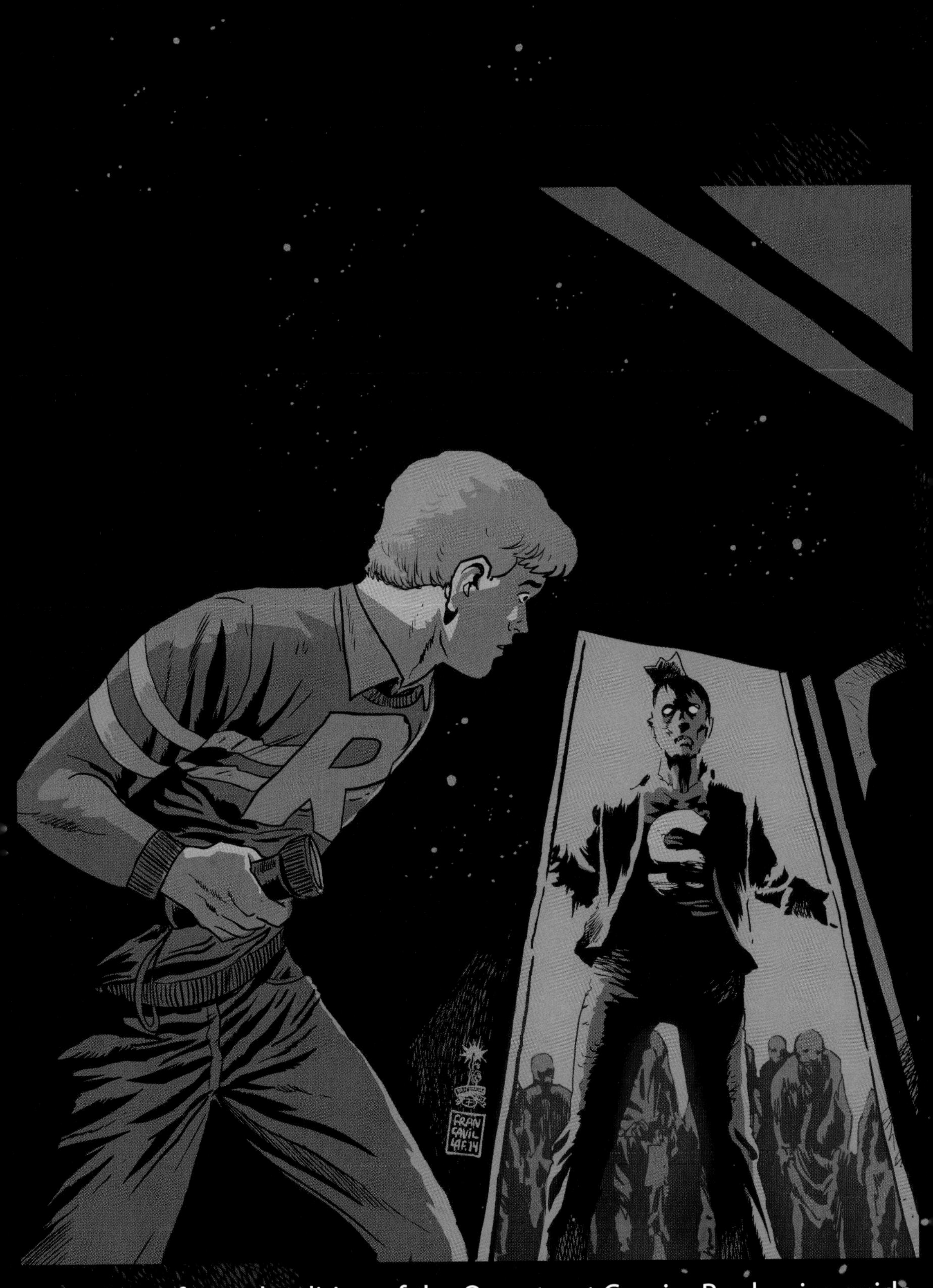

Cover for 44th edition of the Overstreet Comics Book price guide. *Here's Jugdead!* In this single image, artist Francesco Francavilla tells an entire chilling story.

Artwork by **FRANCESCO FRANCAVILLA**

SKETCHES OF THE DEAD

A very good day is when an e-mail appears in your Inbox, and it's from Francesco
Francavilla, and he's sending you pages he's drawn based on a Word Document
you e-mailed him who knows how many weeks earlier. Before you get the final
inked and colored pages, you get Francesco's pencils. He usually sends them to
you in two chunks; the first twelve pages, then the second. The pencils are tight—
meaning, they're very close to what the final pages will be. They are gorgeous,
and could be published as is—which is part of the reason they're included here:
Because why should we be the only ones who get a peek into Francesco's process—
his notebooks? Every single page is stunning—and here, in this book, you can
see how even slight adjustments between pencils and finished artwork make an
enormous difference. Compare, for instance, Francesco's first take on the death of
Fred Andrews to his final version. It's still a grid, but it's less repetitious, and the
individual panels tell a greater story. (Truly a "Mondrian of horror" page, which
is how Francesco described it.) When I saw the pencils for that page, I thought,
"Perfect." When I got the inked and colored version, I thought, "How did he make
it better?" It's a question I find myself asking a lot these days.

Roberto Aguirre-Sacasa

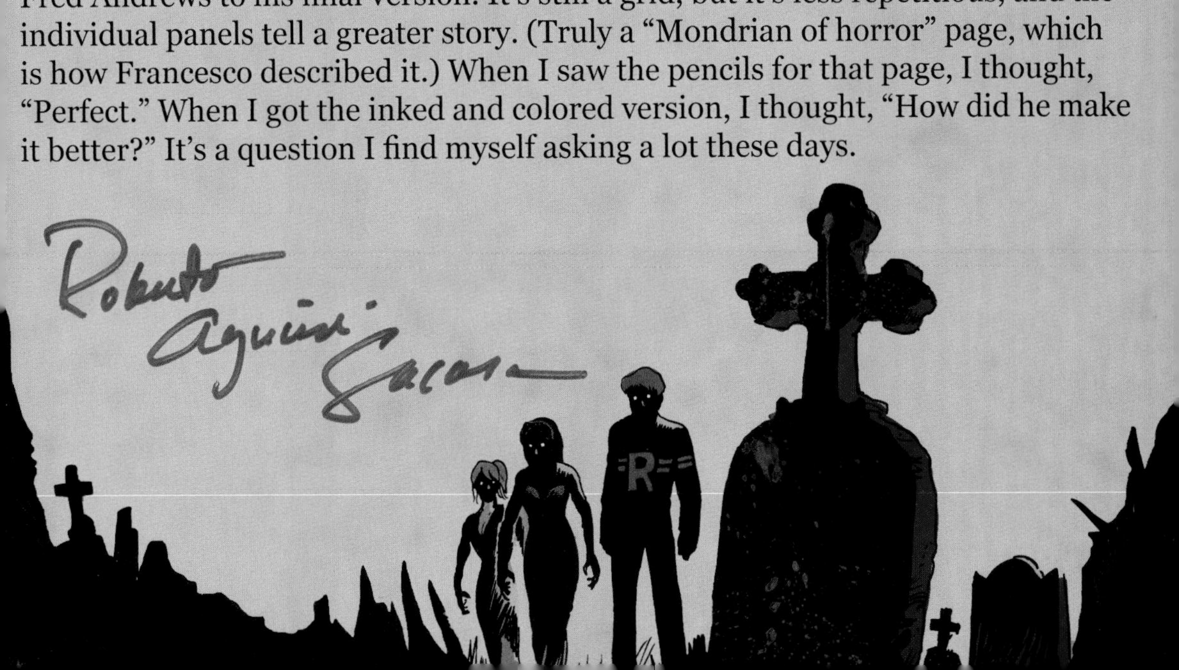

In these next few pages, take a look at the layouts and brilliant framework of artist Francesco Francavilla's gorgeous art for chapters 1-5.

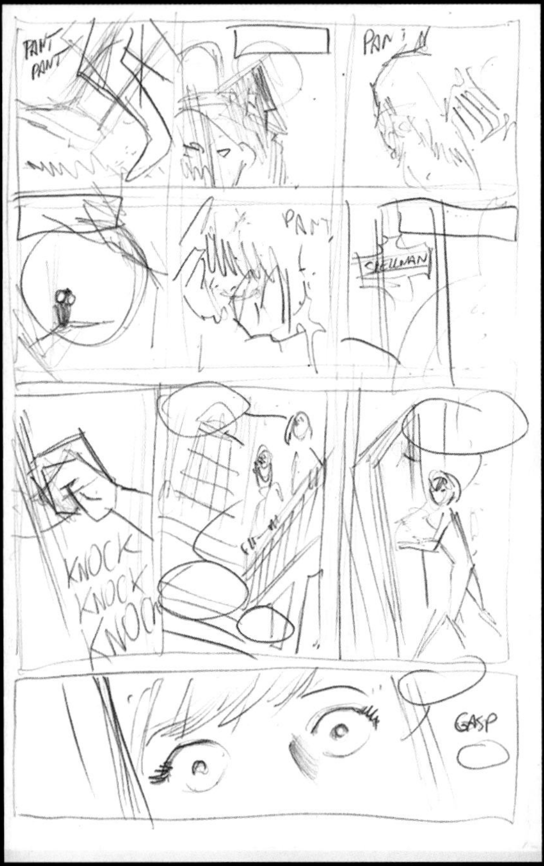
PANT PANT
PANT
PANT
SPELLMAN
KNOCK KNOCK KNOC
GASP

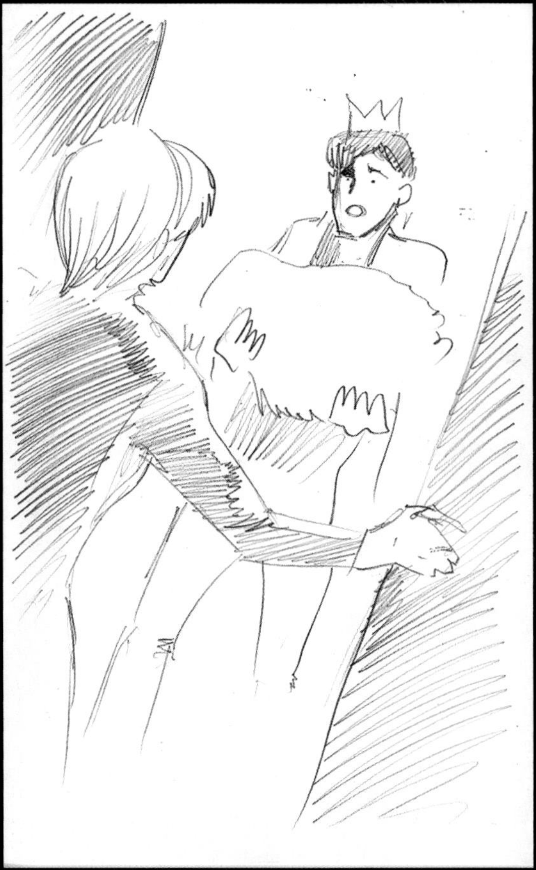

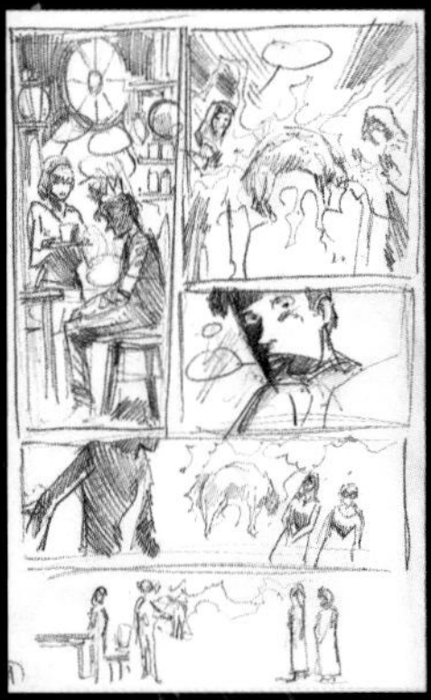

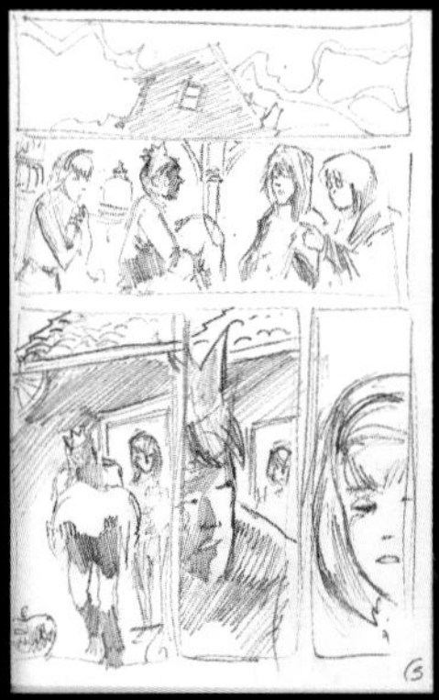

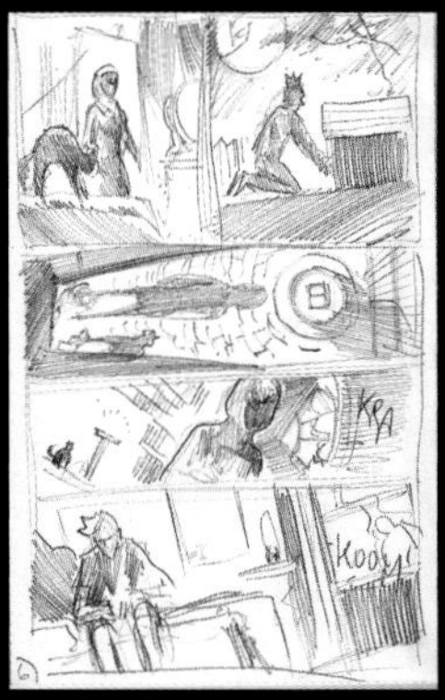

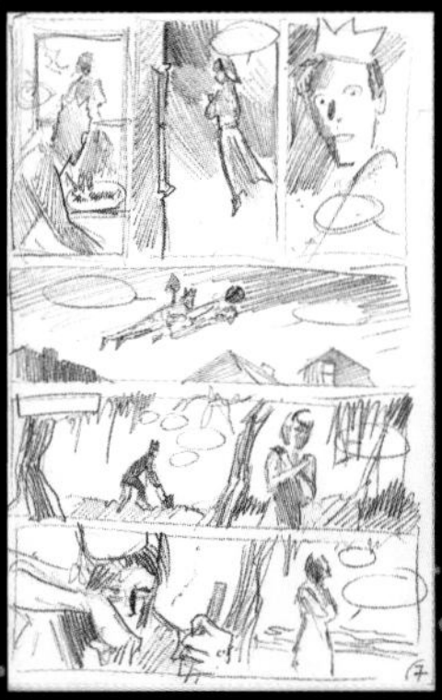

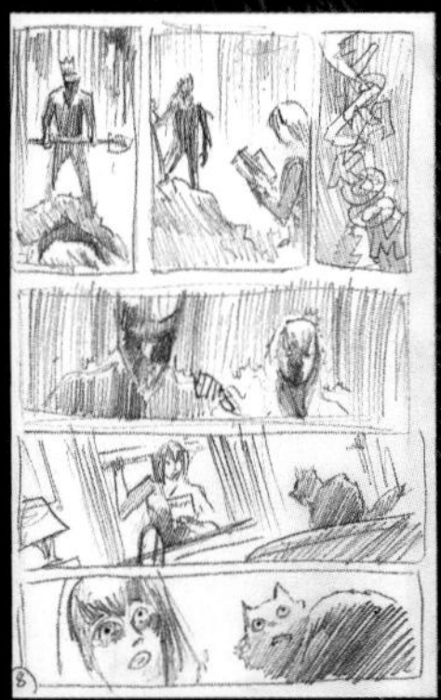

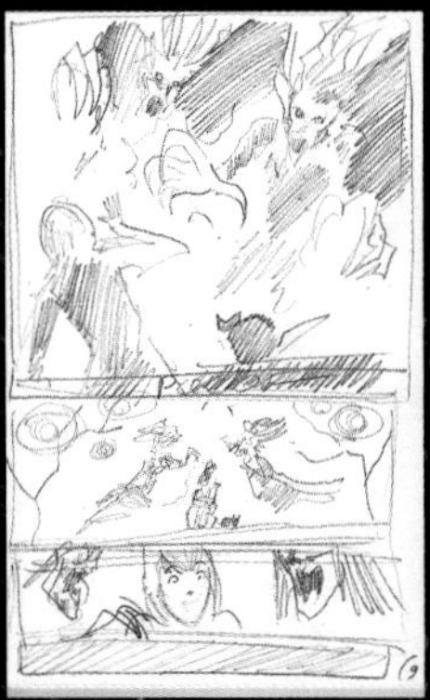

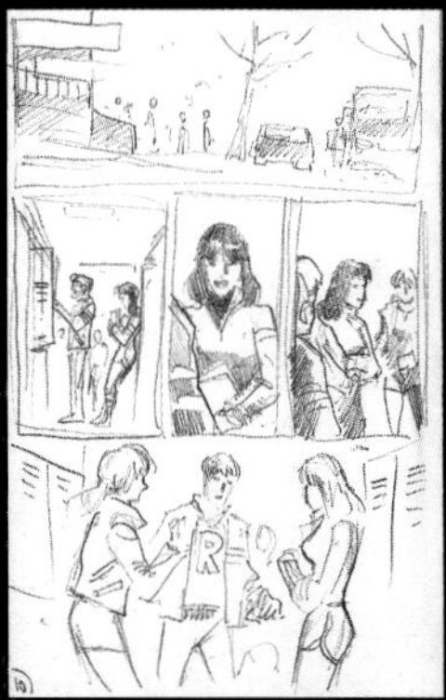

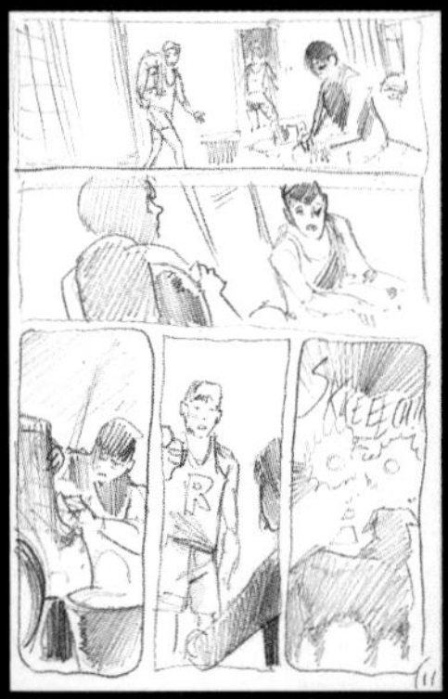

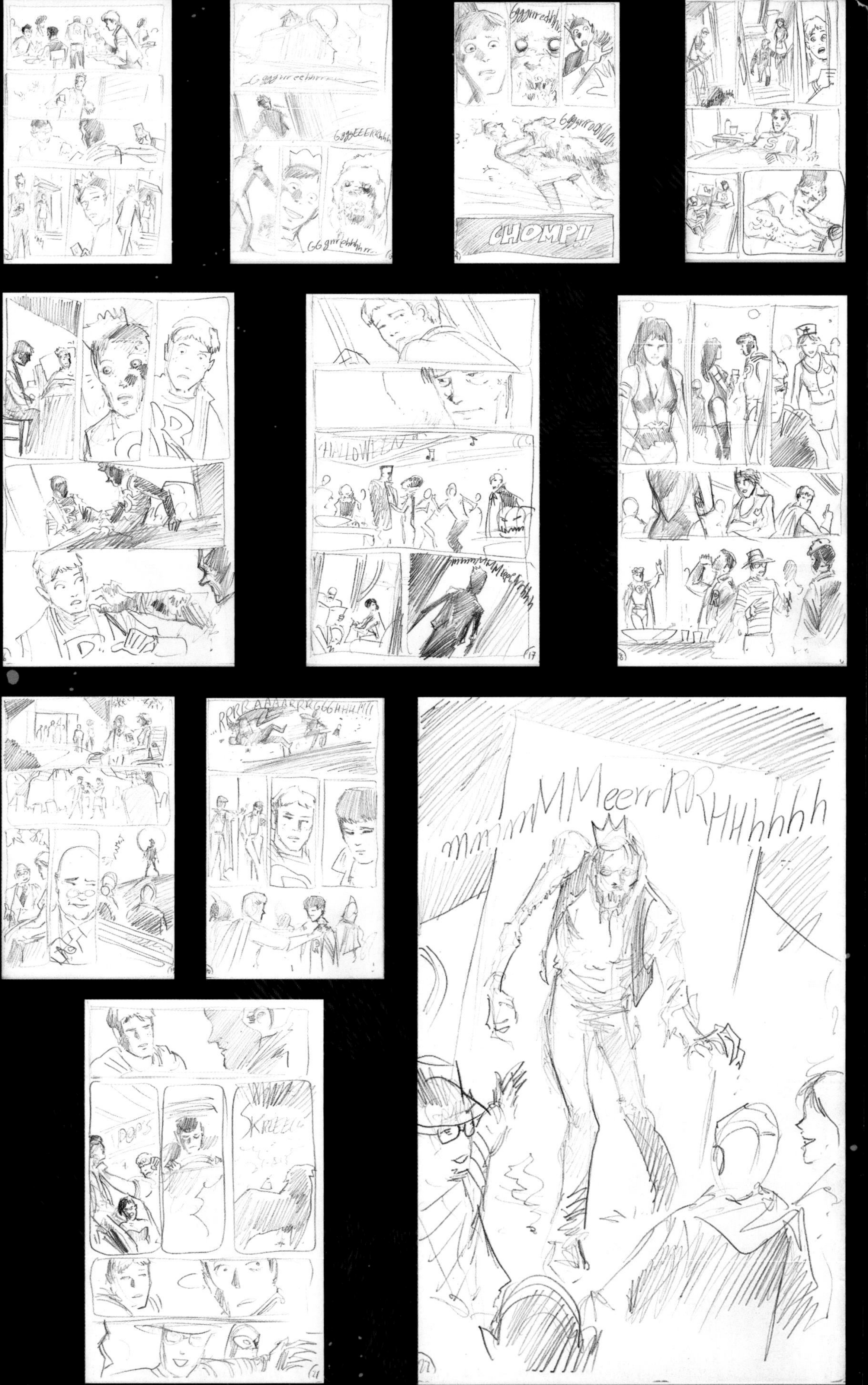
CHOMP!!
HALLOWEEN
MMmmMMeerrRRHHhhhh
POP'S

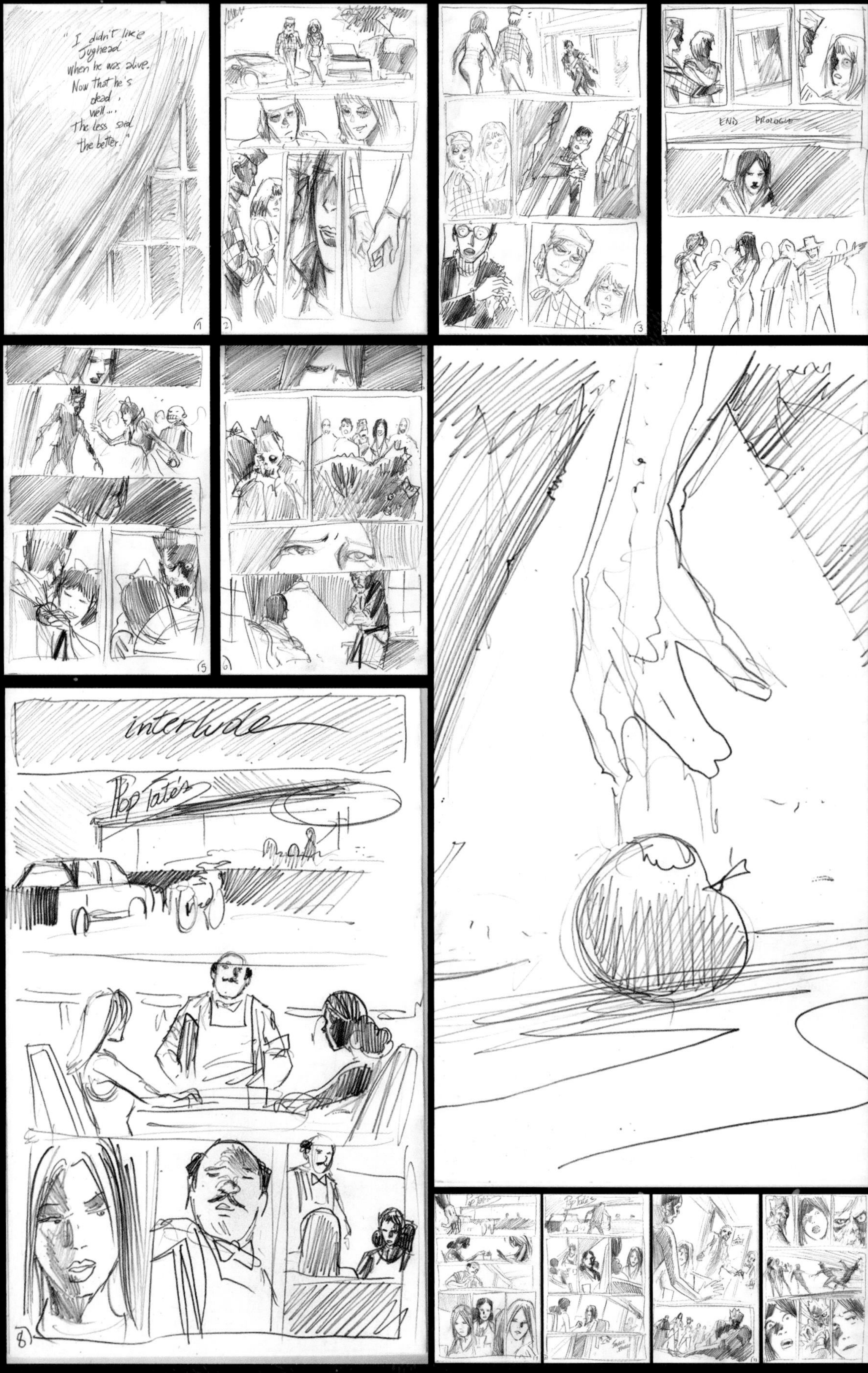
"I didn't like Jughead when he was alive. Now that he's dead, well.... The less said the better."
END PROLOGUE
interlude
Pop Tate's

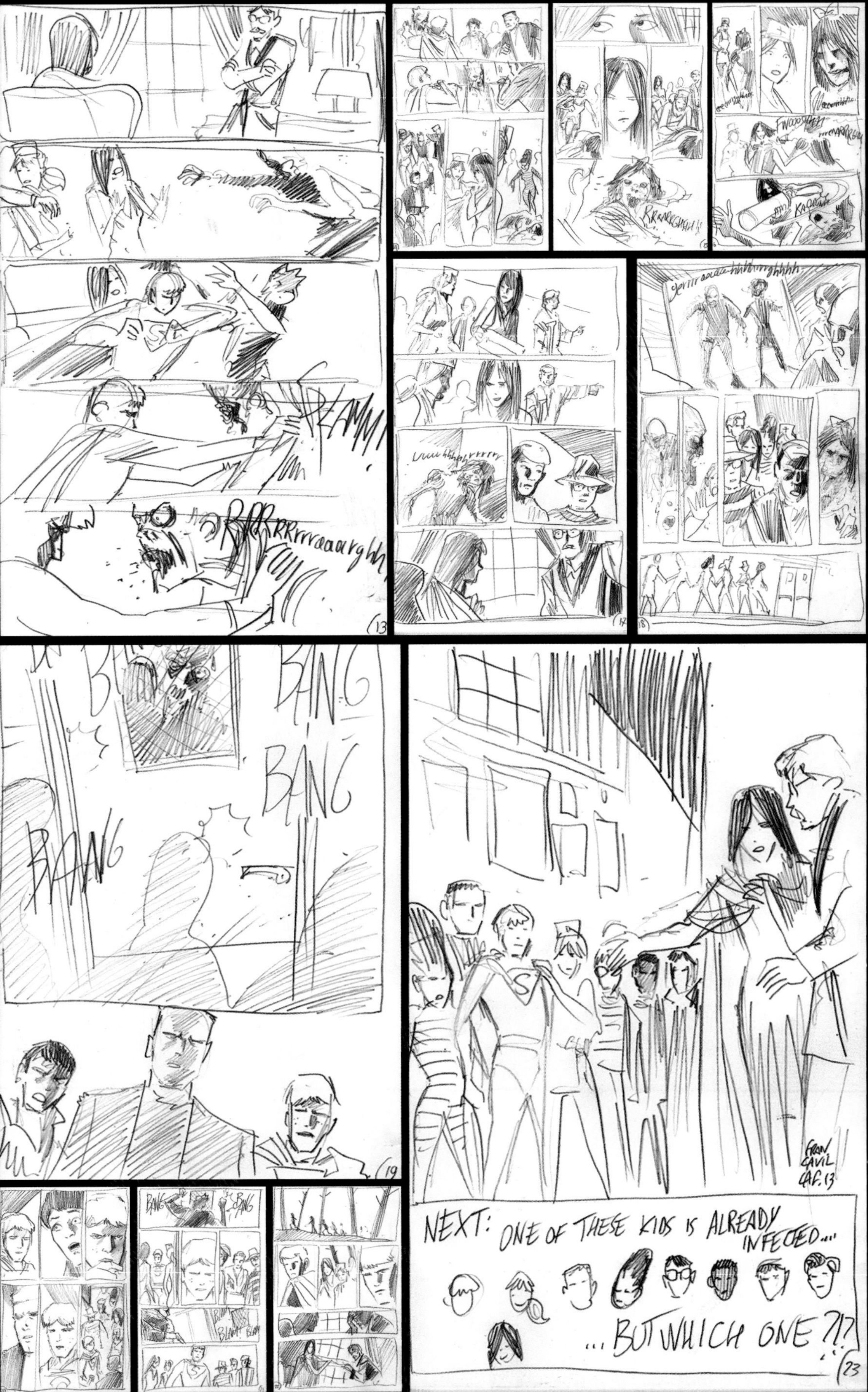
BANG
BANG
BANG
BANG
NEXT: ONE OF THESE KIDS IS ALREADY INFECTED...
...BUT WHICH ONE?!?

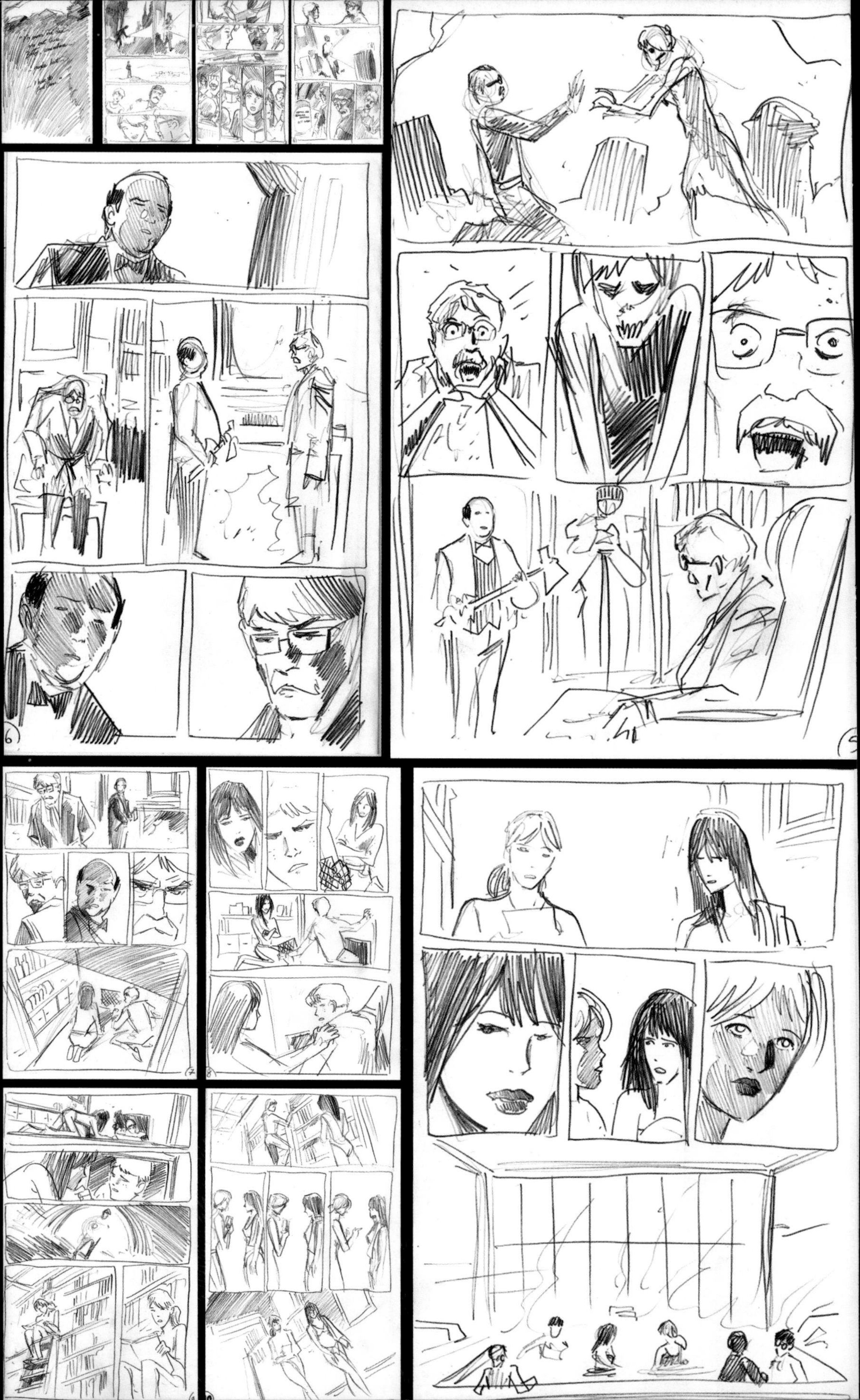

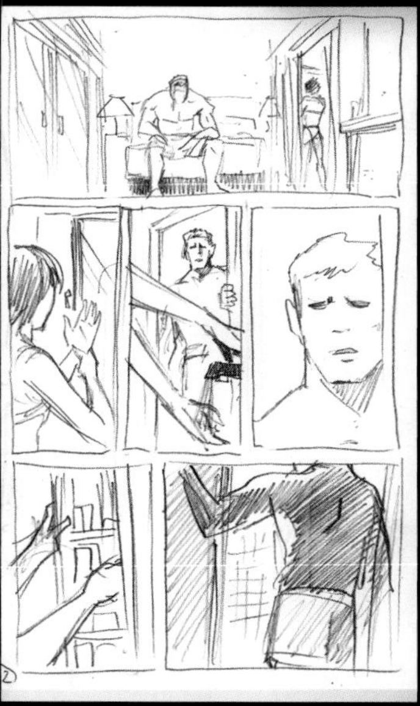
12

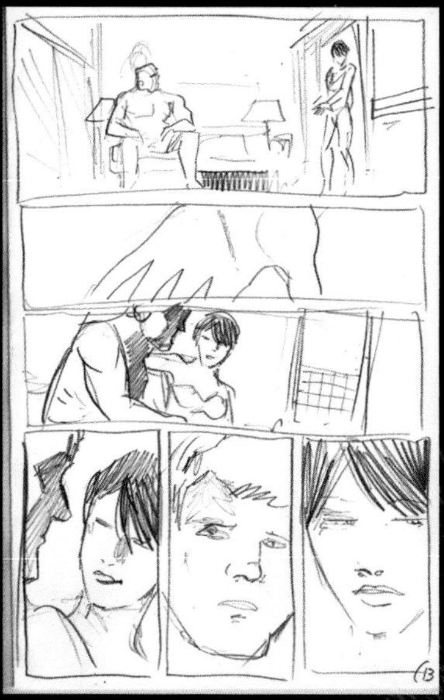
13

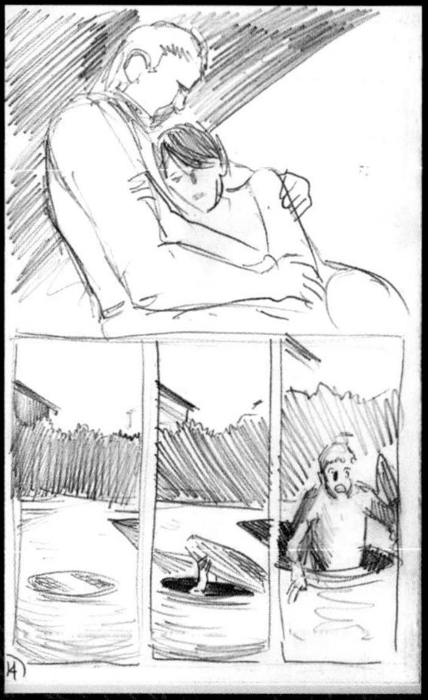
14

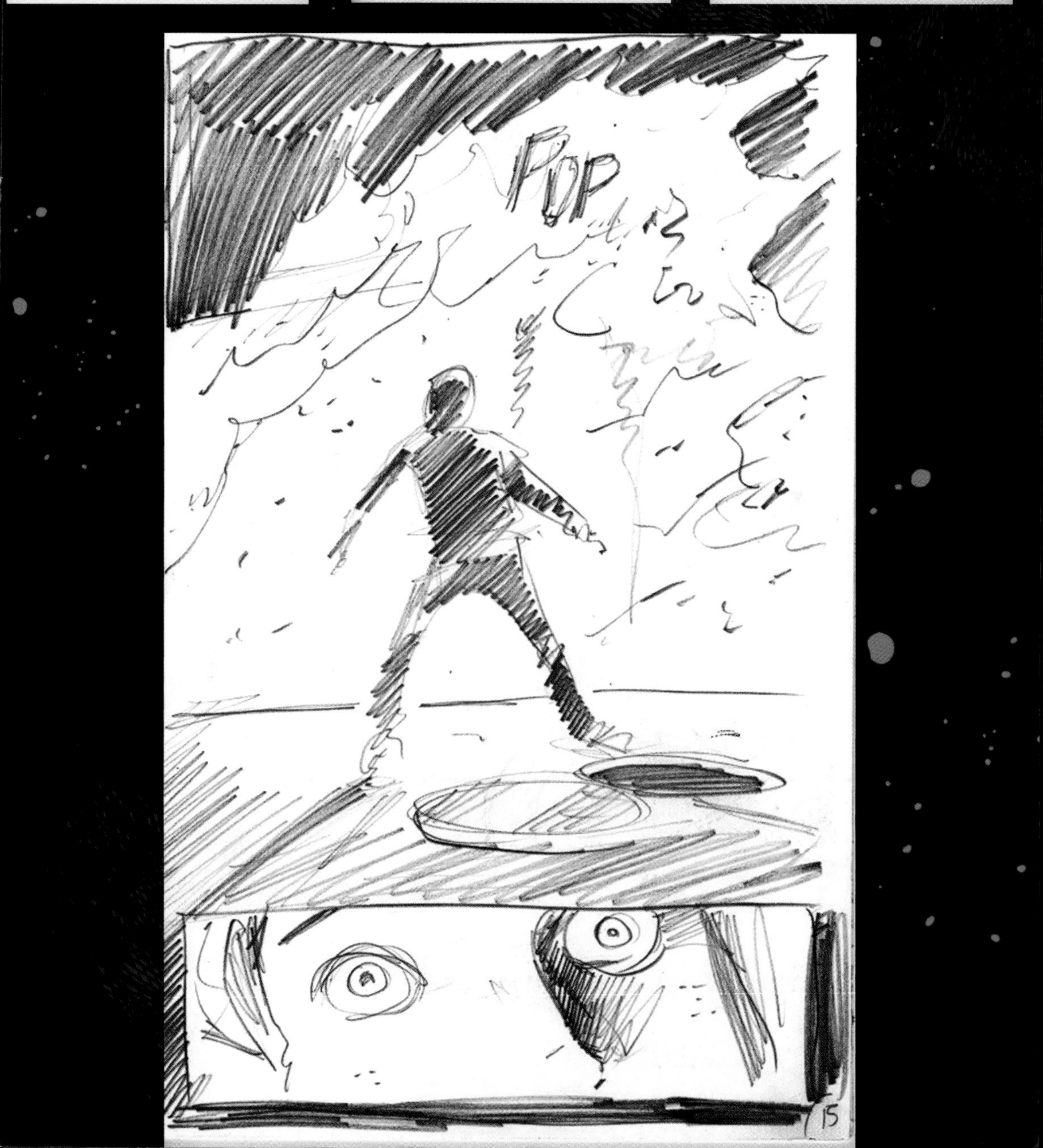
POP
15

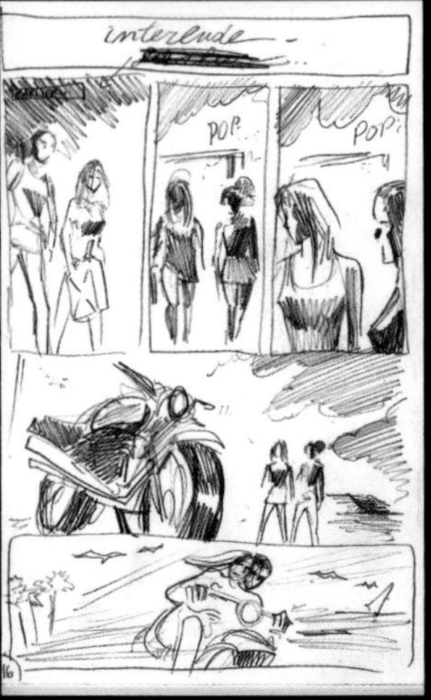
interlude
POP
POP!
16

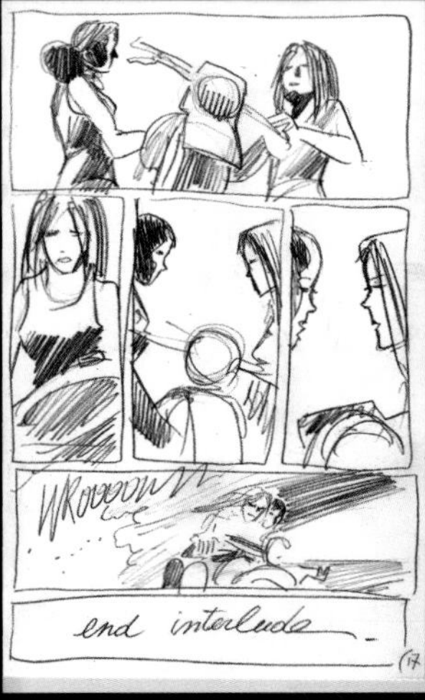
end interlude
17

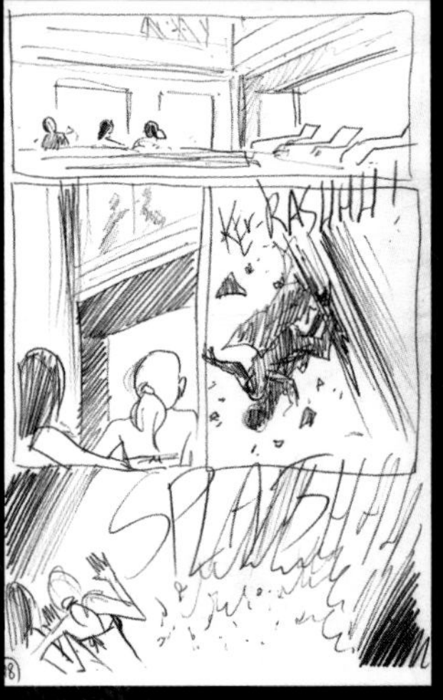
SPLASHHH
18

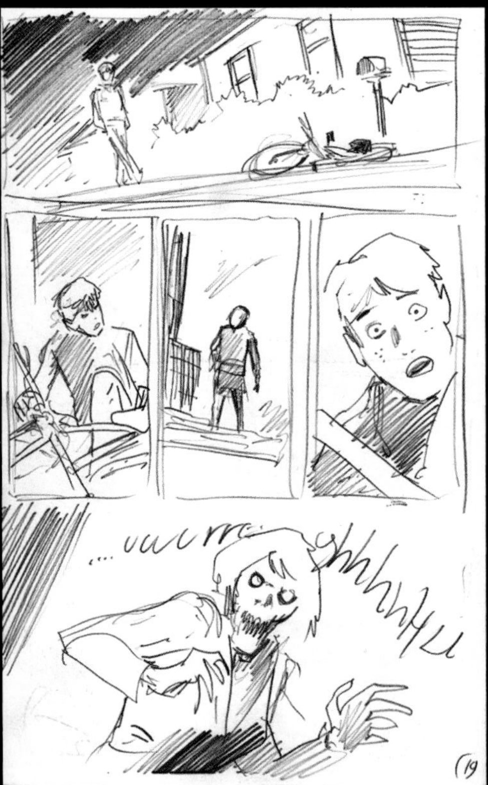
...uuurrrghhhhhhh
19

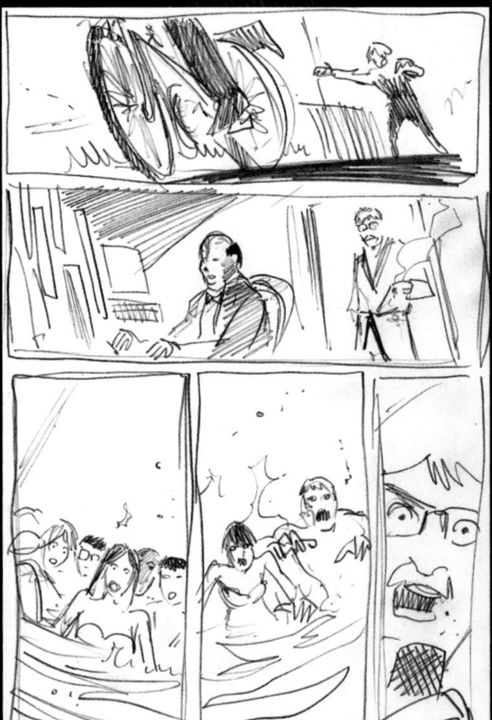
20

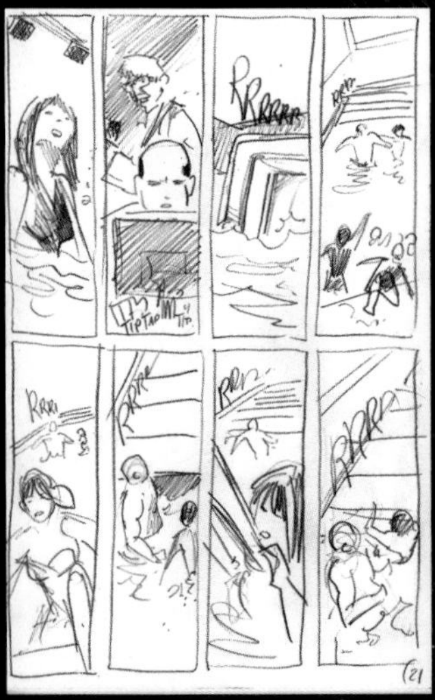
21

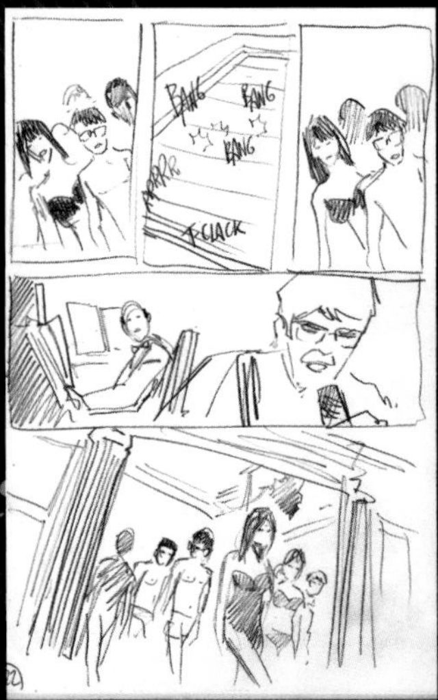
BANG
BANG
BANG
CLACK

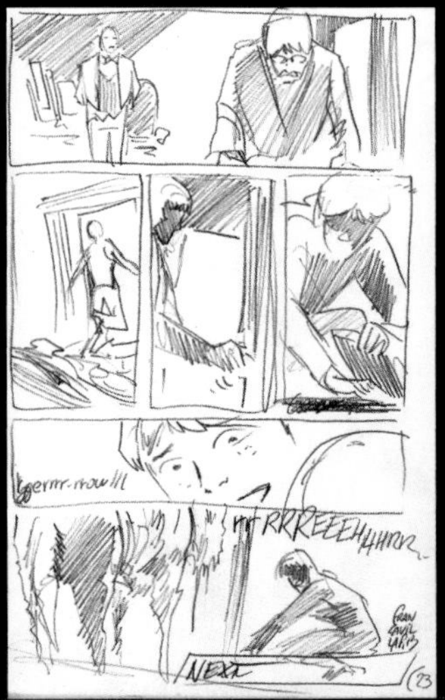
NEXT
23

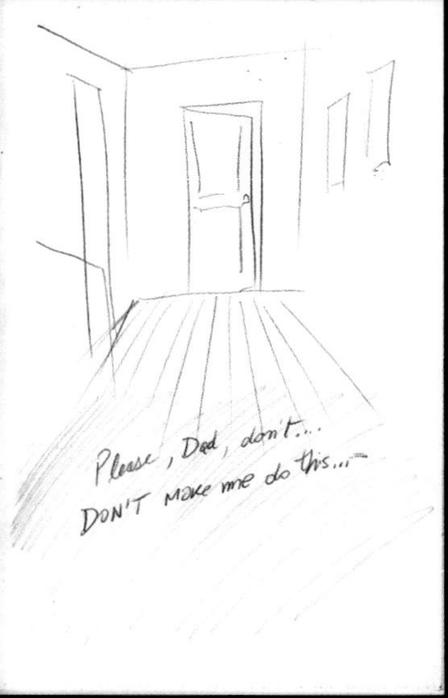
Please, Dad, don't...
DON'T make me do this...

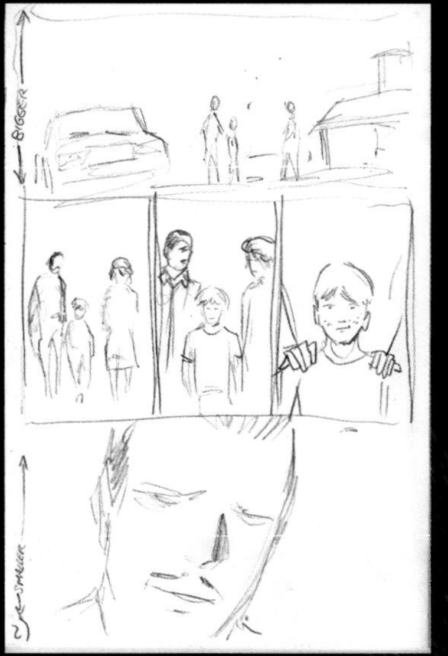

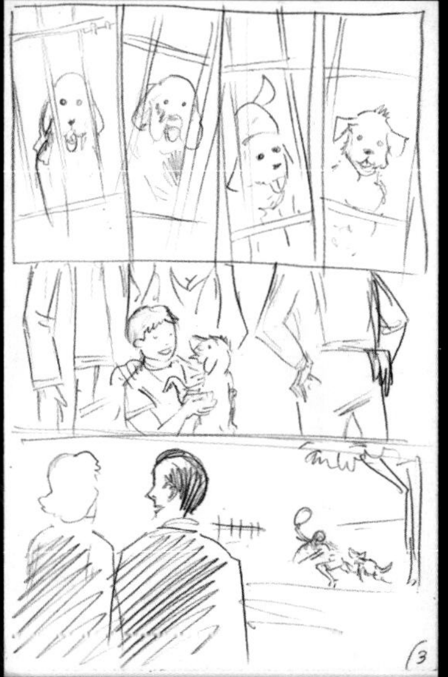

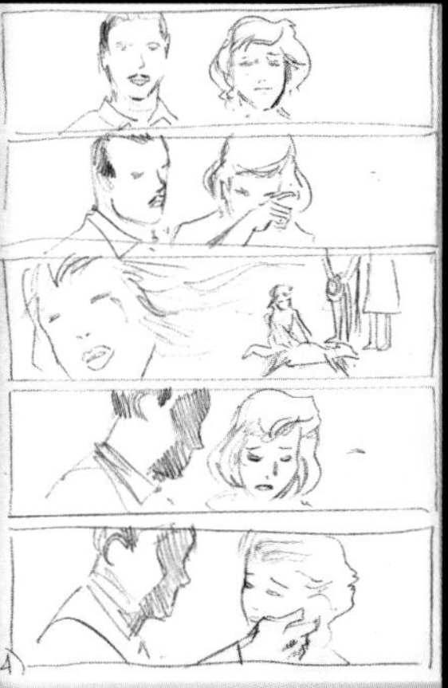

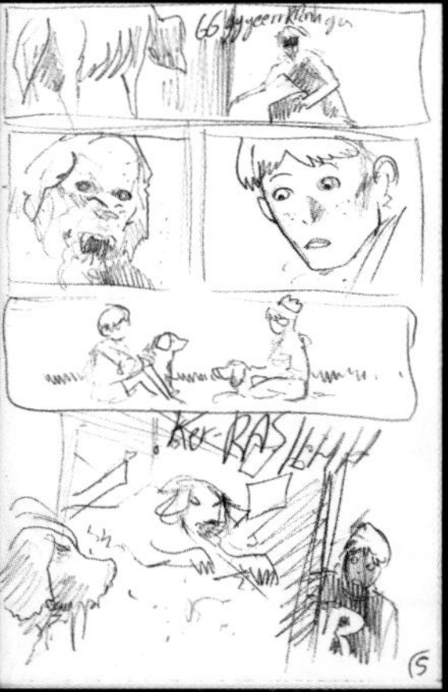

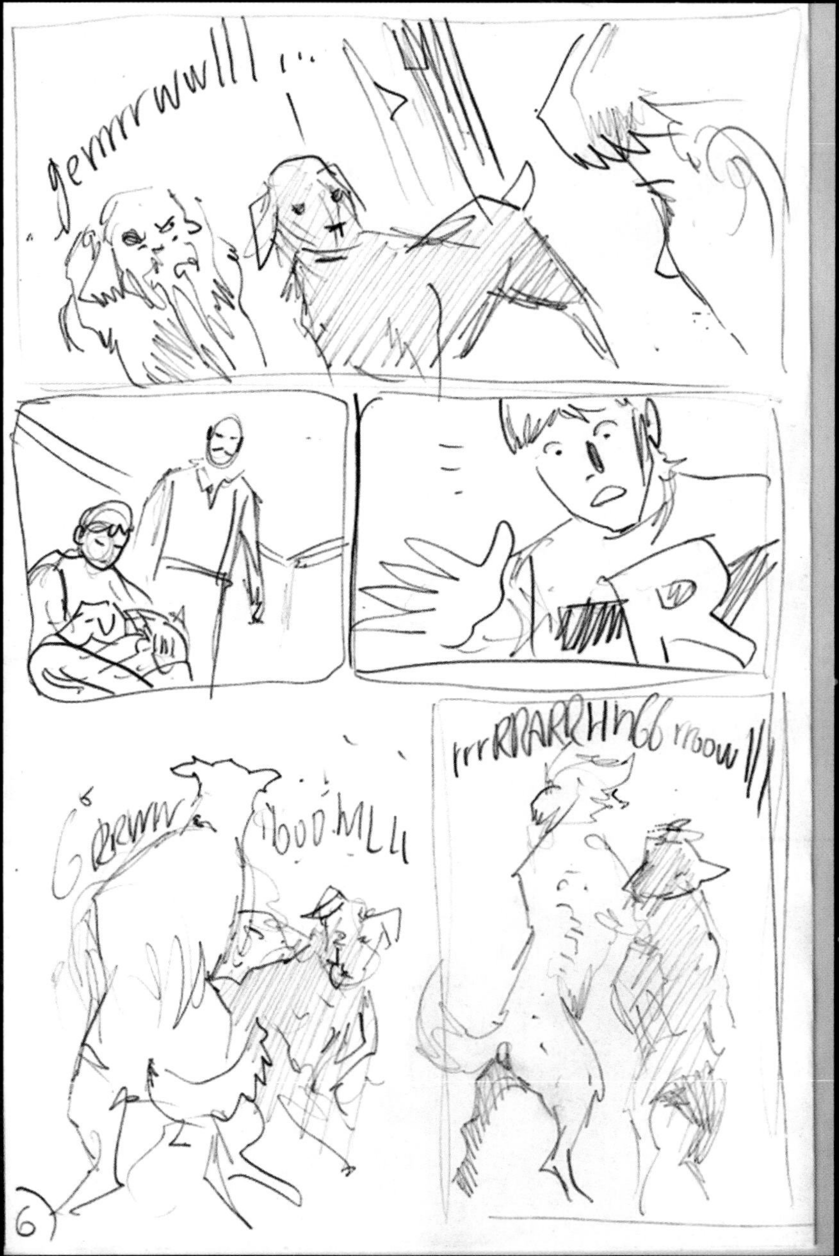

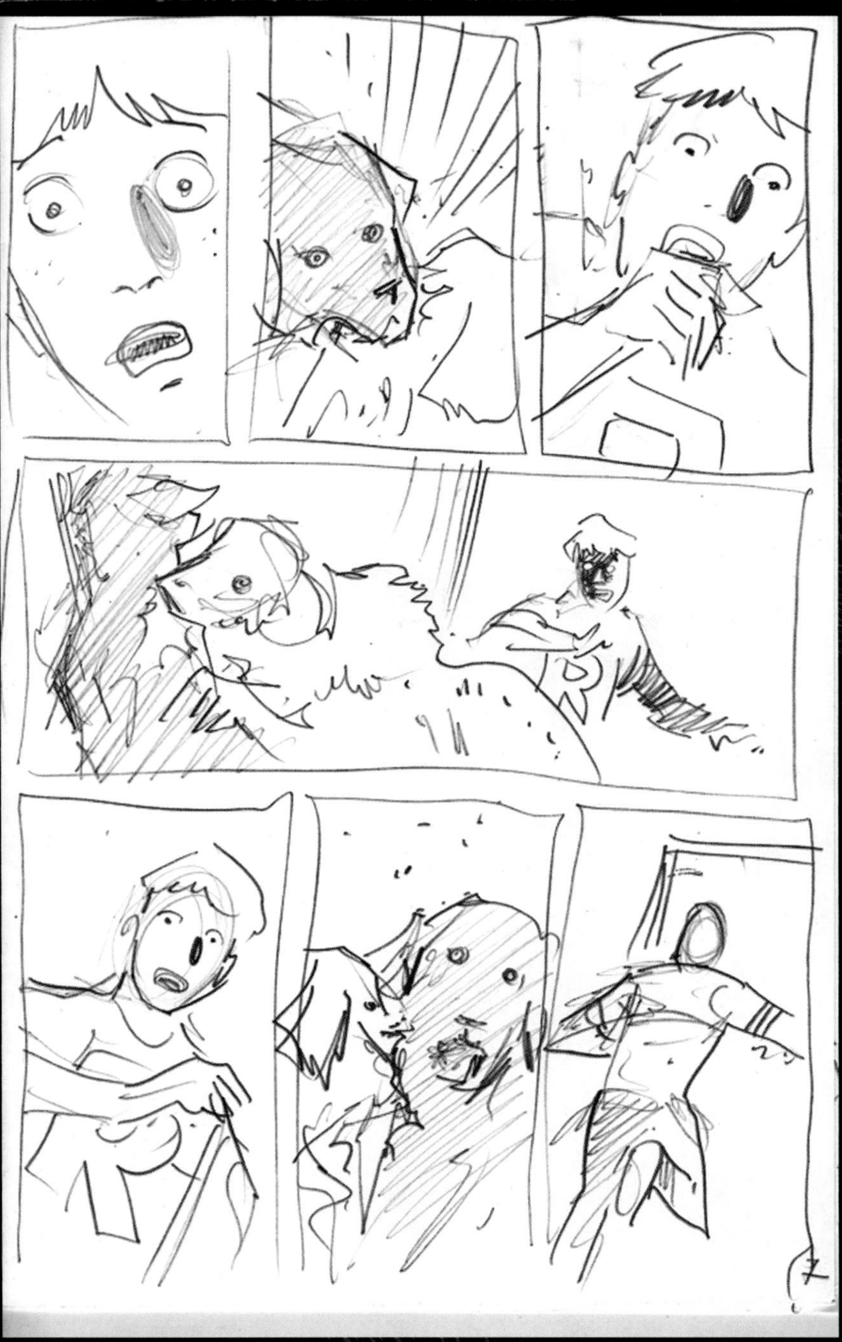
7

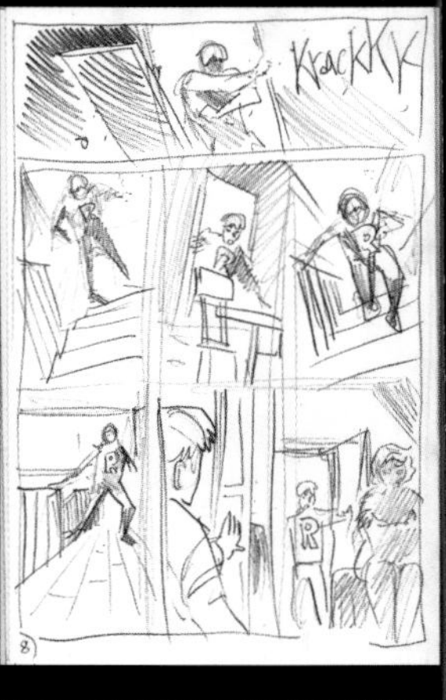
KrackKK
8

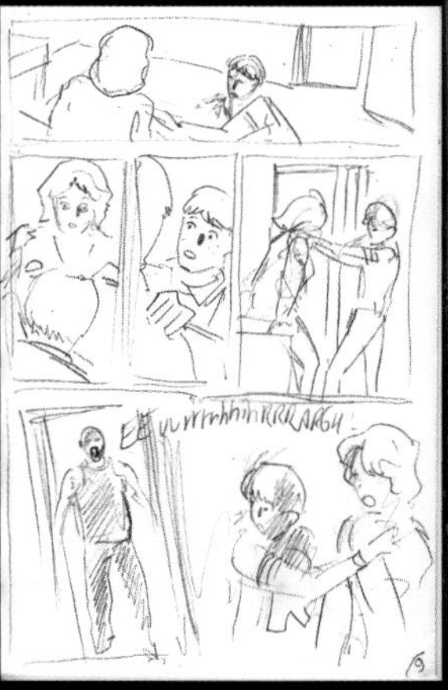
EEUUrrrrhhhhRRRRARGH
9

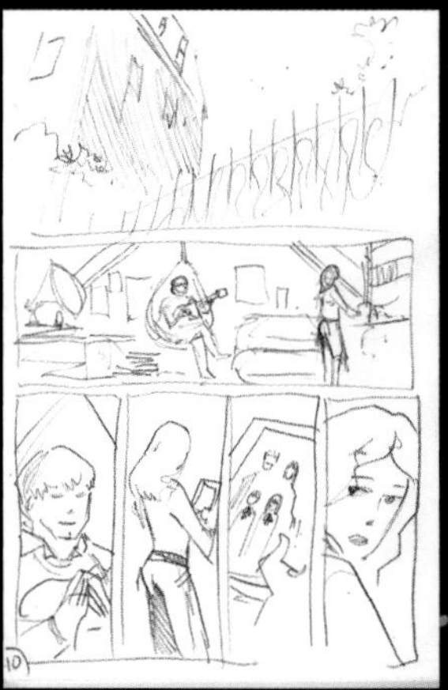
10

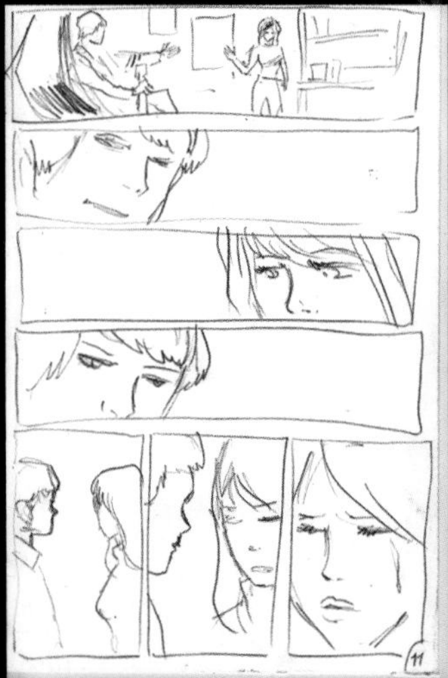
11

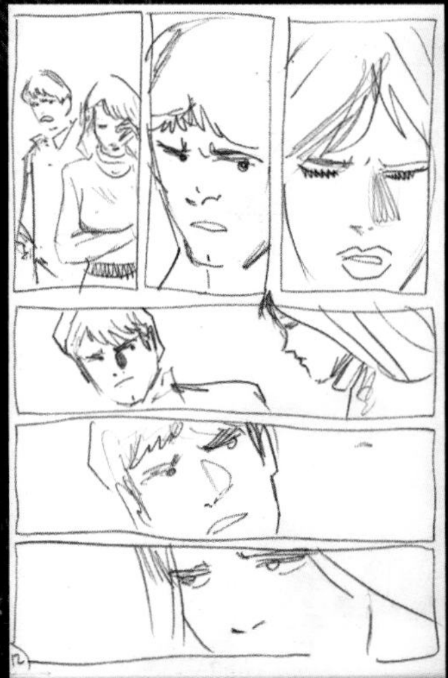
12

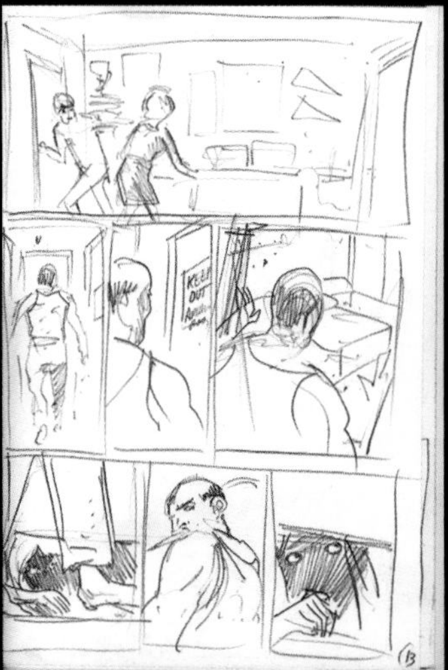
OUT
13

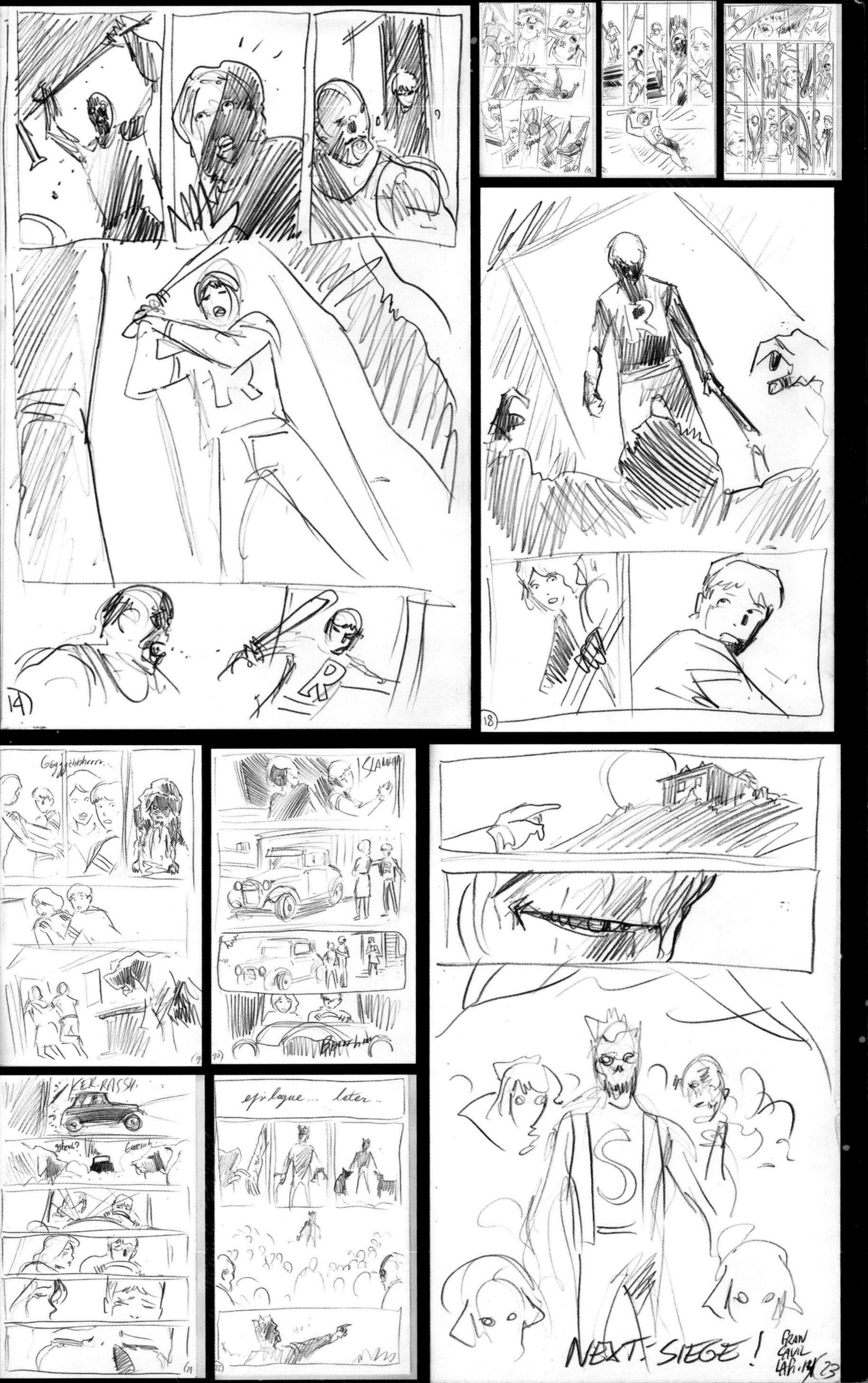
KER-RASSH
epilogue... later...
NEXT: SIEGE!

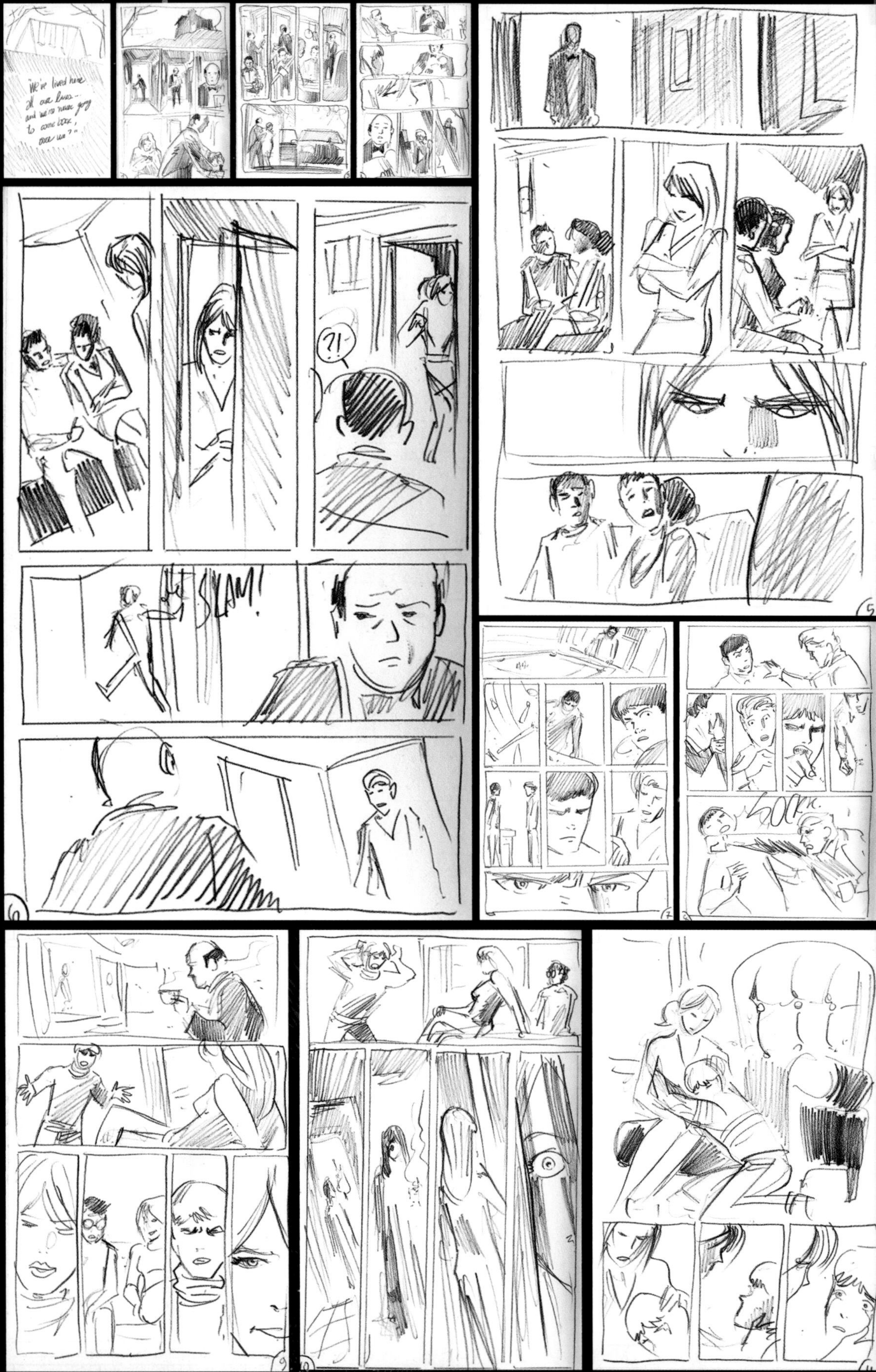

"We've lived here all our lives... and we're never going to come back, are we?"
?!
SLAM!
SOCK

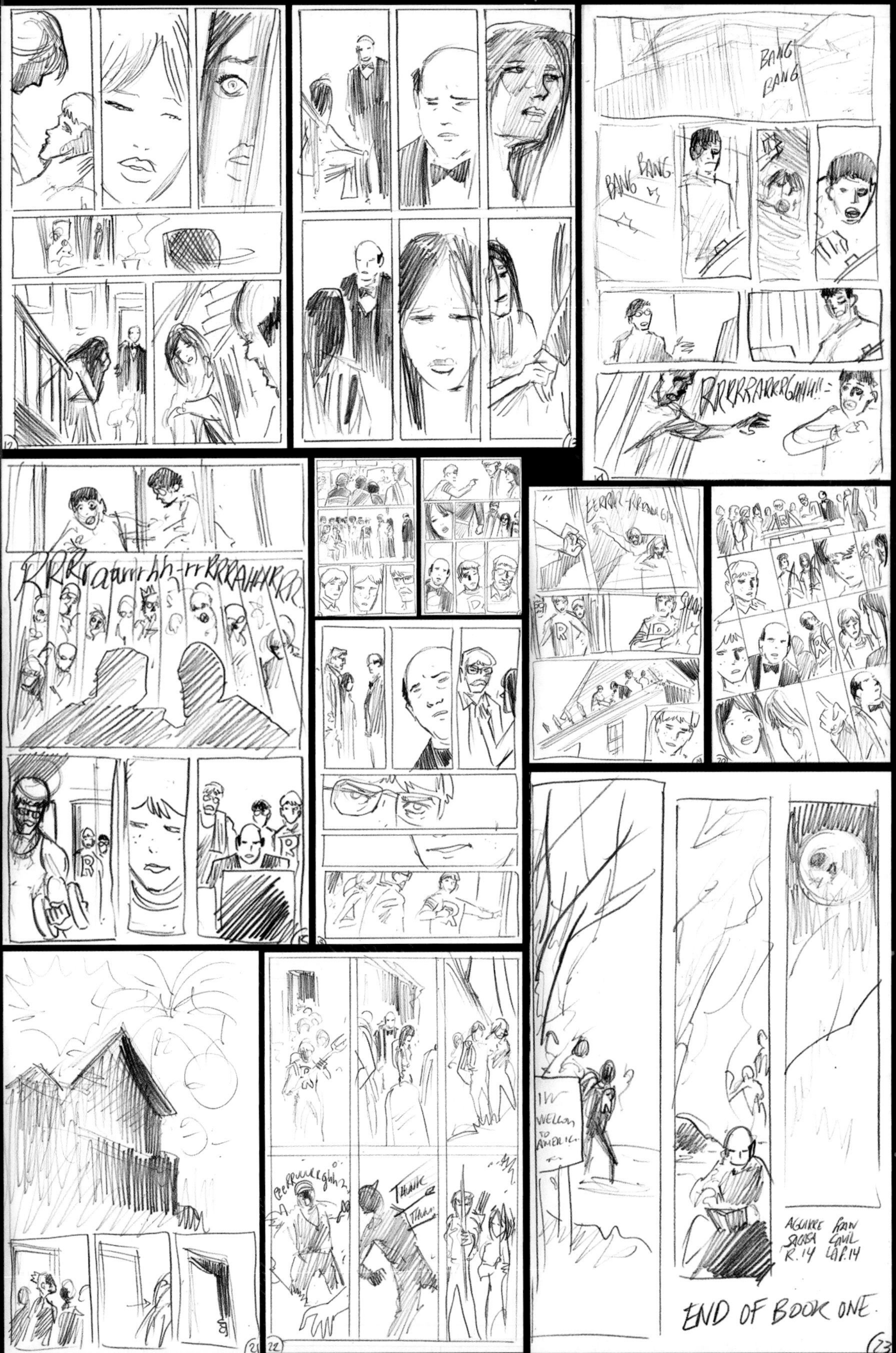
BANG
BANG
BANG BANG
RRRRRARRRGHHH!!
RRRraurrhh-rrRRRAHHRRR
THUNK
WELCOME TO AMERICA
AGUIRRE SACASA R.14
FRAN CAVIL LA F.14
END OF BOOK ONE.

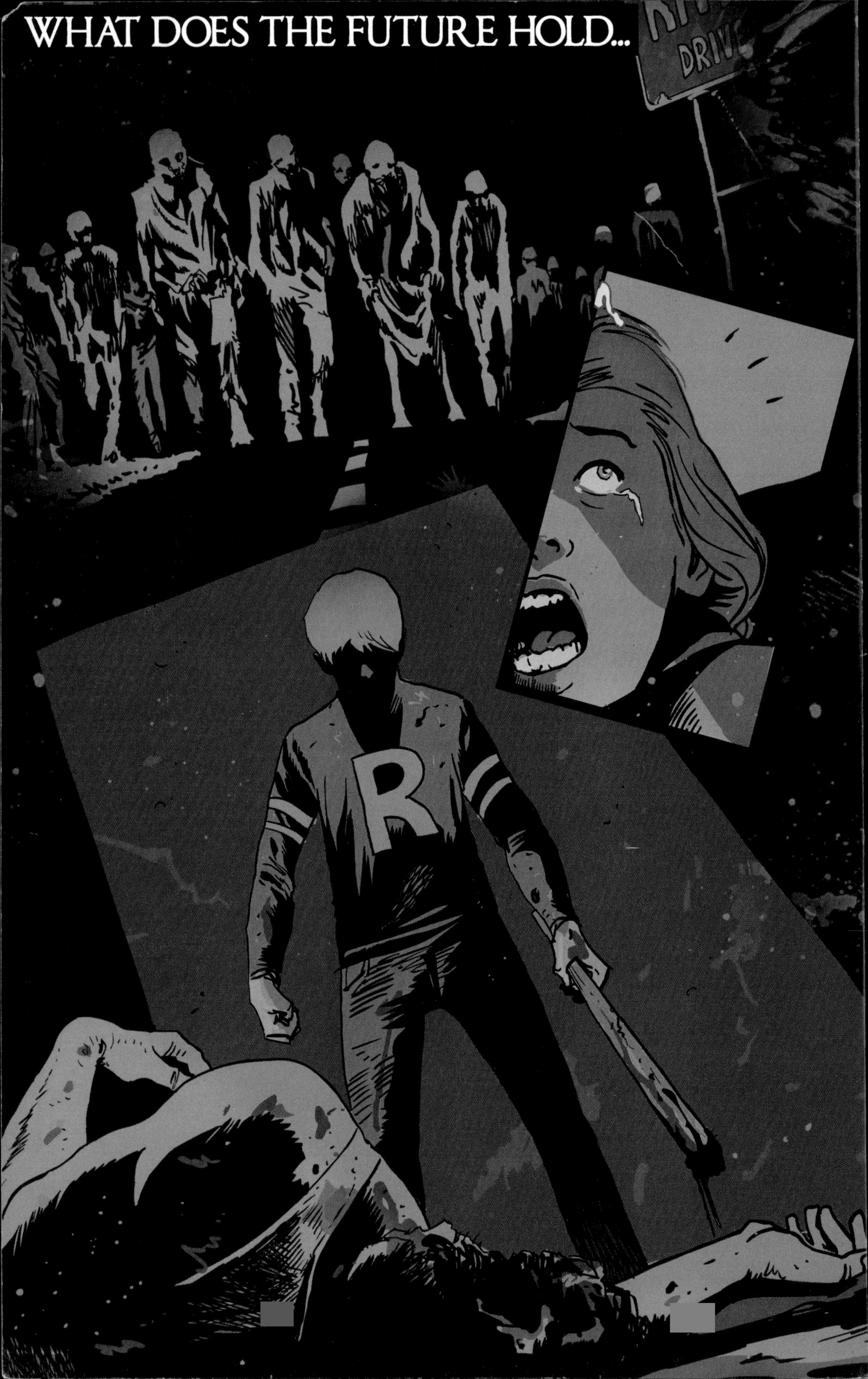
WHAT DOES THE FUTURE HOLD...

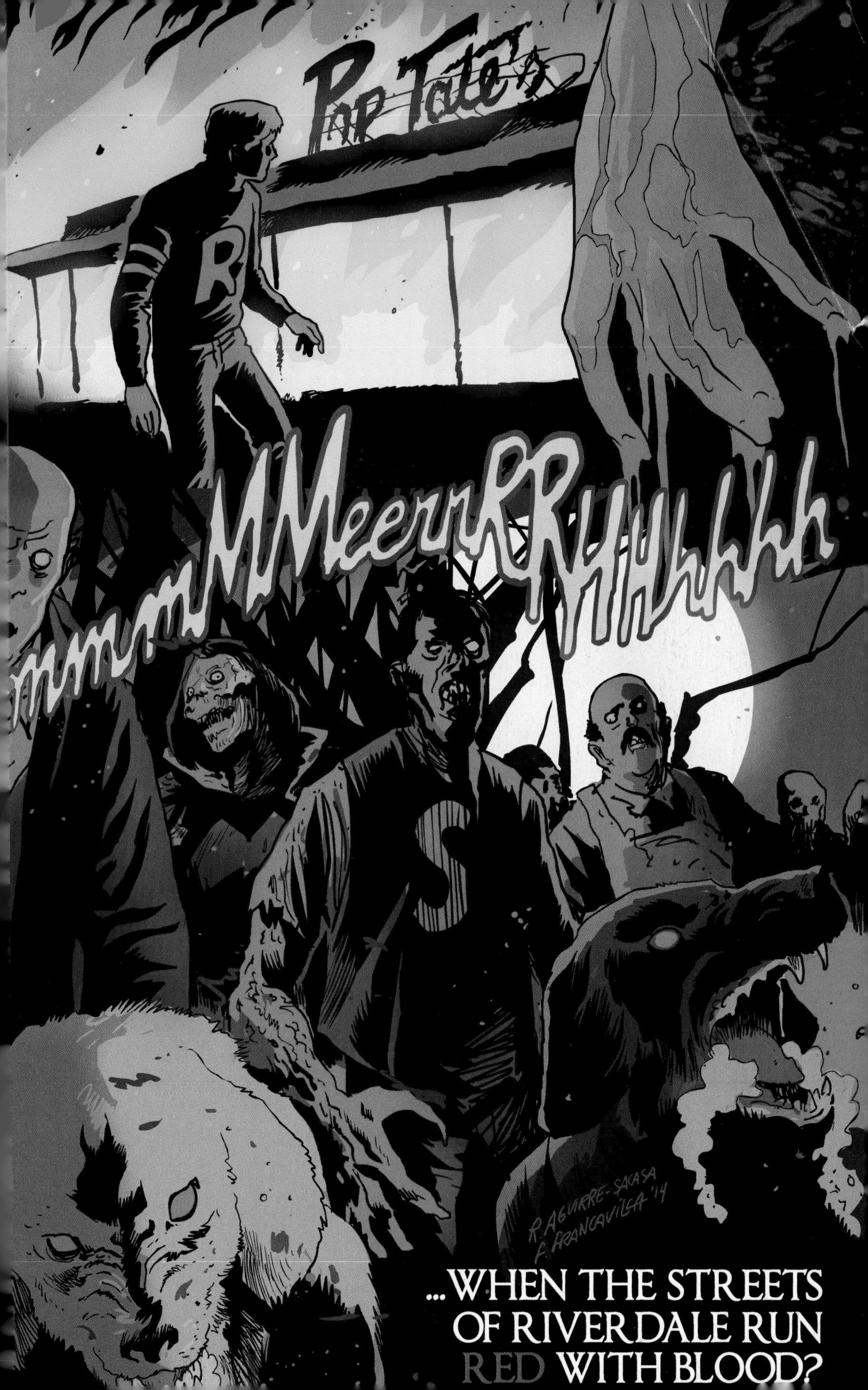
Pop Tate's
mmmmMMeerrrRRUHhhhh
R. AGUIRRE-SACASA
F. FRANCAVILLA '14
...WHEN THE STREETS
OF RIVERDALE RUN
RED WITH BLOOD?

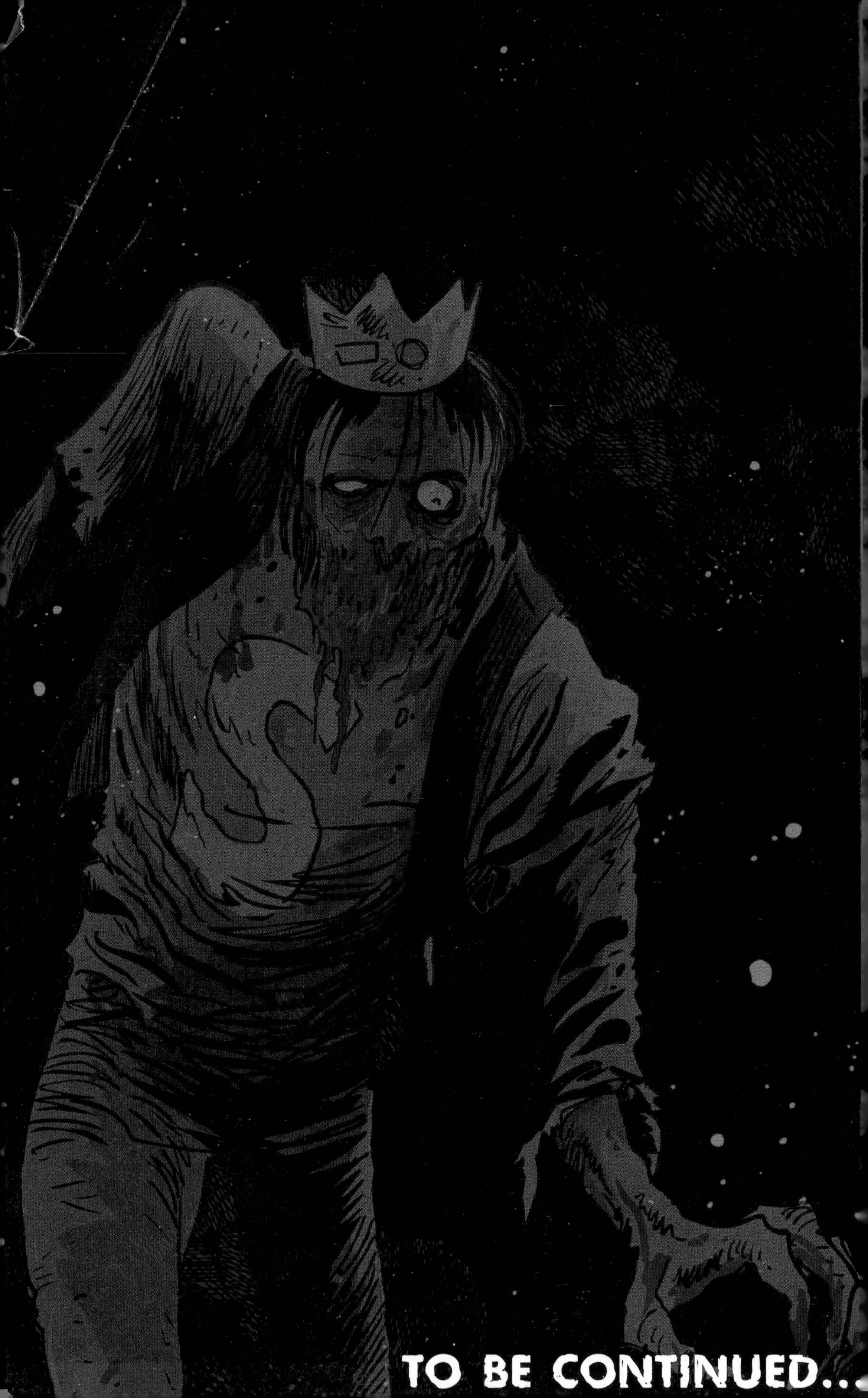
TO BE CONTINUED...